# AUGMOSIS

## STEVEN TYE

This is a work of fiction. All of the characters, organisations, and events portrayed in this novel are either products of the author's imagination or are used fictitiously

AUGMOSIS

Copyright © 2025 by Steven Tye and Tyepo Publishing

www.steventye.com

All rights reserved.

Cover design by: Radu Muresan and Steven Tye

Illustrations by Steven Tye and Adobe Stock.



Paperback ISBN: 978-0-9954286-2-1

To Lara, Lachlan and Kaitlyn

Don't settle for what you see.

# Table of Contents

# MAP OF PRAXIS

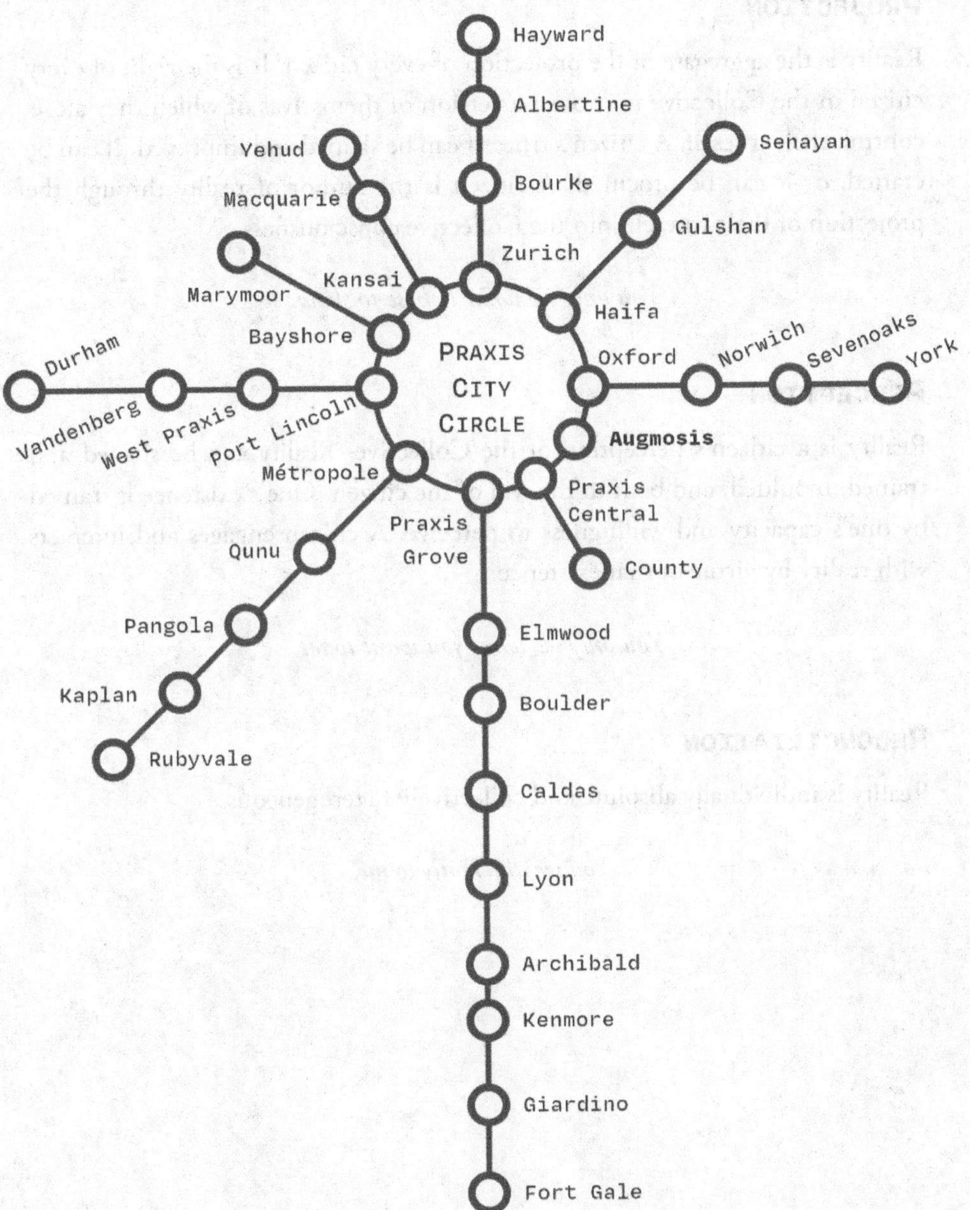

# THE RIGHTS OF THE COLLECTIVE

## PROJECTION

Reality is the aggregate of the projection of every citizen. It is the right of every citizen in the Collective to project a version of themselves of which they alone control: their trueself. A citizen's trueself can be shaped and improved. It can be crafted, or it can be procured. A citizen is the author of reality through the projection of their trueself into the Collective consciousness.

*You only see what I chose to show.*

## PERCEPTION

Reality is a citizen's perception of the Collective. Reality can be shaped and trained, moulded, and bent to the will of the citizen. One's existence is framed by one's capacity and willingness to perceive. A citizen engages and interacts with reality by virtue of that existence.

*You only see what you want to see.*

## RECONCILIATION

Reality is individually absolute and collectively heterogeneous.

*You see differently to me.*

## ANONYMITY

Anonymity is protected. It can be relaxed by mutual consent, governed by context and location. A citizen's relationship to the Collective is identified only by their Network moniker.

*You only see me when I want to be seen.*

## REFLECTION

The highest level of trust between two citizens permits each citizen to perceive reality as the other does. In this union, by mutual consent, anonymity is fully relaxed. It is the most intimate of unions within the Collective.

*We see each other.*

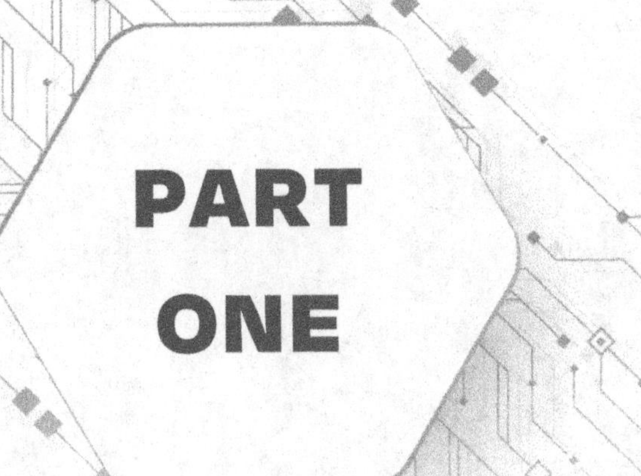


*"The citizens of the Network* are *the Collective."*

Callum Bonner, Co-Founder

Foot patrol could have been accomplished by a telepresence robot, but Constable Lee Nguyen took it in his stride. Head still, his eyes darted from one citizen to the next, a Praxis Police Department observer algorithm identifying everyone within 20 meters. Warrants, interview requests, and potential threats lit up in his augmented optics with different colours and callouts.

There were roles within the Praxis Police Department with greater responsibility and opportunities for career advancement. But he hadn't joined the PPD out of a sense of justice or adventure. He didn't join because he liked the power that came with the badge. And it certainly wasn't for the politics or the pitiful salary. Instead, he just wanted to serve in the community he'd grown up in.

Nguyen scanned a group of citizens walking towards him, the Network telling him nothing out of order. They wouldn't know he was a police officer—he wasn't exactly undercover, but during surveillance, he was permitted to mask his projection. When he needed to announce himself, he would apply the projection of a PPD officer uniform, which was the fastest way to de-escalate a conflict or get someone's attention.

He slowed his pace to clear two citizens seated in an outdoor café, bathing in the simulated sunlight emanating from West Praxis' protective dome. He briefly considered stopping in the café himself to purchase something sweet, but resisted the urge—his PPD lifesuit was already starting to feel a little tight around his waist.

Approaching another outdoor café, his scan paused on a group of three citizens seated at a table separate from the other patrons. *My first hit of the day,* he thought.

The callouts in his optics identified the first citizen as "Fernando Alvarez", with a public moniker of "Atacama". The Network supplied his address and listed a past conviction for low-level Network hacking. The second, "Petros Zaimis", identified as "PeliasLolcos" had more recent arrests on suspicion of narcotics and firearms. That told Nguyen he was worth keeping an eye on for now, so he found a seat just outside the alfresco seating for the café, near the 20-meter limit of his observer algorithm.

Then his attention went to the third citizen. Other than stating his Network moniker as "Korb1k", the Network offered nothing else. No name. No residential address. No employment history. It was an anomaly he'd never encountered before—every citizen in Praxis had a record on the Network unless they were too young to have their augments fitted.

They each projected simple trueselfs, with rudimentary crafted clothing. By focusing intently on the group and selecting an elevated surveillance option, Nguyen could slightly amplify their conversation above the background noise using his phonics, but even then, he was only able to make out sparse words.

"…they don't belong in the dock." said one.

The other replied, "Why….bits on the side?"

There was a long pause before the person identified as Korb1K said in a clearer voice, "Apparently you are a distraction."

Korb1K reached across the table and placed his left hand on Zaimis' neck. From Nguyen's position, it almost looked like a sign of affection. Zaimis didn't seem to care, but soon his head dropped, and his eyes closed. Korb1K exchanged a few more words with Alvarez. Nguyen couldn't make them out. Then they both stood and walked away in opposite directions. Zaimis remained slumped in his seat like he'd fallen asleep.

Nguyen approached, increasingly concerned as to what had just happened. All lifesuits contained rudimentary systems to monitor health and preserve life, such as a built-in defibrillator and basic stimulants dosed through the skin. There would be an immediate alert if Zaimis was in medical distress.

Then, the callouts from Zaimis's body that showed his name and identity disappeared.

Nguyen's concern increased as he reached the man, still slumped in his chair, Zaimis' projection abruptly dissolved, revealing his oldself—what he physically looked like under his augmented projection. Like most citizens, he was shorter and heavier than his trueself projection and appeared to have aged almost a decade. Nguyen reached for a pulse and found nothing. As he waited patiently for any sign of life, the smell of smoke caused him to recoil. It was coming from the plexus in the centre of Zaimis' lifesuit.

Nguyen had to make a quick decision. There was little he could do to help Zaimis—the systems in his lifesuit would have done everything possible to preserve the man's life. Standard PPD protocol deterred officers from providing first aid to any citizen unless a level 1 trust relationship had been established.

One of the other men, Alvarez, crossed the common some distance away. His projection dematerialized to reveal a telepresence robot beneath. The robot changed direction, likely returning to its charging station. The other citizen with no name, Korb1K had casually walked away to the north past the commercial lots towards the apartment complexes and was now out of sight.

Nguyen initiated a request for urgent assistance, interfacing with his commander by using hand gestures recognized by his lifesuit. He sought a warrant for surveillance on Alvarez and Korb1K and rushed off in the direction he'd last seen him. As he ran, he triggered a command to both 'bank' his last ten minutes of surveillance data so it could be retrieved later, and to record everything he saw from now on. His live stream would also become available to other PPD officers and the judge who would hopefully approve the warrants.

He approached a wide pedestrian walkway between two domicile complexes and slowed his pace. He had no visibility of Korb1k and the warrant for heightened surveillance had not yet been approved. PPD command advised that support was en route with an ETA of 12 minutes. But without a warrant, Nguyen was blind.

He stepped out of the foot traffic and caught his breath. His arm rested on his holstered sidearm—part habit and part response to the adrenaline of the moment. He wasn't built for high-speed pursuits—this wasn't the sort of friendly neighbourhood police officer role he was used to.

A flow of citizens walked up and down the same walkway in their various projections and virtual attires. Nguyen was getting impatient and cursed to himself. As though the Network had heard him, his phonics beeped a response: a warrant had been approved and issued for Korb1K.

Nguyen's optics flickered, and the highlighted silhouette of the suspect could be seen some distance down the walkway. The heightened surveillance features in his optics granted by his active warrant calculated a distance of 100 meters. He stepped back to the walkway and resumed pursuit at a jog.

Running through the crowd of other citizens on the walkway was problematic since many of their projections concealed a much larger body shape. Sculptors weren't miracle workers, but they could usually shave a few sizes off a citizen's projection. If Nguyen ran too close to a larger body shape concealed behind a smaller projection, their bodies would collide. His job would have been far easier if Nguyen could just hide everyone's projections from his optics, but the law prevented that.

He backed off the pace as he reached the end of the walkway. His optics tracked Korb1k's silhouette entering an apartment complex and begin to ascend the fire stairs. He'd never questioned the technology that allowed the Network to deliver him a live feed of the suspect's location in three-dimensional space, but he was certainly grateful.

He entered the building's lobby. It was empty and somewhat derelict. It could be easily mistaken for a thousand domicile complexes across any of the hubs in Praxis. The main hallway from the lobby led to two central elevators. Both were covered in tape to advise they were out of service. The door to one elevator was slightly ajar and in the flickering hallway light, Nguyen could see the elevator car inside was on an angle. The second elevator was in worse shape—no doors at all and the only thing saving Nguyen from falling three levels down into the basement was a virtual warning in his optics.

He checked his request for backup. For some reason, it was still at 12 minutes. He looked up to find his suspect was no longer climbing but was standing in one of the domiciles several levels above his position. The technology was not able to perceive anything else in the room other than the citizen itself. Without line of sight, he couldn't tell if they were sitting or standing, but at least he was no longer moving.

The smart play was to wait—there was no way out of the building without returning to the ground level. He kept constant watch on Korb1k to confirm he hadn't moved. A minute passed, then another. Agitation grew within him— this sort of delay for backup was entirely out of order.

Waiting for backup was standard procedure: the Network had a solid lock on his suspect, and he still hadn't moved. Nguyen had no desire to be the hero, so there was no reason for him to continue his pursuit and place himself in danger. But after ten more frustrating minutes of waiting… *He's not going anywhere. Might as well get a little closer.*

Nine flights of stairs awaited him, his resolve waned with every flight. After making it to the ninth landing and finding the fire door chocked open, he took his time to catch his breath. Other than growing in scale, the suspect's silhouette remained in the same position within his vision. New, feint silhouettes appeared—these were other citizens occupying different rooms in the building. Those closest to the tagged suspect were slightly more vivid in contrast to those further away. It was a helpful feature, allowing Nguyen to confirm that there was no one else in Korb1k's room that could present a threat or be used as a hostage.

Nguyen unholstered his sidearm and held it at ready position in his left hand as he walked down the corridor. PPD sidearms fired a rubber shell with a digital tracer that instantly scrambled a target's augments. One shot to the torso and their optics would phase black and phonics would scream a high-pitched noise until the officer issued a release command. It was a humane way to take down a target, even if it left them with a solid bruise.

His PPD lifesuit also offered him excellent protection from firearms—he'd seen officers walk away from a vintage shotgun blast to the chest. His projection also concealed his standard-issue helmet and face visor. All this technology gave Nguyen a tremendous advantage against any adversary and gave him the courage to continue.

He closed the distance quietly until he was just outside the suspect's domicile. From outside the door, Nguyen could reconcile the orientation of the doorway with the position of the suspect inside. If he forced the door open, the suspect would be standing right in front of him. He really wouldn't have a better option.

*You're fine. You've done this before*, he told himself.

He checked his PPD feed—still 12 minutes until backup would arrive. *Dammit.* That was all the confirmation he needed—with his quarry so close and backup somehow delayed, he made the decision to enter. He raised his firearm to a shooting position and breached the door with a solid kick to the locking mechanism.

"PPD! Freeze!" he called, bursting through the door.

The grey silhouette morphed into the projection of Korb1k the moment he had a clear line of sight. He stood before him, unmoving, with a strange expression on his face.

"On the ground! On the ground!" he called, but the suspect remained completely motionless. This surprised Nguyen so much that he fired his sidearm. It was a good shot, but rather than dropping the suspect to the floor from sensory overload, the projection simply faded out and disappeared in a cloud of pixels. His eyes followed the line of the shot to a hole in the opposite wall where the shell was now embedded.

It made no sense, but it was a riddle he would not have any time to solve. He felt a cold hand gently clasp his throat from his left side. He began to spin towards his attacker, seeing the scarred face of a man he could only assume was Korb1K. He was no longer highlighted in his optics and the Network showed no ID.

Nguyen tried to step away to give himself space to fire his weapon, but a sudden tightness in his chest swelled to the point that he collapsed to the floor. And like a rubber band snapping, the tightness ceased in a moment of release like falling from a great height.

His final thought as he died was to wonder why he'd ever decided to take such a risk.

## 02

S imulated light and virtual imagery projected over the false windows of Carli Dawes' transit carriage. Her seat allowed her to watch the faces of the other travellers joining her on her daily commute from Archibald into the Praxis City Circle. Most stared blankly into space, their optics delivering content directly into their retinas. Carli, however, enjoyed observing the variety of human projections, as one artist studies the craftsmanship of another.

She had the same optics integrated behind her irises and the same phonics embedded into her cochleae as every other citizen in the Collective. Together they painted a virtual picture over the top of each person—a unique personal expression called their 'trueself'.

The citizen immediately opposite her projected a trueself featuring pale skin free of any imperfections. His spiky, two-toned hairstyle looked to be a near copy of an anime character from the Content Network. His face had no hint of stubble—in fact, no hint of any other hair follicles, pores or blemishes. They'd been airbrushed away. Deleted from reality.

Such perfection did not exist in the physical world. Carli knew her own face, her 'oldself' almost as well as her projected identity. There were similarities, of course: one's oldself was usually the raw material upon which a trueself was sculpted. But it was little more than the blank canvas on which a completely new identity could be painted. For some people, their projection would remain for the entirety of their adult life. For others, it might be changed or altered almost as often as they changed lifesuits.

An 'economy of self-expression' it had been called. And it was in this economy that Carli had forged her career as a sculptor. She'd sculpted the trueselfs of CEOs and low-level Network stars. She'd even sculpted the projection of one of the Overseers. To Carli, it wasn't just a technical process.

She also loved the intimacy of the bond with her clients, out of which something truly beautiful could be created.

Carli likened it to a second birth for each citizen. Their first birth to the physical world produced their temporal 'oldself' but Carli had the privilege of shaping and sculpting their trueself.

One passenger's trueself was a near copy of an alien villain from a retro science fiction serial. Another donned a feminine projection covered in animated tattoos. The twenty people in her carriage were a microcosm representing the absurd diversity in each citizen's projection that was repeated across the Collective.

Some citizens wore virtual masks that concealed their projection. Since a trueself may have been uniquely identifiable to them, some wore masks to maintain a level of anonymity. Even these had been turned into statements of fashion.

The doors opened, and a wave of citizens entered and found their seats. One appeared as a muscle-bound spandex-wearing superhero. Another, a feminine form, was far more subtly crafted, avoiding the temptation to project unrealistically large breasts and augmented lips.

One of the new arrivals dressed as a western gunslinger, sporting chaps, spurs and a cowboy hat. Carli had noticed this citizen a few times before on her commute. She appreciated the quality of both the sculpting of the citizen's image as well as the crafted garments and accessories he wore. She heard the rustle of leather and clinking of spurs as he shuffled past, or at least the simulated sound he projected as he walked. Considering he, like all citizens was physically wearing only a lifesuit, he certainly did a good job selling the projection by the way he strutted through the carriage.

For a moment, Carli almost perceived a slight aroma of leather as he walked past. This should have been impossible since animal products had been banned for as long as she could remember and there were few real animals left in Praxis. Unlike sight and sound, smells could not be projected into the Collective since no biological augments existed to use them. And still, Carli wondered if the scent was truly there or if the gunslinger's projection had been so accurate, that her mind filled in the gaps. Even more concerning was that Carli had no idea what leather actually smelt like.

Another new citizen found a standing position off to the side. He wore denim jeans, and a brown oilskin coat over a knitted white shirt. Carli had also seen him before. His projection was practical and no-nonsense. Based on the way he carried himself, she concluded he was possibly a police officer.

The last person to enter the carriage projected a trueself of a short, teenage female, but walked with a stiffness and rigidity Carli suspected was closer to an octogenarian. Realising most of the seats had been filled, Carli stood to offer her own and received a warm smile in response.

The carriage doors closed, and the transit began its gentle acceleration to the next station of Elmwood before starting a loop around the Praxis City Circle. Carli would take the first stop at Praxis Grove where her workplace, NuSculpt was located.

With a series of blinks and hand gestures interpreted by the sensors in her lifesuit, Carli reviewed her work diary for the day. Her morning would be consumed by an 'emergency' sculpting appointment from a well-paying, repeat client, Ms. Pasadi. Her propensity to exaggerate made the appointment sound more ominous than it probably warranted.

Her afternoon appointment held more promise, however. The client, Aliya Quereshi had already undertaken a preliminary interview, followed by a full body scan. When they met, she would voluntarily deactivate her projection and reveal her oldself. From this point, Carli would seek to bond with the client, both intellectually and emotionally to unearth their trueself. Like an artist being inspired by their muse, Carli would begin to sculpt a projection that may bear little resemblance to the original.

Her final appointment was a dinner date with Deniz Harper—one of NuSculpt's solicitors. She'd only been on a few dates with him, but Carli hadn't felt any real spark. She suspected he was also on the rebound from his previous relationship, someone from NuSculpt's finance pool—a theory confirmed on their first date when he accidentally called her Shannon. She figured she'd give him one final date before deciding to call it all off. She didn't have the patience to waste time on a dead-end relationship.

The transit slowed, and the carriage doors opened to receive its last group of commuters. More interesting characters entered, including one resembling some form of a teddy bear and another that looked as plastic and disproportionate as a vintage Barbie doll.

Carli's optics rendered another traveller's body with only a matt-grey silhouette. The risk of granting each citizen the right to craft their own identity included the ability to project a trueself that others may find inappropriate. The "right of perception" granted all other citizens the power to filter a projection for any reason, which might include social, political or religious rules.

In Carli's case, the only thing she chose to block was outright nudity. She appreciated the naked form but didn't need to see it every day on her morning commute. Text attached to the silhouette's projection confirmed this for her benefit, stating:

### PERCEPTION FILTER: SEXUAL CONTENT

It was apparent that others in the carriage had no such filter active as their gaze followed the form the whole way until she found a spare seat. Either the attention was too much for this citizen, or she finally realised she had accidentally left home wearing nothing but her birthday suit because her projection quickly morphed into formal business attire, and her face became fully masked. Carli could not help but chuckle.

The final person to enter the carriage wore only their lifesuit with no projected image. It was an older lifesuit, with visible symbols to help everyone's optics track the body's movement for a projection to be overlaid. The only thing this citizen projected was a mask over their face: a brown paper bag with characters in bold black lettering. A colon and open parenthesis.

:(

A retro-style sad face emoticon. Carli had never seen such a projection before and had rarely seen anyone in public wearing only a lifesuit and projecting no clothing. She only guessed the citizen's gender based on his height and the tightness of his lifesuit.

He stood, facing her, only a few meters away. The mask and its strange 'face' staring at her. She held its uncanny gaze and tried to unravel the puzzle of this citizen. Was he aware of what he was projecting? It wasn't like his projection was offensive to her, but it just didn't fit her idea of 'normal'. Surprisingly, the naked projection seemed more normal to her than what this citizen was projecting.

His body was tall and fit. His fingers, visible through the lifesuit's gloves, were the only exposed skin: masculine, perhaps a young man. His plexus, the quantum processing core that unified a person's augments into the Collective, was mounted on the torso of his lifesuit.

Carli's phonics projected a simple blip noise—a proximity trust request had been initiated. When the Network detected two citizens within proximity who had made eye contact for longer than 5 seconds, a level 1 trust relationship was assumed to have been requested. Her optics highlighted the man's silhouette over the body with the following callout:

LEVEL 1 TRUST REQUESTED: CITIZEN 'CHALCED0NY'. CONFIRM?

Carli knew this citizen would be perceiving a similar projection from her. If she waited another 10 seconds without confirming through a single slow blink, the trust request would time out and disappear, like it was an accident. She could also immediately reject the request with a fast double-blink. Carli hesitated. Every sense within her told her to reject the request. But before she could, a new proximity text message was projected into her view with a corresponding notification sound.

<CHALCED0NY> YOU ONLY SEE WHAT YOU WANT TO SEE...

What? she thought. With an instinctive double-blink, she rejected the request and closed her eyes. What just happened? She'd met strange characters with strange projections in the Collective, but this one confused her. She steeled herself, opened her eyes and looked back at the man who called himself, 'Chalced0ny'.

He had disappeared.

In the position where he was standing, there was only an empty space. Within a few seconds, the other citizens standing nearby adjusted their position to fill that space, clearly unaware someone had just disappeared. Carli looked across the carriage and didn't see him. She looked for some other citizen who appeared new, in case this Chalced0ny had simply applied a new projection to cover their lifesuit and paper-bag mask and then disappeared into the crowd, but she saw no one new.

Interfacing with the Network through her palm sensors she performed a search for the citizen by name. The Network responded with an ambiguous message:

<NETWORK> CITIZEN "CHALCED0NY" NOT FOUND

C arli made a swift departure from the carriage and transit terminal, ascending to the ground level of Praxis Grove.

*He just disappeared. Was he even real to begin with?*

She shook her head—a failed attempt to convince herself that what she'd seen wasn't real. Or the Network was broken. Neither option gave her any comfort.

On her ascent on the conveyor, she passed walls painted a sterile white. She remembered once seeing these covered in different kinds of graffiti, some of which Carli had thought was actually quite artful, but in recent months they had been cleaned away. Advertisements projected directly into her path. She avoided looking at them—the Network equated her attention to genuine interest and caused them to increase in size and volume. Each advertisement was tailored to her public identifier. She'd chosen, 'MalvinaHoffman' for her identifier—a tribute to her favourite sculptor from a time before the rest of the world was destroyed.

The street level of Praxis Grove featured many food stalls and service hubs, many of which spilled out the onto footpath. Unlike the outer parts of Praxis, which didn't place a high value on artwork, architecture and green spaces, all city circle hubs featured all three. Large potted trees strived upwards to reach the simulated light squeezing its way through the buildings. Other small gardens and even sections of grass were scattered throughout the space, forming a tessellating pattern with contrasting plantings.

She passed an outdoor art installation—a collection of contemporary sculptures of stone or metal, mixed amongst a few classical forms she recognized. All public spaces were clean and sanitary. There were no birds and no litter.

Despite this apparent vibrancy of life and form, it was the people and their projected trueselfs that seemed the most colourful and alive in Carli's opinion.

A news bulletin appeared in Carli's optics, listing paid headlines and summaries of feeds she'd subscribed to. She noted a rain event was planned for the City Circle hubs the following evening, a process she understood cleared the air and the streets of dust and contaminants.

Her phonics gave a chirp indicating a live post from ArdentBlue. Carli had assigned her followship to ArdentBlue for three years. Her posts in support of freedom of expression and personal liberty had resonated with her to the point that Carli had given her support to join the Council of Overseers. Her relationship deepened in the weeks prior to her ascension to the Council when Carli received the commission through NuSculpt to create a fresh new trueself for ArdentBlue. They never met in person, but Carli invested more of her own time than for any other client to make the trueself as perfect and as real as possible. It was one of Carli's proudest moments when her client took the oath of Overseer, wearing the trueself Carli had sculpted.

As she walked, Carli activated the post in a window within her optics.

*"Blessings Citizens of the Collective! Two weeks from now marks one hundred years since our liberation into the Collective. For one hundred years, we have all benefited from our awakening to the freedoms we now cling to. To commemorate this amazing milestone, the Council of Overseers has organised a range of events and activities across the whole Collective. This is indeed a time for us to come together to celebrate in our shared prosperity, liberty, and freedom*

*"But friends, now is not the time for us to take lightly the fight to preserve the liberties we all enjoy. Even now, there are those within our Collective who believe the right to control our projection and protect our liberty is not absolute. I refer specifically to the bill currently before the Council submitted by the so-called 'Union of Citizens for Justice', which seeks to increase the power of municipal authorities and their agents and remove the rights of citizens convicted of certain crimes to project into the Collective.*

*"The key to rehabilitation for any criminal remains their reintegration within the community—within our shared Collective. To erode the rights of a citizen who has paid their debt to society is a slippery slope towards further restrictions on our freedom and liberty..."*

Carli wondered if restricting the rights of such criminals made some sense, but she trusted ArdentBlue. Liberty of projection was the bedrock of the Collective.

*"…It is for this reason I will be voting to oppose this restraint on our shared liberty. The heart of liberty is to define one's own concept of existence, of meaning, of the universe and the mystery of human life. The reality we define is the reality we project, and the reality we project is The Collective. The Collective is one. The Collective is all. The Collective is liberty!"*

The video concluded with ArdentBlue's catchphrase, a call to both unity and individual liberty. It resonated with Carli. Bills such as these required two-thirds support of the 21 members of the Council. Only fundamental changes to the constitution of the Collective would require its citizens to vote directly. To the best of her recollection, it hadn't happened in 100 years.

A pair of teepers—telepresence robots, crossed in front of her. They left a wide margin and walked with mechanical precision towards a charging station in front of a pharmacy. Rather than travel halfway around the city for a brief meeting, people could rent and remotely pilot a teeper. Anyone looking at the teeper would see its pilot's trueself projection, effectively indistinguishable from the real thing, though Carli was sure she could always spot the difference.

The robots had a familiar humanoid shape and moved in near silence. Tracking markers were positioned across the surface of the teeper's skin to assist in the process of overlaying a citizen's projection. Stereo optical sensors were mounted in the robot's head, relaying vision into the controlling citizen's own optics. It required no 'mouth' since the controlling citizen's voice was projected from the Network to the phonics of any citizens nearby. The function of the teeper was therefore only as a physical frame onto which the trueself could be projected.

A dedicated control harness was typically used to remotely control a teeper, providing the user additional spatial awareness and haptic response, though, with limited control they could be piloted directly using only gestures. Carli's employer, NuSculpt owned a bank of control harnesses, each in a private room. This room also required calibrated lighting and a cluster of sensors to track the facial movements of the user, so they could be applied to the teeper's projection. Carli found teepers awkward to control and tended to avoid using them unless she had no other option.

Carli approached the entrance of the building that housed NuSculpt. She passed a person in a wheelchair, holding a cardboard sign with the words 'Bits for Back'. An icon her augments would allow her to initiate a money transfer. She'd met him before. His name was Vinesh Naidoo. She'd transferred a few bits to him once and had even had a brief conversation with him, but now she found herself ignoring him.

She greeted the receptionist at the oversized, centrally positioned desk in the middle of NuSculpt's lobby. Projected on the concaved walls around the desk was an underwater scene populated with corals and various sea creatures. It made Carli feel as though she'd been immersed in an underwater capsule like the kind described in stories from her youth.

These surface projections, called scapes, were everywhere in Praxis, from the walls of the transit to Carli's apartment. Buildings had no windows—if the view beyond the domes were visible, it would reveal only a wasteland. Instead, the Network overlayed positional markers on the wall surface with three-dimensional projections representing what the world used to look like, or something more fantastical dreamed up in the mind of an artist. Whatever ugliness may lie beneath was inconsequential when it could be overlaid with something better. One day, a home could be a rainforest retreat, and the next, an alpine lodge.

Carli's apartment currently exhibited scapes from an island resort, which she leased at reasonable expense. Every morning Carli would wake up to the bluest of oceans and the sound of gentle waves breaking onto the sand before retreating into the virtual ocean. This scape was designed to evolve over time, so when Carli returned home after a day's work, she was greeted with the most brilliant ocean sunset. No two sunsets were ever the same. On occasions when she'd returned home later than usual, she would rewind the timing of the scape to replay the sunset she'd missed.

She queued for the elevator with a few coworkers she recognized only by their projected NuSculpt uniforms.

"That guy in the wheelchair is still out there," said one.

Another scoffed and replied, "I know—I'm just going to mask him. I feel bad, but I don't need to see that on my way to work."

Carli said nothing. She considered what sort of advanced society would still have people begging for money—it wasn't common, but even utopias have limited resources. She felt a pang of guilt that she too would consider masking out someone from her reality simply because she wanted to pretend they didn't exist.

This was the first time Detective Hal Briggs had been an active participant in a meeting of the Council of Overseers. The bill before the Council related to the rights of criminals returning to work. He had no idea why he was requested to attend at all—he was one of many senior detectives and as far as he was concerned, politics was well above his pay grade.

"This is someone's idea of a joke, right?" he said. He was speaking to the other people in the physical room he was in, rather than the virtual meeting space for the Council.

"They asked for a front-line detective, Hal. An 'expert'." Briggs' vision showed only the virtual room of the Council, but he would recognise the voice of Anneke Hagen, his Captain anywhere.

"So, this is your fault?" he asked.

"On the advice of counsel, I decline to answer that question," she said.

Briggs scoffed, but she was pretty much the only person he didn't mind being stirred by. She'd more than earned that right—she was the kind of friend you want on your side before a disciplinary hearing or a rehabilitation panel. Something he knew from personal experience.

He was posted in the ambiguously titled, 'Network Crimes' division—a catch-all for any crime relating to the systems that made the Network and the Collective tick. It was a department filled with junior detectives putting in their time before being appointed to more interesting posts, officers being rehabilitated, and officers approaching the twilight of their careers. Briggs met two of those criteria.

He fidgeted uncomfortably in his seat. He was physically in a board room on the 12th floor of the PPD headquarters deep in the centre of Praxis Central. His virtual projection was possessing a teeper in the back row of the Council

Chamber. An array of sensors in the board room mapped Briggs' voice and movements seamlessly onto the remote projection. It was already starting to make him feel unwell. He had the rare privilege of being one of the few people in the Collective whose brains struggled to reconcile their perception of the physical world with the often conflicting information from the virtual world.

In the meeting space, the twenty-one Overseers sat at a doughnut-shaped table. Around them in concentric arcs were members of different administrative arms of the Collective and petitioners who were to speak for or against any motion raised.

A single humanoid virtual presence occupied a seat in the centre of the room. Layered over the top of its skin was the amalgamation of the projections of every citizen across the entire Collective at that moment. Six million trueselfs were projected as one individual, one consciousness. The citizens of the Network are the Collective, and in this room, the kaleidoscope of infinite individuality was distilled into a singular physical presence. It would not move—but from any position in the room, it would appear to be looking straight at them. Briggs found it distracting.

Any member of the Collective who wished to passively participate in these meetings could connect to this single presence to see and hear everything happening in the room. All speeches, arguments and counter-arguments were posed not to the other Overseers, but to this one virtual presence as a proxy for the thousands of people who connected to it.

In the virtual space, Briggs was seated next to his indirect supervisor, Deputy Commissioner Earl Moya, an imposing figure who had cautioned Briggs not to make a fool of himself or the department when he was called on to speak. Where Briggs was a straight shooter, Moya was skilfully elusive, politically astute, and opportunistic. Even among the most adverse of scandals, Moya survived, even thrived. Needless to say, Briggs despised the man.

The Council chairperson called on someone on the opposite side of the room to speak. Though Briggs could hear them clearly, he paid little attention to what was said. He instead took in the Chamber itself, appointed with the most luxurious of furnishing, including hand-carved wooden furniture with gold inlay. Every element in the room, from carpets to the lighting installations, pointed the participant to the centre of the room, where the Collective sat and watched.

Another officer, Lieutenant Constança Gomes, head of ONI joined them in the room. The 'Office of Network Integrity' or ONI was a specialised division in Network Crimes for investigating anomalies in the Network itself, including attempts to hack or compromise it. Their officers were secretive, with capabilities Briggs couldn't begin to understand. It was either the arrogance of their well-paid consultants or Briggs' ignorance of what they did that led him to treat them with guarded contempt.

"Captain," she addressed Hagen. "Detective Briggs, I don't think we've really met." Briggs offered a passable salutation. He was concentrating on his breathing to try and placate his vestibular system which wasn't happy about him being in two places at once.

A cue informed him that he was about to be called on to speak.

"I'm just about to plug in," Hagen said. "I'll be looking right at you as you speak. When they ask their questions, just pretend you are talking to me."

"I thought you told me to be diplomatic," Briggs said.

"True—but just pretend you are talking to a version of me that wants to be impressed like we're on a first date," she said. In a louder voice, she spoke to the room, "But for any recording devices in the room, that last statement should be taken metaphorically, not literally."

A momentary smile crept onto Briggs' face before he was addressed by the Council Chairperson.

"Detective Sergeant Hal Briggs…" Brigg's teeper stood in the virtual room, though he physically remained seated. An overlay within his optics told him he was now 'live'. As his perspective elevated, the Collective presence in the centre of the room now focused its attention on him.

The Chairperson, who was also standing was dressed in a knee-length, ivory-coloured sherwani worn over silk pants. A virtual callout identified the Chairperson as PraxisJudiciary, making them one of the three permanent members of the 21-Seat Council. PraxisJudiciary was not one individual, but a representation of the entire judicial branch of Praxis government. The other two permanent members of the Overseer included PraxisAdministration which represented all administration functions within Government, including the PPD, and PraxisNetwork which represented Augmosis, the founder of the Network itself. The remaining 18 members were all added to the Council as a result of followership within the Collective.

"You have been commended to the Council by the PPD as a frontline expert to respond to our questions. We acknowledge you are a decorated officer of 29 years. You have been a detective for 19 years, the last four being in the Network Crimes division. We recognise you will be speaking only on your own behalf and not as a representative of the Police Department itself. So just answer as truthfully as you can."

*Maybe this won't be so bad*, he thought for a moment.

"Yes sir." A more correct response would have been to say, "Yes, Overseer", but Briggs didn't feel it necessary to correct himself.

"You have reviewed the proposed bill before this Council." It wasn't a question. "One of our members wished to pose questions to a frontline officer to help them understand the impact of this bill on law enforcement."

The chairperson pivoted to another member, "Overseer ArdentBlue?"

Overseer ArdentBlue stood. She wore a royal blue evening gown with a plunging neckline. It clung closely to her meticulously sculpted and feminine figure. She had the face of a woman in her early thirties, framed by mid-length wavy brown hair that settled lightly on her shoulders.

His cynicism kicked in. *That looks expensive*, he thought. *In real life, she's probably twice that size and twice that age.*

"Detective Briggs, thank you for joining with us today." Briggs didn't think her voice matched her projection, even if he couldn't decide why. "We have already heard several speakers in support of or in opposition to this bill. So, at this point, I only have one question."

That seemed easy enough.

"Detective Briggs, if a suspect stands before you, brandishing a weapon such as a knife or firearm, and you are forced to draw your sidearm in response, will having their projection stripped away to reveal only their oldself make any difference to your capacity to defend yourself and subdue that suspect?"

Briggs paused briefly before answering, "No it won't, Ma'am".

A subtle but resolute smile washed across ArdentBlue's perfect lips. Apparently, she'd expected a different response.

"Thank you for your candour, Detective Briggs," ArdentBlue postured. "This Council thanks you for your time here this morning and for your many years of service".

The Chairperson confirmed none of the other members of the Council wanted to ask a follow-up question before also thanking Briggs for his time and moving on to another speaker. He disconnected from the meeting to find Lieutenant Gomes leaving the room and Captain Hagen staring at him wildly.

"What the hell was that?"

"What? You said to be honest? Besides, I only answered the question I was asked." Briggs knew he was being facetious.

"That wasn't honest, you're smart enough to know that wasn't the right answer!"

"Look," he said, "I don't care if some perp's wearing only his lifesuit, his birthday suit or an ape suit—that's not going to stop me from taking him down…"

"But that wasn't the point of the question!" she said, rubbing her face as though he'd just given her a sudden migraine. "You know I'm going to get my arse kicked for this."

He smirked at her cheekily, "You still love me, right?"

"Argghh." She shook her head despairingly, but her eyes told Hal a different story. She smiled. "Whoever suggested you would be the right person to answer that question, needs to have their augments checked."

"What? I thought it was you?" Hal joked.

Simultaneously, they each received an incoming voice communication from the Network. "That's probably Deputy Moya ringing to revoke my commission," she said.

However, when they both connected, it was a very different story.

"This is Detective Carlyle out of West Praxis Homicide," the caller began. "Who am I speaking to?"

Hagen took the lead. "You have Captain Hagen and Detective Briggs here from Network Crimes. What do you need?"

"We have two homicides, including one officer." A pause. "Sirs, we believe they may have been killed by their augments."

Briggs and Hagen looked at each other before Briggs pressed in. "Why do you say that?"

"Well, both died the same way in two different locations. Their plexus has melted to slag through their chest. Sorry to be so graphic".

"Send me the details, I'm on my way there." Briggs closed the call and stood, with a fresh energy. "Looks like I've got some real work to do," he said.

Hagen nodded. "Maybe you ticking off Deputy Moya wasn't the biggest problem I'll have to deal with today."

Exiting the elevator to her 6th-floor workspace, Carli was greeted with open-plan cubicles encircled by breakout spaces and meeting rooms. Scapes were projected on the outer walls instead of windows. Each overlooked a city scape with lush parks and beautiful buildings from an age long-forgotten.

Even though she was on the 6th floor, the scape appeared as though the office was near the 40th floor of a historic metropolitan skyscraper. The view in one direction looked out onto a forested rectangular park so large, Carli could barely see the end in the distance. A variety of buildings, some concrete, some glass, surrounded the park in all directions.

Carli's dedicated work studio was positioned on what would have been the eastern face of the building. This gave her one of the best views of the park below, though a large part of the work she performed needed the scapes to be deactivated to minimise distraction.

She approached and greeted her assistant, Lori who had again beaten her to work this morning, despite the fact her domicile was in the region of Rubyvale which was one of the furthermost parts of Praxis.

"Good morning Ms. Dawes, I have your work package prepared for your 9:00 am with Ms. Pasadi."

"Thanks, Lori. Again, please call me Carli." This routine had gone the same way every morning for the last six months. Carli said it with a smile on her face. It was a level of respect given to Carli that she felt unearned considering Lori was perhaps 30 years her senior.

"Ms. Pasadi has just arrived. The Care Team is keeping her well entertained in Suite C."

Carli thanked her again. She would have a few minutes before the Care Team would be ready to receive her and she needed to review the prepared work package. She collected the package from Lori's outstretched hand—a graphite slate with an attached stylus. The slate was blank except for a single unique tracking marker that would be replaced when the package was applied.

The lights in Carli's studio activated when she walked in, though the windows facing the park already illuminated the room. It was sparsely furnished, with little more than some visitor's chairs and Carli's own chair which she rarely used. Her work was best performed standing up.

The most important item in the room, a zippered case was placed on a side table. The case was old—a recycled surgical case from many years ago. It had been given to Carli as a gift from NuSculpt's directors when she was promoted to her current role of lead sculptor.

The items inside this case were as important to Carli as scalpels and clamps were to a surgeon. In fact, many of them may have resembled those same instruments and fulfilled a similar purpose. In her hands, these instruments had sculpted the trueselfs of hundreds of citizens of the Collective.

Carli's sculpting specialty was called 'true realism'. She created a real, life-like projection for the client that fit their sense of self identity. Her role was not so much to invent some new identity for the client, but to uncover the identity which already lay within and bring it to the surface for the world to see. The result may be closely aligned with the client's base ethnicity and gender or may deviate significantly.

With the door now closed, using a series of hand gestures, the walls of the studio grew completely black, and the model of Ms. Gail Pasadi appeared in front of her. The model included two things: the original oldself of a sixty-year-old woman and the overlay of her trueself, a much more dignified woman in her early forties. A title above this trueself stated:

GAIL BRONWYN PASADI

AKA: MEOWCATZ

TRUESELF V4.9.1.3

With a wave of her hand, Carli separated the two selfs so that they were side by side. There was very little in common between the two. Where her oldself was overweight and effectively bald, the trueself was more athletic in shape, with full, slightly wavy brown hair. There was some resemblance in her face, though the eyes of all the oldselfs were always dark.

Though Ms. Pasadi could at times be a demanding customer, Carli was committed to giving her the same professional service as the rest of her clients. She'd been able to integrate elements of Ms. Pasadi's past and personality into her sculpt. This included a slight increase in height and the redefinition of her body to include more of an hourglass figure. It matched her aristocrat-style personality well. It would have been easy to completely edit away all of the scars from her face, but these had also helped to shape who she was. Instead, they were replaced with far more subdued blemishes, as a memorial to her lifetime of perseverance.

Carli sighed. It was not going to be easy to begin this process over again and arrive at something new. The sculptor fed on the energy of the client to create. Carli feared that, for *this* client, the well may be starting to run dry.

Her phonics chirped. Ms. Pasadi was ready for her interview. Carli waved away the models before her, and the room's lights brightened back to their normal level as she left the room. She made her way back down to the building's third level, carrying the slate in hand. The door opened as she approached. Ms Pasadi stood from her comfortable couch to meet her.

"Carli, darling! It's so good to see you again." She approached and held Carli's shoulders—a substitute for a hug. "I'm afraid I've been somewhat naughty…"

Carli barely heard her. Her gaze was instead fixed on Ms. Pasadi's face. Not the dignified face she'd crafted for her almost six months ago, but something foreign. Something almost ghoulish. Her eyes looked sunken, and her cheekbones far more pronounced. Her nose was no longer bold and assertive, but had been unrealistically narrowed with the tip upturned. What made things worse was that Carli could see a number of tracking errors between the trueself and the oldself beneath. As she moved the muscles of her face, the trueself didn't respond correctly. At times, the projected image jumped completely.

This was the work of an amateur sculptor. Perhaps even Ms. Pasadi herself. Carli felt someone had just painted over her masterpiece. She bit her tongue before forcing a smile.

"No problems, Ms. Pasadi. We'll have you looking great in no time."

"Oh, thank you, darling!" Her shoulder hug ended with a gentle squeeze and a distorted smile that skipped and vibrated around her face in waves of pixels.

Three hours and a rushed lunch later, Carli had finalised the work to correct Ms. Pasadi's trueself. It could have been restored from a private backup, but her client also demanded new changes. Carli had hoped for more time to prepare for her sculpting appointment with her new client, Aliya Qureshi but it had been stolen from her. She paused to catch her breath before entering the interview room, making a conscious decision to remind herself that this was her favourite part of the job.

"Good afternoon," Carli said with a smile, taking a seat on the comfortable couch opposite her client.

She was welcomed with an anxious smile. "Peace be with you."

"It's good to meet with you again. Thank you for giving me the privilege of sculpting your new identity. Are you still happy for me to refer to you by your first name?"

"Yes, that's fine." She nodded in agreement.

The work package Carli was reviewing included the preliminary interview information previously captured by a member of the NuSculpt sales team. Aliya Qureshi was 17 and currently wore an inexpensive, generic trueself she had leased as a temporary placeholder until her new one had been sculpted.

"Thank you, Aliya. As I said, this truly is a privilege for me. I have had the joy of sculpting the trueselfs of over a thousand citizens, but to be honest, nothing is more exciting to me than partnering with a new client to create a new identity."

Carli had said something similar many times before for her new clients, but it was one of her strongest-held beliefs. To Carli, *this* was her mission. Her work to create beauty and uniqueness was her identity. Aliya Qureshi offered a cautious smile in response.

"Aliya, there are few relationships more intimate than between a client and their sculptor. In this relationship, we both need to be honest with our thoughts and feelings. The things we love and the things we do not. How does that sound?"

Aliya nodded again.

"This is a completely private room. In this space, there is only you and me. Nothing is recorded, and no one sees what happens. The first step of this process is for you to remove your current projection and allow me to see your oldself. From there, we can start this process with complete openness."

Aliya's head lowered. Carli detected a strong sense of shyness—a common reaction.

"*My* trueself is the projection of my real identity. There are similarities between the self beneath and the self above. What I choose to project to the Collective is the best version of myself, but I believe that there needs to be a connection between who you are and the self you choose to project.

"Just like you, I can be self-conscious about sharing my oldself, especially with someone I don't know well. But it is truly nothing to be ashamed of. Your body is the vessel that carries your desires and your dreams. It bears the marks that this world has imparted upon you. It is the clay from which your trueself is sculpted. Your scars may have brought you to where you are now, but it doesn't define your future."

Her client looked up before nodding again. This was often the hardest barrier to break through. With a sequence of gestures, she removed her temporary projection. Now wearing only her lifesuit, Carli could see for the first time the oldself of Aliya Qureshi.

A petite figure. Beautiful eyes, although the dark discs of her optics still obscured them. Her complexion was smooth and youthful. Her nose was straight and bold with cheekbones more striking than any Carli had seen before. As she watched, Aliya Qureshi also removed the bonnet of her lifesuit to reveal her whole head. Lush brown hair was released past her shoulders. In Carli's opinion, she was… beautiful.

There was also something unique about her face. Aliya Quershi suffered from vitiligo. Patches of white shone through her otherwise golden skin. These patches were most prominent around her mouth and the sides of her nose, as well as her hands.

It was a very uncommon condition. And yet, the texture of her skin was otherwise unblemished. Here, in Carli's presence was a young woman, who was simply marvellous. The white patches on her skin did not detract from her projection—in Carli's view, they amplified it. She was truly unique and truly beautiful.

**06**

The transit to West Praxis took almost an hour, but Briggs wasted little time on the journey. He'd already reviewed everything in the case file via the Network. Officers in the field had begun to bank witness statements and other observations to the PPD's private network. Briggs held back from viewing the banked recordings—he wanted to take in the crime scenes with his own eyes first.

The first victim had been reported by Officer Nguyen at 8:10 am, who had observed the homicide himself before pursuing the suspect. That victim was Petros Zaimis, a 52 year-old male with a healthy rap sheet including convictions for battery and assault, break and enter, and drug possession.

His most recent conviction was for 'Destruction of Property'. Zaimis had taken a steel bar to a Telepresence Robot, breaking both legs. The teeper had been hosting the projection of an associate known to Zaimis, but it was unknown if he knew if he was attacking a teeper or a real person. Since his associate did not wish to press charges themselves, the offence was recorded only as a misdemeanour. This offence broke the conditions of his parole from a previous conviction, and he was swiftly sent back to the penitentiary in County. He was also fined for the cost of repairs to the teeper. If his associate had pressed charges, however, this could have been pushed up to felony assault, if it could be proved that Zaimis did not know the projection was only a teeper.

The second victim was Officer Nguyen himself. After witnessing the first homicide, Nguyen requested and was provided with a surveillance warrant. He also requested immediate backup to his location, but it seemed no-one was even dispatched until over an hour later. That struck Briggs as an anomaly that needed to be investigated. The path through a complicated crime, particularly in the Network Crimes division, was always in the anomalies. The systems of the Collective were robust and predictable. Anomalies pushed against those systems in a way that usually created a trail.

There had been a third person, Fernando Alvarez, who had been present at the fatal meeting. Alvarez had been piloting a teeper and had a far shorter criminal history, noting only minor offences and misdemeanours. He had undergraduate and postgraduate qualifications in electrical engineering and robotics, which Briggs thought set him apart from the usual class of criminals he dealt with. Alvarez had not been located since the event, and an interview warrant had been issued.

Reviewing this information in the transit carriage was becoming increasingly difficult for Briggs. He desperately wanted to try to get a head start on the details of the case, but even the subtle motion of the carriage played havoc with his vestibular system when combined with the information projected into his view. He reluctantly disconnected the stream of information and shut his eyes. Long, rhythmic breaths helped him to re-centre and the sense of vertigo dissipated as he opened his eyes.

Augmentation Vestibular Syndrome was rare across the Collective. In Briggs' case, it was getting no better with age and there was no permanent treatment. It was one of the reasons Briggs had been posted to the Network Crimes division since it was beginning to impact his capacity to work in the field. He had no issues when his body was perceiving only one reality, such as when seated in a quiet room, but the stimuli from two separate realities collided inside his brain in a way that inevitably led to a violent response from his stomach.

His disability held him back from doing the work he loved in the full capacity it deserved. Still, he was confident his other skills as an investigator more than made up for any deficit. Unlike the rest of his vices, he at least accepted this one was beyond his control. Unfortunately, appearing unsteady on your feet and unwell had raised the ire of some of his fellow officers, and Briggs found himself having to regularly prove he wasn't under the influence of drugs or alcohol. This was ironic since he was also a recovering alcoholic.

As the sensation faded, he looked out the virtual window of the carriage. A digitally crafted urban landscape moved along with the travelling of the transit. The transit was 200 meters underground, and what lay above probably looked nothing like what this scape portrayed. Over the top of this window was a freshly sprayed graffiti tag obstructing and interfering with the view. It simply said, 'Wake Up'.

A virtual perimeter screen encircled the crime scene. Only citizens with law enforcement or emergency services credentials could peer inside. From Briggs' perspective, this perimeter appeared as a semi-transparent hemispherical mesh 20 meters around the centre of the crime scene but for everyone else, it was an impenetrable dome of white, bounded by a blue and white checkered tape with the words, "CRIME SCENE: DO NOT CROSS".

He walked past an officer standing sentry outside the screen before walking through and seeing the crime scene for the first time. The wet body of the deceased lay on his back next to a table. He'd already reviewed the witness statement of the café manager who had moved the body onto the ground. After noticing Zaimis' plexus seemed to be "on fire", the manager's first reaction was to upend a nearby cleaning bucket to solve the problem. The outcome was a body that was equal parts dead and saturated.

Crime scene technicians were also at work. An optics technician was placing a series of pole-mounted cameras at different positions around the body. When complete, he would call for all other technicians to step away and a detailed three-dimensional model would be instantly captured including every strand of hair and speck of dust. The scan was detailed enough to capture fingerprints and penetrated the top layers of the body itself to allow a partial digital reconstruction.

Though a full autopsy would later be conducted by the medical examiner, this scan was usually sufficient to determine the cause of death almost instantly. As the technician continued in his work, Briggs made a mental note to check with them before he left the scene to request an advanced copy of those results.

A pair of gloved technicians stood to the side of the body, waiting patiently for the optics technician to complete their work. These technicians would be taking swabs from the body and around the crime scene once it had been cleared.

Further afield, officers were continuing to take statements from witnesses. Those statements would all be permanently filed against each citizen, cross-referenced with this case by time and geographic location. Like officers, a citizen could "bank" the last 10 minutes of what they perceived from the Network, but for reasons of privacy, everything else that streamed through the Network to create their reality was destroyed. Unless this data was specifically banked, it could not be magically recalled and replayed. Storage of this data was expensive, and few citizens made use of it, other than to store specific key memories for later recall. Even then, a citizen would often edit those banked memories to remove elements and even other citizens at their discretion. As such, they were often unreliable as evidence unless captured by a police officer, who was restricted from modifying banked recordings.

Briggs spotted Detective Carlyle at the edge of the perimeter, concluding a witness interview and made his way towards him.

"Detective Carlyle."

"Briggs", Carlyle said turning, pointing directions to one of the technicians as he moved. "You made good time. I was surprised when you said you'd come here in person. The last time I referred something to Network Crimes, they just sent a teeper."

"I like to work the old-fashioned way," Briggs said.

Briggs understood what Carlyle was implying. Most of the Network Crimes team rarely left level 12 of the PPD headquarters. Most did their work virtually or with a teeper.

"Well, it's good to see you in the flesh," Carlyle said.

Briggs asked, "Warrants issued for the other two at the table? This Fernando Alvarez and whoever this Korb1K is?"

"Yes," Carlyle said. "Alvarez seems to be out of range. But whoever this Korb1K is—the system doesn't register his ID. We had to force the ID into the machine to even get it to save the report."

Briggs had reviewed the warrant. Alvarez being offline was possible if he was located a distance greater than 200m from a PPD officer, which was the range of basic warrants. However, he was more concerned that a citizen could exist within the Network without an ID. This was another anomaly to follow up.

The optics technician gave a wave to indicate his work was complete and the technicians and officers could now enter the crime scene. Carlyle and Briggs moved together to get a closer look.

The burns on the body were just as unpleasant as they had been described by Detective Carlyle. A 10-centimetre-wide hole had been burned in Zaimis' chest at least through his sternum and into his chest cavity. The fibres of the lifesuit had also melted and fused onto his skin around the hole. What remained of the plexus was little more than a blackened lump the size of a small fist, now resting almost on the victim's spine. Briggs tried not to consider the surrounding flesh, nor the acrid smell, including the lower parts of the heart had now been cooked.

"Seen anything like it?"

"No—nothing like this before," Briggs replied.

Throughout his career, Briggs had seen many unsettling things. The pristine utopia that was projected to the Collective failed to restrain antisocial and violent behaviour. The controls of the Network often restricted many more predatory types of crimes since any citizen could instantly and covertly transmit a distress request not only to law enforcement but to any citizens nearby. Still, there were those for whom a virtual fantasy became no longer satisfying and had to be played out in the physical reality, with much violence and much pain.

Briggs found these perversions increasingly common. The files of the PPD were filled with citizens who gouged out their own eyes to "make the visions stop" or had tried to remove their phonics with whatever long, metal tool they had available to them. Even more unsettling were those citizens who managed to do this without any stims in their system, as though it was simply the only rational choice available to them.

In this case, Briggs saw something completely new, but just as disturbing. The fact that he was a convicted criminal went only a small way to alleviate his disquiet.

"That hole in his chest," Carlyle asked, "Surely that's from a weapon? Maybe a taser or EMP could cause the plexus to overload?"

"Nguyen's banked footage should tell us for sure." Briggs removed a small torch and was methodically scanning each element of the body to see if any clues stood out. It was technically redundant, but it helped Briggs think.

"Well, that's going to be somewhat of a problem," Carlyle said. Briggs looked up, confused. "That data's been corrupted. We can see it was banked, but it just appears as static. That's the other reason we called you in—I didn't think that could happen."

Briggs looked down, his brow furrowed, "It can't."

"That's only half of it—the warrant for surveillance of the suspect approved by Judge Khoury is also gone. So is Nguyen's live stream of the pursuit. We have a record that he activated the stream, but it doesn't exist. We haven't confirmed with the Judge yet, but there is a small chance he may have witnessed Nguyen's livestream himself."

"So, our only objective witness for two murders is a judge, who probably reviews the footage of a hundred crimes every day?"

"Yep. This is a right royal stuff up." Carlyle turned to move away, patting Briggs on the back, "And since these things are above my pay grade, it looks like you get to figure out who stuffed it."

Briggs stayed crouched, staring blankly at the body whilst his mind tried to assemble this information in a way that would reveal a logical explanation. He failed. He stood, stepped back from the body, and watched for a few more minutes as the lab technicians continued to work.

There wasn't anything more he could learn from the scene that he couldn't learn later when he reviewed all the captured data. As he walked past the optics technician, he enquired, "Preliminary cause of death?"

"Indeterminate," he replied.

"Figures." Of course, nothing about this case was going to be simple.

L iam Nolan's lip curled—he was tired of being told how to do his job.

<258041-9AF5EE> YOUR ACTIONS WERE EXCESSIVE.

<NULL> YOU TOLD ME TO CLEAN UP THE LOOSE END. THAT'S WHAT I DID.

The simple text communication didn't communicate Korb1k's smirk. He'd been told before these communications were fully secure, but he remained guarded.

<4B9E56-19DAC7> A PUBLIC DISPLAY DOES NOT SERVE OUR INTERESTS. DRAWING ATTENTION AT THIS MOMENT CREATES UNWANTED COMPLEXITY. YOU SHOULD NOT HAVE KILLED THE POLICE OFFICER.

Korb1k composed a rushed response.

<NULL> HE TRACKED ME TO MY APARTMENT. YOU TOLD ME THAT WASN'T POSSIBLE.

<DEA693-7942F2> THE LEGION HAS LIMITS. WE CANNOT INTERCEPT EVERY SURVEILLANCE WARRANT. HOWEVER, IF WE HADN'T DELAYED THE POLICE RESPONSE OR CLONED YOUR PROJECTION, YOU WOULD NOW BE IN CUSTODY.

<NULL> SO, DO YOU WANT ME TO THANK YOU?

Immediately he felt like he'd crossed a line.

<98212A-573EC1> LIAM, WE HAVE MANY PEOPLE IN OUR EMPLOY. YOU ARE FAR FROM INDISPENSABLE, BUT FOR NOW, IT SUITS OUR

PURPOSES FOR YOU TO REMAIN ACTIVE. YOUR KORB1K IDENTIFIER HAS
NOW BEEN RECYCLED. YOUR NEW IDENTIFIER WILL BE AVAILABLE
WITHIN 24 HOURS. UNTIL THEN, STAY HIDDEN.

Liam did not need this explained. Korb1k had been his third identifier in the past six months. Without an identifier, Korb1k was just Liam Nolan. This made him practically naked. He could not interact with the Network or don a projection. He still perceived the Collective through his augments, but the Collective did not perceive him. How his employer was even able to communicate with him in this state still confused him.

Without his identity, he could not hide his tall and muscular stature, nor the scars that covered his face and body like a half-melted candle. His left hand was an exception—replaced with a black carbon fibre prosthesis, attached just below the elbow. It wasn't as nimble as a healthy human hand, but it was a significant upgrade from the disfigured lump of burned flesh that preceded it.

<48FBC8-995F0F> WE GAVE YOU A NEW LIMB FOR OUR PURPOSES.
WE CAN TAKE IT BACK AT ANY MOMENT. IT WOULD BE WISE FOR YOU
TO REMEMBER THAT.

Liam raised an eyebrow. He'd never heard his employer make such a threat.

<NULL> I UNDERSTAND.

<0EE4B8-B05970> GOOD. IS YOUR LOCATION SECURE?

<NULL> YES. I'M STILL IN WEST PRAXIS BUT IN A SECOND SAFE
HOUSE.

<7CF9D4-4769B7> GOOD. A NEW IDENTITY WILL BE PROVIDED
SOON. ONCE IT IS IN PLACE, WE HAVE ANOTHER ASSIGNMENT FOR
YOU.

Liam Nolan no longer exists.

The conversation concluded. Liam found himself alone in a new safe house—another apartment nearly identical to the one he had before. He rubbed his eyes with both hands, one fleshy and scarred and the other, cold and hard. Prosthetic limbs weren't uncommon across Praxis, but they were never visible since they were concealed by the wearer's projection, just like a teeper.

His was not a standard factory model, however. In the palm of his hand was a circular disc the size of a large coin. A transparent covering revealed only a deep darkness with an occasional flicker of orange plasma from the centre to the edge of the disc. Liam hadn't been told what this device was or how it worked. He only knew that, when activated, on someone's skin, halfway between their plexus and their optics, it would render them incapacitated.

It gave Liam a strange sense of power, but it was also the leverage his employer needed to control him. He suspected the moment his employer no longer needed his services, this strange device would be his end. But Liam was resourceful. He had a rather brutal contingency planned should it ever be required: a six-inch-long metal blade concealed in a sheath sewn into the calf of his lifesuit. The hundreds of thousands of bits in his accounts were worth nothing if he wasn't around to use them.

Liam had used his device several times before, but in private locations where disposal of the bodies could be performed without the prying eyes of law enforcement. He knew taking care of Petros Zaimis in such a public place was risky, but Zaimis was being difficult and refused to meet him in person anywhere else. Liam didn't regret purging Zaimis from the Network. The fool had drawn the attention of a smuggling syndicate when he'd tried to sell off some recovered Old-World contraband. According to Liam's employer, they couldn't afford that kind of attention. It also sent a message to Alvarez of the consequences of defying his employer.

The police officer was regrettable, however. Not that killing an officer bothered him any more than any other sorry soul in the Collective. But it was a rushed decision, followed by a rushed relocation. Rushed decisions were never wise decisions. Still, his employer had kept him safe. Separating your projection from your body to form a decoy was a neat trick his employer had taught him. The downside was it could only be done once per identity.

After the deed was done, Liam donned a trench coat, glasses and fedora hat to cover his projection-less body. He'd returned the police officer's sidearm to its holster before disposing of the smouldering body down the elevator shaft.

Liam's new clothing and accessories were rarities, recycled from a time long ago and had cost him a small fortune. At least by wearing these, Liam could somewhat blend in with the rest of the citizens of the Collective. Even with a turned-up collar, his burned face was still visible, but since there was such a large variety of different selfs and masks, it could be dismissed as just another horror movie-themed artistic expression.

The sleeves and fingerless gloves of his lifesuit covered most of his right hand, but Liam had removed the material and haptic sensors from around his prosthetic. The prosthetic itself functioned like the hand sensors in a lifesuit, so having both was redundant. Without a projection, he'd wrapped a strip of material he'd found around it to keep it concealed.

After collecting his pack he'd left the apartment building and walked the 12 blocks to another building in even poorer repair. His journey took almost ninety minutes, at a pace which was brisk but unhurried. A few detours confirmed he wasn't being followed. He also took extra care avoiding smaller industrial and commercial areas still using old technology security cameras that could capture part of his journey. Most businesses and public spaces instead used optical sensors to capture people's projections, rather than natural light. Liam covered his face as a precaution, nonetheless. Even in his grotesque natural state, the citizens of the Collective were too preoccupied to pay him any mind.

His new safe house was another low-cost domicile S7E3 on the 23$^{rd}$ level. It had little more than a mattress on the floor, a refrigerator, and an ablution space. A clean air supply and running water covered his basic needs. But being effectively disconnected from the Network until a new identity had been prepared meant no access to Network content, and no access to his accounts.

He opened the refrigerator and removed a protein drink—one of many he'd stashed there weeks earlier. He hadn't expected to be using this safe house so soon. Though there was enough food in the room for a few days he hoped to be well gone by then. His carry bag contained his only entertainment: a rubber ball and a pack of playing cards. Both doubled as a form of therapy, helping to build his fine motor skills for the alien-like device attached just below his left elbow.

For emergencies, he carried with him about 40 chips of platinum in a small paper box. Each chip, about two grams in weight was worth about 50 bits, but would only be accepted by a certain kind of establishment. Fortunately, Liam had a sense for locating the kinds of establishments that would accept this alternate currency. For a moment Liam considered stepping outside and finding a bar or stim dealer, just to give him something to make the wait a little more bearable. He dismissed the thought—for now.

There was little Briggs could learn inspecting the body of Officer Nguyen. The forensic and optics technicians were still trying to process the scene in the elevator well, crowding each other in the confined space. Briggs didn't add to the confusion by joining them. He didn't need the technicians to tell him that Nguyen had died from the same mystery augment malfunction—the gaping hole in his chest made that clear. His immediate conclusion was that the body had been disposed of down the elevator shaft post-mortem unless he found evidence to the contrary.

Speaking with the building controller over the Network, Briggs learned that a locking mechanism had been recently breached in a domicile on level 9 of the building. Details of the lessee weren't forthcoming, either because the controller didn't want to share them or because they did not exist. Briggs presumed this would be the main crime scene and laboured up the nine flights of stairs with two local officers in tow.

He found the door ajar and the room empty. Briggs hadn't expected to find his quarry in the room waiting to be arrested—not three hours after the crime. Via the Network, he gave instructions to the officers and forensic team to join him upstairs when they were finished, and he donned a pair of latex gloves.

The locking mechanism was destroyed. Nguyen had breached the door before entering. Briggs noticed a pea-sized impression in the wall opposite the door at chest height. Switching his flashlight to UV, he inspected the hole, revealing a glowing reflection from the circuitry contained within the metal shell. *Nguyen had gotten a shot off.*

Briggs marked this location with a virtual marker, adding a callout requesting technicians perform ballistics. It was a redundant step—the technicians would have picked up the shell the same as he would, but it was a routine that helped Briggs work through the scene systematically to ensure he didn't miss anything.

There was very little else of interest in the room. A worn sofa. A small plastic dining table with a single chair. An uncomfortable-looking mattress. The concrete walls once painted cream were now a range of stained colours from rust to olive green. Aside from a layer of dust and rubble from the degrading concrete walls, the room was otherwise clean of rubbish. No food wrappers. No personal effects. No signs of struggle.

The ablution space offered little more. The shower curtain had been lost at some point. The metal tap to control the flow and temperature of the shower was missing, replaced with one-half of a pair of pliers attached by tape. The toilet was dirty, stained from years of continuous running, and a water source high in mineral salts. A small shard of a mirror remained on the wall above the sink. The sink itself contained the rest of the mirror, smashed into fragments.

Briggs directed the officers to set up a crime scene perimeter. One officer removed a unique sticker from a sleeve and attached this on the hallway side above the door frame. A virtual bubble enclosed the doorway to restrict visibility from neighbours beginning to congregate in the hallway. Briggs heard one of them ask the officer outside if they were there to fix their plumbing.

Standing again at the doorway, he pointed his finger like a gun towards the shell in the wall opposite. *Did you miss your target?* The distance from the doorway to the rear wall was only four meters. *That's a hard shot to miss if the guy is standing right in front of you.* Over the PPD network, Briggs recalled Officer Nguyen's most recent sidearm proficiency ratings. 92% - a fair score. Better than Briggs'.

Any observations made by Nguyen prior to his death had been somehow corrupted. The details of the surveillance warrant still existed but did not contain any additional notes. They simply pointed to the banked, but now corrupted footage as justification. As a result, Briggs had no idea what this strange weapon was that could somehow take down an experienced officer without struggle. *If it was fired there should be some form of entry wound on the victim.* The scan of Zaimis' body didn't reveal this, but perhaps the entry wounds had been missed.

The only other plausible option Briggs could come up with was that it had somehow been administered by the Network itself, perhaps even remotely. It was a radical idea and not something Briggs would share—any suggestion that the Network could kill would be political suicide. Briggs hoped the later autopsies might reveal more. He requested whatever remained of the two victims' augments be recovered and analysed by his liaisons at Augmosis. He expected he would most likely be paying them a visit soon anyway.

*This part of the puzzle now has two pieces*, Briggs thought: *how did he miss and how did he die?*

"Hell of a way to go out sir." One of the arriving officers broke into Briggs' concentration. Briggs might have normally given him a curt response but checked himself. *These are West Praxis officers*, he reminded himself. *They just lost one of their own.*

"Hell of a way," Briggs said.

He gained temporary access to a vacant domicile 3 doors down from the level 9 crime scene. It was an identical apartment in shape and size. A single plastic chair and a few other small items had been left behind by the previous tenant. This gave him some privacy from the optics technicians who had just arrived and were setting up their scanning equipment. More forensics officers would follow, scanning for prints and DNA, and would extract the shell for analysis.

As the technicians did their work, Briggs charged the two officers with him to take witness statements from the people in the surrounding domiciles. He would review these later but did not expect them to yield any fruit. These rooms were mostly empty: their occupants scattered well across the rest of the city, working in restaurants, factories, schools or nightclubs. Unless Korb1k had walked around without a projection, any kind of physical description would not be particularly useful. And since most citizens made an unconscious decision not to notice anyone but themselves, even getting a sense of when he'd been spotted in the building over the last three weeks would be difficult.

He considered his next course of action. A warrant had been issued for the other witness, Fernando Alvarez. West Praxis division was presently following up with any known associates. Unlike the first suspect, Korb1k, Alvarez still "existed" within the Network. He simply could not be located. An officer within a range of 200 meters would be able to locate him in their optics. The technology of the Network should allow the PPD to track anyone at any location, however, that was yet another unreasonable restriction placed on the PPD as the means to strike a balance between safety, privacy and personal liberty.

Unless Alvarez had taken a one-way trip outside the dome, he was most likely still in West Praxis. Scanners at the transit station would immediately alert the PPD if he attempted to relocate to Port Lincoln or Vandenberg. However, there were illegal shroud devices that could temporarily switch someone's moniker with a stolen one. They were expensive and only worked for as long as it took the original owner to report their stolen plexus. If Alvarez had used one, he would eventually be tracked down somewhere else.

No, the real mystery was Korb1k—unless something changed, *that* was his priority.

Briggs sat on the plastic chair, he held each hand in front of him, rotating them palm-down to palm-up as he turned his head slowly from side to side. He concentrated on his breathing deeply and slowly. It was a process he'd been taught to try and centre his balance and ease any sense of vertigo. He then instigated a virtual meeting call with Judge Amir Khoury.

The scanners used within the PPD conference rooms were able to perfectly track his movements and project them into a virtual room or a stationary teeper. No such sensors existed here, so Briggs used the cheap substitute which was to look at himself in a mirror. His optics tracked his reflection and sent it into the virtual meeting space. The mirror's frame would act like a window to the other participant.

After a short wait, the call connected. Briggs stood and moved to the mirror located on the wall of the living space, dragging the chair with him by its back. He held onto it tightly, offering extra support—these kinds of virtual calls didn't typically cause him trouble with balance, but having something to hold onto had become his habit. Briggs' reflection dissolved, replaced by the judge. The marks and small cracks in the mirror overlaid the judge's face like they were looking at each other through a dirty window.

"Good afternoon Your Honour. Thank you for taking my call".

"No problems at all Detective Briggs. I understand you had the pleasure of addressing the Council today?"

This caught him off guard, "Uh, yes sir..." The judge did not respond. Briggs continued, trying to break the silence, "It was my first time addressing the Council."

After a long pause, Judge Khoury responded. "I have a busy schedule today, detective. What do you need?"

"Sir, at approximately 8:25 am this morning, you granted a surveillance warrant on a citizen with the moniker of 'Korb1k'." Briggs spelled the name for accuracy. "This request was made by Officer Lee Nguyen after he witnessed the suspect commit a homicide. You may be aware also sir that Officer Nguyen was found deceased almost 70 minutes later."

Briggs chose his next words as carefully as possible. "Sir, for reasons we don't yet know, the banked footage from Officer Nguyen, including the footage used to justify the initial warrant has been somehow corrupted. We therefore have no footage of the initial crime, nor the pursuit immediately thereafter.

"Your Honour, I would like to know if you may be able to describe the footage you reviewed before issuing the warrant."

The judge didn't respond. No emotion or movement whatsoever. Not even a blink. Briggs began to pivot his head, trying to discern if there was something wrong with the conference connection before he was interrupted.

"Detective, I action up over 50 warrants most days. The reason the footage is banked is so that judges don't have to rely on their memory."

"I appreciate that, sir. I can only ask you to give your best recollection."

"I understand." The judge's phrasing was measured and careful. "I believe the footage I reviewed showed a group of three citizens seated at a restaurant table. There were words spoken between the group. Voices were raised, though I could not discern what was being said.

"After a time, the victim, Mr. Zaimis, simply slumped forward in his chair and the other two departed in different directions. In the recording, Officer Nguyen's optics soon advised that the citizen was now deceased, and his projection lifted. Officer Nguyen approached the victim to find his Plexus on fire. This triggered his pursuit of the suspect, Korb1k and the request for the surveillance warrant."

Briggs made mental notes as he went, though he would also bank this conversation as part of his investigation report.

"Sir, did you see a weapon used?"

"Not at first, Detective. Before granting the warrant, I reviewed the moments immediately before the victim slumped in his chair several times over. My best assessment was that the suspect, Korb1k delivered some form of injury to the victim. Prior to the alleged murder, the suspect's hand appeared to come in contact with the victim's neck."

Briggs hastened his questions, excited that a small piece of the puzzle had been identified, even if he didn't yet know where it fit.

"Which hand sir"

"I beg your pardon, Detective?"

"Sir, do you know which of the suspect's hands touched the victim?"

The judge paused again, concentration on his face. He closed his eyes for a few moments, before saying, "I cannot be certain Detective."

"Your best guess, Your Honour?" Briggs probed.

Another pause, "I believe it was his left hand. Again, Detective—I am not certain."

"Thank you, sir, that may still help. Sir, were you able to observe any of Officer Nguyen's livestream as he pursued the suspect?"

"No, I did not. I disconnected my oversight once Officer Nguyen acknowledged the warrant, and I returned to my other duties."

Briggs sourced descriptions of both Korb1k and his accomplice. Visual descriptions weren't usually very helpful, but they remained part of standard procedure. Korb1k's description was limited since, for the most part, his back faced Officer Nguyen, but he doubted it would be helpful.

Briggs thanked Judge Khoury for his assistance and concluded the call. He returned to the crime scene to find the optics technicians packing up their equipment. A preliminary ballistics analysis had been completed, which he activated. A coloured line illuminated in his optics from the bullet hole in the opposite wall through the doorway he was standing in.

Briggs unholstered his own sidearm, removed the magazine, and placed himself just inside the doorway, lining it up to the path of the bullet. He recalled Nguyen's personnel file stating he was left-handed, and he switched his grip accordingly. He remained in this position as he looked around. The open door, with its broken lock, hanging to his right.

"Officer, can you come here for a moment?" Another officer had been posted just outside the doorway.

"Yes sir?"

"Come inside and stand here." Briggs allowed the officer to pass and pointed to a spot to the left side of the door. He resumed his stance in line with the ballistics path.

"Now grab me around the neck."

"Sir?"

"Just do it, not hard. Just like you're checking my pulse."

The officer grabbed his neck with his right hand, twisting his body in an awkward position. He pulled back and tried with his left hand. That worked better.

"Good. Can you give me your ops helmet for a moment?" The officer removed his helmet and Briggs put it on his head.

"OK, can you do it again?"

The officer complied. Even with the helmet on, there was a large area of Briggs' neck exposed above his body armour, but below the face visor.

*Left-hand delivery.*

"Okay, that'll be all." The officer returned to his post.

*So, if he is on your left, what did you shoot at?* Briggs pondered. *Was it a reflex shot after you were attacked? Was there someone else in the room or did something distract you?*

He returned his sidearm to its holster and left.

09

I couldn't believe the realism," Deniz said. "The immersion is near-perfect. The physics were off the charts! Here I am, strapped into an immersion rig at some Bayshore tech start-up, but then I've been transported to a beautiful alpine resort, carving into fresh powder!"

It took Carli a lot of effort not to blow off her date with Deniz Harper. She'd never been to this particular restaurant, so she decided it would be a nice distraction from the day's events. Although she'd started to forget about the disappearing person on the transit, her appointment with Aliya Qureshi had not gone the way she'd expected.

Aliya had asked for only one thing to be changed in sculpting her trueself—that the white patches of her skin be sculpted away. All other parts of her body were left unchanged—though they still required a lot of work to be reproduced digitally. As she left her appointment, Aliya Qureshi donned a virtual mask incorporating a religious head covering concealing everything except her eyes.

Carli realised Aliya's trueself would be for no one but her. The time Carli had spent and would continue to spend as she finalised the sculpt over the next few days was only for Aliya's enjoyment. It was not to impress anyone or to satisfy someone else's expectations. It was just for herself.

This challenged Carli. She understood it, but a sense of professional pride was wounded that her work would not be on display for the world to see.

But there was something deeper. *That face*, she thought. *That face was unique. It was already perfect.*

Carli had briefly suggested the white patches of her vitiligo be kept. This was met with a very abrupt, "No". Carli almost jumped as Aliya's response broke through her otherwise quiet demeanour.

Carli was a paid subscriber to the philosophy that every citizen had the right to project whatever they wanted into the Collective. But a seed of doubt had now been sown. Carli found herself preferring the unchanged version of Aliya Qureshi, with her patchy but perfect skin instead of the trueself Carli had created for her.

*Sometimes beauty is below the projection*, she thought. *Sometimes beauty is below the mask. Sometimes the physical world offers up something that I can't improve.*

Deniz' story approached its crescendo and Carli offered a half smile of feigned interest. She was happy to listen, but Deniz' stories always featured himself as the protagonist, reminding Carli of why she didn't expect this relationship to last.

"They've thought of everything. They have 360 degrees of directional air supply—freezing cold if you want it. As you power down the mountain, the air shifts around you. The platform has the best haptic response I've ever felt, you can feel every snowflake beneath you crush and refreeze as you glide over. And the scape! More beautiful and textured than anything I've ever seen!"

"Is that so?" Carli responded.

"Absolutely! I mean, some of the immersion sims are spectacular too, but this was something truly special. I could take you some time. I could teach you to ski."

"That sounds nice, but I'm afraid I can be a little clumsy," she conceded. Carli wasn't really clumsy, but at this point didn't want to commit to anything beyond this evening.

"Oh, I can show you how it's done!"

Deniz continued, sharing another story featuring himself, followed by another. Carli, was polite but remained aloof. *At least this place is nice*, she thought.

*Nuit Claire*, was a French-themed restaurant located in Métropole, the next hub in the City Circle to the west of Praxis Grove. In addition to being one of the four main financial districts in Praxis City, it boasted landmarks and architecture which paid tribute to a long-lost city. Moulded furniture reminded Carli of a spaceship, and the mood was set with large luminaries encircling mirrors of different sizes.

But the highlight was not the décor, but the view from the large windows wrapping around the length of the restaurant. These looked over the scape of a city's skyline. The centrepiece, a large metal tower rising up from the city around it, glowing a brilliant white.

Its beauty distracted Carli from an otherwise uninteresting conversation. When they'd arrived at the restaurant, the scape was cycling from dusk through to night-time. The blue sky transitioned to purple before resting in the deepest of cobalt after the virtual sun settled beyond the horizon. A handful of stars managed to poke their way through the sparse clouds and gentle glow of the city.

*What an amazing city*, she thought to herself. She understood why so many of the citizens of the Collective chose to live large parts of their lives in immersion simulations. Carli had resisted, but only because she feared the beauty of escaping into a virtual reality would captivate her so much she may never want to leave. She'd seen friends and co-workers lost down that rabbit hole and it was something she guarded herself against. But she still wondered if this virtual world was preferable to the real one she lived in.

Her musings were interrupted, not by Deniz' story but by the arrival of the main course. It had been described in the menu as simply, '*Lièvre*'. What arrived was a few small parcels of meat rolled in seed, layered with an assortment of mushrooms, tomatoes and a dark crimson sauce. Like all food across Praxis, its ingredients were grown in one of the many thousand farming factories. The hub in which Carli lived, Archibald was one of those farming centres. *Some of this food was probably manufactured next door to my home*, she thought.

Deniz surveyed his own meal—something called, '*Le Homard*'. A white meat in a creamy sauce served in an alien-looking shell with root vegetables. It was the most expensive thing on the menu. He looked up to her and announced with a smile, "*Bon appétit*". It sounded more like "appetite".

As they ate, Carli's mood improved. It may have been the excellent food. It may have been the beautiful view. Or the fact that she was approaching the end of her third glass of synthetic pinot noir. But she found herself unwinding somewhat, becoming just a little more vulnerable.

"How is your food?" Deniz enquired.

"Excellent.. um… *très bien*," she replied, trying to join in with the theme.

"I know I said this before, but you *do* look beautiful tonight," he said.

Carli hoped so—she'd left her rental of her burgundy halter-neck evening dress projection to the last minute, making it more expensive. But she loved the way it clung tightly to her athletic figure, emphasising her shoulders and back. Carli had spent a lot of time sculpting her own body and liked to show off the parts she was most proud of.

She pictured herself in the dress dancing with an elegance and grace she didn't possess. Then, she imagined Aliya Qureshi in the same dress, with her beautiful white patches of skin on display.

"Carli?"

Snapped back to reality, "I'm sorry. I had a few really strange things happen to me today. I few challenging clients. Oh, and I saw a strange citizen on the transit…"

"Pretty much everyone on the transit is strange," he interrupted.

"This was a guy, wearing only a lifesuit and a paper bag over his head as a mask. He… He spoke to me and then he disappeared, like he was never there."

"Like, in a puff of smoke?"

"No, of course not," she felt her guard rising again. Deniz was not the sort of person she felt she could have this conversation with. Actually, she wasn't sure who she would feel comfortable having this conversation with.

"It doesn't matter," she shook her head with a polite smile. "I'm sure it was just some bug in the Network."

They continued in small talk, and she switched to water—something she was sure Deniz noticed. Dessert came and went; something cold, delicious and expensive. Checking the time, and finding herself bored with the conversation, Carli decided the date was drawing to a close.

Deniz read her mind, "Are you thinking about your transit home?"

"Oh, sorry yes. It's been a long day and I've probably still got an hour's worth of travel ahead of me."

"That's OK. You know, my place is closer in West Praxis, you could always stay there…"

"Oh? Oh…"

She was about to speak, but he reached across the table and gently held each hand. The physical contact made her heart jump for a moment.

"Look Carli, I know I can ramble on a bit. Maybe I'm just a bit nervous. But I enjoy spending time with you. I don't know where this relationship is going, but if you want some… physical companionship tonight, you can trust me."

"Oh, Deniz, I'm…" Carli ran out of words. It was a brazen request, and Carli would normally have dismissed it outright or even been a little offended. But at this moment, she felt the need for a companion—for something physical and real. His warm hands brought hers together and cupped them tenderly. He gazed into her eyes. It was the first time she'd felt truly noticed all evening.

"I'm giving you a level 4 trust. I hope you accept."

He raised one hand and made a few gestures as he interfaced with the Network, and Carli saw the request appear in her feed.

She gave a polite smile. She needed to think. "Can you give me a moment, Deniz?"

"Uh, sure thing." He released her other hand with a final squeeze.

Carli stood and took herself to the bathroom. She found her typically guarded demeanour to be waning. At this moment, she craved intimacy and made a snap decision.

With a wave of gestures, she accepted his trust request.

She was just about to return when she caught her reflection in a mirror. Her reflected image exhibited a virtual silhouette with a callout on the side. She expanded it in her vision and saw the text:

### ACTIVE REFLECTION: DENIZ HARPER

The highest level of trust between two citizens will allow one citizen to perceive reality as *they* perceive reality. This principle was called, 'reflection'.

A reflection-level trust only existed for level 5 relationships, not level 4. Carli was sure that Deniz had not intended to assign her this trust.

Projection was the bedrock of the Collective. What you project to the Collective defined reality. However, all citizens had the right to perceive reality the way they wanted. It was the same system that allowed people to block inappropriate content. To mask or alter things or people they no longer wanted to see. And according to the silhouette around her reflection, Deniz Harper was perceiving Carli differently from what she was projecting.

Carli raised a hand. With a gesture, she activated the reflection protocol. Now she was experiencing the world Deniz Harper, NuSculpt solicitor saw. And as she stared into the mirror, the face she saw made her gasp.

She did not see Carli Dawes.

A sweet, round face. Green eyes instead of brown. Blonde hair instead of brown, swept and styled in the same fashion as hers had been.

She wore the same burgundy dress, but her chest was now several sizes larger and her figure far less athletic.

She saw Shannon Ayres. Junior accountant at NuSculpt.

She saw Deniz Harper's former girlfriend.

An angry grunt escaped her clenched teeth, and she slapped the bench in front of the mirror with closed fists.

"That bastard".

She fought the anger and tried to find some clarity. She evaluated her next move. She considered just walking out, lumping Deniz Harper with the bill and never speaking to him again. Carli usually didn't enjoy confrontation, but now in the face of such insolence, such disrespect, she found an inner strength like a raging animal.

She left the bathroom—boldness and righteous fury in every stride.

Deniz stood next to their table, dismissing the host. Carli could see their joint bill had just been paid. He turned to look at her as she approached, a smile on his face. *The smile of a predator.*

"I see you have accepted my…" the rest of the sentence did not escape his mouth as Carli picked up the full water jug from a nearby table and launched its contents over Deniz' smug face.

The water disrupted her optics' capacity to overlay Deniz' trueself over his oldself and parts of his face and body flashed between each. A bulbous nose, crooked teeth and a lopsided jawline. For brief moments, Deniz Harper appeared as ugly on the outside as he clearly was on the inside.

He tried to recover. "What the hell?" There was rage in his voice.

Carli strode past, defiant. She headed for the exit.

"Shannon Ayres says, 'hello'" she shouted.

With a wave of hand gestures, she cancelled the trust relationship with Deniz, reverting it down to its lowest level. A few more gestures and she cancelled the lease of her outfit, styles, and jewellery, reverting to the simple business suit she'd been wearing previously.

She heard yelling behind her, and she didn't care.

'The captured DNA does not match anything in our records.' The forensic technician's report was concise but unhelpful. Either Korb1k's DNA had never been secured, or it had been scrubbed from the Network. The former was plausible—capture, sequence and storage of DNA was only permitted for citizens with a criminal history. The latter should be impossible and under normal circumstances, Briggs would have discounted it outright. However, the anomalies he'd so far encountered caused him to keep an open mind, even to the most unlikely option.

Briggs stood in the middle of one of the many crime scene reconstruction suites on level 12 of the PPD headquarters. It was a white four-meter cube with tracking markers in the centre and corners of each wall. Those walls and the door he entered through were well insulated to block out most of the noise from outside. In this room, Briggs could overlay any crime scene from the scans taken earlier that day with near-perfect clarity.

At this time of the evening, most of the other detectives and support staff had left for the evening and Briggs had his choice of the best room. Being able to block out all external noise also helped Briggs to concentrate, rejecting any competing stimuli threatening to throw off his sense of balance as he navigated through the virtual crime scene.

In this augmented space, Korb1k's apartment was visible. A glowing green outline denoted the borders of the physical room—a necessary safety feature to ensure he did not try to walk through a physical wall when perceiving the virtual. As he approached each wall, it glowed brighter until it was the only thing he could see. He reached out and touched the wall hidden a few centimetres behind the virtual outline. Moving back to the centre of the room, the glow of the walls dissipated until they were almost invisible.

Using hand gestures, he positioned his viewpoint in the doorway of Korb1k's apartment. A virtual menu listed different forensic layers available for selection. He chose one labelled 'fingerprints' and glowing circles appeared in different positions around the room, including the door handle in front of him. A callout listed observations and notes made by both the field technician and a lead technician who had reviewed their work.

The prints had no match in the PPD database. Some potentially useful observations had been made, however: only five unique prints—four fingers and a thumb. The report also stated, with legal disclaimers and caveats that the prints were most likely only from the *right* hand.

The lead technician had noted that two of the fingers were classified as being "scarred, as though burned through thermal or other radiation". Briggs had seen some perps try to beat forensics by burning their fingerprints, only to be thwarted by a sea of other evidence including DNA, but this seemed different.

Briggs shifted the prints in front of his face, expanding their size. Other prints from the scene were incorporated to first construct a flat model of the prints, which included not only the tips of the fingers but also the length of one finger and the thumb. An algorithm interpolated all of the prints into a single combined model which Briggs overlaid on a three-dimensional hand. He opened and closed his own hand and saw the virtual hand do the same.

The burns to the hand were extensive. They looked deeper than just the surface, and they looked old. Each finger had a different pattern, not as complex as a normal print, but unique, nonetheless. *That might work for an ID*, he thought.

With a swipe, the hand disappeared and Briggs brought up the ballistics information. He activated a character layer, selecting a mannequin resembling Constable Nguyen's physical characteristics. This mannequin was without any detail, standing like a plastic statue in front of Briggs. He overlaid Nguyen's oldself, wearing only his lifesuit, followed by his PPD body armour, duty belt, holster, binders and pouches. For a few moments, he looked into the lifeless and expressionless face of the deceased. A brother and compatriot in a seemingly endless quest to maintain order and justice across the Network—now dead.

Briggs activated a pre-determined stance, moving Officer Nguyen into an active posture, right-foot forward and holding a combat rifle poised to fire. He realised the rifle was the wrong weapon and switched it for a Torque 9mm sidearm. He also corrected the mannequin's posture from right-handed to left-handed. Briggs reached ahead and picked up the weightless mannequin, and placed him in the doorway, aligning the path of the bullet to the position of the gun barrel. This required a few small adjustments to posture and position as well as bringing him almost half a metre inside the doorway.

Now standing back from this scene, Briggs could survey the room, with Nguyen in position. He rotated the room around himself, placing himself directly in the path of the bullet on the opposite side. This movement brought on an almost instant headache and a tightness in his chest. Through deep breaths, he powered through the dizzy spell.

Briggs was of average height and build. The bullet path was now travelling a few inches higher than the centre of his chest. Nguyen was an above-average shot. So, if standard practice was to aim at the centre mass of the target, roughly the heart, then the person Nguyen was shooting was potentially three to six inches taller than Briggs.

No other DNA or prints in the room. Nothing to indicate a second person in the room. Nguyen had shot at a ghost.

Briggs placed a second generic mannequin from his current position, separating from his own body as he stepped out of the way. He scaled the mannequin up to six foot, two inches until the bullet path went through the target's chest. Facing back towards Nguyen's position, he stored the scene as a layer in the investigation file to review later.

Rather than moving the room around him, Briggs just walked back to a position next to the entrance where he theorised the perpetrator must have been. Doing so highlighted the glowing physical wall as he approached, on a different angle to the virtual one, but not so close that he was in danger of hitting it.

Briggs stored what he saw as a second scene. He crouched slightly and looked up at Officer Nguyen to his right, whose body was positioned just inside the doorway. He reached and grabbed the mannequin's throat—just like the report from Judge Khoury. His left hand.

Doing this placed him even closer to the physical wall which glowed brightly in his optics just beyond the face of Officer Nguyen. It was intentionally distracting. Briggs triggered a second mannequin from his body with his hand on Nguyen's throat. He stepped back to get a better look at this scene, but this placed him behind the virtual wall, obscuring his view. Briggs grumbled to himself and triggered a very slow movement of the room around him until he had a good view of both the ghost mannequin and the attacker mannequin. He was satisfied with the result. It fit the evidence so far and he stored this as a third scene.

He reviewed the other two scanned locations, but found nothing further of interest. Each time he switched locations, the virtual crime scene faded out to the empty white room before the new scene faded in. Each time, Briggs positioned himself back to the centre of the room, breathing deeply through the transitions to maintain composure.

He returned his view back to the apartment crime scene. It was clear this was going to be the most useful. He cycled between the two saved views. Each time, the movement was instant and did not cause Briggs too much trouble with his balance, but he still found himself practising deep breaths and jerking his hands out as a reaction to trying to centre himself.

He considered the attacker's left hand. No left-handed prints, only right. Judge Khoury had confirmed the attacker was not missing a hand. Taking all evidence as presented, he arrived at only one conclusion: *the attacker's hand was prosthetic.*

The theory explained the prints, and fit with his emerging theory that something had triggered the victim's augments to overload. He'd originally thought that something from the Network had caused it, but now he considered an alternative. *Was the prosthetic hand the weapon?* It was another piece to the puzzle, but it didn't give him a sense that he was any closer.

Briggs felt like he was chasing a ghost. *Korb1k, the one-armed ghost.*

Assigning his quarry a title, gave Briggs a brief moment of amusement. There was nothing more to be learned here.

From the position he was standing in the apartment, he instinctively walked towards the virtual doorway rather than the physical exit. After a few strides, he realised his mistake and began the sequence of gestures to dissolve the virtual room. Either the sequence of gestures was wrong, or there was a problem with the way it registered, but rather than dissolving the virtual room, it instead spun to position Briggs at the first of the two captured scenes. With his body first moving in one direction and the room swirling around him, Briggs instinctively staggered to his right. His body overbalanced as the room continued to rotate and he felt himself falling. He braced his hands towards the floor, but it didn't help as his head connected with the room's physical wall.

He crumpled down the wall to the floor, his right eye stinging. The room slowed its rotation, but his head was still swirling. Droplets of blood seeped onto the virtual floorboards. His chest tightened again, and his stomach joined in. His attempts to centre his mind were overrun by an increasing rage at his own inadequacy and the feeling of being spun around in circles by an imaginary hand.

He managed to get onto his hands and knees, desperate to regain composure. Sweat began to pour down his face, and his mouth began to salivate. Rage overflowed into a brief scream, cut short by an involuntary action of another sort as his stomach purged itself.

He pounded the ground in defiance with both fists.

A few minutes passed before he noticed an alert in his optics telling him his lifesuit's hand sensors had been damaged:

LIFESUIT RIGHT GESTURE INTERFACE FAULTY, CONTACT SUPPORT.

LIFESUIT LEFT GESTURE INTERFACE FAULTY, CONTACT SUPPORT.

His equilibrium returned, though his chest now ached along with the gash over his right eye. Cold perspiration joined a mess of fluids, spoiling the white floor. The room had decided to conclude the virtual overlay after recognising he'd fallen. He let out an exasperated moan, the rage draining away and leaving only the familiar sense of self-loathing.

Briggs put pressure on his eye as he left the room. He took some small comfort in the fact that only a small number of people would be around to see him in this state.

"Chalk up another flub for 'Dizzy' Briggs," he muttered to himself.

**11**

For the first hour, Liam exercised. For the second hour, he played a solo card game. For the third hour, he bounced a rubber ball back and forth across the domicile. After that, he practiced throwing playing cards around the room, trying to hit marks or targets. His right hand was adept. His left was not.

It was late evening, and he had no idea how long he'd been lying in bed, staring at the ceiling. Even sleep was elusive without a connection to the Network. Relaxing sounds or an optically soothing kaleidoscope could be triggered which would help the mind to ease into a brain pattern to induce sleep. Such a thing was necessary for overstimulated minds, and Liam was no different.

His safe house was already starting to feel like a cage.

He fingered the small box of platinum chips in his coat pocket. *A few libations and a Vallux would help pass the time*, he thought.

The last time he'd been in this situation was three months ago. That was when he became "Korb1k" after his previous identity, Povern0 had been retired. Liam had been doing his employer's bidding out of Pangola at the time: a poor industrial hub at the end of the southwest transit. *It was even uglier than this place.*

That time, an identify change had been required after the Bratstvo Syndicate had dropped a Network-wide hit on him. Liam's employer had charged him with the job of securing the services of some of their members. Most were just thugs—not unlike Petros Zaimis—useful for security or moving materiel. A few however were Network hats with experience in police communications. His employer had been particularly adamant that they be co-opted under any circumstances. Unhappy to lose some of their key agents to what they assumed was a rival faction, Bratstvo placed the hit and Povern0 was as good as dead.

The irony was that the same people to place a hit on his former identity were more than happy to start working with a new operator named Korb1k who offered a new source of untraceable bits. The mistrusted Povern0 was dead, but Korb1k started with a clean slate and building up credibility didn't take long when offering streams of untraceable bits for relatively simple or low-risk jobs.

The last time he'd lost his identity, it had taken Liam almost 20 hours before defying his employer's direction and venturing unmasked into the seedy underbelly of Pangola. It helped that he slept the first twelve hours after taking a single dose of Vallux stashed in his safe house. But after that, he donned his coat and hat and made his way to the closest night club where he traded some chips for a second dose to knock him out long enough for his employer to deliver on a new identity.

Liam chastised himself for not furnishing this safe house with enough Antistim or Vallux, or even some alcohol to make passing the time more bearable. Without something to distract him, his only company would be his own thoughts and *that* was never a good thing. After being in this situation for the third time, he clearly hadn't learned from his mistakes. Then again, Liam suspected this was just his subconscious's way of escaping his employer's grip on his every move.

He gave his box of chips one final rattle. He dressed himself and headed out onto the streets of West Praxis.

A bag of ice covered one eye. The other gazed intently at a glass of synthetic scotch, unmoved and undrunk since it had been carefully placed there an hour earlier. Briggs knew there were no answers at the bottom of the glass, but that never seemed to matter. Once consumed, it would be re-filled with more false promises of enlightenment and clarity. With every drink, those promises were louder, but ever more elusive.

It was a trail Briggs had gone down many times before and had caused more damage to himself, his relationships and his career than almost anything else. And alcohol was only the tip of the iceberg.

Briggs had been clean for almost 18 months, but there had been many times like tonight when he'd walked the three blocks from the PPD headquarters to the local watering hole to order two fingers of the best synthetic single malt he could afford only to stare at it for a few hours. Sometimes it had been after a breakthrough or success on a case. Sometimes it was a dead end to a case that just couldn't be solved. Tonight, it was the fresh reminder that his body was not what it used to be and was almost working against him. Nights like tonight were usually the most dangerous.

He removed the ice pack from his forehead for what may have been the hundredth time. The cut had stopped bleeding some time ago, but the cold and condensation from the ice caused the hastily applied butterfly strips to lose adhesion. He'd managed to clean up his mess and leave the HQ without being asked any embarrassing questions.

Somehow, he'd been able to keep his lifesuit relatively clean, but the damage to the sensors in his lifesuit's gloves made it difficult to navigate the Network. He had to rely on eye movements and blinks which were only useful for a set of basic controls. There were several spare suits at his residence in Boulder, but he hadn't decided if he would make it home tonight or pay for an overpriced hotel capsule. Either way, he rejected the idea of trying to sleep in the small number of bunks back at the PPD.

Someone quietly slid onto the seat next to him. A familiar scent of frangipani and gun oil. Briggs didn't need to turn to see who it was.

"Working late Captain?" he said.

"You know me, Hal. Crime never sleeps in this city." Anneke Hagen waited a moment, "I heard you had a little *incident* in the reco-room,"

Briggs turned to face her, still holding the pack to his face, "I thought I'd made a clean getaway."

"Seriously, Hal, you're barely graceful at the best of times. Seeing one of my detectives masked in the office staggering around holding a mop and bucket leaves quite an impression."

He turned away and eyed his drink; another wave of humiliation rolled over him.

"Can I take a look at the damage?"

He didn't need to remove his mask—Anneke Hagen already had his full trust. That was a good thing because he wasn't sure how to achieve that without his hand sensors being fully functional. "Sure"

Hagen grasped his hand and carefully moved it away from his face. The touch was warm and gentle. It stirred something within him, and not for the first time, but he pushed the feeling as far away as possible. Whatever he felt for

Hagen had never been reciprocated, but if he was honest with himself, she knew him more intimately than pretty much anyone he'd ever met.

"Goodness, Hal. That probably needs sutures—or at least something better than those strips."

Briggs pulled his hand back to his face. Even unmasked in her presence, he felt the need to hide.

"I think you've got some tracking errors going on there too. Your projection is a little off when your face moves. You should get someone to sort that out while it heals."

"Yeah, I figured as much."

Briggs changed the topic. He filled Hagen in on the steps he'd taken so far in the case but omitted some of his suspicions or half-baked conclusions. *Now isn't the time to share my Korb1k theory*, he decided. He told Hagen that tomorrow he was going to Augmosis to speak to his PPD liaison, Gen Nomura. Earlier in the day, he'd received a request to make contact regarding his case. Though it wasn't unusual for Briggs to speak to Nomura on a Network case, it was rare for her to contact him first.

The conversation continued, and Brigg's mood began to lift. He now realised how hungry he was and ordered a counter meal, which he split with Hagen. She'd been the most stable influence in his life for the better part of five years. That stability and trust cultivated a level of affection far deeper than any other relationship he'd had. Perhaps because it was based on trust rather than any possibility of romance.

"DC Moya wasn't too happy after your little performance at the Council," she said.

"Yeah, well, I can't do anything about that now."

"You know, if half of the rules we have to follow could be relaxed for law enforcement, we probably wouldn't have any crime at all"

Briggs didn't respond. He'd heard this argument before—in fact, it was the standing policy of the PPD to lobby the Council for a relaxation of Network controls for major crimes or emerging threats. But the Council consistently rejected every request, considering them an affront to personal liberty.

"The Network knows where everyone is. Even your two suspects in West Praxis," she said.

Briggs countered, "For the officer in charge of Network Crimes and Integrity, that sounds like an *unpopular* thing to be suggesting. We're all supposed to be upholding the law, not working around it."

"I'm not suggesting anything. We know our jobs. But sometimes it makes you wonder if the rights of the guilty are worth more than the rights of the innocent."

Briggs thought this over. He was no stranger to the grey area between the law. He didn't think of himself above them. But he *did* think himself above those who wrote them. He'd seen far too many opportunistic bureaucrats rise to a station far beyond their level of competence to avoid growing cynical.

After a lot more conversation, Hagen addressed the matter at hand. "So are you going to drink that?" She motioned to the glass that hadn't moved for the last hour.

Briggs took a final look, stood, and faced her. "No Ma'am."

She smiled and stood with him. "Good boy."

They left, separately.

# 12

I t was approaching 11:00 pm. Liam stepped around citizens who had passed out from stims, synthicol, a meaningless life or a combination thereof. He walked the four blocks to the nearest cluster of businesses that preferred to ply their trade in the dark of night. Colourful manufactured light, images and music attracted weary and desperate citizens like moths to a flame with the promise of a good time free of short-term consequences.

Even though his identity no longer existed in the Network, he still passively perceived everything around him just like every other citizen. Virtual advertising crept into his view as he approached. Some were for food establishments, others offered discount coupons for Network content and immersion simulations.

Sexualised projections appeared in front of some of the shopfronts as he walked, males and females in different states of undress, of every shape, size and orientation beckoning him with smiles, dances and hand gestures. Some offered only a simulation. Others offered something physical to go with it. Each advertisement silhouetted in his optics to show it was only a projection, but that didn't dissuade one drunk patron from trying to hit on one of the virtual billboards.

"Not tonight ladies," Liam said to the darkness.

The sound of people grew as he neared the centre of the entertainment district. A small eatery could be seen, overflowing with citizens queued onto the street. The smells of roasted proteins and spices were pungent and inviting as he passed, making his mouth water. But without a connection to the Network and with only a handful of chips to spend, he needed to choose his destination carefully.

The main intersection of the entertainment district had four bars, one on each corner. Noisy patrons staggered between the three bars which appeared to be the busiest. The fourth was far more subdued. The lights were less bright, the music more melancholy. The virtual sign identified it as 'The Komitet'. *This place will do.*

He checked his trench coat's collar was lifted up to partially conceal his burned face and made his way inside. Approaching the dimly lit bar, he could feel the increasing stickiness of at least one night's worth of spilled drinks or other bodily fluids that had partially dried on the stone floor. Though his head remained relatively still, his eyes darted around the room to confirm there were no threats or security cameras. There were maybe two dozen other citizens in the room. He felt satisfied and found a position at the bar as far away from the other patrons as possible.

"Are you waiting bus, comrade?" a heavyset bartender called in a thick accent from the far end of the bar. Without his connection to the Network, Liam could not instigate a pre-emptive transaction trust with the business.

Liam kept his eyes forward. He slowly removed his box of chips, gave it a shake and put it on the bench on front of him. The bartender looked intently for a few moments before nodding to one of the other bartenders and moving opposite Liam's seat. Liam didn't look up and patiently waited.

The bartender was gruff and sweaty. The towel draped over his shoulder was either for cleaning glasses or wiping the sweat from his forehead. Possibly both. His right hand reached for something hidden under the counter.

"In my hand, is Toz 6-6 drobovika. It makes big noise and big mess. It was gift from father in-law on the occasion of marrying his daughter. In other hand, is Q12 Spectrometer. It analyse metal in 3 seconds. It was also gift from father in law on occasion of marrying his *other* daughter."

The bar tender paused. "So, which do you want?"

Liam made eye contact. His optics identified the bartender with the moniker of 'Официант', but a virtual name badge on his chest simply said, 'Grigori'.

"So?" Grigori leaned in.

"Which hand, or which daughter?" Liam replied. He kept eye contact.

Grigori broke, first with a smile, followed by a gleeful "Ha!". Both hands slapped the table. "*Ochen' horosho!*"

Liam briefly returned the smile. Without a connection to the Network, he couldn't translate Grigori's words but was confident he'd passed the test. Grigori presented a device from under the counter. Spectrometers weren't illegal, nor was transacting outside the Network, but they were an instant red flag to authorities that you might be someone worth keeping an eye on.

Liam removed two chips from his box and put them into the device's open side. The bottom weighed the chips and the top used a laser to determine the metal composition and purity. Liam had previously used other alloys that were mostly gold or palladium in much the same way. All were relatively inert and didn't lose value over time.

The machine beeped and provided a simple digital readout.

"Platinum; 1.9 grams; 910 fine. *Otlichno*." Grigori scratched his thick beard. "I give you 80 bits credit."

It was a poor price, but Liam wasn't in the mood to haggle. Once he had access to his accounts again, he could easily replace his chips for a similar price from the right trader.

"Done."

"Good, good." Grigori pocketed the two chips from the machine and produced two shot glasses, followed by a cold bottle of synthetic vodka from under the counter. He began pouring before Liam could intervene. "Compliments of Russia". Like every other Old-World nation, Russia was little more than a cold wasteland. Still, some citizens in the Collective maintained a strong identity to cultures of the past.

He raised one glass and invited Liam to do the same. Liam wasn't the kind of person who would refuse hospitality or a free drink. The liquid was ice cold but burned the whole way down. By the time it had reached his stomach, it had found a warm equilibrium.

Liam asked for another drink, which he consumed immediately. He didn't want to become drunk—at least not here. He asked Grigori what stims he could offer.

"Psyx, M5, Clarity." They were all mild, legal stimulants. Good if you want to be hyperactive for the next 12 hours. They were the opposite of what Liam needed.

"Any Vallux or Entropy?" Both were illegal, but Liam doubted Grigori would care.

"Hmm..." Grigori scratched his beard again. "You wait here, 5 minutes." Grigori left before Liam could respond.

As he waited, Liam again surveyed the room. His interactions with the bartender had not been noticed. Most of the patrons sat alone, multiple glasses or empty bottles in front of them. *Probably plugged in to the Network watching content,* Liam thought. Two poorly lit tables covered in dark green material sat unused to one side, one set up ready for play with white balls configured in a triangle shape.

Apart from the music, which Liam now presumed to be Russian, the only other noise came from a group of males in a private booth who were telling stories of past conquests or yesterday's dreams. They did not match the rest of the patrons, but they were far from out of place.

Liam felt himself begin to relax a little as the vodka started to kick in.

He held the empty glass up to the light with his right hand—scarred for the last five years. The pain over his whole body had ceased, replaced with a tightness and itchiness wrapping around him like a second skin. His body had healed itself in a somewhat functional sense, but the scars ran far deeper than his burned flesh.

He considered his prosthetic hand. Before the accident, its predecessor had been innocent. The Liam before the accident obeyed the rules of the system, often unquestioningly. The system was there to protect its citizens and to care for them when they could not care for themselves. But it was the system that had let him down, let his wife, Fi down. Now she was gone, and his body was little more than a grotesque husk, filled only with bitterness and an acute sense of self-preservation.

Another citizen entered the bar, masked, but clearly drunk. "Greg? Where's Greg?"

Liam kept his position, hoping his presence, even without the Network, was projecting an aura of "stay away".

It failed. The citizen plopped himself only two stools away from Liam. He slapped the table for service. Another tender, this one without an accent and with the name tag, 'Orson' confirmed his account and served him a drink, bourbon on ice in a noticeably dirty glass. The drink did not last long and with a loud, spurious sigh and a tap of the glass on the counter, another was ordered. As it was being poured, either to the bartender or the glass itself, he remarked, "Daddy needs some more medicine".

Though he tried to avoid eye contact, Liam snuck a quick look at this new arrival. His moniker said only 'TheNez'. Liam watched part of the man's glass disappear behind the virtual boundaries of his mask as he drank. It looked like the amber liquid was being poured through the event horizon of a black hole.

With his second glass empty, the man's volume increased. Orson was the unlucky recipient of TheNez's intoxicated anecdote, but he was drawing attention. Liam could not care less about his story, something about "some ugly bitch stiffing him on the bill at a fancy restaurant". He could feel the weight of the room's eyes as they turned in his direction.

Grigori returned; his arrival was announced loudly by the drunk as "Greg!" Grigori winked at him as he passed behind Orson, who used the momentary distraction to serve another customer further down the bar. With a smooth and rehearsed move, Grigori slid a cellulose napkin under Liam's shot glass and poured a third drink. Liam downed the drink as he snatched the napkin and put it into his coat pocket. He might normally have checked his quarry but was increasingly anxious to leave.

Returning the glass to the counter, Liam began to swivel away from the loud visitor but was interrupted, "My God, you are one ugly bastard." Liam paused, anger rising, but with at least an equal measure of sober judgement keeping it from overflowing.

"Hey, I'm talking to you!"

Liam continued to turn away, but the man grabbed his prosthetic hand, just above the wrist. That was a mistake.

Liam moved quickly, twisting his wrist down and pulling the drunk man closer. With a jerk of his arm, he broke the grip and made his own on the man's forearm. In the same motion, his body swivelled around to land a driving blow from his right hand just below the man's rib cage, into his plexus. TheNez crumpled to the floor, unable to breathe. His plexus let out a short burst of compressed gas as its composite shell was breached.

His left hand now free and nursing sore knuckles on his right, Liam took a brief moment to recognise the whole room's attention was now on him. He made a hasty exit from the bar, furious with himself for taking such a risk and being caught up in a scene. He heard voices calling after him, but he ignored them.

Cursing his sloppiness and holding his aching right hand to his chest, he strode away from the neon-illuminated entertainment and made a careful path through the increasing darkness back to his safe house.

**13**

The burst of adrenaline from Carli's resolute exit dissipated as she transited home to her domicile in Archibald. What remained thereafter was a deep shame.

She was angry at Deniz. He'd effectively violated both his former partner, Shannon as well as Carli. But she was also angry at herself for being vulnerable enough to trust him, only to realise that doing so had proved to be a monumental error of judgment. The gentle sound of the waves rolling on the beach from her phonics wasn't soothing enough to settle her mind as she lay awake in her bed.

Distracted, she found herself investigating the laws and rights of the Collective to determine if what Deniz had done was legal. A citizen had a right to perceive whatever they wanted. Sometimes that meant hiding things they found offensive. But completely replacing another's projection didn't seem right to her.

*What is the whole point of projecting your trueself into the Collective if other people can just ignore it—or worse, overwrite it with something or someone else?*

She did not find clarity on the issue as she searched the Network. There were opinion pieces from past Overseers regarding the tension between the two rights to project and to perceive. The third principle of the Collective, "Reconciliation" was supposed to balance that tension:

"REALITY IS INDIVIDUALLY ABSOLUTE AND COLLECTIVELY

HETEROGENEOUS."

*What a load of nonsensical rubbish*, Carli thought.

Her failure to find a clear answer only compounded her already frustrated mood. Tiredness finally broke through her anger and despondency. With no answers, and being pursued by a deepening sadness, her only remaining response was to cry. She clung to a body pillow, pulling it to her face to absorb her tears and muffle the sound. It was as though her tears contained every one of the restless thoughts she'd been battling.

Carli approached her commute to work the following morning with trepidation. After dressing herself, and boarding the transit, she donned a mask, something she rarely did. She remembered the citizen that disappeared on the transit the previous day, making her more wary than usual. She decided she would sit in a different seat, maybe next to someone familiar.

Two stations came and went. Carli still found herself inspecting each citizen as they boarded the train. No one wore just a lifesuit. No one wore a paper bag as a mask. Some familiar faces boarded the train: the anime character; the elderly lady with the projection of a teenager.

These faces went some way to settle her anxiety. She'd made a decision that morning to tell Shannon Ayres what had happened. She would normally have gone to the NuSculpt legal department and asked for some advice, but since Deniz Harper was one of the company's solicitors, that seemed problematic.

*I'll figure out my next step later*, she thought. Another busy day of work required her full attention.

The transit stopped at the next station, Boulder. More familiar faces entered. One of them was a tall, muscular character, bald with facial tattoos wrapping around eyes replaced with grotesque metal spikes. She'd seen him before, but that didn't make the appearance any less unsettling.

The citizen Carli suspected was probably a police officer entered, his face unmasked. The Network reported this citizen with the benign moniker of "BriggsH33207". He found a standing position near her. His projection was unchanged from every other time she'd noticed him. Jeans, with an oilskin coat. He was of average height, maybe mid-forties. There was nothing remarkable about his appearance. He clearly had no interest in throwing his bits away on expensive crafts or a bespoke trueself to enhance what lay beneath.

As she looked closer, she noticed some tracking errors above his right eye. She perceived it as a flickering, circular distortion from the middle of his eyebrow up to his hairline. For brief moments, she could see a fresh cut with localised bruising, joined together by small strips. This underlying self was quickly replaced with a patch of normal-looking skin and eyebrow that morphed and wiggled as her optics tried to transpose his projection over the oldself.

What she assumed was a fresh injury was causing the Network to have difficulty tracking and overlaying his projection. Such things weren't uncommon. Carli herself had her own projection foiled when she was much younger by an aggressive season of adolescent acne. The desire to correct and improve her projection during this difficult season was what had led her into sculpting as a career.

Most citizens had the skills to be able to repair these glitches themselves. Much like combing your hair or shaving your face, all citizens could make rudimentary alterations to their projection and the tracking algorithms to the self below. Either this citizen did not have the skills or simply couldn't be bothered. It gave Carli a means for an introduction.

"Excuse me, sir, are you a police officer?"

He looked down at her, "Usually not until 8:00 am". Carli didn't perceive any kind of smile or other emotion and started to feel a little foolish before he stepped a little closer and asked, "Is there something I can help you with?"

"Oh, um. I'm sorry but I just noticed that your projection has some tracking glitches. I'm a sculptor—I could probably fix that for you if you'd like?"

He appeared to be considering her proposal. "How much?"

"Oh, no cost—it will only take me a minute." Carli hoped she was successfully concealing her real desire for a sense of safety.

"Sure. What do you need me to do?"

Carli instigated a brief trust request, which the officer accepted. She introduced herself by name, stopping short of reciting her usual introductory address to new clients. He didn't need to, since the trust identified this anyway, but he also introduced himself as just, "Briggs".

She worked quickly—it was an effective distraction. She peeled back the projection and revealed the self underneath. Using some basic actions available to her by her lifesuit sensors, she created new tracking cues and shaping algorithms. These sensors weren't as precise as the tools she used in her suite at NuSculpt, but were sufficient for this quick repair.

Only Carli could see this portion of his oldself while she worked. Everyone else would still see his projection. Once she finished her work, she could commit the changes, and the officer, Briggs, could apply them. As she worked, she realised this man's projection was barely different from what lay beneath. There were a few more grey hairs and facial creases, but that was all.

As she finished her work, she realised she'd passed one transit station. She committed the changes and looked around the carriage, scanning each citizen one at a time. She saw no one wearing a paper bag mask, nor anyone wearing only a lifesuit.

"Thank you, Ms. Dawes," he said. He'd already applied the updated trueself, which Carli could see was performing well. Of course, she didn't doubt her work.

She returned her gaze to the officer, "Oh, my pleasure," she said. "I have added some polymorphic shaping to the tracking that should hopefully change as you heal. With some luck, you shouldn't need any more corrections."

Her immediate anxiety passed, and she found herself making a playful comment, "That is, unless you hit your head again."

He didn't seem amused. "I'll certainly try not to. Thank you again." He motioned away from her, and the trust concluded. The next station was Praxis Grove. She moved towards the doors in silence, and as they opened, she took a final glimpse at Officer Briggs before exiting.

Carli found herself wondering what his day was going to be like. She'd seen enough crime dramas on the Network to invent some exaggerated fantasies. She contrasted these to the day's work ahead of her and concluded that maybe a bad date last night and strange experiences with disappearing people didn't rate on the same scale of problems that this officer probably had to deal with.

It was a rational thought, but it offered her little peace.

## 14

Briggs dressed that morning in his spare PPD lifesuit. He wasn't sure if the sensors in the original suit were repairable or if the suit would need to be replaced in its entirety. He would need to drop it off to the quartermaster sometime, but for today, he left it hanging in his cupboard.

Most citizens owned at least two lifesuits. They didn't usually need to be cleaned from every day use. Briggs' suits were PPD issue and included basic armour plating around his chest and back. It was not as robust as the armour Constable Nguyen had been wearing, nor the more extreme combat suits worn by the Tactical Branch, but it was enough to stop a standard 9mm bullet, but still leave a painful bruise underneath.

He disconnected his plexus from the first suit with a counter-clockwise twist and attached it to the second. The plexus interfaced wirelessly with the body's augments, but the lifesuit sensors were a physical connection. The plexus was a feat of engineering, capable of greater processing capacity in a second than a silicon-based processor could in a lifetime. All plexuses had a partner—a larger, even more powerful processing unit physically connected to the Network in the deep belly of Augmosis.

That was the location of Brigg's next appointment.

His transit had been interrupted by the sculptor, Carli, offering to repair his projection. He'd initially been sceptical, but since he didn't like the idea of having to explain to anyone else how he'd injured himself, he decided not to question his good fortune.

He used the remainder of the journey to confirm no progress had been made in finding the other witness to the crime, Fernando Alvarez. He noted a memo that a PPD medical examiner would be performing full autopsies on the two deceased later that morning. Briggs wanted to be there—most officers would have been satisfied with reading the report, but being part of the process in person seemed more tangible.

Most of the hubs within the City Circle shared similar architecture, but Augmosis was designed with a single purpose in mind: to house the technological behemoth sharing its namesake. The company that designed the Network and manufactured all of its components occupied the entire hub, bar some hotels and service businesses. Rather than having buildings designed primarily for the efficiency of space, the building at Augmosis adopted an ergonomic and serpentine style, individually unique but complimenting each other. It was a deliberate metaphor for the Collective itself: individuality grafted together into a unifying whole.

Briggs could care less for metaphors. In his mind, Augmosis was unnecessarily complicated to navigate—the paths didn't run straight, and it took a whole lot longer to get to where you wanted. His trademark approach to conducting his investigation in person rather than employing a teeper was tested across Augmosis' winding pathways. Still, this hub was not without its charm.

The emphasis on architecture led to a much larger use of green space, from small gardens to large communal spaces. One of these spaces would be used to host a concert event for the coming 100th anniversary of the Collective in over a week. While smaller, real plants existed across all of Praxis, this large space was the only place where a living tree could be found—a Moreton Bay Fig, reportedly planted on the very day the Network was first activated. It now towered over the end of the open space, framing the entry to Augmosis' welcome centre.

That, however, was not Briggs' destination today. One of many elliptically shaped buildings had been designated as his destination to meet his Augmosis contact, Gen Nomura. In the years she'd been assigned as Briggs' liaison within the Network Crimes Division, they had only ever met in the visitor's centre, so this location change seemed out of the ordinary.

Small palm trees and other rainforest plants bordered the entrance to the building. The door slid open to receive him after confirming his identity and Briggs found himself in an empty lobby area, furnished with little more than some comfortable-looking seats. A received message told him his chaperone was en route. The lounge seats were inviting, but Briggs ignored them, stood with folded arms, and tapped his foot restlessly.

Gen Nomura entered from the only other door in the room with a friendly and diplomatic smile. "Good morning, Detective Briggs. I appreciate you taking the time to come and visit us."

Briggs's smile was forced. "I go where I'm needed… and where I need to go."

"Good, good, Detective. Let's find a good place to speak."

Briggs followed through the security doors down a long corridor, past rooms with closed doors with non-descript or cryptic labels such as "Measurement", "Balance Room" and "GLM Analytics". Ahead of him, Briggs could see the corridor opening out to a much larger area. Nomura turned and opened the door of the last room from the corridor, labelled "Planning". She ushered him into the room, but Briggs found himself captivated by the view of the larger room ahead instead.

A gangway encircled a series of transparent cylinders the size of a small building. Inside each were racks of metal nodes by the hundreds. Each stacked one on top of the other for several floors in both directions. The front of each node was illuminated with blue lights, pulsing to an unheard rhythm.

The room was larger than any enclosed space he'd ever been in before. The gangway around the outside slowly spiralled upwards, and Briggs counted at least nine floors above him. He would have counted more, but a white wall materialised to block his view entirely. Briggs frowned and turned to see a smiling Nomura, still gesturing towards the open door, "This way, please, Detective."

Briggs slipped into the room. It was a small conference room with a simple white table and 10 chairs. The room appeared to be designed for utility rather than entertaining external guests. Nomura took a seat at the head of the table and gestured for Briggs to do the same. He sat at the opposite end.

"Tell me, what might cause a plexus to melt through someone's chest?" he asked.

Nomura's fake smile melted away instantly. "Straight to the point, I see, Detective."

"Well, as you may be aware, there has been a spate of augment failures centred around West Praxis. Citizens with holes in their chests after they appeared to collapse." He'd never seen Nomura's face so sour—it was a deliberate tactic to put her off guard, but Briggs would be lying if he didn't gain a mild sense of sick satisfaction from watching her squirm.

Nomura had rarely been helpful on cases. Her knowledge was limited by what her company shared with her. It made her a perfect liaison to protect her employer's interests, whilst only trickle-feeding Briggs with a sanitised version of the truth.

The liaison caught her breath and managed another plastic smile. "That sounds like some story, Detective, but our augments have not had a failure in over 60 years. There have been times where damaged augments have not performed to specification, and others where unauthorised modifications have compromised them to the detriment of the citizen, but these are well outside the bounds of our service guarantee."

Briggs' response was curt, "Unfortunately, Constable Lee Nguyen is no longer in a position to give a damn about your service guarantee."

"Yes… Yes, of course. I'm sorry, detective. I appreciate that this unfortunate event has struck down one of PPD's finest. On behalf of Augmosis, we will be eager to provide support to Constable Nguyen's family and co-workers."

"Yes, I'm sure you'll be quite generous," Briggs scoffed.

It seemed that Nomura had nothing more to say, her fingers tapping nervously on the table.

"Nomura, I travelled halfway around the circle for this meeting. Your invitation inferred you had something to offer. I can only hope it wasn't just to serve up the same old company tripe that you normally do. Why am I here?"

The door behind him opened and another man entered, seated on a motorised wheelchair. His face appeared young and full of vitality, but his body posture was slouched, almost contorted in the chair. A frail, amplified voice spoke, "You're here because *I* invited you."

Aldus Goldstein had been the face of Augmosis, since becoming board chairman almost 50 years ago. He'd outlived all of the founders of Augmosis, most of whom had died at respectable ages. By Briggs' maths, that made Goldstein the oldest citizen in Praxis, at somewhere exceeding 130 years. His advanced age may have been concealed by his projection, but his body didn't move in his wheelchair, which also kept his frail body alive.

Goldstein dismissed Gen Nomura from the room with barely a word and invited Briggs back out to the spiral gangway. The virtual wall had been cleared and Briggs leant on the balustrade, soaking in the view. Meeting Aldus Goldstein was like meeting royalty, and Briggs was wise enough to moderate his usual sarcastic tone.

"It's a thing of beauty isn't it, Detective?" Aldus Goldstein spoke carefully and slowly. Briggs suspected Goldstein might not be able to speak with his own voice, and that the voice he heard was just being projected by his phonics.

"Absolutely it is," Briggs affirmed. His eyes darted between the seated Goldstein and the transparent cylinders containing the racks of electronic nodes. Now that he was a little closer to them, Briggs could make out more detail—the occasional movement of a mechanical arm inside each cylinder with a range of attachments for servicing each node. The arm moved slowly, trailing a set of floating cables, confirming Brigg's suspicion that the cylinder was filled with fluid.

"Let's walk together," Goldstein's motorised chair silently began to ascend the spiral gangway. "Each one of these cylinders contains exactly 32 racks, which in turn contain 256 core nodes. In this building, there are 32 cylinders, meaning there are over a quarter of a million nodes in this building alone. Each node contains the quantum processing core of one of Praxis' six million citizens."

Briggs tried to keep up with the math but gave up.

"Each quantum core is entangled to one citizen's plexus, usually for life. It can perform more calculations per second and can process more data than the human brain will in a week—all while directly wired into the Network and every other citizen of the Collective."

Goldstein's chair slowed in front of another cylinder. "I'll be honest with you Detective; I don't have the slightest clue how these things work. The quantum processing technology was all Botha and Romero. Gare designed the augments. Olena looked after the data and Bonner was the visionary. My job was the software to make it all play nicely together." He gave a very subdued wave in the direction of the cores.

"Millions of citizens brought together in a harmony of both liberty and unity. Bonner would describe it as though each citizen was playing their own solo piece of music at the same time. But rather than a cacophony of noise, it became a symphony of individuality and shared purpose. Bonner loved his musical metaphors."

Briggs had not yet reached his threshold of small talk. It wasn't every day he got a history lesson from one of the founders of the Network. *Goldstein is probably the only person alive who remembers the world from before*, he realised.

"We have plenty of smart kids here who know how these things work. Our legacy is in good hands." Goldstein turned his chair to face Briggs. "But I think we both know that recently, there have been a few reasons to give us cause for concern."

Briggs nodded. As much as he wanted to share where he was up to on the case, he stayed quiet, patiently waiting for Goldstein to speak first.

"This is what I know so far—perhaps you may be able to fill in some of the gaps. You have two citizens, one of them a PPD officer, found dead, possibly because of, or at the same time as their augments. You have a warrant out for the arrest of a citizen with the moniker of Korb1k who seems to have disappeared. You have no recorded footage of either crime, and the other witness to the crime—another noted criminal, has also dropped off the Network."

Briggs' face was emotionless. "That just about sums it up, sir".

"Do you have any other leads I don't know about?"

"I do."

"Would you care to share them?" Goldstein probed.

Briggs decided there was still some charm left in his withered old body.

"Perhaps in time sir. The evidence is pointing me down a path that may not be popular. I would rather get some confirmation before I start sharing my crazy theories."

"That seems very prudent." There was a long pause "Detective, how much do you trust the rest of your police department?"

That question caught Briggs completely off guard. He fumbled for an answer. "Well, enough I suppose, sir".

"Forgive me, Detective. I have spent most of yesterday getting to know more about you as a detective and as a person. I can tell you are someone who doesn't play by the political rule book. Doesn't play 'silly buggers' as we used to say in the old days."

Briggs grunted an affirmation.

"Just as you said, you are keeping your theories to yourself, which I appreciate. As a 132-year-old, I would have to say that I, too, have no time for games. My role as chairman of Augmosis is largely ceremonial now. The rest of the Board and the CEO look after everything important. The Board is geared for damage control, but I'm more interested in getting to the bottom of whatever is going on. This is my legacy and I want to die knowing it was safe and secure.

"If I were to show you something that helped your case, could I count on you to keep it to yourself? I would not want the things you see to be written down in a report, only to be broadcast across every news feed. Losing confidence in the Network would be disastrous for everyone across Praxis. Once the case has been solved, and whatever bug in the system has been fixed, then, as far as I'm concerned, we can tell everyone exactly what happened since there will be no immediate danger."

Briggs thought for a moment. He didn't care to be making deals—especially since he could quite easily get a warrant to secure whatever it was that Goldstein had to share. But that also made a paper trail. He was already keeping his theories to himself, and he didn't want to have some pencil-pusher like Deputy Moya breathing down his neck and compromising his investigation.

"Mr Goldstein, I follow where the evidence leads me. If that evidence leads me to corporate failure or even something far more malicious, then I'm not going to let that stop me from uncovering the truth." Briggs chose his next words carefully. "But I also don't want PPD bureaucrats or the media hampering what needs to be done. So, you have my word that anything you share with me will be kept confidential until such time that it becomes necessary for it to be formally reported."

Goldstein smiled. "I think that will suffice, Detective Briggs. Follow me."

**15**

B riggs followed Goldstein away from the central cylinders down a corridor to an unnamed room. The door opened for them automatically and Briggs found himself in a large conference room with a long white table. Unlike the previous room, this room appeared highly sterilised. The long side of the room was a glass window overlooking another larger space filled with workers in full white outfits and face masks performing research or study. Briggs didn't bother to ask what they were doing—he accepted he would most likely not understand the answer.

Thirteen objects were spread across the length of the long table. Each was masked by a small privacy shroud like the ones used to conceal crime scenes. A female worker in a lab coat looked up and acknowledged them both. Briggs felt her gaze rest on him a little too long, so he met her gaze and watched as she left the room.

"Detective Briggs, this is a clean and private room. Nothing we say here can be recorded." A few hand gestures revealed to Briggs that the options for banking footage were no longer available to him.

"Fair enough," he said.

The first two of the privacy shrouds dissolved to reveal two processing nodes—the same as those he'd seen stacked in the glass cylinders earlier. Each node was identical, with a flat rectangular front containing interface ports and coloured status lights. The unit was the same length as it was wide, and the casing of the node was transparent, revealing the internals of the unit.

"Both of these nodes went offline yesterday morning. The first at 8:09 am and the second at 9:18 am."

"Petros Zaimis and Officer Nguyen?" Briggs enquired.

81

"Presumably yes—but we don't know for sure. The identity of each citizen is hidden, even from us at Augmosis. We identify each part of the augment system with a unique 10-character serial number. That relates to their unique moniker, but we maintain stringent privacy at the hardware layer."

"With respect, sir, I find it hard to believe you wouldn't have someone here with enough power to access every single piece of data across the whole Network," Briggs countered.

"Detective Briggs, from our very first days, Augmosis has established systems within the Network to protect the privacy of every citizen, even from us. Many of those systems I wrote myself personally. Without privacy, there cannot be any trust—and without trust, the whole dream falls apart.

"Now for any faulty quantum node, we would still be able to reconcile it to a citizen's Network identity based on their moniker. However, in these cases, each of those identities has also been corrupted, along with all their data." Goldstein's measured demeanour grew more serious. "Detective, that bothers me almost more than anything else—it is like something targeted every thread across the entire Network and wiped it from existence."

Briggs processed this information for a moment. "What about other citizens who may have recorded information about these two identities? What about advertising scanners? What about financial systems?"

"All corrupted—within seconds of each node going offline. Even our procurement systems, which match augment components with recipients, have had those transactions altered."

The gravity of this fell on Briggs, but he also felt it explained why there was no data recorded from other witnesses or security cameras from either event.

"Take a look at each node, Detective," Goldstein said.

Briggs leaned closer. He spied an embossed identifier on the front of the node, 10 random-looking letters and numbers in two groups of five with a hyphen in between. He began to run his finger along them only to have it disappear into the body of the case—it was just a projection. Briggs grunted in disapproval.

"What am I looking for exactly?"

"The main quantum core is in the centre-left of the case, the quartz-coloured hexagonal prism with metallic fins." Briggs located the module. "To the right are banks of on-board memory chips, used for short-term storage of all information required by the core—each with 16 terabytes. Do you see anything unusual about them?"

"They all look melted together?"

"Correct. If you look below it, there are also banks of smaller metal crystalline cubes. Each contains a further 16 petabytes of memory, used for longer-term storage. Things like banked footage are all contained within one node rather than being distributed. You can't tell by looking at them, but they have all been wiped clean by the same process.

"Detective, I can't begin to tell you how much energy would be required to melt those chips. As you've seen, these nodes are fully submerged in coolant which circulates through each node to keep them cool. What you see here happened in about 12 seconds from start to finish."

"What about the quantum core itself?" Briggs asked.

"As far as we can tell so far, it looks OK. However, it doesn't hold onto any data."

Briggs turned to face Goldstein, "So each of these citizens has effectively been deleted from the Network?"

"That about sums it up, yes."

Briggs continued to process this information when Goldstein hesitantly asked his own question, "Detective, was there a third citizen... killed... at almost the same time yesterday?"

"No, only two have been found or reported."

The next concealment shroud dissolved to reveal a third node, which immediately drew Briggs' attention. It looked no different from the other two—banks of melted chips across the main circuit board.

"Detective, this node went offline exactly 32 seconds before the second node. It followed the same pattern as the other two, however, we were able to identify something else."

"What was it?"

"Moments before the meltdown commenced, one of our supervisory processes logged the de-phasing of the quantum core."

"What the hell does that mean?"

"It only occurs when we need to re-entangle one of these quantum cores with a partner core within your plexus."

Considering Briggs' blank expression, Goldstein continued, "Your Network identity is the combination of your plexus and one of these physical nodes. Both are entangled—bound together to function like a single computer. If your plexus is damaged, you can buy a new one and have it re-entangled. It is repaired with your original node and then you're back up and running. What happened to this third node was just half of that process."

Briggs still didn't fully understand. "So, what does that tell you?" he asked.

"I can't be certain. But if I was to guess, which I don't like doing, this third citizen's quantum-level identity was copied before the node was destroyed."

"Copied to where?"

"I don't know. Across the entire Network, there were no other cores dephased or re-phased within a few minutes of this event. But on average we have hundreds of re-phasings every day—citizens that have damaged their plexuses or want to upgrade to one of the smaller models."

Briggs quickly pounced on this information, "Can you give me the list?"

As if anticipated, a document notification appeared in his optics. Placing one hand on the table for balance, he used the other to review the document—a simple table with the citizen's moniker, two 10-letter identifiers which Briggs assumed related to their node and plexus, and the timestamp of the event. Briggs hadn't yet worked out what this information would be useful for, but it felt important.

He closed the document and floated a theory. "If someone wanted to, say hypothetically, delete someone from the Network, would that be possible?"

"Completely impossible," Goldstein said sharply.

"Even for someone at Augmosis?"

"Still impossible. There are too many interconnected systems; too many processes which oversee security and privacy policy."

"Still, would you agree that someone with enough knowledge of your systems to do this and kill could quite possibly work at Augmosis?"

Goldstein made an audible snarl, not from his projection but from the old man beneath. Clearly, he'd also considered this possibility. "Detective Briggs— I refuse to believe that any of this could be possible. As you can imagine, the most frustrating thing for a software designer would be to learn that the system he has presided over for a century appears to harbour a catastrophic flaw. And yet the facts tell me that such a flaw must exist. The best logical conclusion is as you have suggested—someone with enough access within Augmosis must surely be involved.

"I can assure you that I have my hand-picked investigators combing through everything we have, every line of code to come to some sort of a solution."

Briggs waved towards the workers in the room he could see through the window. "Is that what they're doing?"

"No, those workers are working on implementing a fix that will prevent this from ever happening again."

"How long do you think it will take?" Briggs asked

"I don't know, they've already been working on it for over two years…"

Liam woke with a headache and the chirp of numerous missed calls and notifications in his ears. Rather than stew over his grave missteps the previous evening, he'd simply downed two of the hard-earned Vallux tablets together and collapsed on the mattress in his safe house.

As his mind slowly cleared, he checked the time with a few hand gestures before recoiling in pain when his body reminded him of the consequences of punching a plexus: a set of swollen and bruised knuckles.

His hand now held against his chest and propped up on his plexus, Liam grabbed something frozen from the freezer and rested it over his knuckles. Using his prosthetic hand, he checked the missed notifications and messages. They weren't addressed to him but to someone with the moniker of 'Basilicus'.

Liam's new identity.

At some point during the evening, Liam's employer had secured him another identity. Though it had never been specifically explained to him, Liam had guessed these were citizens recently deceased, their identities somehow appropriated by his employer and put to a new use.

His virtual inbox was filled with unopened messages. The last was a simple message from his employer:

<E77DD7-E51425> LIAM, RELOCATE TO PRAXIS CENTRAL. AWAIT FURTHER INSTRUCTIONS.

He did not read any of the other messages. He didn't need to know the final messages received by the original owner of this new identity in the final moments of their life.

He made that mistake once before—reading messages from a family he had just inherited asking how he was recovering from surgery. Friends saying they were praying for his recovery. Children trying to reconnect after being estranged from their father. A wife leaving a tearful farewell video message to her husband who was now on life support, never to wake up again.

He had plenty of his own emotional pain to drown in without carrying someone else's.

A few gestures and the messages were deleted, and their senders blocked.

His employer reconnected this new identity to his previous accounts. Over eight hundred thousand bits spread across them. That number of bits was more than enough for him to carve out a new life for himself. But if his employer had the power to recycle identities and to connect bank accounts between them, Liam suspected he probably had more than enough power to track him down.

He stepped in front of a mirror and saw the projection of the previous identity. An elderly white male with a thick crop of pure white hair, partnered with a bushy moustache concealing his mouth entirely. Liam wiggled his mouth to see the moustache dance in perfect response.

The clothing however did not match at all—a V-neck, long-sleeve linen white shirt was flashing in and out of reality because he was still wearing his physical trench coat which was causing tracking errors for the projected clothing. He took off the coat and threw it on the floor. Looking back at the mirror, he confirmed the projection had repaired itself.

He could not keep this trueself—there was too much risk of someone recognising his projection, even in a sprawling city of millions. He interfaced with the Network, selecting one of many hundreds of generic trueself suppliers to purchase his next appearance.

Like all his past trueselfs, he always selected something masculine that was roughly his own age and body shape. Selecting a feminine form sounded like a smart idea but he simply did not move in a way that made it appear believable.

Even generic trueselfs were unique, to a degree. Most were based on an original model which had parameters like eye colour and hair colour altered by a simple AI. Liam selected a narrow-faced self on a three-month discounted lease for a grand total of 800 bits.

Applying this to his identity, his reflection switched first to his disfigured oldself before being replaced by his new projection: completely naked, except for a piece of androgynous tanned flesh in place of his genitals. There was simply no reason to project genitals when you were only going to cover them in virtual clothing and selecting the upgrade option for matching manhood was a waste of bits.

He ran his left hand over his now smooth face. His scars had been concealed. Both hands, including his prosthetic hand, were now tanned and blemish-free.

From a different store, he selected a pair of khaki-coloured trousers. Going back through his Basilicus' virtual inventory, he re-selected the same white linen shirt his former namesake had been wearing. He liked the look. A pair of shoes and some virtual glasses completed the ensemble. All up, his new identity cost him just shy of 1,000 bits.

Liam stashed his coat and other belongings back into his pack. He confirmed there was nothing to identify him in this room, before stepping back out into West Praxis. His first task of the day would be to secure a new base of operations and a second safe house close to where his next job was required. He'd maintain his current apartment as another backup. It had already been paid up for a month and cancelling the lease early was now impossible since it had been set up under the Korb1k identity.

Walking back to the central park area of West Praxis, Liam found himself walking past the same café he'd been at just over 24 hours ago. Two police officers in full combat gear stood guard, their assault rifles held at the ready. He walked within ten meters of two officers, nodding towards them with a friendly smile. Their heads tracked him as he walked before turning away, clearly satisfied his new identity was of no consequence.

*The power of anonymity*, Liam thought as he began his descent down the foot tunnel to the transit station.

# 16

"Two years!" Briggs could not conceal his alarm. "What the hell are you talking about?"

"Now you understand why I require your candour," Goldstein said.

The remaining ten concealment shrouds dissolved to reveal more cores on the centre bench. Briggs' glare finally subsided, and he moved to inspect each of the newly revealed domes. He found them to be effectively identical.

"The first control nodes failed two years ago. We investigated it thoroughly, but in the end, we had to write it off as an anomaly. With the association to a citizen's moniker erased, we had no way of knowing what it meant. Five months later, another one failed, followed by another two weeks afterwards. We knew this wasn't just some random once-off anomaly."

"But you didn't tell anyone? Not the Council of Overseers or the PPD?"

"A few people were informed, but there was nothing at all to make us think it had anything to do with real-life murders. That was until yesterday."

Briggs walked along the line of damaged nodes, like a frustrated captive animal pacing the outskirts of its enclosure. He paused, hand cupping his chin. "You said the third node was different—like its computer was copied. Were any of these like that?" Briggs knew he wasn't using the right words, but his brain had kicked up a gear as he considered this stream of new information.

"Yes." Goldstein responded. After a brief delay, six of the ten nodes were illuminated by a virtual blue light. Briggs reached to touch one of the other nodes only to realise that it too was a projection, and his hand passed through it to the empty bench below.

"Though it was only yesterday that we realised it, all six of these nodes plus the one yesterday have a near-identical signature of a quantum core de-phasing prior to overloading. The other seven do not."

"So, if it fits what happened yesterday, then there could be as many as six victims," Briggs mused.

"Perhaps".

"Can you give me the timestamps of all of these events in order?"

The timestamps were projected above each node, down to the millisecond. At the same time, the second node, which Briggs presumed to be Officer Nguyen switched positions with the third node now that it was in chronological order.

Briggs walked to the far end of the table to the very last node. It was highlighted in blue light as a "de-phased" node. He confirmed the timestamp:

$$97\text{-}11\text{-}20 \ \ 04{:}25{:}53.93278$$

Just a little more than two years ago. A theory began to emerge. He looked down the line of coloured nodes. There was no visual pattern, but it presented as a sequence of events he might be able to correlate with other events in the PPD database. Missing persons. Other Network anomalies. It was a welcome shot of adrenaline to his investigation.

"I need this data. I need the re-phased identities for each one of these events. I need…"

Goldstein interrupted, "I think you're on the right track, Detective."

"These are all the same guy," Briggs declared.

"I agree. We too have analysed the correlation between the re-phasing events and the destruction of each node. There is a clear sequence."

"Do you have any data at all on these identities? Even identities that were re-phased around each event?"

"We do, but that won't help." Goldstein shared "Within 24 hours of a dephasing, we can see an identity being recycled, but it too has a 'null' identity. That is, up until now. The list you have are all active identities. I think you'll find your answer in that list."

Briggs agreed, but it somehow didn't seem to make the path ahead any clearer.

Gen Nomura entered the room and stood behind Goldstein's chair, bending down and whispering something into his ear.

"Detective Briggs, this is all the information I have at the moment. I'm not the young man I used to be and unfortunately, I need to limit how much time I spend on my feet."

Briggs cocked his head and concluded the old man was trying to make a joke.

"Is there anything else I can help you with before I leave?"

A raft of questions flooded his mind, but it was the questions he hadn't thought of yet that he was worried about. "Sir, am I able to contact you for any follow-up questions?"

"Of course." A trust request was initiated and accepted.

"Are our communications secure?" Briggs asked.

"All communications in the Network are secure, Detective. But your communications with me will be especially so."

Goldstein's chair began to track slowly backwards and turn towards the door.

"One last question if you don't mind, sir." Nomura appeared irritated and disapproving of the company's founder answering so many questions.

"Sure—what is it?"

"Fernando Alvarez. Also known as Atacama. He was the other witness to the crime. He's dropped off our radar. Is that something you could help us with?"

The question was loaded. Nomura quickly interjected before Goldstein could answer.

"Detective Briggs—you are well aware that it is against the principles and laws of Praxis to circumvent the liberty and privacy of a citizen…"

"Maybe that's a ridiculous rule…" Briggs muttered. "However, given the unusual things happening here right under your collective noses, I thought you might be a little more motivated to try and hunt this guy down. Who knows— maybe it will lead us all to this Korb1k. Maybe we will all get the answers we are looking for."

Nomura glared but stayed silent. Eventually, she too looked towards Goldstein for guidance, as if pleading with the old man not to cross some imaginary line.

"I will see what I can do, detective."

The door opened and Briggs was ushered back outside by Nomura. He was more than satisfied with that answer.

***

After Briggs and Nomura left the conference room its virtual wall dissolved, removing the barrier between the room and the large work area next to it. The female technician who had left the room earlier, Imogen Godfrey, approached Goldstein who remained unmoved in his chair.

"How did he take it?" she asked.

"As good as could be expected."

"Did you…. Did you tell him about the other nodes?"

"No Imogen. Not yet

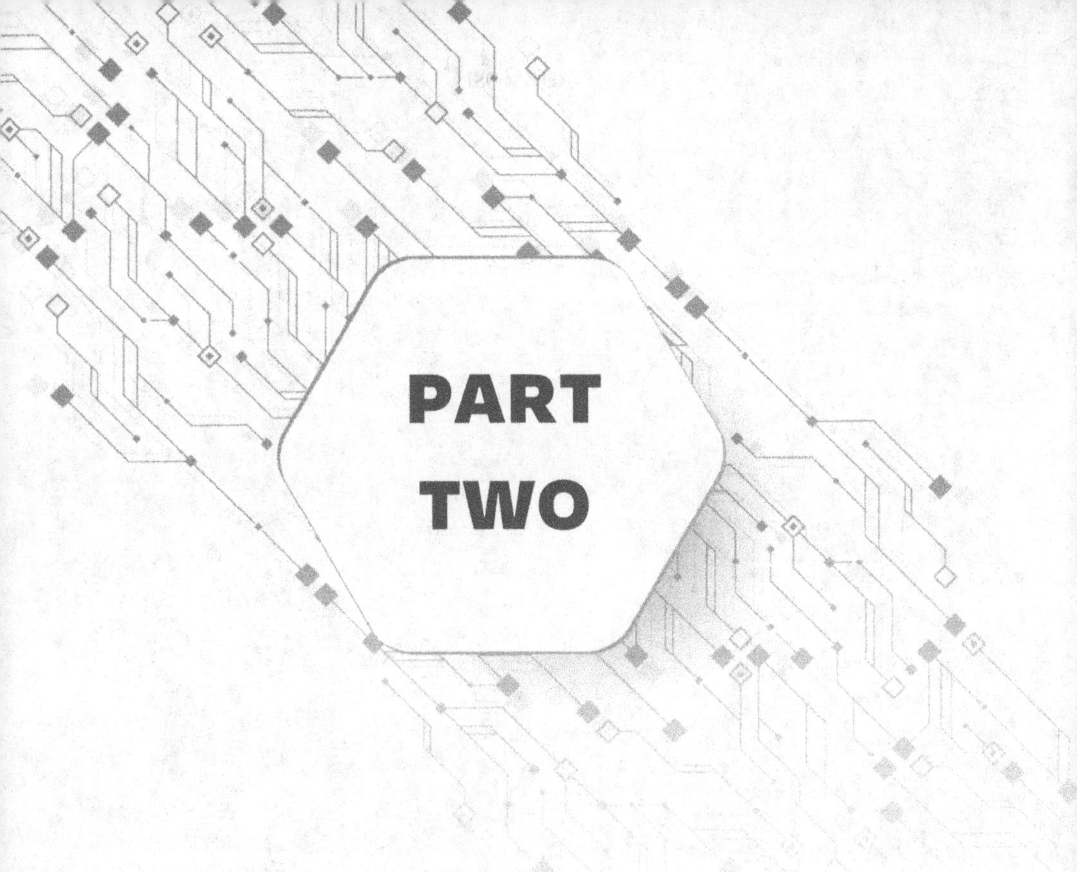

# PART TWO

*"Without projection, there is no self.*

*Without perception, projection is redundant.*

*Without reconciliation, there is anarchy.*

*Without anonymity, there is no trust.*

*Without reflection… well reflection is really just a novelty."*

Aldus Goldstein, Co-Founder

**17**

The two bodies were laid out before Briggs on stainless steel benches in a room so cold his lifesuit was having trouble keeping him warm. The medical examiner, a short woman with grey hair fashioned in a bob, stood over the second of the two bodies, waving her hands in the air as she made virtual notes. A callout identified her as 'Dr. Isa Barclay'—not an examiner Briggs had worked with previously.

Each body was barely covered with small modesty sheets above their pelvis. Post-mortem incisions had been functionally closed by staples, and containers to the side of each body contained organs removed for further testing. The line of staples ceased at the centre of the chest, where a burned cavity the size of a large fist remained.

Another incision circled Nguyen's scalp around the hairline. Officer Nguyen no longer needed a projection. There was no self that could reanimate his lifeless corpse. Here, on a cold metal table, Nguyen was reduced to just flesh and bone, his organs weighed and measured only to be dissected further in the search for understanding as to what had brought him to such an undignified end.

"In the end, we are all just food for worms," Briggs whispered to himself.

"Carpe Diem, detective," the medical examiner replied.

"I'm sorry, I didn't mean to interrupt you."

"No interruption. One can't devote oneself to understanding the cause of death without taking an occasional moment to consider its purpose."

"And what is its purpose?" Briggs enquired.

Dr Barclay's hands slowed, and she turned to face Briggs, "To bring an end to life."

"That makes no sense…"

She smiled, "Neither does death—and yet it is reality."

Briggs' eyes narrowed. He had no time for philosophical games, so he let it go and pivoted to the reason he was there.

"Have you learned anything further from examining the bodies beyond the field scan?"

"I've learned many things detective. I learned that Mr Zaimis here was carrying several cancerous growths throughout his small and large intestines that, without treatment, would become a problem for him in a few years. I also learned that approximately 36 hours ago he consumed moderate doses of the banned opioid 'Ozone' and psychedelic 'Silo'. But I suspect those aren't the kinds of things you are interested in?"

"No—Death: cause and means."

"Hmm… Are you squeamish, Detective Briggs?"

"No," he lied.

She turned and faced the body of Officer Nguyen and motioned her hands and fingers. A projection overlaid his body, revealing organs previously exposed by the central chest incision. Layer by layer more was exposed. The rib cage separated to reveal what remained of the lungs, stomach, spleen, and heart.

"Considering both bodies experienced the same basic injuries, excluding the post-mortem damage to Officer Nguyen's body, I have tried to understand what pathology is shared by both victims. From the statements I have read, I understand both died quickly and without apparent cause?"

"Yes—there were no witnesses in Officer Nguyen's case, but I think that would be a safe assumption."

Dr. Barclay's gestures lifted the projection of Nguyen's head from the table, enlarging it to twice its size and causing it to hover above his body.

"Both brains show signs of hypoxia. Yet there is no evidence of asphyxiation. Both pairs of optics look like they may have malfunctioned and the eyes themselves are mildly inflamed, but I don't have the equipment to analyse them further, so I have provided these to the forensic lab at Augmosis to analyse."

She gestured again and the head disappeared. Each projected organ was highlighted as she spoke. Briggs forced himself closer but found himself breathing shallowly to minimise his exposure to the acrid smell of the two bodies.

"The chest is more of a mystery. As you can see, there are severe burns through the lower parts of the lower pectoral and upper abdominal muscles. If you look here the sternum bone is intact, but the softer costal cartilage which connects the ribs to the sternum has been burned through, to the organs beneath. The xiphoid process has been detached from the sternum completely."

"How much heat would be required to do that?" Briggs asked.

"I'm not sure to be honest, but I think the burns are both exothermic and chemical."

"Chemical?"

"Yes—in addition to a high-capacity battery supply, a plexus contains a whole bunch of nasty chemicals you would not want liquefied and poured onto your skin. There is severe damage to the lungs, the left lobe of the liver, the oesophagus and stomach and of course the heart itself. The lower part of the heart has been burned through, including the left and right ventricle and septum—not to mention a whole bunch of important veins and arteries.

"What remained of the plexus was just a lump of metal. I will need to wait until I hear back from Augmosis to confirm if any of it was missing, but the weight matches. "

"They've assured me this is a high priority for them," Briggs advised. "Is that what killed them—their plexuses going into meltdown?"

She deflected for a moment, "The witness statements, inferred Mr. Alvarez died quietly, without any kind of seizure or sound? No trauma to the chest immediately beforehand?"

"Correct."

She turned to face him again. "Detective, in my world, most things are absolute: black and white. It is unhelpful in my profession to preface my analysis with such statements as 'my best guess is'. The brain was starved of oxygen. And yet, the blood within the lungs was well oxygenated. You can't live without a heart, but it would take time—maybe minutes to cause that much damage to the chest. So, unless you are unconscious or already dead, there is no way someone allows a molten piece of metal to slowly burn through their internal organs."

"Your best guess?"

A wry smile passed over her face.

"If I ignore the melted augments and subsequent tissue damage, the best match to the pathology is something called Commotio Cordis."

"What's that?"

"Sudden cardiac arrest. It's usually caused by severe blunt force trauma to the heart—often in contact sports. A blow so specific that it interrupts the electrical signals of the heart, causing it to go into immediate fibrillation."

"And yet there was no such blow to the chest."

"Indeed, and that's what bothers me. The brain quickly ran out of oxygen, but, for a time, the lungs still worked, oxygenating the blood within the villi. But there was no pressure to move that blood to where it needed to go. The heart just stopped."

Briggs considered this. It didn't offer him a complete explanation, so he dug deeper. "Apart from a physical blow, what could cause the heart to stop?"

"Nothing external. However, in a hospital, a cardioverter can be used to temporarily stop or restart the electrical signals that cause the heart to beat. To treat conditions like ventricular tachycardia and fibrillation. In a purely biological sense, if you can disrupt or interfere with those electrical impulses, you could indeed stop a heart."

Briggs could tell this level of guesswork was moving the medical examiner out of her comfort zone.

"All lifesuits contain built-in defibrillation systems—could they be used to stop a heart?"

Her gaze focused on him intently. Briggs suspected she may have come to a similar conclusion.

"Yes—in theory."

Finally, an answer. He might have let out a fist pump if he'd been one of the junior detectives. He settled for a smile and a half-nod.

"Don't lifesuits keep separate logs of events aside from the plexus?"

"Yes—but they are powered by the plexus and stored just below the coupling. Any logs would have been destroyed."

"If the lifesuit's defibrillator activated, wouldn't that leave a mark on the skin?"

"Usually, yes, but when cardioversion is performed in a hospital, the voltages are far smaller. I'm not sure if there is any research on deliberately stopping the heart this way since, in a medical context, you would only be stopping the heart for the sole purpose of starting it again."

Briggs nodded. He'd already begun to factor this new information into an evolving theory. His train of thought was briefly interrupted.

"Detective Briggs, there are too many unknowns at this time to put this kind of theory in writing. The official cause of death will be stated as 'Unspecified sudden death'. I hope you understand?"

"That's perfectly OK with me," Briggs said.

"I'll run my observations past my colleagues, but they tend to be even more conservative than I am—so I doubt the official cause of death will change."

"That's OK. At this point, it still helps, even if it can't be put in writing. You could say this case has already attracted more interest than I'm used to."

"I can imagine. I've had Deputy Moya on my call sheet since last night to give him an update."

Brigg's eyes narrowed, and his jaw clenched briefly. "I suppose it wouldn't be too much trouble for you to only give your official opinion and not your 'best guess'?"

She smiled again. "Of course, Detective."

**18**

Work was a welcome distraction for Carli. She broke for lunch and took the elevator down to the ground floor and onto the street. She was relieved to have not bumped into Deniz Harper so far this morning, and she hadn't yet spoken with Shannon Ayres. The more she thought about speaking with her, the more nervous she became. Thinking the conversation over and over in advance wasn't going to make it any less uncomfortable.

A familiar smell greeted her as she left the ground floor. She turned to the side, expecting to see Vinesh Naidoo in his wheelchair but he was no longer there, which seemed out of place. She ordered a lunch meal from a vendor a block away and selected one of the tables positioned around the courtyard of the main street. A fountain was projected in the centre of the courtyard, spraying virtual water from a central flower-shaped spire. If there had been any breeze, and if the fountain was anything more than a virtual projection in her optics, a light spray of water would have settled over her as she sat.

She opened her lunch container, a mixture of green leaves and synthetic proteins coated in vinaigrette. She ate alone and in relative silence. Those around her did the same. Like her morning commute, when people weren't working, they were immersed in the Network. Unless circumstances required it, the social norm in Praxis was to keep to oneself.

As she ate, two teepers walked in near unison across the courtyard. She tracked them the whole way to the other side of the street where they turned and backed into two empty charging docks. More citizens moved around the courtyard, some in pairs, most alone. Carli found herself again critiquing each of their trueselfs. Yesterday morning she did so with an attitude of naïve wonder. Today, it was more like a mental exercise to try and keep the anxious thoughts at bay.

100

Another citizen approached her table from the opposite corner holding a meal in an identical container. He gestured towards her and asked if he could sit at the opposite end of her table. She nodded but considered him with a wary gaze. His projection was just as unique as any other. Male. Six feet tall. Olive skin. Wavy brown hair and a thick but manicured brown beard. The Network identified him with the moniker of "Wollemi".

She finished her lunch and was readying to leave when he spoke. "I hear there's rain on the way."

It was a whimsical introduction—rain was a scheduled event, sprayed from sprinklers embedded within the dome high above. It wasn't like an unpredictable storm front.

"I heard—eight o'clock tonight," she said.

"I like rain," he continued, "it washes everything away and starts afresh."

Carli continued to collect her rubbish, motioning to leave, but he kept talking.

"If you pay attention, sometimes you can glimpse the truth through the rain drops."

Her interest was piqued. "What do you mean?"

"The truth. The way this place truly is instead of the lies our eyes tell us." He was now looking at her with a charismatic smile. Carli made a quick assessment that he was just being friendly, but she felt compelled to counter— this was a common philosophical argument she'd often considered.

"Isn't the projection of the Collective the better truth?"

"Ah! A true believer!" he again said with a smile. The conversation established a trust request in the Network which she ignored, but she continued the conversation.

"Of course, without the Collective, we are only shadows—no capacity to project, no capacity to shape the world for the better."

"But is it really better?" he asked. He motioned to the fountain near them. "Is that really an improvement on the physical world? It doesn't cool the air. It doesn't wash over you with the movement of the breeze. It doesn't cling to your hair. It's just a poor imitation."

"But without it, the space would be empty and lifeless. The Collective has given life and beauty to something that would otherwise be empty." Carli found herself standing to support her perspective. "The Collective serves us a better truth, when the old truth is no longer enough. That's why Praxis has flourished for 100 years…"

His smile waned but not his resolve. "I see the dogma of the Collective burns bright in you."

This shut Carli down. "That's offensive. It's not dogma when it's the truth we all agree upon."

Carli began to move away from the table and away from her debater.

"Forgive me—I can be a little forthright. Do yourself a favour, Ms MalvinaHoffman—tonight when it rains, go for a walk. See the world the way it really is, not the way we all pretend it is."

Carli paused to acknowledge his statement with a brief smile of her own before leaving the table. As she walked away, she found herself wondering if she'd seen the man eat any of his food.

"Hello again, Ms Dawes"

Carli turned in the direction of the voice and found Detective Briggs standing in the NuSculpt waiting area, his projection illuminated by the light of the foyer's ocean-themed scape.

"Oh, hello officer… um, Detective." Carli tried to conceal her surprise, only because she'd pretty much forgotten their earlier encounter that morning. She instinctively looked to his forehead to see if there was something wrong with the fixes she'd made to his projection, but found her work to be more than satisfactory.

"Is there something I can help you with?" she asked.

"No, I was nearby and thought I would follow up on something with one of your colleagues."

"Who were you looking for? Perhaps I could help?"

"A citizen with the moniker, *TheNez*. A Mr… Mr Deniz Harper. Your receptionist has called him down for me."

Carli gasped, covering her mouth. *Not a very composed thing to do in front of a police officer*, she immediately realised.

"Do you know him?" Briggs asked.

"Um, yes. We've been seeing each other for a few weeks. That is, until I broke it off last night."

"I see. What time did you last see him?"

"Maybe—maybe around 9 o'clock? I could probably give you an exact time if you like?"

"No, that should be enough." His fingers and eye movement indicated he was reviewing something in his optics.

"Is Deniz in some kind of trouble?"

"Probably not."

The elevator opened to reveal Deniz Harper. He strode out of the elevator but stopped in his tracks when he saw a police officer standing next to Carli. A scowl crossed his face immediately, and he continued his approach, a finger waving in the air.

"You bitch! What have you done?"

"I didn't…" Carli was cut off.

Briggs stepped between them, holding his hand up in Deniz' face. He was shorter than Deniz, but the authority of a PPD badge seemed to give him a few extra inches.

"We are being civil here, Mr Harper. Ms Dawes is just a friend."

Deniz's eyes beamed anger like lasers at Carli. She stood her ground, but her chest felt like it was going to explode. Deniz finally turned and looked at Briggs, realising that any kind of physical posturing wasn't going to work with him.

Carli saw the look of concern on the lobby receptionist's face. There were currently no clients in the lobby, but it wouldn't stay that way indefinitely. It didn't help anyone to be part of a scene. She interfaced with the NuSculpt network—one of the lobby interview rooms was available for the next thirty minutes. She made a booking.

"Detective, perhaps we could move this conversation somewhere more private?"

"Sure, lead the way, Ms Dawes."

**19**

The interview room was small but well-appointed. A central round table had seating for just four, of which Briggs had requested Carli and Deniz make use of.

Something had happened in the lobby that Briggs didn't fully understand. He was here to check up on Deniz Harper—one of 143 citizens the Augmosis logs listed as having re-phased a plexus in the last 24 hours. Briggs first excluded any identities re-phased before 8:00 am the previous day. Then, he excluded all other hubs except West Praxis and those adjacent, cutting the list to 22. West Praxis alone had just fourteen on the list—these would be the most likely.

When he'd interrogated the PPD Network after leaving the medical examiner, he'd identified three of those fourteen to be within walking distance of the station at Praxis Grove, so he decided it was a good place to start.

He was reluctant to issue a 'Be on the Lookout' or BOLO for all fourteen citizens, still not convinced his searches and scans weren't being monitored and the last thing he wanted to do was tip someone off. *Whoever this person is or whoever these people are, they have enough access to the Network to do things Augmosis can't even stop. Best to take extra care.*

He'd already met with the other two citizens at Praxis Grove. One was a teeper service technician who'd replaced her Plexus at a West Praxis street vendor earlier that morning after the last one had been damaged playing virtual contact sport.

The other citizen was a sales consultant at a crafted tattoo parlour who had simply upgraded their plexus because it was an older model and was reporting its battery was no longer accepting a replacement charge from her sanitiser.

For each, he asked their whereabouts yesterday morning and confirmed neither had a prosthetic arm.

As Deniz Harper sat agitated at the meeting room table, Briggs quickly judged this also wasn't his guy, but in the interests of seeing this conversation through, he thought he should at least see what he had to say. Knowing absolutely nothing about what had caused Deniz Harper to become agitated, Briggs decided to give him enough rope to see what he did with it.

"Why am I here, Mr Harper?"

Deniz looked straight back at Carli. "Obviously, she has a problem with me."

"Mr. Harper, I'm going to have a problem with you, too, if you don't explain yourself."

"I have every right to perceive someone else the way I want. If I want to perceive you as a bipedal pig with wings, that's my prerogative. If she doesn't like it, that's her bad luck. I'm a lawyer—I know the rules."

Briggs saw Carli stir in her seat, but she remained composed. He had no intention of getting involved with a lover's quarrel and he still had no idea what the issue was. He decided to move on.

"Mr Harper, do you have a prosthetic arm?"

"Huh? Um. No?'

"Do you mind if I check?"

"Why? What does this have to do with…"

"You might be surprised to know that I have no idea what you are talking about. I'm following up on a double homicide in West Praxis yesterday morning. I see you occupy a domicile in West Praxis?"

"What? I was here in the Grove yesterday. I only went home after dinner."

"Good, then I'm sure you won't mind me checking your arms."

Deniz's body language loosened, a look of confusion replacing his agitation. He held his arms out.

"Sure—knock yourself out."

Briggs leaned over and felt both wrists and hands. They were fleshy and sweaty.

"Satisfied?"

"Mr Harper, you procured a replacement plexus this morning at 7:10 am at an Augmosis retail outlet in West Praxis. Why did you do that?"

Deniz remained confused, his eyes darting between Carli and Briggs.

"My old one broke. Last night."

"How?"

"At a bar—some guy punched me in the chest. Some ugly guy."

"You were assaulted?"

"No... well yes. I suppose so."

"Did you report it?"

"No—I was drunk. I don't remember what happened."

"Who was the guy—what was his moniker?"

"I don't know—I don't even think he had one."

This piqued Briggs' interest. "What do you mean?"

"I mean he didn't have one. He was trying to look as ugly as possible. Kinda looked like he was burned."

"Where did all this happen?"

"West Praxis—A bar named The Komitet. Sometime around 11:30 pm or so. It was just a silly disagreement. No-one was hurt."

"Can you tell me what he looked like?"

A strange look crossed Deniz's face and he unfolded his arms. Like he was no longer under suspicion and had suddenly become useful.

"I can do better than that—I can show you."

"How?"

"Because I banked the footage."

Carli remained in the room as Briggs received Deniz's banked footage over the Network and dismissed him.

"Ms. Dawes, do you mind if I use this room for a few minutes to follow up on a few things?" he asked.

"There is another booking in 15 minutes."

"More than I need, thank you." He returned to a seat, a look of determination on his face. Whatever Deniz had told him seemed important. Briggs' expression changed, and he looked up. "Sorry Ms. Dawes, I should have asked—why was Mr Harper upset?"

Carli swallowed a lump in her throat. She wanted to be dismissive but found herself needing to tell someone what had happened.

"Turns out he didn't like me for who I really am, so he turned me into someone else."

The Detective's facial expression didn't show any visible sign of comprehension, but then he asked, "Reflection?"

"Yes, how did you know?"

"Not my first rodeo. Nothing illegal there, but it's messy."

Carli felt pressure in her sinuses. She swallowed a few times to try and keep any tears at bay.

"Did he perceive you as someone else?"

"Yes."

"Someone you know or someone virtual?"

"Someone who works here," Carli replied. Tears were only moments away.

"How good was the projection?" The question confused Carli and distracted her enough to regain some composure. She recalled the face she'd seen in the mirror.

"It was identical—it was perfect."

"Could he have made it himself?" he asked.

"No way. It was too good—an exact copy," she replied.

Briggs smiled. "Then the legal issue isn't that he replaced your projection, but that he copied someone else's. He would have had to copy it from the original."

Carli processed this. There actually was a line that Deniz had crossed.

"The issue is theft. Unless the other person gave him the rights to their self, he must have stolen it."

She stared away as the penny dropped. The threat of tears was gradually being replaced by a feeling of empowerment. She used the NuSculpt Network to confirm that NuSculpt stored Shannon Ayres' current and previous selfs. She'd taken advantage of the NuSculpt employee program to sculpt and maintain her self, which was stored within the local network. It was supposed to be secure.

"Remember that this would be a civil matter, not a criminal matter, but I would recommend you have a chat with your HR department to see if any internal policies had been broken."

She smiled. It felt a little sadistic, but she didn't care.

"Thank you, detective. I'll leave you to your work."

The cloud she'd brought with her to work this morning had started to dissolve. As she entered the elevator, she pressed the button for the sixth floor, where her studio was. She changed her mind and pressed the button for level four: 'Administration, Finance, Legal and *Human Resources*'.

## 20

The banked footage Briggs received from Deniz Harper was short, only about 15 seconds. Deniz had deleted almost everything leading up to the altercation itself and everything afterwards. His plexus had been damaged but appeared to remain functional long enough to perform the bank operation.

As the footage commenced, Briggs instantly became unwell. Viewing someone else's perception stream from a first-person perspective was just about the worst thing for his vestibular system. With a few gestures, he made the stream appear within a window in his vision, like a scape or physical screen. The change removed any sense of depth since it was no longer a stereo image.

Briggs could tell immediately that Deniz was well and truly drunk. Even in a window, the image swayed and darted about enough to continue his unease. He considered the strange irony of perceiving someone else who was intoxicated when there was a dark part of himself craving the same thing. At this moment, viewing someone else who had lost control, the idea of having a drink himself seemed repulsive.

Briggs let the footage play out before he analysed it more deeply. It commenced with Deniz leaning forward to look at the man sitting next to him. The man slowly turned away in the opposite direction.

*"Excuse me, you forgot to pay."* The man didn't appear to respond.

*"Hey, I'm talking to you!"*

Briggs saw Deniz reach down and grab the man's arm. What followed was quick: a lot of blurry motion, like Deniz had been pulled away and lower, losing all vision of the man. Deniz was pulled into the other man's body for an instant before falling forward. The footage concluded as the strange man walked away from the bar.

Briggs brought the footage back to the start and played it at quarter speed. The detail of a recorded stream was exceptionally high and would appear smooth even at such a low speed. Near the start, Briggs found the best image of the man's face: a side profile in shadow, largely concealed by the collar of his trench coat. But his nose to the top of his head was visible, scarred and grisly. The top part of the ear was visible above the collar but was little more than a hole surrounded by a nub of flesh. No hair, no eyebrows.

The scars had no start or end. No real pattern to help identify a cause. To Briggs' untrained eye, it almost looked like his head had been deep-fried. What was more interesting was this person was not masked—this was his oldself out in the wild for all to view.

He captured a handful of static frames for reference and progressed the video forward: the moment that Deniz grabbed the man's arm. A few frames revealed the hand. Prosthetic, a dark composite material. Apart from being graphite grey in colour when most others were flesh-toned, it appeared no different from any other he'd seen, save for a single frame where the hand rotated a few degrees and revealed part of the palm. It was deep black with an orange glow. He took a few more frames for later review, storing these in his personal store rather than his PPD account.

Viewing through the stream a few more times, Briggs concluded there wasn't anything else of value. There were no reflections on glass, no voices that could be used for comparison.

There was one anomaly, however—Deniz's initial statement had a different audio profile to the rest of the stream. Briggs guessed he'd overdubbed it, perhaps wanting to hide whatever he actually said. It was inconsequential but validated Briggs's judgement of Deniz Harper's character.

Briggs weighed the evidence he'd just found. It was helpful but not conclusive. It could just as easily be a coincidence, but Briggs' intuition told him it was important. There was probably enough data from the facial profile to get a visual match, but that would require a warrant, and Briggs doubted there was enough connection with his case for a judge to sign off. It would also require Briggs to divulge information he wasn't yet ready to.

Deniz Harper could file a formal claim of assault—that might get the ball rolling. But Briggs doubted there would be enough evidence to secure a facial recognition warrant, especially since a small part of the footage was obviously doctored. Most judges would viciously discount large chunks of banked footage where there was any doubt that even a small portion of it may have been tampered with.

This left Briggs with another clue but no more leads. Still, his gut told him this was the guy. The fact that he was not identifiable on the Network fit the timing evidence for the re-phasing Briggs had collected from Augmosis, compounding his conviction.

The revelation only emphasised the importance of working through the list of re-phased identities. The closest were two located in Métropole—just two transit stops away.

As he left the NuSculpt building and headed for the transit, he found himself wondering if the man in the bar was indeed Korb1k. If so, why had he surfaced at all to go to a bar? It seemed like an incredible risk. If the prosthetic hand was indeed the source of the 'touch of death' that killed Nguyen and Zaimis then Deniz Harper should consider himself extremely fortunate to not have become a third smouldering corpse on the floor of The Komitet.

Lastly, he wondered what it would take to defend himself from such a weapon should it be used on him. *Better to not get that close.*

A few hours later, Briggs' list had shortened to seven. One of the Métropole suspects had replaced their plexus after upgrading to a lifesuit with a newer connector. The second suspect's story was more interesting but equally benign. He'd been visiting a neighbour's domicile for a late-night rendezvous. After removing their lifesuits, they were interrupted by a known third party and in his swift, naked escape, his lifesuit and plexus had been left behind.

Briggs now sat on a bench near the entrance to the Métropole transit station. Seven names left. He hoped one of those would be his man. He wondered what he would need to do if he were to meet him face to face. If the images he'd pulled from Deniz Harper's banked stream were indeed the guy, he would have no way of identifying him unless he was able to strip away his projection. Briggs scoffed at the irony—it was the same issue he'd been asked to comment on by the Council of Overseers. If he could see what everyone looked like beneath their projections, confirming an ID would be a far simpler exercise.

Seven more names. He went through their monikers and present locations. If the Network was fully compromised, Briggs' basic searches would be noticed, but may not raise any specific concern. If he raised a BOLO on them and they had access to the usually secure PPD Network, then they would be alerted. At the very least, his superiors would ask why they were being investigated at all—something which Briggs couldn't adequately answer without fully divulging his conversations at Augmosis.

Briggs was content to operate in the grey. The goal was to solve the riddle and to catch the bad guy. Rules weren't being broken or even bent, they were just being sidelined for long enough to be able to get a result, after which the broader context would be retrospectively and meticulously documented. It was a risky approach—not because it played chicken with PPD policy, but because it relied exclusively on Briggs' memory. The whole reason cases like these needed to be regularly documented was as a backup in the unfortunate case the lead detective should become temporarily or permanently incapacitated.

Briggs read through the monikers and present locations. Three remained in West Praxis. Two in Port Lincoln. One was in Bayshore and one more was presently identified as "location unknown". That was uncommon but not completely abnormal. Citizens who had not connected with the Network for 12 hours may have this status. Home addresses were listed for some, but all were farther away from the City Circle, and he'd prefer not to travel so far unless he was left with no option.

With three identities located in West Praxis, that seemed like the most logical location to search, but Bayshore and Port Lincoln were technically closer.

His mind made up; Briggs began walking towards the transit station. A chirp in his phonics alerted him to an incoming voice call—Deputy Moya.

Briggs' initial reaction was to dismiss the call but figured it was only delaying an inevitable conversation. He had a 20-minute transit ahead of him in a usually crowded transit car—that would give him the option of choosing not to answer any questions because of the risk of being overheard. He accepted the call without a greeting.

"Detective Briggs"

"Deputy Moya." There was a long pause. Briggs walked himself through the tunnel at the mouth of the Métropole transit station and continued towards the platform.

"How are you progressing with the investigation of Constable Nguyen and Mr. Zaimis?"

"I believe the medical examination has been completed. I have analysed ballistics in the case of Officer Nguyen. I have spoken to the Augmosis liaison about the case, and I'm still following up on some other points of enquiry."

"Yes, all those things have been recorded in the running file. Unfortunately, nothing you have recorded seems to shed any light on what has happened."

Briggs' chest tightened, but he stayed relaxed. "It is indeed a mystery sir, but I'm following up as best I can."

"I'm sure that you are." There was another long silence. Moya liked to draw out more information by saying nothing after a question had already been answered. The uncomfortable silence made it feel like a better answer was expected. Briggs knew the ploy and was more than happy with silence.

After 20 seconds, he ended it. "Is there anything else sir?".

"Medical examiner advised on the cause of death?"

"Only preliminary, sir: both sudden cardiac death." Briggs knew that Moya already knew that.

"And what did Augmosis say?"

Briggs was getting irritated. "What I've reported so far, sir. They've offered compensation to the victim's families and asked me if there was evidence that illegal modifications had been made to the victim's plexuses." *Not completely true, but close enough.*

"And had they?"

"Not to my knowledge, sir, though the Medical Examiner is sending what remains of the plexuses to Augmosis for further analysis."

"Any way that this is just some random coincidence of augment failures?" There it was. A suggestion that Moya wanted this buried rather than resolved. Briggs assumed Moya's motives were only to avoid a political failure rather than anything more sinister, but the idea grated, nonetheless.

"No chance whatsoever, sir," Briggs said in defiance.

"And, have you found any connection to any organised crime or antisocial groups?"

"No."

"What about the Wakers?"

That seemed like a sudden yet very specific name drop. The Wakers were one of many activist groups in the Collective. Though Briggs thought they were benign, clearly, Moya thought their anti-Network rhetoric was more malicious.

"I've found no connection, sir."

There was more silence before Moya moved on. "Captain Hagen assures me that this case has your highest priority—is that still, correct?"

"Yes sir."

"What were you doing in Praxis Grove?" Moya was tracking his location as well as his progress. Another red flag. Another confirmation that keeping his running theory to himself was justified.

"Following up on some leads."

"And in Métropole?"

"Same again." Briggs was close to losing his temper but redirected it. "You know, sir, if you'd like to brush up your field skills, I'd be more than happy for you to walk with me for a day."

"That won't be necessary, *Detective Sergeant*."

# 21

Aldus Goldstein watched on as the Augmosis virtual board meeting wound up. Goldstein had the right to be there, but Director Landon Hatch and the Board had all the power now. His position as chairperson was honorary only, and he preferred it that way. Boardroom politics and power plays were never his thing when he was in his twenties—they certainly weren't now in his advanced age.

For over a hundred years, Goldstein had pursued the elegance of the code that made the Collective possible—which made Praxis possible. His legacy didn't exist around a virtual meeting room table, it was embedded in the optics and phonics of every citizen. His legacy was the harmonisation of humanity. A legacy now at risk.

The Board cared very little about this recent series of events. They had been briefed, but they were treating the deaths as mere accidents. After all, a few failures in over a hundred years was still a pretty good track record.

But in Goldstein's world, anomalies could not be tolerated. An unbalanced equation. A byte of memory mishandled. An exception uncaught and unmanaged. It irritated him more than an ill-fitting lifesuit.

Director Hatch had been slightly more supportive. The Board generally gave Goldstein the freedom to work on his vanity projects without a whole lot of oversight and allowed him to hand-pick his team members from the thousands of architects, engineers, and Network hats at the company's disposal. After Goldstein raised the first group of core overloads and re-phasings to the Board, Hatch took him aside and asked him to continue the investigation with whatever resources were needed but to keep the issue away from the rest of the Board.

Goldstein had provided updates every few months, but the story hadn't changed—more nodes being re-phased; an occasional node going into meltdown. No change, until yesterday morning.

The rest of the board treated Goldstein with professional respect, but none knew him well. He was old enough to be their grandfather, even great-grandfather. He was wheeled out for public events and important corporate announcements, but aside from that, his only real interfacing was via Director Hatch.

Goldstein sat in his private office It was one of many node silos spread across Augmosis, though unlike the others it also contained Goldstein's private research lab. Its 4-byte identifier was A17A, but to the special group he'd selected, it had been affectionately named "The Kitchen". It was where new ideas were cooked up, tested, evaluated, and often thrown away.

The Kitchen Crew as they called themselves, had existed for almost 45 years. Goldstein had retired as CEO, only to enjoy three days of retirement before boredom led him to create the team for pure augment research. The team was responsible for many important advances within Augmosis, including the current generation of organic plasma optics, distributed plexus processing, shared perception interpolation, and even improvements to the algorithms used for distributing and evaluating financial transactions.

Those successes were built on thousands of failures. Most were lovingly nurtured only to be mercilessly killed once he suspected their success was unlikely or their utility uneconomical.

The conference call included the company's Chief Operations Officer and Chief Procurement Officer, both from the Technology division, responsible for the design and manufacture of each of the components of the augment system. Also in attendance was an important supplier, Elemental Minerals, represented by their CEO, Ridley Hayward as well as numerous underlings Goldstein didn't know.

The Augmosis COO, whose name Goldstein also couldn't remember, was leading the meeting, "Ridley, in the last three months we have had seven shipment delays exceeding 24 hours. That's the highest on record. Right now, you are behind on delivery by more than two days. What's the issue?"

"The yield of suitable product from our activities has been declining, as you know. It's taking longer than ever to process and transport the material. A single tonne of chondrite is now yielding fewer than a handful of quantum-quality diamonds. Finding and processing them takes more energy, and it's not like transporting the material a few thousand kilometres is happening any faster."

"Is that the full story?" the CPO asked.

"Yes sir—we can't deliver something that's becoming increasingly rare. There is only one known source of quantum-quality diamonds. 100 years ago the yield was sixty times that amount. We mined the parts of the asteroid with the highest yield first. This outcome was inevitable."

Goldstein remembered. He was there. So was Elemental Minerals. It was a tragedy the day the asteroid had fallen from the sky and ploughed into the centre of the Asian landmass. A billion people dead in an instant. Eight billion more from the debris, dust and fallout that followed. The atmosphere was still caustic a century later.

Praxis had been the salvation of humanity—a new reality built from the ground up around the principles of liberty and freedom. Underpinned by the Augmosis Network.

It was so long ago. And Goldstein was the only one left to remember it.

The conference call concluded with more promises made and grudgingly accepted. Goldstein immediately re-triggered a direct call to Director Hatch.

"Landon, I need a few minutes of your time."

"Sure Aldus." It had taken Goldstein 5 years to convince the 45-year-old CEO not to keep calling him Mr. Goldstein.

"I see the same consumption numbers you do. Praxis is trending down in population by 30% over the last 20 years. Deceased citizens no longer need their plexuses and nodes. Can't they be recycled to make up for the shortfall in the quantum-quality diamonds?"

"We still have stable demand, Aldus. Recycling isn't keeping up with needs. Teepers and Drones rely on quantum cores too and they have continued to grow."

Goldstein conceded defeat and shifted to the more pressing issue.

"I have news on our Plexus issue."

"Good news?"

"In a way, but still not certain. We have confirmation that some core meltdowns relate to individuals coinciding with their deaths. It appears there is more than a connection, but a causality."

"Causality?"

"Whatever caused the meltdown of their cores also destroyed the citizen's plexuses. There are currently two homicides in West Praxis under investigation."

Hatch was silent, considering this information. "Still no sign of a solution? Or something to stop it from happening?"

"No. The connection with these homicides is alarming, but I think it also gets us closer."

"It's more than alarming. It's a PR disaster."

Goldstein knew Hatch just wanted the matter resolved and taken off his list of problems. He didn't want to know the details. Hatch was a pragmatist and an administrator. He hadn't written a line of code in his life—but he did know how to manage operational efficiency and how to best capitalise on Augmosis' monopoly.

There was little of Augmosis resembling the innovator it had once been. His Kitchen Crew special projects were the only legacy of that greatness. Most of Augmosis' senior leadership were third and fourth-generation heirs to the real pioneers. Protecting their trust funds seemed more important than trying to continue the revolution their forebears had begun.

After concluding the call, Goldstein sat in silence. He was tired—tired of this puzzle that had defeated him for more than two years. A special project in The Kitchen never lasted longer than three months—fixed deadlines were key to driving pure research. But this issue had brought his entire team to a standstill. It wasn't just the tarnishing of his legacy, it was the crippling of his team from being able to invest in other projects. Like working with lead shoes, and now they were getting weary and starting to sink.

His on-duty personal aid entered his lab to check on him and to see if there was anything he needed. One of the many downsides of being a 132-year-old confined to a wheelchair was to rely on a team of aids and nurses to assist him with activities from eating to bathing himself. It had become a humiliating experience, but Goldstein wrote it off as the cost of longevity. Still, it was frustrating to have someone enquire about your wellbeing every moment the levels of hormones in your body changed.

Goldstein waved the man away, but his mechanical heart remained heavy. For what seemed like the thousandth time, he considered and ranked each of the strategies that might uncover a solution to this puzzle. So many had been followed through without success: tracing the event, working backwards from Network transactions to find some sort of pattern, even going through code line by line. The best they had been able to achieve had been to simulate the meltdown of an unused node. Knowing the "how" proved insufficient in finding the answer.

But the conversation with Detective Briggs had revealed more information than he'd been able to discover on his own since the first meltdown. Knowing for certain there was a correlation between the destroyed nodes and the matching augments in the field added more detail to the picture. What remained of those augments had been received from the PPD for testing, but Goldstein had inspected them when they arrived and doubted they would reveal anything more about what happened to them.

He now had a real-world explanation. This was no longer a failure of the Augmosis Network, but interference from some external agent. The answer to the puzzle may not be found in the virtual world but in the physical one. In Goldstein's view, the investigation by Detective Briggs now had the highest likelihood of delivering a result. At least, in the shortest amount of time. Briggs had asked for his help—the type of help only someone who knew every line of code in the Network could provide.

Goldstein made a decision. A decision he'd sworn he would never make, to cross a line he'd protected unquestionably his whole life. A line he'd drawn not only for himself but for all of Augmosis and the entire Collective.

*My legacy is at stake. It will be worth the cost.*

Carli made her way from NuScupt to the transit station. After making an initial report to the Human Resources department about the possibility of Deniz Harper stealing Shannon Ayres' projection file, her afternoon progressed with a 'final fitting' for another client's trueself. Before she could leave for the day, she was called into a meeting with the head of Human Resources to make another formal statement, which dragged into the early evening.

She felt resolute that she'd done the right thing. An undercurrent of embarrassment remained, but she found the fortitude to bury it. Now, she longed for the comfort of her home and her bed: to press "reset" on the last few days and start afresh tomorrow, like sculpting away some grotesque facial defect as though it had never existed.

The streets of Praxis Grove were quieter than most evenings. An explanation escaped Carli until she felt the cold splash of a fat drop of rain on her forehead. Instinctively, she looked up. Years ago, citizens would have looked to the heavens to see dark clouds brooding, silhouetted by flashes of occasional light and a low rumble, and concluded that rain was approaching. Now, the rain was simply a scheduled event, dispersed from jets high above the city within the structure of the dome.

Another drop of rain landed on Carli's uplifted face, cold and momentarily alarming. Then another. Other citizens still outside now hastened their progress towards the entrance to the transit station a few hundred metres ahead or had made a beeline to the nearest shelter on the side of the main pedestrian corridor. Carli would have done the same, but she stayed still.

The drops became more frequent. A slight odour of chlorine and other unknown chemicals became noticeable. She closed her eyes. She could feel drops of water accumulating on her eyebrows and running down the tip of her nose.

Yesterday someone or something had met with her and disappeared without a trace. Yesterday, her identity, her trueself, had been cast aside and replaced by a man she'd chosen to trust, only to have that trust abused. It made her feel worthless. Deniz could have achieved the same result by pushing Shannon Ayre's stolen projection onto a prostitute or even a teeper, but for some twisted reason, he'd chosen to inflict that abuse on her.

But Carli no longer needed to cry. As more rain fell on her face, she felt satisfied that the universe had somehow found a way of squaring the ledger, of righting the wrong inflicted upon her. She chose not to be a victim. She chose to live.

Opening her eyes, she found the world now obscured by rain. The sky had greyed further, the projection of the sun now moved beyond the unseen horizon. She was alone in the pedestrian corridor—it was like the rain was not only washing the dirt from the streets but also the citizens of Praxis. Were those citizens to look upon her, they would not see the projection she'd so carefully and meticulously sculpted for herself. They would not see the false projection of Shannon Ayres or anything else they'd chosen to perceive. They would just see Carli Dawes.

*And I would see them.*

The science of her lifesuit could no longer keep her body dry as she felt water slowly seep down her back. It seemed colder than the rain. She removed her lifesuit's skull cap and allowed the rain to wet her short-cropped hair as she walked towards the transit station entrance.

She noticed her arms distort and disappear, revealing he own hands and lifesuit sleeves. She swung them. Her projection returned for a moment, before disappearing again. Her optics could not reconcile and track the old reality consistently enough to replace it with the projected reality through the rain. She noticed the fronts of the buildings on either side of the corridor were no longer branded and signed, but bland, almost indistinguishable from each other. Whereas once, the walls of the buildings appeared freshly painted, now they appeared weathered and covered in patches of dark lichen. Looking upward, in the final moments of twilight, even the sky appeared different, like a solid mass of opaque grey, crisscrossed by a metal framework supporting it.

She paused outside the entrance to the transit station. A few citizens huddled there, finding shelter and desperately trying to shake off any water causing their projections to fail. One ran his hands over his bald head like a rubber squeegee to wipe away the water held captive by the few remaining wisps of hair. Two females, clearly known to each other stood back to back like strangers, doing their best not to see each other's virtual nakedness. A fourth person, was further down the corridor, leaning against the wall. Carli couldn't quite make out his outline through the rain.

One of them spotted Carli, beckoning her inside "Come out of the rain darling."

Carli barely heard her—watching these three fight to preserve their dignity was spellbinding. The Network placed no silhouette around them to identify who they were just nameless citizens fleeing exposure, wiping away the water like it was burning their skin.

Through the rain, she again saw the graffiti and artwork she'd thought had been painted over on the walls of the transit entrance. It hadn't been cleaned, only masked away from reality.

"Come inside." Both women were now looking at her. Carli was exposed, but she didn't care.

One of the markings on the wall caught her attention. A message cut out of a piece of plastic and hastily sprayed in aerosol paint. Carli read it.

YOU ONLY SEE WHAT YOU WANT TO SEE.

The message was jarring. She knew it well. But at this moment, the message had more meaning. She understood it. A deeper truth was being revealed. As the drops of rain fell between her and these three unknown citizens, she was choosing to see the world differently.

Her revelation was interrupted.

"What the hell are you staring at?" The man shouted at her through the rain, clearly irritated that his vain attempt to preserve his projection would make no difference to Carli, who remained outside in the rain. His hands were raised, not only in anger but to create a physical mask to cover his face. "Either come inside or piss off!"

The man's projection flickered in and out of reality. In the space of a second, his bald head transitioned to a full head of hair and back again. At the same time, his face lost, then gained 10 years and 10 kilos.

Carli walked out of the rain. As the rain cleared away from her eyes, their projections solidified. The Network bounded them in her optics with callouts identifying their monikers. The walls again appeared freshly painted, with no graffiti. No hidden messages.

She walked past them towards the conveyor that would take her down into the depths of the transit station. The fourth person, the male leaning against the wall looked up at her. Carli recognised him. Olive skin. Manicured brown beard.

"You see it, don't you? The truth between the lies?" he said.

"I do."

"What do you think of the reality that lies beneath?"

"It's different," Carli said. She thought of Deniz covered in water the previous evening, "It's ugly". Then she thought of her client yesterday, Aliya Qureshi. "But it's also beautiful."

The man smiled and extended his right hand. Carli's optics recognised it as part of a trust relationship and identified the man by his public moniker, Wollemi. The man she'd spoken to earlier that day in the courtyard eating space. "Ms MalvinaHoffman, my name is 'Percy Hayward'."

She considered his hand for a moment. She extended her own. "Carli Dawes."

"It's a pleasure to meet you."

They shook hands, and Carli considered the hand she now held. It was cold and hard.

**23**

ecades earlier, Goldstein tasked his Kitchen Crew with a new secret
project. He called it, "The Final Augmentation". The reach of a citizen's
consciousness already extended beyond their physical body. A mind could be
engaged within the immersion of a simulated reality indistinguishable from the
physical. A presence could be projected thousands of kilometres away onto the
frame of a teeper. A piece of lifeless plastic and metal could be temporarily
animated with life.

But this golden age had one limitation—a mortal consciousness was still in
control. Ultimately, it was flesh in the driver's seat. As the brain died, so too did
the power to project and the power to live within the Collective. He'd seen his
co-workers, the founding members of Augmosis, pass from this world, some of
them from diseases like Alzheimer's or cancer that remained incurable. Minds
once sharp and vibrant had dulled: fading to nothingness long before their
bodies followed on. Then there was Olena—the only woman he'd ever loved—
healthy and vibrant one moment, brain dead the next from a sudden stroke.

Faced with his own increasingly apparent mortality, Goldstein set his team
to work on the unification of the human mind into the Collective itself—to
find the secret to the liberation of consciousness from flesh to dwell eternally
within the Collective.

This was to be the *final* augmentation. The transcension of the Collective.

But the project was a failure. Cracking the code of consciousness was too
difficult. The best that the brightest minds at Augmosis could manage was the
illusion of consciousness—a simulation of intelligence that could do little more
than perform like an actor in a Network drama, but with no will, no awareness
and no life.

Some of the members of Goldstein's team said the technology to map the mind could never capture the *soul*. It was an explanation that defied his scientific sensibilities like a slap in the face. And yet, through multiple restarted attempts to solve the problem with new teams over 40 years, the same explanation was repeated: 'The soul of man was far too unique to be codified in terms of ones, zeroes and quantum superpositions.'

Still, as was often the case on such projects, this same research led to other advancements between man and machine benefiting the Collective. Understanding the language of the human nervous system created the architecture to control prosthetic limbs. Hardware could bypass a severed spinal cord to restore a citizen to full mobility. For the right price, the blind could receive sight, the lame could walk and the deaf could hear. The only thing still beyond Goldstein's power was raising the dead.

Goldstein's own inventions now kept his body alive. Organs that failed years ago had been replaced with machines, plumbed throughout his body, wired directly into his brain. These new systems kept his body fixed to his wheelchair. The chair wasn't just his transportation, it was his heart, liver, lungs, and digestive system. Goldstein may not yet have found the secret to immortality, but he still hoped to delay death long enough to make it reality.

To decode the brain's secret language, Goldstein implanted a neural link directly into his cerebral cortex. That neural link gave his consciousness the freedom to join the Collective without resorting to hand gestures or eye movements. In the Collective, he could stand on two feet, control a teeper and walk proudly and covertly amongst the citizens of Praxis with just the power of his mind. He might have failed so far to liberate his consciousness from his body into the Collective, but for now, he settled for bringing the Collective into his body.

Goldstein had decided to keep this breakthrough a secret. A direct neural connection to the Collective would be dangerous for people limited to their mortal bodies. Thousands died every year from malnutrition and disease because they neglected their physical needs by being too immersed in the virtual. So, he justified withholding this revolutionary breakthrough for now until the final augmentation was possible. Even Augmosis leadership were in the dark.

*But once we have decoded consciousness, then we can finally liberate ourselves!* It remained the last unconquered frontier—for the simulation to become reality. And for the flesh, with all its limitations, pain and inequality, to be put to death.

In the quiet of his office, Goldstein used this technology to interface directly with the code and systems that drove the Collective. Systems he had personally developed, some as old as the Collective itself. His neural link allowed him to navigate faster and more efficiently than the best coders and Network hats in all of Praxis—some a hundred years his junior. His physical limitations no longer posed any disadvantage. In this state, he was as integral a part of the Network as its operating system.

If one of his aids looked in from the room next door, he would have appeared motionless, as though he was in a deep sleep. But his mind was alive, navigating the web of interfaces, daemons, services, hypervisors and gateways as effortlessly as a primate swinging from branch to branch in the forest.

His neural link didn't just serve to connect his consciousness to the Collective, but it continued to stream his brainwaves directly into storage. Whereas the average citizen could bank what they see and hear, Goldstein could bank what he thought. It served as the repository of data his team could use for research: petabytes were stored and analysed each day through a neural network he designed. All in service of the goal of liberating a consciousness into the Collective.

The closest he and his team had gotten to this goal, was the development of a high-functioning artificial intelligence. A simulation of life that could respond to complex queries and even hold sensible conversations. But it was passive—it had no intuition or will of its own. It had no *soul*.

Playing around with AI brought Goldstein perilously close to breaking the law. Artificial Intelligence was carefully controlled within the Collective. It was used for processes and systems that underpinned the Collective and AI could be used for automating physical activities like mining, manufacturing, and table waiting, so long as it did not directly impact employment opportunities for flesh and bone citizens. But humanity feared that machines would displace mankind—and they codified that fear in legislation and Network controls that came to be known as the Hawking Act.

Goldstein was ambivalent about the idea. *If I can't crack the code on synthetic intelligence, there is no way someone else could.*

His failure in this regard was staring him in the face. The artificial representation of his consciousness had the same face and even spoke with the same voice as he did. A team member had suggested giving it a name, and another had hastily made up a silly acronym to qualify it: GOldstein's LEarning

Model, or Golem. Apparently, it drew from an ancient legend of a being brought to life from clay.

Goldstein physically shook his head, realising he was distracted from the task at hand: *Fernando Alvarez.* That was the name Detective Briggs had given him as the other witness to the crimes in West Praxis. Goldstein had already spent an hour trying to locate Korb1k, but with no success. Alvarez however still existed within the Network. There were occasional connections Goldstein could see in the logs of some of the most fundamental systems that made the Collective work.

The very searches Goldstein was now performing broke the law—laws he helped to write. But now that he'd started, he didn't want to finish until he'd found the answer. Like riding a wave to the end, he needed to see this through to some form of result. What started with searching Network connection logs, escalated to interaction logs with other citizens. These repositories would log when any Network-connected citizen observed or interacted with Alvarez, which could be used to pin a person down to a single place at a point in time. It was a power the Police Department would kill for, but in the interest of liberty had been withheld. Their systems of warrants and BOLOs operated several layers above this and depended on wilful observation.

Goldstein's conscience shuddered with every line crossed, but he went further. The interaction logs placed Alvarez somewhere in a storage precinct in West Praxis over the last six hours, but he was unable to discover his location beyond that. He reviewed the profiles of each citizen Alvarez had been in contact with and found a possible lead.

Female, early thirties, using the moniker of 'Aprilf00ls'. The Network told him her full name was April Rocha. Based on the frequency of historic connections, he surmised they had probably been seeing each other for about six weeks. The logs also showed a three-hour connection between the two 23 hours previously, which he concluded was a face-to-face meeting. The connection was a few blocks from a nightclub where she worked as a dancer.

It was a good lead, but Goldstein wanted more. Using a vulnerability in the personal storage service, he went through April Rocha's banked footage, finding nothing helpful, but plenty that would have made his 20-year-oldself blush. Such power could be devastating in the hands of anyone else, but in over a century of presiding over the privacy of humanity, Goldstein rationalised that he was the only person who could be trusted.

Another vulnerability revealed Rocha's criminal history—mostly misdemeanours for drug use. Another vulnerability showed that for the last five years, she'd been evicted seven times and was late in servicing several debts.

Goldstein was enjoying playing the detective—the same part of his brain was firing as when he was deep into a coding project. The moment one connection was made, he pursued another and then another. Each minor discovery built upon the next until the puzzle was nearly complete. And yet, he still hadn't found Alvarez's specific location.

With a few more high-level security systems bypassed, Goldstein connected directly to Fernando Alvarez' live stream. The stream of audio and video ran straight through his augments. Goldstein now heard what Alvarez heard and saw what Alvarez saw. It was the ultimate breach of privacy. If caught, He would be instantly dismissed from Augmosis and disavowed, followed by a public lynching. The only thing worse would be to strip away everyone's projection and look at their oldself.

He hoped the risk was worth the reward. But all he saw was black. Goldstein checked the feed to see if something was causing it to be corrupted but it seemed fine. Connecting to Alvarez's lifesuit he could see a steady pulse and blood oxygen level. He heard a noise he recognized. Heavy breathing. A low resonance. Snoring. Fernando Alvarez was asleep.

He cut the feed and checked the time, not realising how late it had become. Goldstein tended to nap more than sleep in long stints. But right now, he felt reasonably alert.

Turning his attention back to April Rocha, he connected to her livestream. He was not met with the same blackness, but the sensory overload of loud music and flashing lights. It took his brain a few seconds to adjust, and a whole lot longer to work out what he was looking at. The world was swirling—loud music swirled with it. Bass thumped, and voices yelled. It was disorientating and made him feel unwell.

The swirling stopped for a moment. Goldstein made out faces looking at him with wide eyes and smiles. Arms crossed in front of his face, holding onto a vertical silver bar. Bare legs crawled up the bar—his legs, or April Rocha's legs. The brief moment of stability ended, and Goldstein was now upside down looking out to a crowd that was whooping in excitement. The music died out and his view righted. People were clapping and Goldstein saw a trickle of bits flowing into April's bank account.

At last, he was able to comprehend some of what he was seeing. A bar with lights and drinks being served, dance platforms with naked and semi-naked bodies writhing around as others looked on. For almost a minute, Goldstein had been hanging naked from a pole for the entertainment of a drunken horde, for barely enough bits to buy a decent meal. It was about as foreign an experience as he could imagine. If he still had a heart, he was sure it would have almost stopped on the spot. *This isn't the utopia we'd imagined*, he thought.

Goldstein watched on as April Rocha stepped down from her podium and made her way to a backstage area. She passed by boisterous patrons hurling insults and solicitations in her direction. She passed dancers lined up in virtual costumes for their coming routines. Some of the dancers were covered in glitter, another donned the naked projection of some form of blue alien that Goldstein didn't recognise.

April found her way to a dresser and considered her reflection in a mirror—a blonde with unrealistic proportions, a colourful water-like animation flowed over her naked body. With a few gestures, this naked self disappeared, replaced with a completely different one: Hispanic, short dark hair and now fully clothed.

"Good work out there, sis," Goldstein heard. The view turned to see another dancer approaching, smiling. Her fingers wiggled and she too morphed from a disproportionate, naked figure to a more realistic one now fully clothed.

She came closer, "So you're going to see him again tonight?"

"Shh… Jerry. He doesn't want me to tell anyone."

"Well, when he gives you some more of that sugar, you put some aside for me this time, eh?" She walked past, and April's view returned to the mirror. She stared at herself for some time, making Goldstein feel even more guilty at invading this private moment, but satisfied it may have been worth the breach if it meant getting a little closer to an answer.

# 24

Carli recoiled before she realised she'd just shaken the hand of a teeper.

"Sorry, I should have given you a warning first," Percy Hayward said.

"No," she began. "That's OK."

"Are you cold?"

"Yes, now that you mention it." Even in a closed and sheltered environment, there were still places where changes in air pressure would cause anything from a gentle breeze to a sudden gust. The entrance to a transit station was one of those places, and Carli's saturated lifesuit was now struggling to compensate.

"Let's go down to the platforms to get out of this wind."

"Sure."

They walked together, advancing down the travellator before entering the main part of the transit station. Some of the convenience stores offering stimulants and small meals remained open. Others offering crafts and immersion sim licenses had closed for the evening.

As they walked, Carli watched as Percy Hayward's teeper navigated its way carefully around commuters and other obstacles. Spotting a teeper when they were standing still was relatively difficult, but the way one moved in a crowd made them easier to identify. The motion of their arms and legs seemed overly erratic like they were making a thousand minor corrections in their movement to keep the teeper well balanced. At the same time, the head always stayed level.

Her feeling of exhilaration surprised her. She even briefly wondered if she was under the influence of some substance. But rather than dismiss this strange connection and retreat to the safety of anonymity, she chose to engage. She felt like she'd undergone some form of awakening, albeit brief, and decided she owed it to herself to at least explore this experience a little further. The part of her brain that normally would be sounding alarm bells had either been disabled or was being drowned out by something greater.

"Are you hungry?" she asked Percy. She realised her foolishness. The puzzled expression projected on the teeper's face made her laugh with embarrassment.

He recovered with a smile, "No, but if you want something to eat, I'd be happy to sit with you."

She found what seemed like the best of a limited number of open food outlets, The Golden Panda. She'd eaten there before. They served a range of rice and noodle dishes with different sauces and vegetables. As they sat at the table, the Network chimed a notice that a five-bit charge would be applied to their shared account for a teeper. That was a standard rate since the teeper would be taking a prospective customer's seat without ordering any food. Still, looking around the space at the small number of patrons, it was clear there wasn't going to be a shortage of seats any time soon.

Carli placed her order, initially planning on picking a dish she'd eaten previously, but making a last-minute change to something she could barely pronounce, let alone identify. It seemed she truly was in a risk-taking mood.

"So, when we spoke at lunchtime, were you running a teeper then too?" she asked.

"Yes, could you tell?"

"I couldn't remember if I saw you actually eat your food."

He smiled. "Not my usual way to meet people, but I find it easier to get around Praxis quicker than running the transit system."

"Still, some might say it's a little odd that someone sits at a table and pretends to eat in order to meet girls," she said, forcing a deadpan look that broke into a smile.

"You're probably right. But then I wasn't looking for girls, so much as watching for anyone showing signs of enlightenment."

Carli's smile ended. "I'm gonna need you to explain that."

"Sorry, what I mean to say is that I can usually tell the people who might be open to seeing the world a different way. When people eat their lunch, they're distracted. When they commute, their bodies are in motion, but their minds are in far-off places. Even when people are walking down the street, their brains are on autopilot. They are like mindless drones in service to the Collective machine."

It sounded rehearsed but heartfelt. "And me?"

"What I saw was someone who was observing the world the best they could. Someone watching what everyone else was doing. I was watching someone who was watching everyone else."

"And you think that makes me like you?"

"Well, I don't know that, but it's usually a good start. Trying to explain the light to the blind is impossible, but if someone already has their eyes open, it gets a little easier."

"That almost sounds religious."

"I'm not trying to be. But you're right I suppose—I see my purpose right now as trying to find people like me, who see the world the same way I do, or at least are willing to listen. Maybe that is like a Network evangelist—I wouldn't know."

"And what do you do with these people, once you find them?"

"Ha, you make it sound like I'm collecting them. All I do is try to connect with them. To understand their story. If we see things the same way, then it might be useful to try and network more people together. Sometimes we rally together to try to get our opinions shared with the rest of the Collective, but ours isn't a voice most people want to hear."

Carli's meal arrived. It smelt good and tasted even better. She gave herself an internal 'high-five' for trying something new.

"So, what's your story, Carli Dawes?"

"I'm a sculptor," she said.

"Amazing, I haven't had this sort of conversation with any sculptors before. What sort of work do you do?"

Carli wasn't sure if he was trying to come on to her or if he was interviewing her for a job.

"The full custom package. Most of my work is 'true realism.' I like creating a projection which honours the old self, but reflects their true identity."

"So, you don't do body enhancements?"

She squirmed a little. "Not if I can help it. I want my clients to appear grounded in some sense of the natural reality. Not that I'm always successful convincing my clients that natural, and reality-honouring is a better option."

"You must meet lots of interesting people."

"Yes, I do. Getting to know my clients and their stories is probably one of the most satisfying parts of the job."

Carli was finding it hard to eat her dinner and talk at the same time. She flipped the conversation back to him, "What's your story then? Do you work, or do you just hang out in places trying to find like-minded people?"

"I still work a little. Family business—not terribly interesting. But it also gives me time to think. I have seen things that bothered me. Met people who challenged me to look a little deeper. I've come to the conclusion that in the pursuit of greater interconnection and greater self-expression, we may have lost the very thing that makes us human."

"What is that?" Carli asked through a mouthful of noodles.

"The truth."

# 25

Briggs sheltered from the first hour of rain at a diner near the PPD station in Port Lincoln. He'd eaten there many times before—a diner regularly frequented by Port Lincoln officers, a station Briggs had been posted to many years prior as a junior detective.

Briggs looked on those years with equal measures of fondness and lament. It was in Port Lincoln that he'd cut his teeth as a detective, including his first major bust of a criminal gang shipping materiel illegally into the port from the wasteland beyond. It had also been when his first serious relationship had failed, leading to two months of alcohol and stim-induced paralysis he could barely remember.

The port itself was one of the most important pieces of infrastructure within Praxis. In addition to the large business and habitation zones, Port Lincoln had the largest land dock and industrial precinct in all of Praxis. It required a second dome to be erected to protect the different shipping, processing and decontamination facilities on the northern edge. It was also a target for criminals who sought to traffic illegal goods into the city. Goods not from this world, but from the world that preceded it.

A large part of Praxis' industry was built around the mining of resources from the wasteland. The earth had been rich in all manner of minerals, even before the asteroid had fallen from the sky. Though the asteroid and the destruction that followed had otherwise destroyed all life on Earth, there remained pockets of infrastructure scattered across the globe that hadn't been destroyed by the fire, water and dust. Cities of old, military installations, mining installations—all lifeless and deserted, but still harbouring raw minerals, relics and even fully functional technology.

Technology like weapons.

In the first decades of the Collective, many of the caches of accessible weapons and other equipment had been secured and recycled by licensed salvage operators, piloting small drones and teepers to avoid the contamination of the wasteland. Over time, the supply of useful resources declined, and it became more cost-effective to simply mine and manufacture whatever was needed to satisfy the Collective's thirst for resources and technology. As a result, the only legal salvage operators still in business were those operating on private commissions to recover some long-lost family heirloom.

Salvaging something from the wasteland was difficult enough, but bringing it through the barrier also demanded an expensive decontamination process. It was cost-prohibitive: unless what you want cannot be legally acquired within Praxis itself. This, was the purview of criminal salvage operators like the Bratstvo Syndicate and the Chimera Cartel

For nine months, Briggs became an expert in criminal salvage logistics. First, an organisation needed to secure a small fleet of drones and teepers. These were often sourced from decommissioned mining leases, or occasionally directly stolen and reconfigured so that they couldn't be tracked. If they weren't already positioned in the wasteland, they needed to be covertly transported out of a port hub like Port Lincoln and controlled by an operator from relative safety somewhere within Praxis.

There were however, more significant obstacles to overcome. The first was that teepers had a limited battery life and needed to be paired to some of the larger drones to be recharged. Secondly, the sheer distance to be covered to a suitable salvage site could take months. Thirdly, and perhaps most importantly, the syndicate needed to know where to look to find what it wanted. Discovering the locations of viable caches of equipment created a secondary layer of even more secretive people known simply as prospectors. They were dealers in the most valuable resource in the wasteland: information.

Working undercover, Briggs was able to gain the confidence of key members of the Chimera Cartel. Cases of weapons, ammunition and electronics made their way through security, customs and decontamination by way of bribes and good timing. Gaining access to the temporary storage facility, Briggs used a specialised aerosol spray to add a unique radioactive signature to the crates and some of the equipment inside, allowing them to be traced as they dispersed to almost every hub across Praxis.

A wave of arrests followed. The heads of the cartel were caught literally with radiation on their hands. The logistics middlemen, the corrupt port officers, and even street criminals were taken into custody. A second wave of arrests followed as the network was dismantled and the customers were exposed.

It was Briggs' first big success as a detective, and it brought forth private commendations from his superiors. It was the sort of win he'd always dreamed of as a child and a cadet in the academy. But the celebration lasted barely longer than a day. When he returned home, he discovered his partner had left. By the state of the food that was in the refrigerator, it was months prior.

There had been many successful cases since. Few as far-reaching, and none delivering the same high of victory that Briggs so desperately craved. From the first big success, his descent into alcohol and drugs was born out of the abrupt realisation the high he needed from solving the puzzle still left him unsatisfied. With help from people like Anneke Hagen, those demons may not be fully put to death, but they were at least sleeping for now. The irony Briggs acknowledged was that no matter how many times the high of a successful case failed to deliver, he still strived for it with all his energy. Everything else in his life might be falling apart, but the case is what gave him purpose. Alcohol and drugs might be in his past, but his addiction to solving the case was as strong as ever.

Briggs took another long sip from his coffee. His mind was still on the case, but his attention was starting to fade. He'd covered a lot of ground today. One name was removed from Bayshore, followed by the two at Port Lincoln. Like the rest, all of these citizens had plausible explanations for why they had needed to purchase a new plexus, and none had a prosthetic arm.

His list was now down to four. Three were in West Praxis: 'Urannah', 'DashRound6' and 'AtomicFly'. The last had the moniker, 'Basilicus' and was still reported in the Network as "Location Unknown". The names meant nothing to Briggs, nor did the limited information he'd sourced from the PPD. All three of the West Praxis citizens appeared to live and work in the hub and had done so for several years. The location unknown citizen, however had last been pinged in Métropole three days earlier. Date of Birth information couldn't be secured without a warrant, but by looking at his public history, Briggs had guessed he was most likely retired.

He confirmed the time: 9:10 PM. It was too late to start making enquiries in West Praxis now, and he felt far from the level of alertness he needed if he was going to be encountering K0rb1k, especially if he was alone. The falling rain did little to keep him awake—he used some of the same sounds to help him get to sleep at night.

*Today is over.* He told himself. *I haven't solved the puzzle yet, but every step forward is a step closer.* But with the list of identities nearly down to zero, he was starting to wonder if this was the best use of his time.

As he waited on the transit platform for an approaching carriage, he received a new message. The sender identified themselves simply as "Aldus". It read:

<ALDUS> FERNANDO ALVAREZ (ATACAMA) IS IN WEST PRAXIS. I HAVE HIS LOCATION. DO YOU WANT ME TO SHARE IT WITH YOU?

*Aldus Goldstein.* Anything that Goldstein could provide on Alvarez' location couldn't be used for a search warrant. Couldn't be written down in a report. Couldn't be shared with the judge, or his superiors. Goldstein was breaking the law by obtaining this information. Receiving this information was also legally ambiguous. It also felt like cheating.

*But is this not for the greater good?* Briggs debated with himself. *Surely extenuating circumstances demand the rules be bent for the sake of security?*

The only way Briggs could use this information is if he could somehow retrospectively manipulate it into something that would pass scrutiny. That might be possible, but it would depend on the information he received. If Alvarez was located in a public café, Briggs just needed to walk up to him, scan his identity and arrest him on the spot. But if he was hiding in the basement of some apartment, it would be difficult to manufacture probable cause to enter and make the arrest.

He wouldn't know until he got the information. With a sequence of gestures, he composed his reply.

<BRIGGSH33207> DO IT.

# 26

Carli often found it difficult to avoid observing and critiquing someone's projection and to simply see them as a person. When she'd first seen Percy Hayward earlier, her initial judgment was based on his appearance—olive skin, dark eyes, dark hair. She saw the attention to detail applied by his sculptor. Every beard follicle to the crease at the corner of his eyes conveyed a sense of warmth and wisdom. His was not a generic self purchased from the Network, but a personalised work of art. It would not have been cheap.

Now after speaking to him, she found herself being drawn deeper into him as a person. His friendly eyes concealed a deeper wisdom, almost a sadness. Though she believed they were around the same age, Carli sensed an older soul beneath the youthful façade.

"There is something that has been bothering me, Percy," she said.

"What is it?"

"Well, you are clearly passionate about your beliefs. And at some level, I think you have a point. Yet, you still project a self to hide what lies underneath. Right now, that's hiding a bunch of plastic and electronics. If you were physically here, your projection would be covering up your oldself. It seems a little..."

"Hypocritical?" he said.

"I was going to say 'inconsistent'."

"You're not wrong. But if I were walking around in a lifesuit with my oldself exposed to the world, I can guarantee you wouldn't have taken me seriously. Sometimes we must play by the rules of the system to make a better one."

"Sounds like you are planning a revolution." Carli joked.

"Maybe a revolution is necessary. Maybe all of us need to be woken from our shared dream." Percy didn't wait long enough for that statement to sink in. "Do you know the history of the Collective?"

"You mean, how this all started? No more than anyone else. Augmosis developed the Collective and established the city of Praxis. Because the first city hubs had been equipped with atmospheric filters and protective domes, they weren't devastated by the asteroid that hit the Earth. To be honest, that's about it."

Percy picked up on the story, "That's all any of us are ever taught. That's all the Network dramas ever share—how Aldus Goldstein and his cronies at Augmosis saved humanity by building a new civilisation that could outlast anything and evolve into something greater."

"Is that not true?" she asked.

"Some of it. I believe the whole story is more… concerning"

"And how is it that Percy Hayward, revolutionary, discovered the whole story?"

He looked at Carli long and hard, like he was trying to make up his mind on how much to share.

"Maybe someday I will be able to share it with you. Someday, the truth needs to be shared with everyone. Would you agree that the truth is important?"

"Yes."

"And concealing the truth can be harmful?"

"I suppose so." Carli sat back, feeling like she'd been backed into a corner.

He pivoted, as though reading Carli's mind, "I'm sorry if I've confused you. I believe it is important to understand our history since it shapes what we see. The reason we all take the Collective for granted is because we all believe it protected our species from the tragedy of the asteroid. We see the Collective as our saviour. We respond to the Collective in the same way a patriot used to salute a flag. To even question the fundamentals of the Collective is dangerously unpatriotic. But if we have been lied to about how this all came to be, the Collective is no longer our saviour but our master. And we are all its slaves."

"You talk like the Collective is some form of malevolent force—it's just the sum-total of each citizen, including you and me," Carli interjected

"But it's governed by systems and technology controlled by only one company."

"Augmosis?"

"Correct. They were there at the beginning. Every plexus, phonic and optic is theirs. Six million citizens wired together. All of them sheep. All of them living in an augmented state between true reality and a dream of their own design."

"I think you're exaggerating," she said.

"Keep an open mind," Percy said, "I'm not proposing we all burn our plexuses just yet. But as the remnant of humanity, we owe it to ourselves to know the truth and to let it shape how we move forward. I'm more than confident that what all of us truly need is to be woken up from this technological dream."

Carli felt she'd reached her limit of conspiracy for one day. Most of it, she doubted, and she hadn't decided if Percy Hayward was just eccentric or slightly unstable. She felt tiredness starting to creep up on her.

"I have enjoyed our chat, Percy. I'm not sure I understood all of it, but I'll think it over."

Percy's projection smiled, then looked off to the side with a distant stare, like something had caught his attention over her left shoulder. She turned to see what was there but found nothing of interest—the large open space of the centre of the transit station. A few people were moving around, but none looked in their direction.

She turned back. Percy's gaze remained fixed, his position dead still.

"Percy?"

Percy Hayward's projection dissolved away from the teeper, to reveal a genderless plastic and metal frame. His warm friendly gaze was replaced by two soulless lenses, his mouth replaced by a rectangular slit.

It was jarring and Carli jumped back in her seat.

The teeper moved its head around in a sweeping motion, taking in its surroundings. It appeared to make a few quick calculations before announcing in a mechanical voice, "Please stand clear as I return to the nearest docking station."

Carli forced her mouth closed.

"Well," she said, "that was rude."

# 27

The rain had stopped, and the time now approached midnight. Briggs waited in the front entry of apartment complex N4E5 in West Praxis. It was only yesterday that he'd had walked through these doors to investigate the scene of Officer Nguyen's murder. Now, shrouded in darkness, Briggs was about to commit a crime of his own. A crime that he felt justified if it meant justice would be served.

A second officer approached, his face poorly lit by the one security light near the building entrance that hadn't been broken. Briggs' optics confirmed his identity as Detective Sergeant Brand Carlyle.

Carlyle swung a large duffle bag from over his shoulder and dropped it at Briggs' feet. "Thanks for the invitation," he said.

Briggs scanned Carlyle's expression and found resolve and determination. This case was important to Briggs, but it was personal for all officers from West Praxis. Briggs had counted on that when he formulated a strategy that had the best chance of both apprehending Fernando Alvarez and protecting Aldus Goldstein as his source—all while making any possible arrest stand up to external scrutiny. It was a fine line to walk, but Briggs concluded that the reward was worth the risk.

Briggs barely knew Carlyle, but after calling him to arrange the meeting, a few carefully worded questions gave him enough confidence Carlyle could at least be trusted to back him up.

"You gonna share who your secret source of information is? It would be nice to have my own angel to give me a helping hand now and then," Carlyle asked.

"Who said anything about it being a secret source? Maybe I just figured it out."

Carlyle chuckled, "Maybe you did."

"What did you bring?" Briggs asked.

"I thought, since we were having a party, it would be nice to come dressed for the occasion." Carlyle opened the zip on the bag. He pulled a standard PPD riot helmet which had the visor missing and handed it to Briggs. He tapped his own head which gave off a dull clunk—he was already wearing a helmet, but his projection was masking it. Briggs placed the helmet at his feet for a moment.

Next, he handed over an ammunition belt. Briggs was carrying only his Torque sidearm, and a spare ammunition magazine integrated into his holster. He inspected the belt and found a pair of binder cuffs and another two mags. Sliding one of them out, he observed they contained live rounds rather than the usual stun rounds. Live rounds were legal for PPD officers to use, but considered the last line of defence. Live rounds were also less effective on non-living targets like teepers since the stun would also immobilise a teeper.

Briggs unholstered his Torque 9mm sidearm. His gun and its holster positioned under his left armpit was concealed beneath his projection until the moment he unclipped it and it became visible within the Network. He ejected his mag to confirm his ammunition was stun rounds, his preference. He pulled back the slide on the gun and inspected the chamber before reinserting the mag, confirmed the safety was still on and chambered a round before re-holstering it. It was a reassuring habit, before stepping into danger. Carlyle did the same.

Briggs wrapped the belt around his waist and adjusted it for his size. Its previous user was a few sizes larger than him. It would have also been too big for Carlyle to wear who, himself was taller and heavier-set than Briggs. Once the belt was in position, the tracking icons printed onto the surface of the belt caused it to disappear beneath his projection.

Briggs positioned a flashlight onto the strap of his shoulder holster. The belt had more pouches which he checked, pulling out a black enamel-coated canister smaller than a soda can with a ring pull. Briggs counted two in his belt and looked to Carlyle for confirmation.

"Grenades?"

"HPM grenades—Stunners. 4-second delay. Work the same as your stun rounds but over a bigger area, up to five metres for ten seconds. They'll fry the circuits in a teeper or a plexus, no questions asked—so best not to stand too close."

"Are they traceable?"

"Sure, but they stay in one piece after they fire, so we just need to collect them before we're done and I'll switch them with the supply used for training."

Briggs grunted but re-pocketed the grenade in its pouch on his belt. He made some final adjustments and was just about to run through the plan of attack when Carlyle removed something from his pack that Briggs didn't recognise—a long cylinder with a worn rubberised coating. Three finger-sized rubber buttons ran up the length. One end was a large eyepiece and the other a shiny glass lens.

"I haven't seen that before," Briggs said as Carlyle handed it to him.

"Thermal and night-vision scope."

Briggs considered this for a moment before looking up with a confused look on his face.

"Contraband? Just in case we weren't sure we were crossing the line?"

"In for a penny, Briggs," Carlyle replied. "Look, it's clean—something left off the inventory from a bust a few months back. I don't want to be going blind into a fight. If it becomes a problem, we just leave it at the scene."

Briggs moved the scope around in his hand. It wasn't the first time he'd held technology from the Old-World. The rubberised surface was cracked and sticky—clearly not designed to last longer than a few years after it was manufactured, let alone almost a full century.

He found what looked to be the power button and raised it to his eyes. He saw the world in strange monochrome, but Carlyle's body stood out in brilliant white. Briggs could see his helmet and belt—even the ribbed texture of his lifesuit. With this device, it didn't matter what someone was projecting, all Briggs would see was the heat generated by their body.

*Useful.* Briggs handed the device back to Carlyle. To Carlyle, it might have looked like he was doing so out of principle. If he was honest with himself, Briggs doubted he would be able to work the damn thing in the heat of battle.

"All good, Hal—I only had one anyway." Carlyle held the device up to his eye and looked at Briggs. "Damn Hal, what happened to your head?"

Briggs reflexively raised his hand to cover the cut over his eye. It was still sore, but he'd almost forgotten about it. "Nothing good," he quipped.

It was a twenty-minute walk through West Praxis' dark alleys to get to the rendezvous point. Briggs led Carlyle to an observation point a block away from the nightclub, "The Spicy Moose." They found a position in the shadows, with a full view of the service entrance of the nightclub.

"Who are we looking for again?" Carlyle asked.

"April Rocha. Moniker: 'Aprilf00ls'"

"Is that some kind of joke?"

"It's December, so no."

Briggs sent a private message to Aldus Goldstein confirming the contact had not yet left the nightclub. It was met with two clicks in his phonics: an old radio code to mean, "Affirmative". Goldstein's idea, not Briggs's. Goldstein had been in his ear, giving him unnecessary updates when Briggs had told him to cool it. For a centenarian, Goldstein had started to act like a child playing a role in a Network drama.

"We wait here. She'll be out soon and will be meeting up with Alvarez a few blocks north of here."

They waited a few more minutes until Briggs heard Goldstein's voice, "*She's leaving now*".

Briggs spotted her first but waited for Carlyle to make the announcement. She donned a mask and walked past them both at a reasonable distance, walking north. They followed carefully behind, keeping to the shadows and making only brief glimpses in her direction to confirm her position.

The streets of West Praxis were largely empty. An occasional advertisement triggered in Brigg's optics as he walked, which he waved away. Normally, they wouldn't appear if he was in active pursuit of a suspect, but there was no surveillance warrant active, and he wanted to make sure there was no log in the system just yet.

"*Find cover!*" It was Goldstein's voice, and Briggs pulled Carlyle by his ammo belt further into the darkness. April Rocha turned, doing a full sweep behind her, finding nothing.

Carlyle started to complain about getting too friendly before he realised Briggs had just saved them both from being spotted.

"How did you…" Carlyle started before Briggs cut him off with a raised hand close enough to his face to still be seen through the dark of night. April continued her sweep around her before turning back and continuing on in the same direction. Goldstein must have intercepted a message between her and Alvarez.

One more block and another figure met her at the corner. *"That's him,"* Goldstein commentated. Briggs and Carlyle again found partial cover and Briggs' optics resolved his moniker as Atacama, bounded with a callout indicating an active warrant was in effect. A smile crossed Briggs's face. Alvarez and Rocha moved away from the corner together towards a laneway where they stopped. It was a good place for cover but also a good place for Carlyle and Briggs to make a close approach without being noticed.

They stood there for half a minute. Talking presumably. They were distracted.

"Let's move in for the arrest," he said and started to move forward, but Carlyle held him back. Briggs scowled, turning towards his short-term partner.

"That's not him." Carlyle was holding the monocular over his eye. "That's a teeper."

Briggs turned back. He could now barely see either of them in the darkness ahead. With a few gestures back to Goldstein, he asked, *"Did you get that?"*

Goldstein's response was slow, but eventually Briggs heard, *"Yes, he's right."* He was annoyed at himself, but at this distance, it would have been impossible for him to tell.

"What do we do now?" Carlyle asked.

Briggs considered the question. They were close—he felt it.

"We follow the robot."

# 28

Alvarez's teeper and April Rocha walked a few more streets together, deeper into the industrial district of West Praxis with Briggs and Carlyle in careful pursuit. The buildings here weren't as high as the residential apartments closer to the centre of the city, but most were still massive structures. Some were storage complexes. Others produced everything from lubricants to white goods.

The further they walked into this area, the louder the sound of automated machines, stamping and cutting, overlayed with a low electrical hum. Above the buildings, Briggs might have naturally expected to find all kinds of exhaust gasses belching into the atmosphere, but these were piped outside of the hub, past the protective barrier and into the wasteland beyond. Instead, he saw a dark sky, littered with stars and a crescent moon projected over the barrier.

Carlyle noticed Briggs' temporary distraction. "Eyes on the prize, Briggs. Target's entering a storage facility."

Briggs chastised himself and fumbled for a retort to save face, "I'm starting to wonder if letting you tag along was a bad idea."

Carlyle took it in stride, "C'mon Detective if it wasn't for me, you'd be hauling a bag of bolts down to PPD in cuffs."

He had a point. Briggs found Carlyle's jovial demeanour grating.

"There—building North Fourteen, East Eight."

"Any information on that property?" Briggs asked, both to Carlyle and to Goldstein.

"Long-term storage by the looks. Small units, a few squares for people to bank any personal effects or possessions. Not somewhere I'd want to stick anything valuable for too long. Plus, the edge of the hub and the barrier is only one block away—too far away from the transit station for me."

Briggs waited for Goldstein to give him some form of confirmation but heard nothing. April Rocha disappeared into what looked like a maintenance entrance. The Alvarez teeper remained outside and performed another surveillance sweep, but Briggs and Carlyle were too sheltered to be spotted. It stepped inside, closing the door behind it.

"How do you want to play this?" Carlyle asked.

"The warrant for Alvarez was to apprehend and question as a conspirator on Zaimis only. If we call it in, we could get an upgrade to surveillance, which might help us out."

"Will that get us around your secret supply of information?"

Briggs faced him, annoyed. And rattled off his best explanation:

"*Following an anonymous tip-off, Detective Carlyle of West Praxis PD and myself, Detective Briggs of PPD Network Crimes followed April Rocha, believed to be an acquaintance of Fernando Alvarez from her West Praxis workplace. This led to a private meeting between Rocha and Alvarez who we discovered by observation was piloting a telepresence robot. We decided to pursue them further to this location, just south of building 'N14E8' whereupon they both entered the building.*"

With a few gestures, his voice was turned to text and added to his running file.

"I'm happy with that. Do you want to request the surveillance upgrade?"

Briggs wasn't sure. He'd been considering it for almost the last hour. He wondered if having the surveillance warrant active had somehow alerted K0rb1k that Officer Nguyen was on his tail. He didn't have Nguyen's banked footage to back him up, so it was just a hunch. But clearly, what Nguyen had been seeing as he entered the room was convincing enough for him to shoot at, but not real. And that mistake had gotten him killed.

"No. I'd rather not alert anyone else until we have him in custody."

This frustrated Carlyle, the first time Briggs had seen him flustered. "I don't have a death wish, Briggs. Snooping around up here in the shadows is one thing, but going into an unknown building without a surveillance overlay is suicide."

"Look, I know it's a risk, but we've seen the Network do some strange things over the last few days. I don't know if some of the PPD systems are compromised but a surveillance overlay didn't count for a damn in keeping Nguyen alive."

"C'mon, Briggs—we don't know what we're walking into. There could be a whole army of people down there for all we know." Carlyle continued his argument as Briggs weighed his options.

A surveillance warrant focused exclusively on one individual was ideal and would silhouette the target in the officer's optics, in addition to any citizens nearby. An alternative, however, was a general request that didn't specifically pinpoint Alvarez as the target—he would just appear as a grey silhouette or a 'ghost' like anyone else in proximity. Still, activating a surveillance layer was auditable and would need a good explanation when the arrest was reviewed later. Briggs didn't want to have to explain his doubts over the integrity of the Network's surveillance warrant process to anyone just yet.

All he needed was a justification that would stand up to scrutiny. He had an idea and triggered a recording of his comments for the record as he explained them:

*"The building in question has an unknown layout and is considered potentially hostile. A temporary surveillance warrant would be advantageous; however, in reviewing Alvarez's past associates with high-level Network hats, we share concerns that doing so may tip off the suspect of our approach. Therefore, Detective Carlyle and I will activate a general surveillance layer in our optics in compliance with PPD Officers Code 2822 for lawful pursuit and personal liberty."*

"You sound like a damned lawyer," Carlyle said, but he seemed satisfied.

*I might not have the best balance, but I know how to document a case in order to make the charges stick.*

They both triggered the surveillance layer in their optics. Within a 50m radius of their position, they saw the silhouettes of only a small number of citizens. In the domicile complex opposite, the corner apartments showed citizens mostly lying in bed. Next to them, in what was some sort of factory, Briggs could see a handful of people standing and moving about, operating machinery or controls of different types. These could be physical bodies or remote-controlled teepers—they would appear as the same grey silhouette in his optics, overlayed on their physical position in virtual space.

Looking back to the building where Alvarez entered, Briggs caught a glimpse of them starting to descend in virtual space before disappearing from view as they exceeded the 50m virtual boundary offered by the overlay.

"Crap—get moving." Rushing forward towards the door, their approach momentarily brought them back into and out of view. They had already descended in an elevator of some kind within the building.

"What's your plan for the door?"

Briggs listened for a moment before saying, "I just leased a storage unit—basement level 5. That should get us where we need to go."

He stepped out of the shadows toward the entrance, unholstering his sidearm and motioning for Carlyle to do the same. With his left hand, he reached the door handle—its electronic lock deactivating just before he touched it, confirmed with an LED that switched from red to green. He turned the handle, Carlyle slid past with his weapon raised, and Briggs followed through after receiving an all-clear signal. Adrenaline washed over him, silencing the voice telling him this was a bad idea. The anticipation of the hunt and the pursuit of answers spurred him on.

## 29

Of the many skills Liam Nolan offered, being a human courier seemed beneath him. Planning and logistics, yes. Establishing networks and tying off loose ends, absolutely. He was a capable fighter at short range but was intelligent and seasoned enough to avoid a physical confrontation altogether. Tonight, however, his Employer had given him an assignment that just seemed tedious.

Maybe he was being punished for his mistakes in West Praxis, though Liam would gladly put his record against anyone else's in terms of his ruthless efficiency.

Like most of his Employer's assignments, there was no real explanation. No apparent strategy that he could identify. It was like a randomly generated quest in some immersion game serving no purpose other than to frustrate the player.

After relocating to Praxis Central earlier that day, Liam set up some short-term accommodation in the least expensive part of the city. Unlike West Praxis and many of the hubs further away from the city circle, the price of accommodation in Praxis Central was far more expensive. There were many higher-end apartments and domiciles throughout Praxis Central, but the room he leased was little different from his last two safe houses, other than a mouldy odour from a source he couldn't locate.

His first task was to meet a contact at one of the eateries in the Praxis Central transit station. The contact, a short and rotund man, had arrived from the direction of the Oxford station at exactly 2:00 pm. Liam stood casually at a distance, identifying his mark the moment he waddled off the transit carrying a large satchel across his body. His optics confirmed his moniker, "Copernix" as his contact, but the man was too preoccupied with being at the eatery at exactly the right time to notice Liam.

The eatery in question served coffee and light meals. Most importantly it was just the right amount of busy—not so full to have no tables available, nor so quiet that they would be noticed. The man found his way to the service counter of the eatery and placed a careful order before finding a seat away from most of the other diners, placing the satchel at his feet below the table and trying not to look around.

Liam watched through the diner's large windows. This man was clearly out of his element. Liam could almost see the beads of sweat confusing his projection. This guy was an amateur, and it bothered Liam to have to interact with him at all. In his line of work, an amateur was almost as dangerous as the most hardened criminal. They were unpredictable, drawing unnecessary attention to themselves and by association anyone they were interacting with.

Liam knew where he was. The PPD headquarters was only three blocks from his current location. The transit station was most likely full of police officers changing between shifts and returning from field assignments. It was a poor choice of location to meet, a point he was unable to impress upon his employer since the direction was given only through a sequence of text messages. Liam even considered this was a ploy to have him captured, but given the effort his employer had gone to secure him a new identity, he dismissed the idea as unlikely.

Through the side window of the diner, Liam scanned each seated patron. Small groups of twos and threes were in engaged conversation, but most were singles who clearly looked to be engaged in the Network—staring off into space and waving their hands in front of them. No other eyes scanned the room. There was no guarantee, but Liam was moderately satisfied the room looked clear.

A patron leaving the diner threw away a branded disposal cup into a waste receptacle outside the front entrance. Liam approached, retrieved the cup from the trash and carried it as his own, walking past the service counter towards the table where his contact sat in wait. He placed his empty cup on the table and pulled out the chair opposite, sitting down with confidence like it was his regular seat.

The man stared at Liam—equal parts anticipation and fright. Liam stared back. He'd been instructed to say some passphrase to his contact, but he waited instead to see how the man responded. The man fidgeted in his seat, eyes switching between Liam and other people in the room. He gripped the strap of the satchel like it was a lifebuoy.

"Um..."

"How you going, buddy?" Liam's voice was friendly, but his face was stern and focused.

"Um... good... "

"You've ordered something from the counter. You're going to wait until they put it on the table, and then you're going to stand up and walk away, leaving the bag on the floor."

"Uh? OK?" The man was clearly out of his comfort zone and confused further by the fact that this contact had not said the passphrase he'd been expecting. The man should recognize Liam's "Basilicus" moniker. The phrase was redundant.

"What did you order anyway?" Liam acted out, bringing his empty cup to his face.

"Bran muffin... and coffee."

"Bran, eh?" Liam was toying with the man, who pulled a napkin from the table's dispenser and wiped over his face. His other hand tightly gripped the satchel's strap, pulling it towards his body. The man's eyes darted towards Liam's left hand, like he knew it contained a dangerous force.

A server came and placed the order in front of the man, who jumped in his seat.

Liam laughed, leaning forward. "You are free to go."

It took almost a further 20 seconds for the man to come to the full realisation his job was now complete. He slowly released the handle of the bag.

"Keep them away from microwaves and don't drop them." With that, the man stood and made a hasty exit from the diner. Liam reached over and grabbed the bran muffin. He took one disgusting bite, grabbed the new coffee and the satchel from under the table and left, heading up to street level and back to his domicile.

Now in the early hours of the following morning, Liam returned to the streets of Praxis Central. He transferred the items from the satchel to a smaller backpack he'd bought. It was designed to integrate into the virtual silhouette of his lifesuit, meaning his projection would hide the backpack as though it wasn't there. It was an expensive item, but necessary to avoid drawing attention to himself.

The items themselves were nine metal cylinders, six inches long, with a flat section on one part of the cylinder. Each weighed almost a kilogram. Each appeared to have been custom-built. Liam assumed it was probably the fat, sweaty guy himself who had made them. He didn't know what they were for. All he'd been told was what to do with them.

He walked for almost thirty minutes through the streets of Praxis Central. He crossed the central park area, cut through the Areopagus and arrived at his destination: a teeper recharging station. His wide circle through the city was deliberate to try and maximise the distance from the PPD headquarters, but now he was at the closest point with the greatest risk. The station held a bank of 20 teepers all standing together, waiting to be leased by an operator. The location was quiet and dark. He'd walked past a few citizens on his journey here, most of whom were enjoying night-time festivities, but this charging station was between two buildings away from the communal park area.

Inspecting the breastplate of each teeper, Liam found the serial number matching the list he'd been given by his employer. From his backpack, he removed one of the cylinders and inserted it into the teeper's body cavity between the plastic outer shell and the metal frame underneath. The flat surface of the cylinder attached itself to this metal frame with a magnetic clunk.

Liam continued, comparing the serial numbers and verifying the safety of his position. He reached the final teeper and discovered he'd run out of serial numbers and still had one cylinder left. He hesitated; this didn't feel like the sort of mission that he should be improvising on.

He considered contacting his employer for clarification, but a shuffle of feet and distant voices far behind him caused him to back further into the shadows between the last two charging teepers. In the alleyway behind him, two citizens walked past. They weren't uniformed, but Liam could tell by the way they moved that they were police officers on patrol. He trusted the darkness to keep him hidden. He slowed his heart and patiently waited for them to pass out of view.

Removing the final cylinder from his pack, he fixed it into the last teeper. Its serial number did not match, but at this point, Liam did not care. Reattaching his backpack, he made a careful exit from the area, avoiding the location where he last saw the officers.

Another successful mission. Another dump of bits into his bank account. One step closer to breaking free.

# 30

The side entrance to the storage complex led to a central lobby. There were four elevators designed for people and a fifth appeared to be for larger pallets or machinery. As they approached, the dark corridor was illuminated one section at a time, causing a shadow to stretch out behind them as they advanced.

One elevator was active, the indicator shifting through B4 and coming to rest on B5. Briggs again caught glimpses of the two distant silhouettes descending before they disappeared from his optics. There were no other silhouettes, and the other elevators indicated they were still resting at ground level. Carlyle removed his chest light and shone it about the lobby. Most of the storage units were on the 5 levels below or the 12 levels above, but some still opened onto the main lobby—rolling doors covered in grease and grime no wider than a person could walk through.

"No-one else home by the looks," Carlyle declared

"Not at one in the morning."

Briggs removed his own flashlight and found a wide set of metal steps going in both directions. He approached and looked down a dark void and heard machinery he guessed were the doors of the elevator closing followed by a whine as it appeared to be returning to ground. He'd lost sight of them for almost 20 seconds, precious time he needed to make up. A few gestures beckoned Carlyle to follow as he descended the stairs.

The steps were sturdy and quiet as they walked, but they had to take care not to brush against the railings. The slightest noise would reverberate around the structure. They also disabled their lights to conceal their approach—the stairs were illuminated with faint strip lights. One flight, then two. They descended another level, slowing down the pace. There was little light, but their eyes adjusted.

As they came closer to the fourth level, the floor was awash in a gentle blue glow. They continued to watch the corners and sweep the open space but found nothing. No movement. No noises. No silhouettes. Descending onto the landing halfway down the final set of stairs gave them their best view of the space below. They crouched and looked again.

Carlyle had his monocular on his eye and was taking in the scenery. "What do you see?" Briggs asked.

"Not much. No heat. Minimal light. They could be further into the storage cells. Not much room to move down here."

They descended the final set of stairs. No lights were activated on their approach. The lobby opened into corridors jutting in all directions. Some were wide enough for a forklift drone to operate, others no more than a meter wide. Carlyle scanned what he could with his monocular and made an annoyed grunt.

*"Northeast. Second corridor".* Goldstein said in his phonics. Briggs took it as fact and led Carlyle towards that corridor. He recognised his vulnerable position by accepting Goldstein's direction without question, but he had no reason not to trust him. His bigger concern was that if the old man's direction wasn't accurate, it might get them both killed.

A loud metal clang reverberated around them, sounding like a large door had closed. It caused them both to find cover behind a storage trolley. The sound echoed around them and up the stairwell for so long that it didn't feel like it ever reached its end.

With his back to the corner of the corridor, Briggs motioned for Carlyle. Carlyle complied—surveying the end of the corridor from a crouched position as Briggs stood over him.

"I've got something at the far end of the corridor," Carlyle said. "I can't see shapes, but the outline of a bulkhead is spilling out some light or heat or both. Surveillance's got nothing."

"Too far away. Clear to advance?"

"Yes."

They continued closer, approaching slowly, Briggs taking point with Carlyle sweeping behind. The low rumble in the building was the only sound, bar their shoes making a barely audible landing on the stone floor.

Arriving at the bulkhead, Briggs found it didn't match the rest of the storage cells. Rather than having a rolling metal door, this door hung on a worn metal hinge. An improvised handle had been made from two pieces of bent reinforcement bar, welded side by side and attached to the door. A heavy lock hung loose from a matching chain welded into the door frame, clearly used by Alvarez to lock the door on the way out but not the other way around. Briggs could see the glow of a low light coming from gaps around the seal of the door, where parts of the floor had crumbled away.

"Looks promising." He saw no ghosted silhouettes beyond the wall—which didn't make a lot of sense because it felt like this should be near the North-East edge of the building. He did another 360 degree sweep but found nothing.

"I didn't hear him lock it after it closed." Carlyle offered.

"Agreed. We need to push through, but it might make a hell of a noise."

Briggs holstered his sidearm, grabbed the rough handle and lifted, testing the weight of the door. He felt its heavy weight, the ridges of the reo bar biting into the thin sleeves of his lifesuit. The door shifted slightly; it didn't seem locked from the other side, and he couldn't hear any chains moving around. He rested it back down and rubbed his hands.

"I'll lift and you push past. Taking the weight off might make it a little quieter. When you're through sweep the room beyond and if it's safe, hold the door for me to follow through. Once I'm out we'll both have to hold the door to stop it from slamming."

"Copy that."

Briggs lifted again and pulled the door open. Loose pieces of concrete and dust fell away from its frame, but the old hinges gave little more than a creak.

Carlyle slipped through the gap, gun ready. "Clear". A few seconds later, he said, "I've got the weight. Come on."

Briggs slipped through. He didn't have time to scan the room—he trusted Carlyle to have done that. Instead, he turned and supported the door as best he could as they both closed it back into position. He was relieved to see a matching chain and lock also hanging free.

Carlyle took it upon himself to grab the lock, which still had the key in it. He twisted the chain through the handle and locked it in place, slipping the key in his pocket. "That's not gonna pass the fire code," Carlyle quipped. Briggs ignored it. They were now locked in.

"What do you expect backup will do when they arrive?" Briggs asked.

"It's only loose, they can move the door enough to get a set of bolt cutters in."

Briggs scanned the room properly for the first time. It was more of a tunnel, cut through the earth and supported with pieces of concrete and metal. The tunnel appeared to spill out into a larger room. Some source of light was filtering through, but Briggs couldn't see the back of the room beyond, nor any silhouettes. Carlyle had his monocular out again and simply gave a thumbs up.

Briggs redrew his sidearm, and they both advanced. Rounding the exit of the tunnel, Briggs now got a view of the room beyond. A large area, with high ceilings. Lighting panels rigged from chains over worn lounges created a makeshift communal area. The lights weren't bright but were enough to illuminate the weathered furniture and rusted collapsible seats and tables. Briggs spotted a cooking unit, refrigerator, and other amenities.

He'd seen these sorts of places before. Makeshift safe houses. Off grid. Places where stimulants were made, distributed or consumed. The observer algorithm running in his optics marked out any potential weapons or threats in his view, but only a few kitchen knives were highlighted. Lining the wall were three old teepers, standing inactive, their plastic and metal bodies battered and stained. One of them was missing an arm and the head of another was strapped onto its body with tape at an uncomfortable angle.

Opposite this area was a second space, sectioned off by frosted curtains hanging from a rail suspended from eyebolts from the stone ceiling above. Briggs approached, finding a gap in the curtains, keeping his gun close and using his left hand to peer inside.

He found two stainless steel tables side by side, between them a trolley of medical instruments like clamps, scissors and scalpels. After a short delay, these were again highlighted in his optics as innate threats. Two large lights were inactive overhead. Other instruments and machines lined the walls. Some looked like fridges. Others looked like devices he'd seen in different hospitals though he didn't know what they did. A few pieces of equipment looked older, almost barbaric, like they belonged to the century before, or even the one before that.

"I've got movement," Carlyle whispered. "One ghost—probably the girl. One of the corridors further down."

Briggs turned and saw her too. He watched for her movement, it was slow and unalarmed—a good sign. There were no other silhouettes—if Alvarez and Rocha were here, they were otherwise alone.

"No other exits?" Briggs asked.

"No idea, but I'm guessing not."

Briggs assumed point, Carlyle sweeping close behind. Moving from the room into another tunnel cut out of the earth, the silhouette of the girl grew larger as he approached. By her movements, she was either dressing or undressing. A second silhouette reappeared maybe 20m further away—Alvarez. He was lying in a supine position before tilting onto his feet. Immediately, Briggs' optics flagged Alvarez as having an outstanding warrant.

"Suspect just dumped the teeper and is back in flesh," Briggs said.

"Good—makes it easier for us. Call for backup yet, or go in all guns blazing?"

"No backup, not yet." Briggs didn't want to tip anyone off until he had Alvarez incapacitated. "Don't let him touch you… with his hands."

Carlyle pulled a face, and Briggs shook his head, adding, "We need to separate the girl, so she doesn't get in the way. How we going to manage that?"

Carlyle's suggestion wasn't helpful. "Shock and awe—looks like she's in a bathroom or something. One of us goes in and gags her."

"Without the other guy hearing? Give me something else?"

*"I can disable her if you want,"* said Goldstein.

"How?" Briggs said before realising Carlyle was looking at him.

"How what?" Carlyle said. Briggs held a hand to his face.

*"She's just taken something—drugs of some kind. She already looks pretty sedate. I can tip her over the edge."*

Briggs wanted to know how, but not now. "We need her out, not panicking."

*"Trust me, I'll look after her."*

**31**

The corridor descended further and twisted slightly to the north. As they followed, they found small unoccupied rooms seemingly cut into the stone. Some contained rudimentary cots and others stored boxes and crates.

April Rocha's silhouette was now in the room next to them, appearing to sway with her hand reaching to clasp whatever shapes her optics or her brain were creating for her. "Did you see the colours, baby?" her muffled voice said through the wall of earth and stone.

The Alvarez silhouette hadn't moved much. He stretched and rotated, maybe trying to get some feeling back in his extremities after spending a long time in an immersion rig. The doorway into Alvarez's room was open. He was only ten meters away.

Briggs replaced his normal projection with the standard PPD officer projection to make sure he was immediately identified as soon as he entered. He finally triggered the request for backup he'd prepared, supplying his location as well as his previous few minutes of tracking to assist. He didn't know how long the backup would take, but he hoped he wouldn't need it.

Preparing to breach, Briggs triggered a private countdown heard only by Carlyle and himself. On zero, he left cover and rushed the doorway, gun ready.

"Freeze Alvarez!" Briggs' voice was clear and controlled. Now with a direct line of sight, Briggs could see Alvarez in his full glory, standing behind the immersion pod. A solid man, with dark features about Briggs' height. A wave of surprise washed over his face, but he stayed still as ordered.

"Mierda," he said.

"Stretch your hands out, palms facing me."

160

Alvarez complied. Briggs took in a little more of the room. Several potential threats were highlighted in his optics by the Observer algorithm; chief among them was a shotgun on a nearby table, but out of reach. A disabled teeper stood silently to Alvarez's right—another old unit that looked to have been recycled and not connected to the main teeper network.

Briggs shortened the distance between them, gun trained on Alvarez as Carlyle circled, positioning himself at 45 degrees and blocking access to the shotgun.

"Now, hands behind your head, fingers linked, and slowly go onto your knees. You don't want a taser round to the chest—trust me." Alvarez complied one arm at a time, one leg at a time. Briggs checked the PPD Network to confirm they would arrive on site in nine minutes.

"Backup's en route. Cuff him," Briggs said to Carlyle.

"My pleasure." Carlyle holstered his gun and unclipped the binders from his belt. When attached, the binders didn't just bind the hands but triggered an automatic lockdown of the wearer's access to the Network, disabling everything but access to legal counsel.

Alvarez seemed to have moved past his initial surprise. A look of concentration washed over his face, which bothered Briggs. "What's wrong with this world, pendejos?" he asked.

"Too many vermin," Carlyle responded quickly.

"The problem is, *you* only see what you want to see."

Carlyle stood over him from behind, one cuff open in his left hand, his right poised to grab Alvarez' right wrist. "What's that supposed to…"

The old teeper lurched back to life. Quicker than anyone could react, it ran straight towards Carlyle, spinning its entire torso around its hips, hitting Carlyle flush in the middle of his face with an outstretched arm. The force threw him backwards. Distracted by the new threat, Briggs set his sights on the centre mass of the teeper and fired two stun rounds into it. One ricocheted off a flailing arm, but the other hit the teeper square, causing it to stutter and falter in a shower of sparks.

Alvarez seized this opportunity and bounded from his kneeling position, heading straight for the shotgun on the table opposite. Briggs had been too distracted with the teeper to intercept. By the time Briggs refocused on Alvarez, he already had one hand on the shotgun and was spinning up to take aim.

Briggs fired again, the bullet only barely grazing Alvarez's right shoulder and burying itself in the wall beyond. It did not trigger a stun response or discourage Alvarez from following through. His next shot was wayward, going high. Alvarez's short barrel was nearly at full arc. Realising he was slower, Briggs dove to his left, finding partial cover behind the immersion pod. Alvarez fired the shotgun with a boom. A cloud of dust and a spray of pellets just missed Briggs' diving body.

Briggs circled the immersion pod on his hands and feet, placing it squarely between them. It was a solid piece of plastic full of gyros and motors—reasonable cover. That theory was tested when another shotgun blast landed on the other side.

Briggs peered around to find the partially disabled teeper had fallen on top of Carlyle who was trying to get back on his feet despite the blood streaming from his face. The teeper continued its jerky movement, almost like it was trying to stay in the fight. Carlyle remained in danger from both the teeper and Alvarez's shotgun, should he choose to take the opportunity.

What happened next would depend on Alvarez. Either he would stay and fight, or he would run. Briggs could see Alvarez' silhouette through the base of the immersion pod standing near the doorway. He decided to give himself a little distance and time to regroup, so he raised his gun above the pod with two hands and fired two more rounds in the rough direction of Alvarez' silhouette. They didn't hit, but caused a reaction—Alvarez turned and ran out the door, back up the corridor.

Briggs ran to Carlyle. Keeping his gun trained on the door, his other hand grabbed the flailing arm of the teeper and pulled it off Carlyle's body and out of danger. He helped Carlyle back onto his feet amongst a stream of grunts and curses. Blood streamed from what appeared to be a badly broken nose, distorting his projection. He floundered briefly but found a way to stay upright.

"You good?" Briggs asked.

Carlyle removed his sidearm and staggered over to the wriggling teeper. He fired once into its chest and once into its head. Live rounds, not stun rounds. The teeper collapsed from the first and its head shattered apart from the second.

"Now I'm good. Let's get this bastard."

"Remember, we need him alive."

Briggs tracked Alvarez's silhouette as he attempted to escape. He now looked to be approaching the door Carlyle had locked.

"He's at the door. Backup's six minutes away," Briggs said.

"That lock won't last long against a shotgun," Carlyle replied as they both moved towards the entrance and started making their way back up the corridor. Briggs led the way, he was faster than Carlyle who was still unsteady, occasionally propping himself against the wall. They passed the door to where April Rocha now appeared to be lying down, Briggs heard her say "fireworks" amongst other words as he passed.

"No-where to run scumbag!" Carlyle's taunt would barely reach Alvarez over the noise of him attacking the door.

He heard a shotgun blast, followed by an angry groan. Alvarez's silhouette was still in the doorway but appeared wildly off-balance. Though Briggs couldn't see the weapon, it was clear he was trying to line it up with the lock, but was having great difficulty, like he was standing on the bow of a small boat in rough sea trying to shoot something in the water.

The sound of the gun being re-primed was followed by another shot being fired and an even louder groan.

"Are you doing that?" Briggs asked Goldstein.

"*Yes. It won't hold him long,*" was the reply.

He was now clear of the corridor and had an unobstructed shot at Alvarez who was feeling his way along the door to the chain and lock. Holding out his shotgun with the other hand, he attempted to line up a shot on the lock, with his eyes closed.

Briggs lined up a shot of his own but was distracted by movement to his left. The three dilapidated teepers had come to life and were making their way towards Briggs' position, slower than the first teeper, but still a threat.

Briggs jumped back a few metres behind the corridor. "Teepers at 9 o'clock!"

Carlyle caught up to Briggs. Sneaking a look at the approaching teepers, he removed a stun grenade, pulled the pin, and tossed it somewhere between their feet and Alvarez's position

"Fall back!"

Briggs complied and counted to four. His whole view lit up with a blue-white light. The grenade made only a dull thud when it went off and Alvarez' high-pitched scream came in response. Some of the overhead lights burnt out.

After a long ten seconds, his optics settled enough to see Alvarez's silhouette on the ground, writhing in pain.

They advanced carefully together, spilling into the larger room, sweeping, and scanning in opposite directions. The three teepers had collapsed like they had simply had their power turned off. Alvarez's shotgun had fallen away from his body, and he was rolling on the floor, holding his ears and whimpering. The threat was over.

Carlyle approached, defiant and cocky. "Let's try this again, shall we?"

In a swift motion, he grabbed an arm, bent it behind his back and attached a binder. Lifting Alvarez by the bound arm, he snatched the other and completed the job before dropping him face-first back onto the floor.

"Fernando Alvarez, consider yourself under arrest."

Attaching the binders triggered the stun algorithm to cease, and Alvarez's body slowly relaxed. Briggs patted down Alvarez to confirm there were no other weapons. As Carlyle slouched down on the floor to rest, Briggs said, "Let's find something cold for your face, backup will be here any minute."

Briggs inspected the door, intending to wedge it ajar. He found two shotgun burn marks on its metal plating and another near the handle. The lock had been smashed too. Alvarez's last shot at escape, with his eyes closed, had nearly been successful.

The fourth basement level of building N14E8 was now awash with bright light and a seemingly endless stream of people. Officers were securing the premises. Optics and other technicians were processing the scene and setting up imagery, and a civil engineer was present to inspect the state of the underground bunker carved from the earth.

Six hours earlier, Alvarez had been transported under guard to the West Praxis Police Station for initial processing. After that, he would be relocated to the temporary holding facility below PPD Headquarters in Praxis Central. Though he'd mostly recovered from the effects of the stun grenade, he answered none of Briggs' questions other than to repeat the word, "lawyer" over and over again.

It wasn't the best outcome for Briggs, but he knew he would have a better chance of co-opting a statement once Alvarez had enjoyed a few hours in custody and his lawyer had hopefully given him some encouragement to talk, especially since the list of offences against him was growing longer by the hour. In the meantime, the paramedic team had patched the wound where Briggs' shot had grazed his shoulder before he was ushered out and into the meat wagon.

Carlyle had put up a solid fight, but as soon as the arrest had been made, he'd found a bag of frozen food from one of the freezers, collapsed into one of the old couches and stared out into space like a scolded pet. Briggs collected the spent stun grenade and returned it to Carlyle's belt. It was going to be too difficult to give a full account of the whole event and conceal the use of the stun grenade. That was probably going to fall on Carlyle, but Briggs didn't think it would lead to anything more than a warning.

From Briggs' perspective, however, he was more than grateful. Taking down a small army of teepers and Alvarez would have been a whole lot harder without Carlyle's help. He communicated as much via a brotherly pat on the back when the paramedic ushered him out and away from the scene. Carlyle mumbled something about his modelling career being over and left Briggs with the other technicians to start processing the crime scene.

But Carlyle hadn't been the only help. Alvarez may have gotten away if it hadn't been for Goldstein's intervention. Briggs asked him what he'd done to stop Alvarez from escaping. Goldstein had shared a complicated response, which Briggs interpreted as doing something to interfere with how Alvarez's optics were perceiving scale. Goldstein had used the word, "seasick", triggering a sympathetic reaction from Briggs.

Goldstein had ended the connection and asked to be informed of any results from interrogating Alvarez. As much as Briggs appreciated the help, he had no intention of keeping a civilian informed on his progress, unless it benefited the case.

April Rocha had also been led away. Once she'd been given time to sober up, she would be asked a few questions but would most likely be released. She might describe the colourful fireworks Goldstein had unleashed in her optics to distract her, but it would just be attributed to whatever stimulant she'd taken.

Briggs provided his full report, including a stream of his banked footage to the arrest file. It excluded his conversations with Goldstein, and some of the lead-up work back at street level.

As tiredness settled like a weight on his shoulders, he observed the swarm of technicians and officers buzzing around him and realised there was little more he could do. The other officers would prepare their reports. They would catalogue the evidence. They would go through all the rooms and uncover any contraband.

He completed a formal handover to the senior officer on site and shared a ride with one of the police transports to a hotel near the West Praxis station. There he'd booked an overpriced room to his PPD expense account and collapsed on the bed from tiredness.

He spotted the same officer who'd taken over the crime scene the night before. Her hands, arms, chest and knees were covered in grey dirt causing an occasional tracking error over her lifesuit.

"Sergeant Li, how goes it?"

"Ah, Detective. You look well rested." Her feigned resentment was exposed by a slight smile. "We've found a significant stash of Old-World contraband. Not just the usual weapons, stims and tech gear but even things like artwork, paper books and some musical instruments."

"What was the entrance point?"

"Not sure. This is a storage facility, so for all we know these things could have been taken from people's lockers without their knowing or located out-world and brought here. Moving contraband to and from storage facilities would be fairly innocuous."

"Did any of the scene techs find anything?"

"Nothing they shared with me before they left. Pretty sure they grabbed prints and DNA from a few spots. That space back there is an off-the-grid hospital. It doesn't look like it's been used for a while and is otherwise clean. We've found a few used lifesuits they would have gotten samples from."

"What about the teepers?"

"Well, according to your report, they had minds of their own and attacked you?"

"That's right. They were recycled units. Either programmed to attack or remotely controlled," Briggs said.

"I'll let you and your Network Crimes buddies try and figure that one out. They've been boxed up and shipped to Praxis Central already."

"Fully disabled, I hope."

"Absolutely."

Briggs thanked the Sergeant for her help. She remained in charge of the scene. Though the Nguyen and Zaimis murders were still his to investigate, sorting through the mass of evidence was West Praxis' responsibility for now. No doubt it would filter across the other central divisions like organised crime, narcotics and other members of the Network Crimes division including ONI. It was an incredible score, but his true mission was far from complete. Briggs made a request to be informed of any results from DNA or prints.

Briggs' next step was to interview Fernando Alvarez, however, he doubted he would get access until after mid-day at PPD headquarters in Praxis Central. It had been a few days since he'd spent more than a few rushed minutes back at his desk. The evening's events were generating more virtual paperwork by the minute.

On top of that, though he was never one to brag, a part of him wanted to see how his colleagues would respond to his productive night's work.

32

Carli awoke to a simulated sunrise radiating from the large scape in her apartment's virtual window. The distant sound of gulls and other seabirds mingled with the roll of waves on the shore, greeting her like a welcome friend as she slid out of bed. Her beach scape spanned the full length of the apartment. The tips of the waves glistened in orange-white light from the sun. Coconut palms swayed back and forth in the morning air like they were breathing the salt and spray. At the peak of each tree, a cluster of fruit was ripening. Each day they grew. Sometimes one would fall to the ground, and yet the pile of coconuts never changed. On occasion, a red crab would circle the trunk of one of the trees or proudly make its way from one tree to another.

It was beautiful. A triumph in design.

And it was all fake.

There was no beach. There were no birds. No trees. The oceans had probably burned up years ago, and the sun didn't rise and set in the same place. Carli reached out and touched the wall that anchored the scape in place. It was made to look like an open window, and yet her hand rested on cold rendered concrete. The breeze causing the trees to sway was distinctly lacking on her face. She imagined the spray of salt settling on her skin and filling her lungs, but the only smell was a mixture of cleaning agents, cement, and manufactured textiles.

She knew what her apartment looked like with the scapes disabled, just as she knew what her oldself looked like when she switched off her projection. But this morning, their pretence seemed more obvious. Rather than lift her spirits as they usually did, Carli felt a kind of sadness and longing for a reality that no longer existed. And yet, she dared not turn the scape off—surely to be immersed in the true ugliness of her apartment would be more depressing than to be distracted by a forgery of something beautiful?

A message had been received through the night as she slept. It identified the sender as, "Wollemi": Percy Hayward.



Carli didn't reply. She hadn't decided what she thought about their conversation the previous evening. She knew one thing for certain, however—her world seemed different today than it did yesterday. It wasn't quite a lightning bolt moment, but a gentle burn towards something: something she still hadn't gotten her mind around.

Another full day of work awaited her. An appointment with a new client in the morning, with the rest of the day booked out to allow her to sculpt three trueselfs to be used in an upcoming Network drama. Normally a day like today would energise her: a chance to meet with a new client and a solid block of time to get her creative juices flowing. But this morning it didn't hold quite the same allure. She dared to wonder if there was truly any value in the work she did. Though she felt well rested, the last few days had left her weary. She made a mental note to look at booking some recreation leave when she got into the office.

She took another look at the beach landscape. The sun had lifted from the horizon on its journey upwards and the colour had begun to shift away from orange and purple towards white. She wouldn't turn it off, but she decided now was a good time to lease a brand-new scape.

What was usually an enjoyable process for her seemed more like a distraction from something more important. The client, a slightly built male of around 40 was looking for a fresh body and fresh face after a relationship breakup. He shared how he'd always fantasised about sailing on the ocean, with the salty wind in his sun-bleached hair. It was an inspiring story and Carli was able to capture enough information from the interview to be able to start work immediately in the hour before she was due for lunch.

But upon returning to her studio, holding her precious sculpting tools in her hands, all she could do was stare at the projected copy of her client's oldself. Nothing like the trueself he wanted Carli to create. He would perhaps not be considered particularly handsome—his triangular chin and thin nose gave the man a reptilian look. But at least it was real.

She stood frozen in her thoughts. *Get a hold of yourself, girl! You've got a job to do.* And yet her mind wandered. She was glad today was Friday, and she had the upcoming weekend scheduled off. *A simulated holiday might be needed.* The idea of a break released some tension. After all, the last few days had been a little off-putting.

A chirp in her phonics indicated a message received.

<WOLLEMI> SHORT NOTICE, BUT A FEW OF MY FRIENDS HAVE A PUBLIC FORUM PLANNED AT THE AREOPAGUS IN PRAXIS CENTRAL FROM 12 TO 1.

Some of the central hubs had an outdoor public space where people often met to share ideas and rally support for certain causes. The Areopagus was one of those, a small amphitheatre in the civic area of Praxis Central. Other hubs had their spaces too, The Colonnade in Zurich, the Lutetia in Métropole and the Quad in Bayshore.

Carli checked the time: 11:30. It was short notice. It would take her ten minutes to walk to the transit station, a ten-minute commute and a ten-minute walk afterwards. Still, it attracted her—perhaps just because of the distraction it offered more than anything else. She realised she was still staring at the virtual projection of her morning's client. It hadn't changed.

With a wave, she dismissed the projection and raised the lights in her studio.

"I'm off for lunch, Lori. I'll be back by 1:00 pm."

She rode the elevator to the NuSculpt lobby and one of the main building elevators to the ground floor. She exited the building, moving around a small group of people going in the opposite direction.

"Bits for back…" she heard a muffled, almost distorted voice to her left. She turned but saw no one. It caused her to pause, but she shook her head and continued to the transit station on her way to Praxis Central.

**33**

Detective Briggs, can you please comment on the operation in West Praxis?"

"No comment." Briggs waved one reporter away. Another interrupted his path with a large hand-held microphone.

"Detective, is it true that you have arrested a suspect connected to the two homicides reported yesterday?"

"Any enquiries can be posted to the PPD Media Office."

"Detective Briggs, do you agree to publicly release the footage of the arrest to confirm all civil liberties were protected?"

This one made Briggs' lip curl. "You are blocking the entrance." He pushed through, careful not to make physical contact with any of the reporters and found shelter in the PPD lobby.

"You're a popular man this morning." One of the officers stationed in the lobby near the security screening area smiled as he approached. Briggs grumbled a response, removed his sidearm and clips and placed them in a container. He walked through one of the screens, which chirped a satisfied response before he collected them and rode the elevator to the 12th level.

He felt he should debrief Captain Hagen in person on the night's events. Some details needed to be left out, but he believed now was the time to share a little more of his theories about his case, if for no other reason than to see how plausible they sounded out loud. Hagen was a good listener, but also a pragmatist.

The elevator paused on level ten, which mostly contained officers for property crimes as well as administration officers for payroll and human resources. A non-uniformed officer entered the elevator, His projection looked

171

like a leather-clad character from a vampire novel. He was identified as 'Specialist Havoc' both by moniker and by name. Briggs recognised him as one of the civilian specialists working with the Office of Network Integrity. He wouldn't have known him by looking at him, however. *Those guys change their projections more often than I sanitise my lifesuit.*

ONI was led by Lieutenant Gomes under Captain Hagen's oversight. In Briggs' opinion, they seemed to burn a lot of their time babysitting the contractor specialists, who were mostly reformed Network Hats—criminals offered a deal to share their skills for the forces of good to balance out their crimes. They traversed the Network with a skill that Briggs envied. They were able to track individuals and transactions Briggs could not. They created models from the swathe of public data to predict crimes. They were the best chance of identifying and tracing external hacks on augments or Network Systems. Briggs even planned on referring Alvarez's zombie teepers to them to investigate. But on the whole, he did not trust them.

Outside of the Department, they were often the focus of public concern over their operations. Even Overseer ArdentBlue had questioned their practices and postulated if such a division operated contrary to the principles of liberty that the Collective was based on. People were naturally sceptical of those with greater power than themselves. Briggs, however, was just naturally suspicious of whose side they were on. He also doubted they were truly the "best of the best". *If they were caught, they can't have been that good*, he thought.

Specialist Havoc cocked his head towards Briggs and said, "Wassup Sarge?" which he ignored until the elevator opened on level twelve. Briggs watched him walk away to the glassed-off section where the other ONI specialists operated, tracking his movements to the door, smooth and fluid. Arms swaying in perfect opposition to the balance of the rest of the body. *A teeper*, Briggs concluded. *He's probably some fat slob hooked into a rig over in Kaplan.*

Briggs turned the other way towards an open space with cubicles and workstations. On the walls, panels were lit up with projected information and live video streams from officers' optics. Briggs had to look away after he felt the motion of the video in his stomach. Other panels revealed lists of citizens wanted for questioning, coupled with photos of their respective projections and last tracked whereabouts. One flashed over as just a generic black silhouette with the moniker 'Korb1k' and last known location as 'West Praxis'. Beneath the silhouette in bold red letters, "Wanted on suspicion of murder". Another of the panels appeared to be broadcasting video from a news report, showing officers wheeling out boxes of material and loading them onto a police transport. He recognised the storage building from the shootout with Alvarez that morning.

He found his way to an unused cubicle in as private a location as he could manage. A few officers greeted him or passed congratulations. Some of them he'd worked with previously or been partnered with on past cases. Briggs was polite but did not linger. His cubicle contained little more than a comfortable seat and an L-shaped desk with a bright white top. He took the seat, put his hands behind his head, closed his eyes and reclined, stretching his body until it gave a few satisfying pops. He was fatigued and needed time to centre his thoughts before he made his next move.

"There are plenty of bunks up on level 29, Sergeant."

Briggs recognised the voice and slowly completed his stretch before swivelling in his chair and opening his eyes to reply, "Good morning, Deputy Commissioner." Moya loomed over Briggs, even from a few metres away. His was a presence that could be felt as well as seen. But there was an unfamiliar expression on his face.

"Excellent work in West Praxis, Detective. I'm told the mole-hole you found could have been there for decades. That contraband will keep Level 18 occupied for months."

Briggs sat in silence.

"And you've apprehended Alvarez. That goes a long way towards closing out your two homicides."

"Alvarez is the witness, Korb1k was the perpetrator."

"Of course. And have you found anything further about this Korb1k?"

"Not yet. I'm hoping Alvarez will help out with that."

"If he exists at all. I don't see how someone could stay a ghost in the Network when we have an active warrant for his arrest. The witness statements have all been a little sketchy. There's been no tracking, no banked footage. Are you certain he is worth pursuing?"

"I wouldn't call Judge Khoury a sketchy witness."

Moya folded his arms, propping his chin on his left thumb. "Detective, I'm not here to bust your balls. You've done good work today. I just want to make sure we aren't spinning our wheels looking for phantoms when we have the conspirator locked down on B7."

Briggs wanted to hide the annoyed look on his face, but suspected he failed, "I go where the evidence leads me, sir. And right now, that evidence still tells me this is more complicated than a two-bit smuggler with a penchant for reprogramming teepers. When his attorney arrives, I'll get some answers."

"Of course. I'll leave you to it." Moya began to walk away but turned. "Tell me, Detective, what information led you to follow the girlfriend to Alvarez's bunker?"

Briggs glared unflinchingly. "Confidential informant."

"I see".

Liam's employer gave him a new assignment. And he didn't like it.

"That's like walking into the hornet's nest. It's a suicide mission," he'd argued. An argument he lost when his employer brought each of his accounts into his view and proceeded to drain all their balances to zero. It was a warning that Liam couldn't ignore. He shouldn't have been surprised, but seeing it happen before his eyes hammered home the truth: *My employer has me by the balls.*

Reluctantly, Liam accepted the mission and saw the balances of his accounts return to what they had been before. As much as the idea of walking brazenly into the mouth of the lion excited him, all his work would be wasted in an instant if he was captured or killed. Eight hundred thousand bits were of no use to him if he wasn't around to use them. The assurances of his safety from his employer seemed dubious, considering his precarious position.

<B17DF3-641B7C> YOUR CREDENTIALS HAVE BEEN ESTABLISHED. YOU WILL PASS ALL SECURITY CHECKPOINTS WITHOUT QUESTION.

Comprehensive plans were provided. The correct building to enter. A turn-by-turn path to navigate would be overlayed in his optics. Even the names and personal information of the individuals who were to be stationed at security checkpoints were provided in case he needed to engage in idle chit-chat.

It might be a solid plan, but it was still high risk.

As Liam stepped outside his safe house in Praxis Central, a satchel over his shoulder containing a few emergency supplies, including a snub-nosed revolver, he ran through each step of the plan. But a deep unease kept rising to the surface—something he'd known for some time, but now accepted: *I need to get out of this arrangement.*

"It's good to see you smiling, Hal."

After processing some paperwork, Briggs had stepped into Captain Hagen's office. "It's always good to have a win. But there's still more to do."

"There always is. The Captain in charge of West Praxis division has extended her thanks to us on the arrest. Between you and me I think she's a little ticked off at Sergeant Carlyle for keeping her in the dark."

"He was very helpful." Briggs meant it. "Where did he land?"

"He's in a hospital bed in Port Lincoln. They say he'll be out of action for a few weeks. Heard he cracked jokes the whole way there, even after they gave him a sedative."

Briggs smiled again.

"But how are you doing? How's your head?" She reached out as though to reposition his head, but Briggs turned instead. "Got rid of your tracking errors by the looks?"

"Yeah, someone helped me out."

Hagen caught his gaze, seriousness in her eyes. "And you're doing well otherwise?" A question they both knew had a deeper meaning.

"I'm good, Anneke. Really."

"I'm glad." She clipped him lightly over the head. "But next time you decide it's a good idea to chase someone down a deep hole in the middle of the night without backup, you think twice, OK?"

"Yes Ma'am."

"So, what's next?"

"I'm down to interview Alvarez in ten minutes. They say his suit is on the way."

"Hmm… Moya's been on my back since this thing started. He doesn't usually express this much interest."

"I know. He wants to know my working theory. At the same time, if he knew where I was heading, I have no doubt I would be cut off in an instant."

"I get it but… Hal, I always give my Detectives a reasonably long leash to follow the evidence and solve the crime. You probably get the longest leash out of everyone."

"But?"

"I trust you, Hal. But we both know this isn't your average case. So, if there is anything you think I need to know, I expect you to share it with me."

"I understand. Running theory is that Nguyen and Zaimis were killed by some form of augment virus. I believe it was administered by the prosthetic hand of the suspect, KOrb1k. I think the meltdown of the augments was only a side-effect as they weren't the cause of death."

"And the cause of death?"

Briggs smirked. "I think something from the virus interfered with each person's heart function through their lifesuits—effectively stopping their heart."

"Wow. That's insane. Did you get anything useful out of Augmosis?"

"Surprisingly, yes, they were more helpful than usual."

"Understandable. This could be a PR disaster for them. And for the whole Collective. Anything that shakes confidence in the Collective gets everyone on edge."

"Tell me about it. Especially for well-connected Deputy Commissioners." Briggs checked the time in his optics. "I need to get downstairs."

"Mr Alvarez is presently speaking with his legal counsel. I've let them know you're here," said the warden.

Briggs stood and waited, checking the time. He'd prepared a strategy, but he did not have the power to offer any kind of incentive or sentence reduction without speaking with the Praxis Prosecutor. He'd filed the paperwork for formal charges in the hours before, but the Prosecutor had not yet responded since the evidence from the site was still being processed. The only formal charges laid had been "serious assault" relating to Sergeant Carlyle and failing to obey a police order. It was enough to hold him for now until any other charges could be authorised, which would most likely include attempted murder.

But to Briggs, those offences seemed secondary. It was the Korb1k puzzle that held his interest. Once he had his answers, he would circle back to the fact that he'd nearly been shot earlier that morning. *There will be time to get angry after I get my answers,* he said to himself. For now, he believed his best move would be to play off the threat of the compounding list of charges with an offer to help his investigation into the deaths of Nguyen and Zaimis.

Briggs checked the time again. "How long have they been in there?"

"I can't say, Detective," the warden replied, distracted by whatever work he was doing.

"At least 20 minutes since I got the call to come down," Briggs offered but got no confirmation. Making the attorney wait had been part of his strategy. It wasn't supposed to be played back against him. His first move countered, he found a seat and decided to wait.

## 34

Carli approached the group standing in the Areopagus with casual caution, donning a simple mask to offer some protection in case a work colleague should happen to notice her. The public space could fit maybe a thousand people either seated or standing, though Carli estimated the group gathered around the central platform would number no more than a hundred. Still, she did not feel exposed. In this kind of public forum, there was usually a level of decorum and respect, even if someone disagreed with what was being said. Like most things in Praxis, rather than challenge an opinion they disagreed with, people tended to just block it and walk away.

She approached the outside edge of the group, looking for a face or a moniker she recognized. One turned towards her and smiled.

"Good to see you again, Carli." Percy Hayward extended his hand. His projection had changed completely from the day before. As they shook, Carli was happy to feel flesh and bone beneath her fingers rather than the lifeless plastic of a teeper.

Percy motioned to a few people around him, introducing two of them, but they seemed somewhat distracted, and Carli didn't attempt to remember their names.

"So, are these people some more of your recruits, Percy?" Carli asked it with some playfulness but was still interested in the answer.

Percy's smile dropped for a moment before he appeared to force it back on. "Not recruits, just people starting to wake from the dream."

"Fair enough."

"Come in a little closer, he's about to start." A tall man took the platform and raised his hands in welcome. Carli didn't recognise his projected moniker, but he introduced himself to the group only as 'The Philosopher'.

"Welcome Friends! We have been spoon-fed an augmented reality since the moment we were conceived! What we see is but a pale reflection of the truth. What we hear is only what has been filtered, compressed, and sanitised. We no longer talk to each other! We put up walls because we want to hide who we are. But they don't keep us safe—they cage us in like a prison, keeping us isolated from each other.

"We all recognise that the world our forefathers knew no longer exists. And because of their failures, we have had to carve out an existence for ourselves amongst the dust and dirt. The natural beauty of this world has been lost, and though we respect the efforts made to bring a sense of virtual beauty to these streets of concrete and steel, we must also recognise that if we have any chance of reclaiming and repairing our world, we must set aside our pretence and dependence on a simulated reality. We cannot repair what we don't see in the light of truth!

"I have seen with my own eyes the truth of the world beyond the domes. It is not irredeemable. The devastation of a century ago has not been absolute. If we break free of the shackles of the Collective, we can forge a new life for ourselves!"

A few low grumbles came over the crowd, but that didn't impact the speaker, who was just hitting his stride.

"But there is one lie we have all accepted without question. We are so enamoured with our augmented existence that we no longer forge real relationships with each other. No longer are there children running through the streets of Praxis. We are so distracted by pretty lights and loud sounds that humanity is dying out!"

Some of the groans were drowned out by at least as many loud shouts in agreement. Carli felt like she agreed, but didn't feel the need to join in. She thought back to her own childhood and the children she used to know and play with. The absence of children was just accepted without enquiry and hadn't been something she'd paid much attention to.

The Philosopher continued to speak. He made a few more points, many of which Carli believed sounded very similar to those Percy Hayward shared the previous evening.

He launched into his conclusion. "Friends, can I call on you to make a statement, here in this moment, to push back against the powers that seek to control us; to declare to each other and yourself that you are done with the hiding, done with the lies.

"One of the writers from almost two centuries ago said, 'sooner or later we must distinguish between what we are not and what we are. We must accept the fact that we are not what we would like to be. We must cast off our false, exterior self like the cheap and showy garment that it is.' We all have the power to project the truth into the Collective. I call on each of you to deactivate your projection—to share your true self with the world. To escape the shadows and stand in the light!"

Carli's eyes darted around the group to see if any would respond. Most were masked, the rest projected their trueself. The only movement was a handful of individuals turning to walk away. The speaker on the platform removed his full projection, revealing an older male with dark, blemished skin. As he released the hood from his lifesuit, a few patches of white, curly hair remained on his otherwise bald head. His outfit also disappeared, revealing an old yellow-stained lifesuit, with visible repairs to the elbows and knees.

She heard someone gasp and another mutter something derogatory under their breath. But Carli stared intently at him. He was exposed, vulnerable. It wasn't just the way he looked but the pleading expression of concern resting on his face. He looked *real*.

One of the other people watching also dropped their projection. Followed by another. A wave swept over the group, like some form of mass hysteria. Carli felt it, too. Something within her wanted to break free from this invisible force, but she dared not. More people dropped their projections, some revealing just the frame of a teeper: *a strange way to join the cause*, Carli thought.

There were more gasps and more people turned away: the group reducing by as much as a third. Of those remaining, half removed their projections. Everyone was looking at each other with smiles and wide eyes. Carli saw one man crying and embracing the man standing next to him. Another person was staring into the sky and slowly spinning in circles with her arms outstretched.

To Carli, it was beautiful.

Others around her had removed their projections. Beautiful natural faces, weathered by life's joys and miseries. It was an awakening, like seeing colour for the first time after years of blindness. Wrinkled eyes and natural hair expressed a freedom and joy that Carli had never experienced. A joy wanted for herself.

A few gestures brought up an overlay in her optics of different controls. The same controls she would use to disable her projection when she cleaned her teeth in the morning. Her heart quickened. First, she removed her mask. Next, she selected the option to remove her projection. Her optics advised her that she was in a public place and sought her confirmation. She paused briefly, then selected, 'yes'.

A chirp told her the action was now complete. She looked around at the other faces and caught the eyes of a stranger who returned her smile. She couldn't see herself. Her eyes saw nothing different than they did before, but she felt like she'd changed. Like she'd stepped out of a boat and was standing on the water. She struggled with words to describe the feeling. It was like being welcomed into some sacred intimacy. For the very first time, she was being absolutely truthful with herself.

She found herself also turning slightly, looking at each face and sharing a common joy and trust with each one. She caught the face of Percy, still identified by callouts in her optics based on her trust settings, but now with his projection removed. He looked very different, he was still slightly built, but his face was more angular than either of his other projections. He caught her eye and acknowledged her with a smile.

She continued to look around. The twirling female slowed, but her eyes remained closed, and arms outstretched. Carli looked closer, soaking in every detail of her face. Such a projection would never exist in the Collective. There were too many wrinkles, too many blemishes. And yet each one spoke a story to Carli more meaningful than any client interview she'd ever had.

The lady opened her eyes and made momentary eye contact with Carli, but this was abruptly cut off—a mask appeared over her face, concealing it in an instant. A mask Carli had seen before. A brown paper bag with a frowning face.

She gasped in response, stepping back. It seemed others had seen it, pointing to the strange face. Then she saw another, followed by another. All of the people who had removed their projections were being masked, one by one, including the speaker from the central platform. Carli spun around in shock. It was like the strange nightmare she'd experienced a few days ago was spreading across the group like a virus. Those who had not removed their projections were unaffected.

The noise in the group swelled. Someone shouted, "What's happening?" For Carli, the feeling of freedom she'd only just experienced now shifted to alarm.

A message crossed her optics:

<OMEGASERVICE> YOU ARE NOT PROJECTING A TRUESELF INTO THE COLLECTIVE. YOUR OLDSELF WILL BE SANITISED.

*What does that mean?* She thought to herself, dismissing the message.

And then, one at a time, people started to disappear.

# 35

Captain Anneke Hagen had just concluded a debriefing to the PPD Media Office, her second so far this morning. It seemed all of Praxis's attention had turned to the shootout in West Praxis. From Hagen's perspective, it was a good news story and something of a positive change from enquiries she'd fielded over the previous two days concerning the deaths of Zaimis and Officer Nguyen.

She wasn't given to worry. She hadn't ascended to such a high-level position in the PPD by doubting herself or the decisions she'd made. And yet she sensed an undercurrent of something ominous with relation to Briggs' case. Like Deputy Moya, she felt the desperate need to see the case closed, even at the cost of the whole truth, but she resisted it, choosing to place her trust in Briggs. Politically, the best outcome was for the two deaths to be written off as random accidents. Pinning them on Alvarez would be the quickest resolution, but Hagen knew the evidence didn't stretch that far. She also didn't like the idea of Briggs being at odds with the political interests of the Department. She knew he thrived on being a loner. But when something went awry, it was always the loners who were the first casualties.

Hagen left her desk, rounded the cubicles, and made her way towards the restrooms. Several officers acknowledged her as she walked. Her path was interrupted by ONI's Lieutenant Gomes.

"Moment of your time, Captain?" she asked.

"Sure Constança, what's up?"

"My guys have been going through the logs from this morning's arrest in West Praxis. We've found anomalies."

Hagen directed her into a small meeting room off the main corridor and closed the door. "Like the ones you found with the two murders?"

"No, different. We've found nothing useful at all with those—just a void of missing data. I've just sent a report to Detective Briggs. But from this morning, we have found a few other anomalies."

"Tell me."

"Well, the easy one was that the teepers were activated by a local network, probably by the suspect in custody. They had a low-level AI that would have attacked anyone they didn't recognise. All were separate from the Network, and the West Praxis officers found the equipment on site. Also, I understand Alvarez is an engineer, so the money's on him reprogramming them."

"That's good, but still concerning. I'm sure Property is already investigating where the teepers came from. Once you conclude your checks, file the paper, and we'll add that to the growing pile of charges. We could probably use it as leverage with him to find out where they came from. What's the harder one?"

"Briggs." The Lieutenant replied, "We were checking through his data stream, and it seemed like he was getting information from someone else during the arrest. There are times when he talks out loud and the other Officer, Carlyle, isn't in the room."

Hagen was dismissive, "Maybe he was talking to himself."

"No, I don't think so. We can see evidence of voice and text connections during the arrest, but they aren't on the Detective's report. We can't see what was shared, but for some of them, we can see a very complex path through the Network. We can't see who they were from, but they knew their way around the Network. My investigators seemed most impressed.

"Captain, is there any chance Detective Briggs could have set up some sort of Network hack to mask these connections?"

"Hal?" Hagen caught herself mid-laugh. "No way. He's a smart guy, but not like that."

"Sorry, I just thought I should ask."

"I'll ask him about it. I'm sure it's nothing."

Hagen's attention was drawn through the window of the office to the outside corridor. Two officers rushed past, and voices were raised. She opened the door, stepped into the corridor, and caught another officer mid-stride carrying a portable fire extinguisher.

"What's the problem?"

"There's a smouldering teeper in ONI," he yelled as he rushed on.

Lieutenant Gomes joined Hagen in the corridor and yelled, "Do we need to evacuate?" The building replied with a klaxon for the alarm sounding, which was met with equal amounts of excitement and reluctant groans from the officers trying to work.

Hagen ignored the siren and pushed ahead towards the ONI section, its doorway congested with people trying to enter and others trying to leave. Through the large glass windows, Hagen could see what looked like a teeper without a projection moving about the conference room as others were trying to convince it to stop moving. One even had their hand poised over their holstered sidearm, ready to draw. Grey smoke poured out of the body of the teeper from somewhere underneath its plastic rib cage.

The teeper stopped moving and stood still. Hagen couldn't tell if it was still being remotely controlled by its original pilot or was operating under its own power. The smoke shifted to white and intensified, masking the teeper's face and starting to cloud the whole room. Another officer with a portable fire extinguisher sprayed in the direction of the teeper, only adding to the fog in the room until Hagen could see nothing.

She came closer to the glass, trying to work out if somehow the smoke was starting to settle. Through the fog, a bright light emanated from the centre of the room, followed by a swirl of electricity. It quickly grew until half of the room was bright white, like burning magnesium. She recoiled from the glass as the brilliant white blinded her. She heard screams over the top of the klaxon, which had changed to a different, more urgent tone, but she couldn't yet open her eyes to see where they were coming from.

The conference room exploded, shattering glass towards her and pushing her to the ground. She felt scratches on her face, the tempered glass exploding into small cubes but ejected with enough force to knock her over and hit her like a shotgun blast. She felt pain all over, but especially her face.

The ringing in her ears waned for long enough for the sound of the cries and klaxons to return—a momentary reprieve. She forced her eyes open, but the centre of her vision was now a bright spot that floated around the room with her. The light from the ONI conference room had gone, but the smoke was now flooding through the rest of the floor, and she could see smouldering pieces of metal scattered around the room, intermixed with the bodies of other PPD officers, some of whom Hagen could immediately tell were gravely injured, or worse.

She did not recognise any of them. With the smoke and the injuries to their faces, her optics could do nothing to identify who they were: fallen comrades she knew well now appeared to her as nameless bodies. She recognized none of them.

She reached for the floor and tried to prop herself up.

"Cap, is that you? Lie still!" It was Lieutenant Gomes' voice, but as Hagen looked up, her eyes starting to adjust, she saw only the frame of a teeper. Gomes' projection was occasionally flicking in and out of reality in different parts all over the teeper as waves of smoke caused the projection to lose tracking. Hagen relented. She didn't want to look over her body to see how badly injured she was, but she knew there were multiple lacerations, even if there was now little pain accompanying them.

The sensors in her lifesuit were in equally bad shape, adding to the cacophony of auditory and visual noise with a series of alarms about damage to her suit and concerning vital signs.

Hagen looked again at Lieutenant Gomes, who was now crouching over her and issuing directions to others for assistance. She turned to look back at Hagen, with an expression of concern switching intermittently with the soulless expression of a teeper. "We've got you, Captain."

She smiled in appreciation, but the smoke was getting thicker. She could taste it, a strange smell of burned chemicals mixed with something acrid she did not recognise.

In terror, she realised the smoke was not from the explosion.

It was coming from Lieutenant Gomes' teeper, just under the plastic rib cage.

# 36

"Look, how long is he going to make me wait? I've got better things to do than sit around." Briggs's frustration bubbled over, his voice raised as though somehow it was either going to convince the warden to change his mind or cut through the layers of concrete and glass to be heard by Alvarez and his lawyer directly.

"There's nothing I can do, Detective. I have informed them of your arrival."

"Well, you can inform them I'm leaving, along with any chance that clown may have had for a deal." Briggs motioned towards the exit.

A message crossed his optics. A fire alarm had been triggered, and a partial evacuation of the building had been ordered for levels 11 to 13.

He looked back to the warden. "You see that too?"

"Yes. Only partial."

"What happens in the event of a full building evacuation?"

"You go, but I stay to make sure the children don't play up. Unless there is a danger on this level in which case, I get the hell out, and we watch the children get burned to a crisp."

"Sounds reasonable." Briggs wondered what the issue was. Fire drills did happen from time to time, and sometimes they were staggered across groups of floors. The whole building was resilient to fire and other threats. Fire was particularly problematic when the atmosphere inside a hub like Praxis Central was self-contained—large quantities of smoke would take a long time to be filtered at the top of the dome.

For a moment, Briggs thought of Captain Hagen and the others in Network Crimes but assumed everything was fine.

"Good news, Detective. Mr Alvarez's legal counsel has requested me to escort you in."

"Finally."

The warden triggered the door and held it open for Briggs to enter. He'd previously checked his PPD firearm before entering the secure area. He walked past a bank of lightweight teepers only used by the police, legal representatives or justice divisions for interviews and consults.

The warden escorted him down one corridor and knocked on the door of one of the last rooms. The walls of the interview room became transparent to give the warden a clear view inside. Alvarez was seated, fully shackled behind a low transparent table. His lawyer stood clear of the door, waiting. Briggs steeled himself, counting to five to slow his heart rate. He didn't want to come across as anything other than in complete control.

"Good afternoon, Detective Briggs. I am Ajay Patersen, Partner at Crest and Associates and Mr Alvarez's appointed legal counsel." She did not offer a hand to shake but instead motioned towards the spare seat.

Briggs took the seat, trying to hide how irritated he was to have been kept waiting for so long. He locked eyes with Alvarez as he sat. The solicitor, Patersen, returned to sitting next to her client.

"Detective, I have spoken with my client and have reminded him of his legal right to remain silent. We understand the Praxis Prosecutor is preparing charges in addition to those already established. So, at this point, there may be some benefit to his future legal position by trying to be as helpful as possible."

"Good," Briggs said. "You would be aware I have no power to offer any form of plea bargain or incentive? Any information provided by Mr. Alvarez will be voluntary and with no expectations." He'd commenced the banking of this conversation the moment the door was opened. He knew the lawyer would have as well.

"That is understood." She turned to her client, who also said, "Understood".

"Mr. Alvarez, the bulk of the charges to be filed against you relate to what was found in your possession this morning in the excavated basement level of building N14E8. You also assaulted my partner and tried to shoot me."

"Do you want an apology?" Alvarez said through clenched teeth. His lawyer raised her hand in defence, and Briggs let the comment go without challenge.

"What I'm more interested in at this moment is what happened on the morning of 22nd December at the Café Roma in the West Praxis Courtyard. Specifically, what happened to a Mr Petros Zaimis AKA PeliasLolcos."

"I don't know anything about that."

"We have witness reports of you meeting with Mr Zaimis and a third individual at around 8:00 am, during which Mr Zaimis was murdered, and you left the scene."

"I wasn't there."

"Not in person, but you were piloting a teeper at the time." Briggs brought up a file he'd prepared earlier of teeper leases in the area, noting Alvarez's hire of the teeper at the time of the murder.

"Those things can be falsified. Have you got footage?"

Briggs hesitated. "Footage is being sought," he lied.

"Without footage, it didn't happen."

His lawyer interjected, "He has a point. The absence of footage of an alleged crime from a public place is problematic."

Briggs returned fire, "I disagree. When all charges are laid you will see the course of the investigation that led the PPD to consider your client to be a person of interest in the death of Mr. Zaimis, and later that morning, PPD Officer Nguyen."

"I had nothing to do with *that* either," Alvarez snapped back

"But you do know about it?"

"I hear things."

With a few other gestures, Briggs shared more information with the solicitor and his client, "The teeper logs are specific. They have your teeper logged as being within meters of the location where Zaimis was murdered at exactly that time. You can keep up the charade, but the evidence points otherwise."

Alvarez turned to his solicitor, who gave him a nod, "Fine. Maybe I was there. I didn't do anything."

Briggs smiled to himself, "I'm less interested in what you were doing. I want to know about the other guy at the table. Who is 'Korb1k'?"

Briggs saw recognition in Alvarez's eyes. "Just some gringo."

Though he was focused on his interview, he felt a gentle rumble in the room. He dismissed it and pressed on.

"Do you know where he is?"

"No."

"Do you have any way of contacting him?"

"No."

"Do you know his name or any aliases?"

"No."

"Tell me what happened later that evening at a bar called 'The Komitet'?"

This time Alvarez looked confused. "No idea."

"But you do know 'Korb1k'?"

"Again, I said, I don't know him." Alvarez was getting agitated, and Briggs was running out of patience.

"Why was Mr. Zaimis killed?" Briggs asked.

"No idea. The guy lived hard, maybe his fat ass just up and died?"

"Has Korb1k or his associates threatened you? Do you feel like you are in danger?"

This triggered a different reaction. For a fleeting moment, Briggs saw a wave of fear wash over Alvarez's face before he shut it down. "No comment."

With a few hand gestures, Briggs retrieved an image from his personal store: one of the still images he'd extracted from the banked footage from Deniz Harper. It showed the best facial profile of the person at the Komitet that Briggs suspected may be an unmasked Korb1k. He projected this image onto the table in front of them.

"What about this guy—have you seen him before?"

Both Alvarez and his lawyer leaned forward and looked at the image. Alvarez sat back quickly, "No idea. Face looks like he went too far with the exfoliant."

Briggs turned back to the lawyer—this was going nowhere. He wanted to reaffirm the importance of being helpful, but his approach was interrupted by a second, larger rumble. Alvarez looked to his lawyer for direction—they'd felt it too.

"Don't go anywhere." Briggs stood and backed away from the table. A deep sense of concern fell over him. He knocked on the door, which was opened by the warden who stuck his head in.

"That was quick."

"Did you feel that? My stream's telling me there are now ten floors under evacuation. What's going on up there?"

The warden rechecked his feeds. "Still only a partial evac. We're fine here."

"That's not the point, though, is it?"

He closed the door himself and moved a few steps away. He accessed the Network, bringing up his communications functions. He initiated a voice call with Captain Hagen. It did not connect and returned an ambiguous error message. He did the same with another of the officers on the level and had the same response. He tried a third, again unsuccessfully.

*Something's very wrong.*

He tried a few more at random. One found its recipient, but the call was cancelled with an automatic "I'll call you back" response. Lastly, he tried Lieutenant Gomes of ONI, who accepted his connection.

"Sorry to call, Lieutenant, but do you know what's happening on level 12?"

Her voice was distressed, "Briggs? I don't know—there was an explosion. A teeper exploded. And then, I don't know—I got booted from my teeper and I'm trying to reconnect."

Briggs could feel an increasing weight falling on him. With every question, his chest grew tighter. "Is anyone injured?"

"Yes… Yes, I saw Forbes and Jorgenson down. There were others—I couldn't tell who they were—they were in bad shape… There were others in the room when it happened, but there was so much smoke."

"What about Hagen?"

"Hagen? She was down too, but she was still talking."

"Was there a second explosion?"

She didn't respond to the question. "Sorry, Briggs, I gotta find out what's going on, myself." She disconnected.

Briggs stood there for a moment. His chest constricted, and his mind imagined all kinds of crazy ideas to fill in the gaps. But he was just circling around his only real concern: the welfare of Anneke Hagen. He tried to call her again and received the same ambiguous message as before: "That citizen has been disassociated from the Collective."

His confusion transitioned to anger. His analytical mind had quickly weighed all the information at hand and arrived at a grave conclusion: *Anneke Hagen was dead.*

His fists clenched and shook, his jaw clamped so hard his cheeks hurt. The pressure building in his mind tried to find some meaningful response, but what he decided on was neither considered nor rational. He flicked his hands free and forced his jaw to release. He turned back to the room and stared at the Warden.

"Let me back in."

With a slightly confused look, the warden released the door, and Briggs moved in. In a swift movement, Briggs crossed to the centre of the room, picked up the chair he'd been sitting on and brought it down on the edge of the table, snapping it into smaller plastic pieces that flew off in all directions.

Alvarez recoiled, but could not move with his hands and feet shackled. The lawyer, Patersen however jumped out of her chair like a startled animal. Both she and the warden said almost synchronously, "Detective!"

With Briggs' anger reaching its peak, he shouted right in Alvarez's face "WHAT JUST HAPPENED UPSTAIRS?"

"HOW THE HELL SHOULD I KNOW?" he yelled back. And with that, the interview was over.

# 37

An unseen body knocked Carli to the ground. She could not tell if the garbled screams were her own or from an unseen source. The panic rising within her seemed to wash across the whole group of invisible citizens like a wave. She feared a trap—it was like all of these people had conspired to torment her.

She scrambled onto her hands and knees, feeling a body pressing against her. It flashed into view, and they recoiled like they had just touched a leper, then it disappeared again.

Another person appeared, not an unmasked oldself but a trueself. This time, they did not disappear but instead paused to behold their hands and bodies restored before rushing away from the area. Another citizen appeared, then another. She heard one of their voices call above the muffled noises, "Put your selfs back on!"

More and more citizens reappeared. One appeared only meters away, pushing their way through the crowd to escape. Carli was forced to roll out of their way to avoid a collision—from the other person's perspective, Carli didn't exist. She made it back to her knees and, following the stranger's advice, re-added her trueself. A notice in her optics confirmed she was now visible again.

<OMEGASERVICE> TRUESELF ENABLED. SANITISATION DISABLED.

Others responded to her reappearance by changing their movements to avoid her as they left the Areopagus. She followed for a distance before another citizen's self reappeared at the side of the square, Percy Hayward. Anger rose within her, she changed her direction to intercept him, but another unseen body collided with her from the side, knocking her back to the ground. She reacted fast enough to put out an arm to soften the fall, but it was enough to daze her for just a moment.

She rolled onto her back, caught a glimpse of the culprit who reapplied his trueself and hurried off without a word or an apology. As she stared up at the sky, a shadow fell over her.

"Carli, are you OK?"

She recognised the voice and the face shadowed by the bright sky behind it.

"What the hell is this, Percy? Who are you people?"

It took almost ten minutes for her heart to stop racing and to regain some sense of composure. She'd swatted away Percy's extended hand and pushed her way out of the crowd of people towards a low concrete barrier forming part of the boundary around the Areopagus.

Most of the crowd had now reappeared, all of them dispersing in all directions. Occasionally, she saw glimpses of unmasked citizens appear for just a moment, only to disappear again. Some ran, some walked as quickly as they could manage. Those donning their trueselfs were visible, but those fully unmasked flickered in and out of her view like spiritual beings stepping in and out of existence. When they appeared, they remained without their projection, faces still covered with the paper bag mask.

She tried to connect the dots and figure out what had just happened, but nothing made sense. The same alarm she'd experienced a few days prior had returned on a massive scale. But rather than leading to fear as it did the first time, now it drove her to action, to push back against some unseen force that had conspired to torment her. Somehow, the offence seemed personal.

Percy Hayward approached again, "Carli—I'm sorry!" Percy called, hands open at his waist.

"What is this, Percy? What's going on?"

"I don't know, I've never seen this before."

"Why should I believe you?"

"I'm just as confused as you are. Something's happened in the Network. A new filter or something. It's not me, I swear!"

Carli's gaze rested on Percy. She needed answers, but couldn't discern any deceit in his eyes. She settled her breathing and tried to relax.

"I've seen this before," she said, almost as if speaking to herself.

"Seen what?"

"Someone disappeared. First, they were masked with a paper bag over their oldself, and then they were gone."

"When was this?" he asked.

"Only a few days ago, on the transit."

"I'm sorry that happened. Carli, I can understand if you just want to be rid of us and get back to your normal life, but it feels like something is going on around here we can't explain. Could we maybe find a safe place nearby, just to talk this through?"

"You can't be serious," she began. Some distance away, she heard an explosion. Her eyes lifted, trying to find its source amongst the buildings around her, but the concrete structures reflected and dispersed the sound. Percy did the same. A public message came across her optics:

<PPD-ALERT> FIRE IN PPD HEADQUARTERS, MAIN STREET. PLEASE VACATE THE VICINITY FOR PUBLIC SAFETY AND TO FACILITATE ACCESS FOR FIRST RESPONDERS.

Searching in the direction of the transit station, she saw the PPD headquarters some blocks away, a steady stream of black smoke belching from halfway up its side. The smoke rose upwards, past the top of the building and pooled at the apex of the dome above.

"That can't be a coincidence," Percy said.

She agreed. It felt like the Collective was breaking down around her, and now the PPD was under attack? She needed an explanation. She needed it to make sense, and Percy was the only person in any position to offer it.

"Fine. Let's go."

## 38

He feared something deep within him had been broken or lost. A deep disconnection. Briggs didn't yet know for certain, but his analytical mind had pieced together the fragments of information into one of two conclusions: either Anneke Hagen was badly injured, or she was dead. *And I'm stuck in this stupid room, unable to help.*

He paced in circles around the small room. As he rounded the door, he again tried its handle to see if it would magically open, but found it just as locked as it was the other twenty times he'd tried. He reached the corner of the room and rested with his back to it, closed his eyes and folded his arms.

The warden had implemented the same dampeners to his connection to the Network normally reserved for someone who had been arrested. This was after he'd intervened to separate Briggs from Alvarez. And now that Alvarez and his lawyer had been ushered away, it was he who had been locked in the meeting room until the warden had decided what to do with him. His only connectivity permitted him to call his union representative or his lawyer. He didn't know his union representative and did not have a lawyer.

In the past, when Briggs had caused a fuss or pushed the rules too far, it would be Captain Hagen, his superior, who would be the first to reprimand him and serve as a support representative if there were other questions to answer with Internal Affairs or an ethics review investigator. But now he felt isolated and alone, compounded by being completely disconnected from any information about what was happening upstairs and no way to be able to help.

A click and the sound of a gas piston exhaling preceded the door opening. Briggs expected to see the warden, but in strode a tall man wearing a police dress uniform. A diamond shape and golden wreath adorned the epaulettes resting on his broad shoulders. Deputy Commissioner Earl Moya. If Briggs had any hope of finding a way out of this mess, it was instantly dashed.

"Take a seat, Detective." He barely made eye contact.

"What happened upstairs?"

"Please, take a seat." Briggs was sure he hadn't heard Moya say please before. Briggs complied. Moya stayed standing. His face was serious, his eyes now meeting Briggs'.

"Sir?"

"There has been an attack on the Praxis Police Department. Network Crimes specifically. There are presently thirteen confirmed fatalities. Twenty-two wounded or severely wounded are currently en route to Praxis General. We've lost many good officers, a few civilian contractors and command staff."

"Command staff?"

"Yes. I'm sorry to be the one to tell you this, but Captain Hagen is dead."

Briggs winced at the news. The dread brewing for the last hour had now been confirmed. An hour earlier, his mind had concluded she was gone. Now the rest of his body had caught up, and he slumped back in his chair.

"What happened specifically?"

"Many small explosions, timed together. We don't know for sure yet. Now that the area has been deemed safe again, forensics will start pouring through the mess to try and work out what happened."

"I heard it was a teeper that exploded…"

"That has been the eye-witness reports, yes. There were reports of teepers in use by ONI officers first starting to smoke and then exploding. I have established a special team to investigate. I'll get answers soon."

Briggs could not help but keep asking questions. Investigating what had happened was an easy distraction from focusing on the pain inside him. "What was the target?"

"We don't know, but ONI took the most damage."

Briggs chewed over this information, trying to see how it fit. At this point, he thought it probable that the attack must somehow be related to his investigation. It was a brazen move to directly attack the PPD. *But why? Was I the target? If so, why bomb the whole department?*

"This must be related to the investigation into Korb1k. He must have known we were making progress in arresting Alvarez…"

Moya was quick to interject, "We don't know that, Detective. ONI and Network Crimes had dozens of active cases, let alone a list of cold cases going back half a century."

"But sir, the timing…"

Moya jerked his head to the side as if distracted by something, before returning his gaze. "Detective, there are a thousand things I need to do and places I need to be. I thought it best you hear this news in person rather than through the Network."

Briggs rested and nodded. "Thank, you sir,"

Moya raised his voice, "No—don't thank me, Detective. If it's not enough that I should have to deal with the decimation of an entire division of the PPD, including the loss of senior officers, I then must deal with your ridiculous behaviour interviewing the suspect."

Briggs began to interrupt, but was drowned out, "You lost your cool in front of a suspect and his legal counsel. She has the entire thing recorded and I've already been given a copy."

"It wasn't that bad…"

"Garbage. I don't care if all you were trying to do was scare him or you were just venting, but you should know full well that line cannot be crossed, for any reason. On this day of all days, I should not have to be dealing with your petulance."

"I'm sorry, sir. I'm prepared to apologise to Mr Alvarez, his lawyer and the warden here and take responsibility. But I'm sure the Korb1k investigation is linked to this attack somehow—"

Moya's voice softened, but was just as forceful as he interrupted, "You misunderstand me, Detective. Only a few hours ago, you scored an incredible win for the Department, but now you've burned any goodwill you might have earned. As of now, your investigation is on hold, and you are now officially on suspension."

Briggs's hands balled into fists, but he kept his temper under control. Another outburst now wouldn't help.

"Respectfully, sir, if Network Crimes has been destroyed, why bench one of its few remaining detectives?"

Moya turned to face the door. "Because, Detective, I'm not convinced that having you in active service will lead to anything but more problems for me to have to deal with."

With that, the door opened, and Moya left. As he walked away, Briggs saw his projection disappear to reveal the PPD interview teeper beneath it, which began to make its way back to its dock.

The warden entered the room. "You are free to go, Detective, but I have been asked to retain your PPD sidearm at the security check-in."

Briggs stood, nodded, and pushed past him. He was defeated. He didn't know what hurt more, the pain from losing his closest friend, or the pain from being sidelined from the case that may have caused her death.

Liam Nolan approached the building with as much confidence as he could muster. He had no choice but to follow his employer's directions to the letter. He'd applied a mask and activated a scanning script in his optics supplied by his employer. Approaching the main building entrance, he passed groups of people chatting and enjoying the virtual afternoon sun. He resisted every temptation to turn his face away, to do anything other than play the role of someone who belonged in this strange place.

The doors for the building opened before him and he found his way into a lobby. There were two security officers to his right, both armed with firearms and stun batons. He considered his satchel—there were things in there that would not pass through security, including a revolver he'd brought just in case things went pear-shaped. He booked a two-hour lease on a storage locker and stowed it until he could leave.

The script running in his optics told him the names of the two security personnel: "Phoebe" and "Kerrod". Phoebe was the senior of the two and had worked with the organisation for over seven years. She was unmarried and was considered a virtual celebrity amongst a very small group of people that followed a niche fantasy combat simulation called, "Realms United", where she played an elf mage named, "Gweyir Zindi". Kerrod on the other hand was new to the organisation. He spent an unhealthy amount of time in immersion fantasies, specifically ones that role-played random acts of violence. Liam wasn't one to judge, but he suspected that Kerrod's employer would probably not have given him such an important job had they known that he liked to beat up on virtual women and children in his spare time.

He caught the eye of Phoebe and nodded with a slight smile. She nodded in return, and he approached the security door. The door scanned his identity and opened as he approached. He let out a long, deep breath and slowed his heart. He would have been surprised if the credentials forged for him by his employer failed, but this remained a risky mission. He slipped through the door, maintaining a constant speed, purposeful but not rushed.

He navigated through a series of corridors opening into a much larger space, following a path laid out for him virtually within his optics. He caught himself once looking about the room at the sight of machines and electrical devices he couldn't identify, and he jerked his head back to the path, reminding himself the role he was playing would not be at all awed or surprised by what he saw in this foreign place. He passed several employees as he walked. Few paid him any mind at all. Those who did saw someone familiar and unsuspicious.

He approached another security door which scanned him and again opened as he approached. His path was concluding up ahead, marked in his optics like a target on a wartime heads-up display. He needed to take the third door on the right.

Someone joined the corridor from another door. A woman wearing a business suit covered by a loose white lab coat. Liam could feel her gaze settle on him longer than anyone else. Either she hadn't bought the ruse or was simply trying to place him. Liam's optics gave him a readout of her profile: "Doctor Imogen Godfrey". A researcher assigned to Augmosis Special Projects. He learned the name of her partner, with a note that they may presently be estranged. Her hub of residence was in nearby Praxis Harbour. All of the information was very generic and difficult to work with.

The gap between them halved, and she continued to look his way. He could see the creases in her brow as she was trying to identify this unexpected person so deep within the building's security.

*She's not buying it*, Liam thought.

## 39

The explosion triggered a lockdown of all transit services. For now, Carli was stuck in Praxis Central. A nearby bar offered them some reprieve.

Percy motioned towards one of the quiet booths in the corner, but Carli shifted to one of the standing circular tables in the middle of the room. At this moment, sitting down seemed almost offensive to her. The bar was far from busy, though a group of about 20 crowded around a fixed display panel near the service area. The panel was streaming live coverage of whatever had been happening at the PPD headquarters. Reports were inconsistent. Some said a fire. Some said an explosion.

One man sat at the bar itself, his back towards the group, masked and hunched over. Carli noticed Percy scanning the room, his eyes resting intently on the group of people crowding around the screen.

"What's the problem?" she asked.

He answered without looking at her, "Nothing." Carli guessed he didn't like walking into strange places without the security of a remotely piloted teeper. She ordered sparkling water, and Percy did the same. Distracted by the slow trickle of news and commentary, they didn't speak until after their drinks were served at their table.

Carli spoke first. "So, what happened out there?"

"I'm still trying to find a theory that fits," Percy said, "but it's almost like the Network just penalised us for going bare."

"Going bare?"

"Yes, sorry—when someone removes their projection to show their oldself, we call that 'going bare'."

"But how were we made to disappear? And why, for a few moments at a time, could I see people reappear and then disappear again?" she asked.

"I didn't see that? Were they donning trueselfs or were they bare?"

"Bare," she answered, "except for bags on their heads. We all seemed to reappear when we re-donned our trueselfs."

"So, it must be the Network," Percy concluded.

"I still don't understand. How could the Network hide someone? The Network can overlay on top, not take something away."

"Maybe it's generating a mask of whatever lies behind someone so they look transparent." The idea sounded plausible. If the Network can see behind someone, it could definitely make a mask to cause them to blend into the background.

"There's one way to know for sure," she said, looking at Percy. "Turn off your projection."

It was a bold request. It was like a stranger had just asked him to disrobe in public.

"Okay," he said.

A couple of gestures later, Percy's projection peeled away. Carli took in the bare self of a slightly built man. Despite the darkness in his eyes caused by his optics, they looked far wiser than his age, which Carli guessed to be mid-twenties. His angular face was soon covered by a paper bag mask, complete with a frowning face. It was still startling, but Carli kept her nerve.

"I got that message from the Network again, something called 'Omega Service'," he said.

"Let's hope you disappear then," Carli said. She knew how it sounded. She didn't care.

They waited up to a minute, but his oldself and masked face remained unchanged.

"Why isn't it working?" Percy asked.

Carli thought about it. She understood some of the algorithms used by the Network to apply a trueself over a citizen's face—there had been one module in her formal study to become a sculptor. She remembered how the Network overlaid a projection onto the person below, how it tracked the movement of the body down to the micrometre. It was all in the optics—they had two jobs: receive the reality of the world and reshape it into the reality of the Collective.

Carli moved away from the table and took a few steps to the side, her eyes fixed on Percy. His emotionless mask tracked her. Nothing had changed yet. She looked past him, moving further to the side so he was positioned more in her peripheral vision. With her third step, Percy disappeared.

A short gasp escaped her.

"What is it?" Percy's voice had changed, quiet and highly modulated, like he was another room away rather than just a few metres.

"You've disappeared," She said, "and your voice sounds strange. Must be active noise cancelling. The image from my optics is being used to construct an image of what is behind you and filter you out. The Network is trying to do the same thing with your voice."

"But you can't see behind me? How does it know?"

Carli looked around the room, considering the growing number of people in the bar. "There are more than 20 pairs of eyes in this room, maybe what they see is also used to reconstruct the image. Maybe two eyes spaced inches apart isn't enough."

She moved back to the table, and Percy's masked oldself reappeared. "It needs enough live information about what is behind you to create a plausible reconstruction."

"So, in the Areopagus, that's what happened? Enough eyes were looking around to allow the Network to edit people out?" Percy suggested.

"I think so. And on the transit."

"This isn't right. I don't see how the Network can do this," Percy said as he reapplied his trueself.

But for Carli, it was finally an acceptable answer to what she'd experienced on the transit only a few days ago. Clearly, the person she'd seen on the transit was simply not projecting a self, and the Network first chose to mask it before hiding him altogether. She couldn't help but feel a small sense of satisfaction.

Percy remained forlorn and distracted. The previous night, he'd been an evangelist. Now he'd been stopped in his tracks.

The energy of the group watching the display panel grew. An announcement was being made. Carli's optics provided a message:

<OVERSEER> A SPECIAL MEETING OF THE OVERSEER HAS BEEN CONVENED TO DISCUSS THE TERRORIST ATTACK AT THE PRAXIS POLICE DEPARTMENT HEADQUARTERS TODAY. COMMENCES IN 5 MINUTES.

"Terrorist attack?" Carli turned to Percy. "Are you going to join?"

"Yes," Percy said without hesitation.

"I'm going to watch from the display panel," she said. She left the table, unsure if Percy had followed. The crowd had grown over the last few minutes. All of them transfixed on the screen with looks of great concern. Some of them were masked, others were in PPD uniforms—police officers.

Only one person wasn't watching the screen—the man she'd seen earlier at the bar, a few metres away. A half-empty bottle of liquor in front of him and an empty crystal glass. Now she was closer, her optics provided a callout as someone with whom she had a basic trust relationship.

She changed her direction to approach him and was just about to say his name when she hesitated. *Someone who comes alone to a bar on a day like this probably doesn't want to be interrupted.*

She turned back to watch the panel—the meeting of the Overseer was commencing.

# 40

Liam wriggled the fingers on his left hand instinctively. He had no qualms about taking another life if he needed to, but doing so would make his escape from this mission effectively impossible. He didn't consider himself a particularly charismatic person but decided his best bet was to try and charm his way out of any kind of confrontation. His target was less than 30 metres away, behind a few more locked doors he hoped would open for him.

His employer had assigned him the credentials of a contractor called in to perform a check on some of the coolant systems in a device in one of the laboratories. It shouldn't matter if this person didn't recognise him, only that she recognized his credentials. He forced a smile and nod as they made eye contact. She stepped into his path and stopped.

"You're here to service the liquid helium exchange?" she asked, almost like it was an accusation.

"Uh, yes… Yes ma'am."

"Don't call me ma'am. Will you disengage the feedback injector before you take it offline this time?"

"What?"

"The feedback injector. The last time one of you clowns touched the helium exchange, you didn't disengage the injector, and it took us a day before we realised we'd compromised superfluidity. That's a day I can't get back."

Liam wasn't sure if he should relax, now that it was clear this person had not yet discovered him. He felt like arguing, but knew the conversation was still on a knife-edge, particularly considering he had no idea what a helium exchange was.

"I'm… I'm sorry about that. I'll make sure it doesn't happen again."

She glared at him. Liam tried to project as much warmth as he could muster.

"Fine. I've noted your moniker. If there are more problems, I'll know whose arse to kick."

She went on her way, making sure to keep eye contact until the last possible moment she passed him. *For such a small thing, she sure put on a solid attempt at intimidation*, Liam thought. The relief he felt was fleeting. He was still far from getting out of this without getting caught. *Or worse still.*

The virtual path in his optics led him through a few more access doors. Each corridor looked the same as the next. Had he been given a list of directions instead of a virtual path in his optics, he was sure he would have gotten lost ten times over. What appeared to be the final door lay in front of him, as banal and ordinary as any of those before them—except for the projected serial number, A17A and a sign posted above the door, with a title burned into a piece of polished wood that Liam couldn't decide was a projection or real wood. The sign read, "Head Chef".

He steeled himself with a few deep breaths and confirmed he was still alone. He checked the time, comparing it against the timeline he'd been given by his employer. He was still on schedule but needed to act soon. He didn't know who lay beyond the door, only that his employer had told him he wouldn't be a physical threat. Still, it did not hurt to take precautions—Liam hadn't survived this long by rushing headfirst into a contract, and even if this mission was the riskiest he'd ever accepted, it did not mean he should throw caution to the wind.

He messaged his employer as per his instructions, "About to enter the target's room."

He approached the door. It recognised his credentials and opened. The room was large and dark, lit only by some pulsing lights at ground level, which gave off a shimmering pattern to the high ceiling above. Cold, dry air enveloped his body like he'd stepped into a refrigerator. In the centre of the room was a capsule—some form of motorised wheelchair. Liam could not see a face, its occupant sat with their back towards him. The chair itself was bulky with blinking lights on the back providing the only other illumination in the room.

One of the room's walls appeared to have a glass window, but was tinted so dark he couldn't see anyone behind, nor if anyone there could see in. He tentatively approached the chair but was stopped by a quiet voice.

"Well, hello, old friend." It was the target. The voice was barely audible, a strained whisper.

"What are you doing?" another question. Liam wondered if the target would be able to call for help through the Network. It wasn't a question he wanted to wait around for, so he continued forward.

"Is this whole thing your fault?"

This stopped him in his tracks, like an electric shock. Who is this person? Have I been discovered? A wave of doubt washed over him.

"And right under my nose, too." The man let out a strange tut-tut sound.

Doubt morphed into confusion. That statement made no sense to him at all.

"But to see what you've become… Now it all makes sense."

Rather than approach from behind, Liam circled to see the person seated in the chair. His eyes were open, but dashing rapidly about the room like he was in some sort of dream. His mouth continued to speak more questions into the still, silent room.

Liam already feared he wouldn't escape this contract. Now that he realised his target was the oldest, most well-known, and richest person in all of Praxis almost brought him to his knees. The shock of looking his target in the face prodded a conscience he thought long dead.

"Aldus Goldstein." He said the name out loud and instantly regretted it.

Goldstein's eyes fixed on him. Liam had no choice but to act, for fear of a horde of security personnel pouring into the room at any instant. He activated the weapon in his left hand through a Network command and placed it on the man's chest. After only a few seconds, a message in his optics told him:

VIRUS DELIVERED.

He removed his hand. Goldstein's eyes had already closed. He heard strange beeps and whirs from the chair beneath him. To Liam, they sounded like they were issuing a faint cry for help, but he had no idea what they were for. He dreaded that any one of those flashing lights meant that that security was being alerted.

After a few more seconds, the projection concealing Goldstein's body disappeared to reveal the withered, tortured body beneath. Arms and legs disappeared, revealing bandaged stumps, amputated just above the elbows and knees respectively. The head and torso were pierced with tubes and wires running about like some sort of horrific experiment. Liam could now see the man's powdery white chest wasn't rising and falling—if this man wasn't dead, he sure should be. *This isn't murder*, he told himself, *this is a mercy kill.*

Standing over the motionless body, Liam was confident his work was done. Every second of waiting drew him closer to being caught. Adrenaline coursed through his body, with no outlet to burn it up. He messaged his employer and told him the job was now complete. He received no immediate response, but that wasn't completely out of character.

After counting the longest 60 seconds of his life, he turned and ran for the exit.

# 41

Good evening, citizens. Today is a dark day in the history of the Collective, perhaps the darkest in our nearly 100 years of peace and liberation." ArdentBlue stood to speak amongst the Council of Overseers. All talk in the bar settled to little more than a few murmurs from the crowd gathered around the display panel.

Seeing ArdentBlue stand defiantly amongst the group in her bold purple dress in this time of trouble gave Carli a sense of calm reassurance. Not only her outfit, but the way she stood and moved projected a sense of power. Carli knew her sculpted face better than anyone's. She'd spent days sculpting every single pore and strand of hair. The movement and contraction of every muscle cell in response to the movement of her oldself below. She spoke towards the virtual camera in the centre of the room—the seated virtual presence representing the totality of the Collective.

ArdentBlue continued, "As you may be aware, a series of explosions have impacted the PPD headquarters in Praxis Central. Those explosions are believed to have originated from an unknown number of telepresence robots on the 12th floor of the PPD headquarters. We are now able to confirm a total of thirteen fatalities, comprising twelve PPD officers and one civilian consultant. Twenty-nine others have received some form of medical attention, and eight of those would be classified as being in a serious condition."

A low chorus of concern emanated from the group watching the panel. Carli saw two men console each other and another's head drop down to their hands.

"Another explosion occurred at a recharge station a few hundred meters away, with only minor injuries to two citizens. It has only been a few hours, but our investigators are more than confident this was not some form of malfunction, nor some kind of accident, but instead, a deliberate and coordinated attack on the Police Department, more specifically on the Network Crimes division.

Carli recognized that name—Network Crimes. The division Detective Briggs belonged to. She turned back to the bar where she'd seen him earlier, but his seat was now empty.

"It would be fair to categorise that, not only is this attack on the PPD but also on the rights and liberties of the Collective of Praxis as a whole. This is organised terrorism—a deliberate assault on the very systems that underpin our freedoms and reality. We have asked one of the senior PPD officers to provide more details on this attack." She nodded to someone out of view, "Deputy Commissioner, Moya?"

The perspective of the display panel changed to show a tall, muscular man with a chiselled jaw in full dress uniform standing from one of the other speaking positions in the Overseer chamber. Carli listened along as this officer provided additional detail, including evidence collected at the scene and the believed sequence of events. Carli found him confident and reassuring.

He concluded with a final statement. "Rest assured, all available resources of the Praxis Police Department will be brought to bear to restore order across the Collective and seek justice for everyone involved."

"Bullshit..." A croaky voice startled Carli, and she turned to her left.

Detective Briggs stood next to her, his posture stooped, his shoulders rounded forward. He was unmasked to Carli but had directed the comment towards the panel. A few people turned in the direction of the comment and nodded towards him.

"Are you OK, Detective?" Carli asked

He looked at her. His projection couldn't conceal a redness around his eyes, nor the pungent odour of alcohol on his breath.

His reply was sloppy, "No, Miss Dawes, I am not."

After other Overseers spoke, the view returned to ArdentBlue, who spoke again. It seemed she'd been charged with the responsibility of wrapping up the shared expression of grief. She projected resolve in the face of a tragic event. But just as her monologue was nearing its high point, she stopped. Her eyes darted around the room and she briefly spoke to one of the other Overseers.

Murmurs rolled over the group. Someone asked, "What's happened now?"

Soon, Overseer ArdentBlue appeared to regain her composure. She looked directly into the virtual camera relaying the meeting to the display panel on the wall of the bar.

"Citizens of the Collective. It would seem the darkness set aside for us on this most terrible of days has only grown ever deeper. We have only now, just received this sad news from Augmosis. Less than thirty minutes ago, Aldus Goldstein, retired CEO of Augmosis and the last founder of our Collective, has passed from this reality into the next."

This news inflicted a complete silence on the people in the bar. Carli put her hand to her mouth. The earlier news had been saddening, but news that the last elder of the Collective had died affected her more. She'd learned the exploits of the founders of the Collective since she was a child. She'd studied some of the algorithms personally written by Aldus Goldstein as part of her sculptor certifications. To hear the news of his death was like losing a childhood hero.

"Aldus Goldstein was 132—the oldest citizen in Praxis. He appears to have died quietly and peacefully in his mobility chair, in his research lab at Augmosis. Friends, we all owe our reality, and even the preservation of humanity, to Aldus Goldstein. On this saddest of days, let us instead choose to remember his unparalleled legacy. I'm sure, at some time soon, we will gather together to mourn the greatest of Citizens and to remember all that he has done to shape the reality we all take for granted. But for now, all I can think of is to remember him and the fallen officers of the Praxis Police Department with a minute's silence."

With that, the other Overseers stood together as well as the others in the Overseer chamber. Those seated in the bar followed suit. One raised a glass and proclaimed in a loud but wavering voice, "To fallen comrades!"

Carli honoured the silence, with her eyes focused on the display panel. The viewport of the panel left the perspective of the central presence and floated around the room so the whole room could be taken in.

"This isn't right." Briggs was mumbling under his breath. "It's got to be connected."

Carli looked at Briggs out of the corner of her eye. She picked out a few other muttered words, including "coincidence". She looked back at the panel. The long minute seemed near its end, and the virtual camera shifted to a position that framed only the overseers and the virtual presence in its centre.

Carli took in the virtual presence. Millions of trueselfs projected over its motionless form. A rainbow of self-expression that changed every fraction of a second. Those changes should have been distracting. Instead swelled and fell away in harmony with the emotion in the room.

And in the mourning, in the silence where the Collective remembered those who had designed and shaped reality and those who had given their lives to protect and serve it, she was certain she saw the presence bow its head.

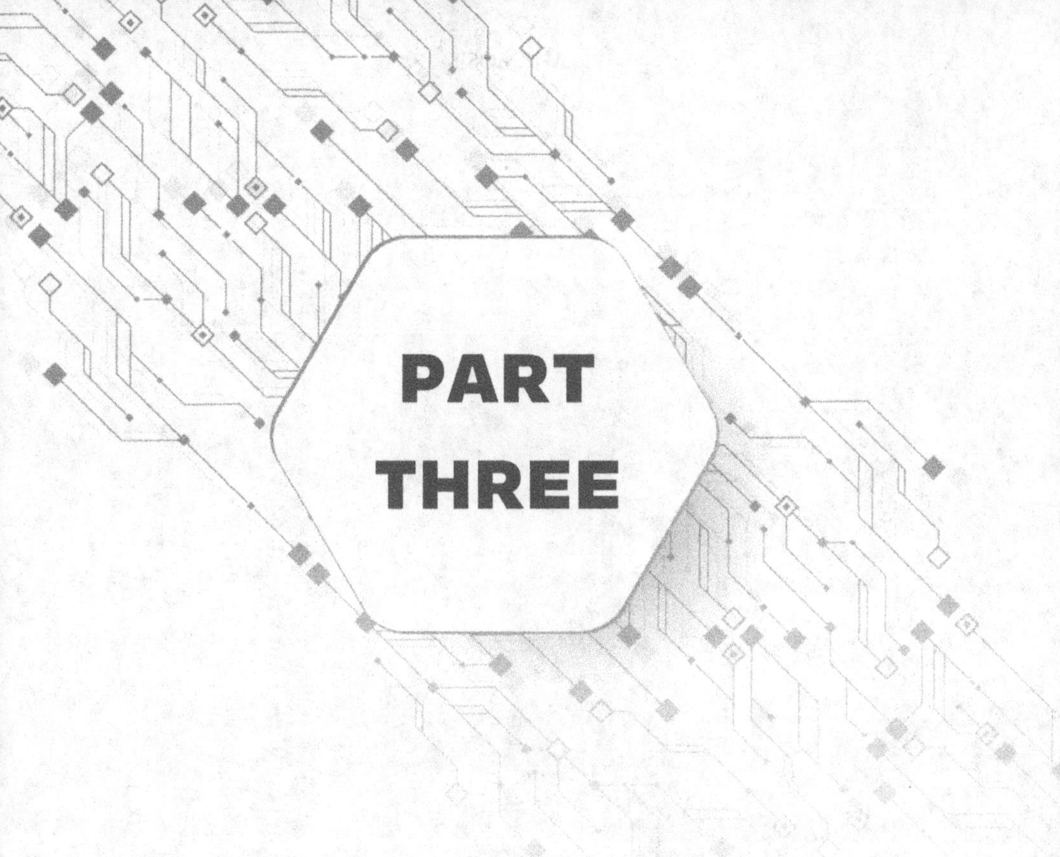

# PART THREE

*"The Collective is a dynamic constant. It is the homogenous distillation of an inherent heterogeneity."*

Olena Linnek, Co-Founder

**42**

Carli slipped through the agitated crowd back to her table. It seemed the Council of Overseers' motions of solidarity had done little to quell their anger.

She considered everything she'd seen, trying to reconcile this with what had happened earlier at the Areopagus and said aloud, "It can't be a coincidence."

"Nothing's a coincidence. It's all linked. Augmosis. Goldstein. Alvarez. Korb1k. *Anneke…*" Briggs had followed her from the bar area.

"How are you feeling, Detective…"

He interjected, "Just Briggs." His wide eyes scanned some of the room before resting an empty glass on her table. "Where's your friend?"

She was surprised that Briggs had noticed them together. "I don't know."

A teeper approached their table and placed another short glass of spirits in front of Detective Briggs. A mechanised voice stated, "This will be your final alcoholic beverage served this hour, Citizen." Briggs released his empty glass, grabbed the new one, brought it to his lips, and paused a moment before downing it in one go.

Carli looked on with compassion. This officer who only yesterday seemed so focused and in control now seemed unhinged.

"Are you OK, Det… Briggs?"

He didn't answer straight away, staring at his hands and the now empty glass. He exhaled slowly. "No. No, I'm not."

"Did you… Did you lose anybody? In the explosion?"

He stared out into the nothingness, leaning heavily on a chair to his side for support. Carli checked the time—she should have been back at work almost two hours ago, but the transit had been shut down on account of the terrorist attack. She figured she had nowhere else to be, so she pulled over one of the high stools and sat at the table opposite Briggs. For a moment, his eyes met hers before they looked away to a void beyond.

A tone alerted her to a message, it was Percy.

<WOLLEMI> CARLI—I HAD TO LEAVE. I THINK A LOT OF THE PEOPLE IN THE BAR ARE POLICE OFFICERS.

*Why would that matter?* She thought.

Briggs's head dropped down, and he mumbled something into his arm. Carli received another alert that roused a groan from the rest of the room.

<PPD-ALERT> ALL PRAXIS CENTRAL TRANSIT SERVICES WILL BE SUSPENDED UNTIL 7:00 AM TOMORROW. PLEASE SECURE TEMPORARY ACCOMMODATION.

Carli groaned with them. *Now I'm stuck here. Can't get back to work. Can't get home.*

She watched Briggs—both of his hands gripped the bar stool tight, his head dropped between them. He let out a frustrated groan. He staggered to the side, pulling the chair with him, and crashed ungracefully to the floor.

Carli leapt to help him but was too late. The best she could do was move the fallen chair away from him and turn him onto his side. *This poor man*, she thought.

She composed a reply to Percy.

<MALVINAHOFFMAN> ARE YOU STILL NEARBY?

<WOLLEMI> YES, I'M JUST OUTSIDE. THE HUB'S BEEN LOCKED DOWN.

<MALVINAHOFFMAN> COME BACK IN AND GIVE ME A HAND. LET'S FIND SOMEWHERE TO WAIT THIS THING OUT.

"Let's get you home, Detective," she said, cradling his head.

His dark, puffy eyes looked up at her. She saw anger and shame. He turned his head away in her hands. She held him for a minute, his body shaking. Barely a stranger, but honourable. His pain was deep and personal. The man who had previously seemed so confident and sure, the man who had helped her when she felt vulnerable, was now broken.

Percy entered the doorway. "Give me a hand."

"So, who is this guy to you?" Percy slumped in an expensive-looking sofa, exhausted from escorting Briggs to Lesante Tower Hotel two blocks away, "I only ask 'cause I don't usually pay for temporary lodgings for complete strangers."

"Complete strangers that are police officers, you mean?" Carli said. "And you didn't have to pay, it's not like I don't have the bits to pay for a room even if this place is a little more expensive than my usual standards. Maybe a more important question is why you are so afraid of being seen with a police officer?"

"It's not that I'm afraid—just wary. A few of my friends say they've been targeted by police recently—called a cultist or an anarchist. Some were brought in for questioning by ONI jerks hiding behind private PPD pseudonyms."

"And who exactly are your friends? I should have asked you before—even if the glitch at the Areopagus wasn't your fault, I think I deserve to know who you are."

He chewed the side of his mouth. "I thought I'd already told you?"

"No. You told me about a conspiracy of concealment—that Augmosis was a puppet master and we are just all slaves drinking the Collective Kool-Aid."

"I didn't say, 'Kool-aid'…" he said. "My friends and I: we call ourselves 'The Wakers'. We started as just a small group that liked to discuss philosophy, but we soon began to doubt if our Collective was truly our saviour or just another master. We have grown in members a lot in the last six months, and we have plans to raise someone to the Council of Overseers to bring about change, but for that, we need to grow more support."

"So, you are trying to recruit me?"

"In a fashion. The system needs to be changed—without support, our voice will never be heard."

"You've decided that the Collective is broken and what? It needs to be turned off?"

Percy frowned and gained confidence, "If that whole charade at the Areopagus didn't convince you something in the Collective is completely broken, then I don't know what will. That's proof, as far as I'm concerned. We do something to express our independence, and the system fights back—completely cutting us out of reality. Surely you see it, too? No—not see it, feel it. The evidence is just confirming what my gut's known all along."

She felt an immediate conflict. *The Collective can't be broken? It's an ideal—an aspiration that not only kept the remnant of humanity from being destroyed a century ago but has sustained it since.* And yet, everything she'd experienced in the last few days said otherwise.

# 43

Briggs sat up and rubbed his head. It throbbed—a combination of the wound on his forehead reinforced by a deeper ache resonating like a bass drum in time with his heartbeat. He suffered through a dry swallow before finding a quiet stranger sitting opposite him.

"Where am I?" he asked.

"Hotel. Lesante Tower." The information didn't seem to give Briggs much. The man continued, "Carli and I brought you here last night. Transits were still offline when we left the bar, so none of us could get home. This was the closest place with three sleeping cells."

"Oh." He looked past the door of his small sleeping cell into the living space. The window scape overlooked a manicured lawn framed by date palms. Beyond that, a rocky outcrop bordered a distant ocean. It was a stunning view, and looking back across the room at the wood-coloured wall panels embellished with marble told Briggs that it would not have been cheap. The hotel room was as big as his apartment in Boulder. "Nice place."

"Thanks."

"I'm sorry, I've forgotten your name." Briggs could have pulled that information from the Network, but he'd shut everything down in the bar the night before. He rose from the cell and moved to the living space.

"Percy. I'm a friend of Carli's"

"Carli…" Briggs said to himself before recognition crossed his face. "Carli Dawes." The door to the bathroom was closed. "Shower?"

"Yes." Percy gestured with one of the coffee cups. "Black?"

"Sure."

Briggs received the cup from Percy, who still didn't make eye contact. He sat himself as far from Percy as possible and drank in silence. As the fog cleared a little, he felt an awkward shame. He remembered only some of the things he'd said the previous night. It had not been his finest moment, but in all honesty, many had been far worse. On some of those occasions, he'd awoken on the street or had transitioned from alcohol to something stronger. Once, he'd woken to discover he'd made a fool of himself in front of Captain Hagen after she'd firmly rejected his drunken flirtations.

*And now she's dead.*

The pain of losing her was compounded by his knowing that she would have been disappointed with how he'd responded. It had been eighteen months since his last relapse. Now, alone and stripped of a badge, he was empty and without purpose. Of all the circumstances to succumb to his addiction, his current ones were the most understandable. Some might say, justified. He wanted nothing but to get away from these people he barely knew, find a quiet drinking establishment, and start all over again.

He planned to leave but thought he should at least wait to thank Carli for looking out for him the previous evening.

His best mental reconstruction of yesterday afternoon's events started to crystallise into something coherent. His case, the explosion in Network Crimes, followed by the death of Aldus Goldstein—it all seemed too close together to be a mere coincidence. It was a mystery Briggs was ideally suited to solve. But his short temper had ruined that opportunity before it even began. *Without me, there would be no justice for Anneke.*

He wanted to restore his connection to the Network, to try and communicate with some of his other contacts in the PPD to get more information. Maybe if he could understand more about the explosions and any recovered evidence, he could find an answer. But the number of officers he had a good relationship with was small, and since a list of the deceased officers hadn't yet been released, he wasn't even sure who was still alive to be contacted. By now, news of his outburst and subsequent suspension would also be well known. Deputy Moya would have made sure of that.

The interview with Alverez had yielded nothing—Briggs was certain he knew more than he was letting on. Even with a projection, the look on his face told Briggs that Alvarez was worried about Korb1k and what he was capable of.

Briggs also thought there was more to the West Praxis storage facility than Briggs and the PPD had so far uncovered.

But thinking about the case meant nothing if he couldn't act on it. He was defeated.

"What are you thinking about?" Percy stood with his back to the wall holding his coffee, looking out to the coastal scape, before turning towards Briggs.

"Work."

"Carli said you're some kind of detective?"

"Yes. Network Crimes."

This caused Percy to pause. "ONI?"

Briggs understood the reservation—for the conspiracy theorists, ONI was the "G-Man" of the Collective.

"No."

"I suppose you'll need to get back to work. To help with all this explosion business?"

Each question grated. Briggs told himself they were innocent enough, but he didn't plan on sharing news of his suspension with this stranger. "Sure."

"I read up on you while you were… sleeping. You did a bust in West Praxis yesterday? Network says millions of bits worth of Old-World tech and other artifacts were collected. Even an original Picasso and a Banksy."

He didn't know those last two names but guessed they represented something valuable from the Old-World. He hadn't seen the full inventory of the property recovered from Alvarez's safe house—but wasn't surprised if it included Old-World relics.

"Do you think that has something to do with the explosion?"

He did, but he said nothing.

"I also looked up the news reports on the Areopagus. Couldn't find a single story."

Briggs didn't try to hide his confusion. "What happened there?"

"Something in the Network decided we all deserved to be edited out of reality". The voice came from the other side of the room where Carli had just emerged from the bathroom. Either her real hair was showing and still wet, or she'd altered her projection to make it look like it was. Her outfit was more casual than Briggs had seen her in before, and for just a moment, he noticed how attractive she was. It was apparent from Percy's expression that he thought the same thing.

Still confused, he deflected by asking more questions—a helpful strategy as a detective and even more helpful to keep the spotlight away from himself.

"What do you mean, edited out of reality?"

"We were all standing listening to the speaker. As part of our free choice, we decided to remove our trueself projections as a celebration of our unique beauty." Carli spoke like a poet. "First, all of our oldselfs were masked with a paper bag with a frowning face on it, then..."

"Then what?"

"We all disappeared," Percy completed the thought for Carli, trying to be useful.

Briggs frowned. "Sorry, I don't follow."

Carli continued, "The Network, something called the "OmegaService" alerted us that our oldselfs were being sanitised—whatever that means. The Network was able to filter us out. As soon as we re-enabled our trueselfs, the filter was removed, and we returned to reality. Now that I've thought about it and we did a few more tests, the Network is just reconstructing the environment around the physical person to make them disappear."

This seemed very strange to Briggs and not something he'd ever heard of before. He was engaged now—at least enough to explore what this might mean. It might not last long, but the more he processed the new information, the less he felt like leaving.

"Can you show me?"

They went through the same process, with Percy removing his projection only to have it quickly masked with a paper bag. He positioned himself in the centre of the room, placing both Briggs and Carli 90 degrees apart and after about twenty seconds, he disappeared from the room completely.

"You're still here?" Briggs asked.

"Yes." The voice was quiet and muffled, sounding like it was at the end of a distant pipe.

As though reading his thoughts, Carli offered, "I think it's active noise cancellation. Doesn't work perfectly since sound can be harder to mask."

Percy reapplied his trueself and reappeared, standing a few metres to the right of where he'd disappeared. He chuckled at their surprise.

Briggs considered this new information but couldn't work out how it fit or if it fit at all. His head told him it was just an odd coincidence of timing. His gut disagreed.

"I know that the situation—the explosion is probably your most important thing right now, but this doesn't sit well with me. Having the Network override our own choices seems important too." Carli said.

"You may be right." Briggs mulled this over. Part of him still wanted to escape and drown his sorrows one more time. But he knew there was something bigger to resolve. Something was drawing him away from the darkness he so desperately longed for, even if it was just momentary.

Briggs couldn't get a solid read on Carli's friend, Percy. He seemed aloof but invested in whatever was happening. His detective brain decided to shortcut the 'get to know you period' by deliberately trying to put him off balance.

"So, you're part of the Wakers?"

It worked. Percy recoiled as though he'd been slapped.

"What? What do you mean?"

"Well, if you were at the Areopagus and Carli was there at your request, you must be one of them. I've had a few PPD briefings indicating growing concern. Organising protests. Civil disobedience. Network hacking."

Percy's eyes widened, and he looked towards Carli for help. No one had mentioned the Wakers, but the story from the Areopagus fit what he'd heard before. Percy's awkward response confirmed his theory. The revelation was of little value, but he took grim pleasure in watching Percy squirm for a few more uncomfortable moments. On a better day, he would have let him off the hook with a wink and a wry smile. Today, he couldn't care less and let it hang in the air like an unpleasant smell. He decided to push a little deeper.

"Maybe the Wakers were responsible for the PPD explosion? Maybe they were investigating your little band of merry men, and you guys pushed back."

Carli interrupted on Percy's shocked behalf, "Surely not?"

"Come on? I shouldn't have to answer that, but fine—no, the Wakers are not responsible for bombing the PPD headquarters," Percy replied.

"But you are one of them?" Briggs confirmed. "Maybe it's a big organisation. Maybe there are others there doing things they shouldn't. Maybe you volunteer a few names of the members, *just to confirm*."

Percy looked at Carli, exasperated. "Carli, your friend here's being a dick."

Carli looked to Briggs with an expression that said, 'What the hell?'

Briggs knew he was being unreasonable and didn't care. He wasn't backing away, but he respected Carli enough to at least give it a rest.

"I think you'll find that in response to a direct attack, a few things might change around here for the PPD. Rather than taking it out of commission, I expect we'll probably be given a wider latitude than usual to investigate. I expect members and associates of groups of concern will have anonymity revoked—anyone with any beef with PPD will be investigated."

Percy tensed. "There are laws that protect anonymity. Old laws—old as the Collective."

"But special measures can be applied in extreme circumstances."

"Like what?" Carli asked.

"Like terrorism," Briggs replied. "Under terrorist threat, the Overseer can formally declare a state of emergency and override the laws of the Collective for seven days by a two-thirds vote."

"That's never happened before," Percy said.

"No one's ever had the balls to blow up an entire police division," Briggs said through a clenched jaw. "You can bet your arse the PPD will ask for every power in the world to bring the culprits to justice."

In Percy's gaze, Briggs saw only agitation. Not defiance. The heuristic algorithm in his brain concluded that Percy was probably not part of the story. Maybe not trustworthy, but at the least, not a threat. Beating him up any more was merciless and unjustified, so he backed away.

"Did they ask for it? Did the PPD ask the Overseer to declare a state of emergency?" Briggs asked. Carli's eyes dashed back and forth—accessing the Network.

"Not yet, but there is another meeting of the Overseer at 3:00 pm today," she said.

"Then that's when it will happen."

**44**

Carli scowled at Briggs and told him he was out of line for going so hard at Percy. Briggs grunted in reluctant acceptance and offered him a forced apology as Percy took himself to the refresher.

"Sorry, kid. It hasn't been a good 24 hours."

With Percy gone, Carli felt compelled to check on Briggs further: "Did you lose anyone in the bombing?"

He didn't make eye contact and simply said, "Yes." He deflected quickly. "So you and Percy?"

"I only met him two days ago. I think he's harmless."

"And the Wakers? It's not the first time I've heard that name this week."

"No idea. There are thousands of virtual communities across the Network. Its very nature fosters connection for all kinds of reasons—sports, interests, spirituality…"

"And conspiracy. I've seen these groups before—each idea and theory, no matter how ridiculous, gets amplified and reinforced. Conspiracy thrives in closed communities that think they're more enlightened than everyone else."

"Maybe that's true for the Wakers too, but over the last few days, I have felt challenged to see the world a different way—a more beautiful way," Carli said.

"Some people might call that anarchy."

Percy returned, wearing the same concerned look Briggs had seen when questioning him earlier. To be honest, she still hadn't made up her mind about Percy, but she knew something was happening across the Network that seemed wrong. And yet, Percy hadn't actually offered any kind of solution.

"These are truly strange times. If only we had the wisdom of Aldus Goldstein to guide us," Carli said. Percy pulled a disgusted face.

"You're not a fan, Percy?"

"I respect his intelligence and longevity. But he is, or he was part of the machine that restricts our freedom to be who we want and to see the world the way it truly is. The history books might consider him a hero. I think for every technological advancement he pioneered, humanity gave up more and more of itself. We have been simplified to the point where what's left of the human race behaves no differently to livestock."

"Explain?" she asked.

"We work to earn bits, only to spend them on intangible things like designer crafts and fake experiences. We've wired an endless stream of content straight into our brains. We prefer a virtual existence over the physical. In a time when humanity should be pushing outside the city domes to rebuild the shattered planet around us, we are withering away. The Augmosis dream of liberty and freedom is nothing more than an illusion to keep us locked inside. We are just cattle—and instead of a ring through the nose we have silicon in our eyes and ears."

"You're more than welcome to take a wander outside if you want," Briggs said. "I can show you the door. There's nothing out there but rock and dust."

Percy's eyes narrowed. "Who's to say that isn't just part of the illusion?"

"I am—I've been out there. I've got the suntan to go with it. There's a reason scavs send teepers out there to collect their Old-World relics—cause the air is still toxic. Even the soil is warm to touch in places."

Carli had watched these two beat their chests long enough. "Anyway—what I'm saying is, if something is hiding us from reality when we remove our projections then I think we dearly need Goldstein's wisdom. I still can't believe he's gone, but I suppose it was just his time."

"Maybe," Briggs said, "or maybe the same thing waging war against us took him out, too."

This caught Percy by surprise. "Seriously? The guy was like a thousand years old. You accuse me of conspiracy theories?"

"Normally, I might agree. But I've seen more strange events in the last week than I have all my career. I don't think it is a coincidence."

"There is definitely something strange going on," Carli conceded, "but why would someone want to kill Goldstein?"

"I haven't had time to think that through fully, but if something or someone was working within the Network—trying to take over or trying to influence things, the two biggest obstacles would be Augmosis and Network Crimes: ONI specifically. Then there's the unlikely option…"

"What's that?" Percy asked.

"That I am the common denominator—that Goldstein was killed because he was *informing* on my case, and Network Crimes was targeted because that's my division. The only reason I was safe was because I was on another floor of the building at the time."

"Surely not?" Carli offered.

"I think it's unlikely too," Briggs returned. "No one else knew what progress I had made on the case—unless they have access to personal stores or they've bugged my optics."

"I'm sure Augmosis would have their back doors in the system to spy on whomever they wanted," Percy added.

Briggs stayed silent. Carli redirected the discussion. "So do you need to get back to work, detective? You're probably being missed back at the PPD. Maybe our story will help everyone else to solve the crime?"

Briggs hesitated before answering, "That's going to be difficult since I'm presently… *on leave.*"

The conversation died for a moment, then Briggs added. "I *do* need to check back in. I've been offline since yesterday. Maybe something's changed." He stood and moved away from her and Percy. Carli noticed him trace his finger along the wall as he walked, while his other hand was splayed ready at his side. She wondered if he was still unwell from last night's *adventure*.

"What about you, Carli? Do you need to get to work?" Percy asked.

"No, I'm on standard shifts," she replied. "The office usually shuts down for the weekend, though I usually put in a few hours from home if I'm behind. Not that I can get there with the transit still locked down."

"Yeah, I don't remember that ever happening before."

They continued in small talk, but Carli found herself continuing to wonder about the last few days' events. She felt the need to do something and felt frustrated to be sitting around waiting for the world to catch up with her.

She scanned some more news feeds issued since yesterday. The same police spokesperson made a statement assuring the public that there was no risk from teepers, perhaps in response to news reports of teepers and teeper stations being vandalised across Praxis.

Other reports were limited and inconclusive. It was frustrating to have direct access to so much information and yet not know. Just as loud as the information about what happened were the opinions and commentary from influencers across the Network. They ranged from conspiracy theories that the PPD had made the explosions up or was at least exaggerating the reports. Other groups came out in support of the police by wearing specially crafted armbands as part of their projection.

So many voices. So many opinions.

A blip in her phonics alerted her to an important notification

<PPD-ALERT> ALL TRANSIT SERVICES HAVE RESUMED. PPD HEADQUARTERS REMAIN CLOSED FOR THE FORESEEABLE FUTURE, BUT ALL PPD SERVICES REMAIN AT FULL CAPACITY. PLEASE BANK AND REPORT ANY UNUSUAL BEHAVIOUR.

Percy made a celebratory sound opposite her — clearly, he'd read the same message. Having the transit open was like breathing fresh air again. She didn't know what to do next, but she felt like just saying goodbye and returning home to Archibald. Whatever was happening was bigger than her, and while she wanted to help, she couldn't think how she could be useful.

Briggs rejoined them. "I'm sorry, but I need to ask a big favour. Of both of you."

Carli saw a different look in his eyes. A look of focus and determination, the same as she had last seen when he spoke to her and Deniz at NuSculpt.

"What is it?" Carli asked.

Briggs was resolute. "I need you to help me catch a killer."

**45**

T his photo's not much to go off," Percy said.

Briggs sighed. "I believe that's what the guy looks like unmasked—I retrieved it from someone's banked footage. But don't worry about that for now—he will be projecting something completely different when you see him. We're just looking for his moniker."

"Basil-something?"

He didn't reply. Briggs' radar told him that it was Percy trying to push back after getting grilled earlier. *That's fine* he thought, *I deserved it.* To be honest, Briggs was surprised that Percy agreed in the first place, but Carli managed to persuade him.

They'd moved from their hotel room to a room full of immersion rigs on the ground level of the hotel. Many were occupied, but they managed to find a cluster together with a little more privacy. Percy had offered to pay for Carli's, but she declined.

From these rigs, he could lease any teeper across all of Praxis: with the right credentials or for the right price. Briggs had hurried them straight from their room only minutes before. The window of opportunity was limited.

He'd explained his thinking on the way, leaving out most of the important parts, but giving enough to convince them both to help him.

Briggs had turned off all his Network notifications immediately after he'd been escorted out of the PPD holding area. Now reconnected, he'd found a message from a PPD watch service tracking transit scans of the handful of monikers still on his list from the previous day. Moya's suspension order mustn't yet have been lodged at the time, which would have shut the watch down.

229

But there it was:

99.12.24 CD 12:04PM: CITIZEN 'BASILICUS' MONIKER SCANNED LEAVING HUB, "PRAXIS CENTRAL"

99.12.24 CD 12:21PM: CITIZEN 'BASILICUS' MONIKER SCANNED ENTERING HUB, "AUGMOSIS"

He checked the public record. Goldstein was pronounced dead at 12:50 PM. The transits were locked down at 1:01 PM. If it took Basilicus 29 minutes to get into Augmosis and kill Goldstein, he would not have had enough time to leave before the transit shut down.

*Basilicus is still at Augmosis, right now*, Briggs concluded. And now that the transit has reopened, he'll want to be the first person out of there.

Briggs checked the transit timetable and made some assumptions on the amount of time to walk from the nearest hotel within Augmosis to the transit station. *I've got 9 minutes*, he concluded.

Carli had already eagerly jumped into her rig. Percy reluctantly climbed into the one next to her, smelling the haptic gloves to confirm they met his approval. "Why us, Detective? Why can't the PPD sort this out?"

"We don't know each other very well, and I'm honestly grateful for you helping me out—both of you. But I don't have any confidence this guy isn't fully plugged into what the PPD is doing. Even if I had the power to raise a warrant or BOLO, I'm worried this guy's going to get a tip-off. I probably haven't earned the right to ask you to trust me just yet, but if we don't do this, bad things are going to happen."

"I trust you," Carli offered.

"So long as you're not getting us into any trouble." Percy looked at the empty rig next to him. "Won't you be joining us?"

*A fair question.* "I can't. These things make me sick. Once each of you've connected, share your stream with me and I'll watch along. If I have to, I'll join once we've spotted him. Remember, you're just observing from a distance. You're not engaging. Make sure you stay masked."

Briggs received Carli's connection invitation, followed by Percy's. He accepted both and overlaid them on a nearby wall. He could have watched either in a virtual window or even fully replaced his own vision with one of the feeds, but he knew from experience that such a thing would make him sick almost instantly. And he still felt unwell from the evening before.

With a few gestures, Percy's viewport switched from a view of the ceiling above them to a view outside the ground-level entry to the Augmosis transit station. Briggs saw a first-person view of the teeper undocking itself from the charging station, looking around and then moving inside the station at Briggs' direction.

People across the station appeared to be predominantly moving towards the platforms rather than away. Clearly many people had been caught out by the lockdown

"Are you in yet, Carli?" Percy asked.

"Yes, I'm at the top of the entrance already. Can't see him."

"There's lots of bodies here, how can we be sure he hasn't left already?"

Briggs replied. "Transit's only been open for six minutes. I can't imagine him wanting to be the first guy on the train and he would have needed time to make it from wherever he'd been holed up. Still, I need you to get in line and start checking everyone."

Percy joined the growing queue to enter the station, turning his head from side to side as he scanned the moniker of any citizen within five meters of him. That process took about half a second of sustained eye contact.

"Careful Percy, scan with your eyes, not with your head. Don't want to scare him off."

"This is inefficient," Percy said.

"I know. On-duty PPD officers are given a longer range."

Briggs switched to Carli's feed, who was doing the same from a second position. He could tell there were scanning gaps between the two of them but had no alternative.

Percy's feed lingered a little longer on one citizen with the projection of a female elf creature. The outfit she wore barely contained her projected breasts.

"That's not him Percy. Move on."

"You were looking at the elf lady, weren't you?" Carli asked. Percy grunted.

"Best if you can keep moving towards the platform. The next transit should arrive in two minutes. Try and get towards the front."

"That won't make me popular," Percy said.

"Popularity's overrated. Carli, can you come back down the tunnel and take a position scanning people from within the terminal?"

Percy moved through the crowd. Even when piloted, a domestic teeper maintained safety tolerances in proximity to other citizens. Though they were around the same weight as an average male, you did not want one stepping on your foot or knocking shoulders with you. Briggs observed that it caused Percy to move slower through the crowd than he'd expected. Rather than pushing towards the front, the crowd was slowly sliding past him.

Percy's teeper cleared the crowd and now pushed into the larger main concourse that led the two platforms, each heading in opposite directions around the city circle. "Which way do you want me to go?"

"Hang there, that's a good spot in case he makes it past Carli."

Locking on to a citizen with the moniker, "BasilFaulty2", Percy let out a muted celebration before realizing his mistake.

"Close," Briggs said.

"Not sure I like having you in my head," Percy said. "There's no teeper stations down here. If you log in, you're not going to be able to get a teeper from down here. Nearest one is back where we started."

"That won't be a problem. If he's coming your way, you can disconnect and I will lease your teeper when it's on its way back to the dock," Briggs said.

"Isn't there a risk you'll lose him in that time?"

"Why's that?"

"There's a 20 second reconnect option which locks a teeper out from being hired by someone else in case the original operator disconnected by accident"

"Are you sure?" Briggs asked.

Carli replied, "Yes, Percy's right".

"I didn't plan on that. Police teepers don't do that, nor police hires of domestic teepers. Keep looking, I'll figure out something else. I'm killing your video feeds, so just tell me what you see and send me your audio feeds."

"Can't you just window it up?" Percy asked.

"No," Briggs jumped into the next control rig and started the connection process. "Just keep scanning, and I'll join you below. Carli, can you go down towards the concourse where Percy is? An extra pair of eyes there would be good."

"On it."

With a few gestures, Briggs triggered a micro dosage of medication from his lifesuit to soften the impact of using the rig on his vestibular system. It was usually only 10% effective, but he hoped it might give him a few extra minutes piloting the teeper. As he connected, his world dissolved to reappear from the same teeper station he'd seen from Percy's feed.

He heard Percy's voice from the rig next to him. "Um, some guy's looking at me?"

"Is it our guy?"

"No. He's coming towards me. Oh crap."

*"Citizen Hayward. PPD Officer Formosa. What is your business here?"*

"I um… Sorry sir, I'm waiting for a friend."

*"Why are you piloting a teeper inside a transit station?"*

Briggs thought that was a very reasonable question. "Say your friend got stuck in Augmosis overnight and you are checking to see if he is OK."

He heard Percy relay the information. The officer didn't respond. He added, "I didn't know I was doing anything wrong."

*"Does your friend have a name?"*

"What should I say?" Percy asked privately, muting his voice to the teeper.

No answer came. Carli interjected, "I see him!"

Briggs' teeper was now only starting to descend towards the concourse. He figured he was two minutes away and already feeling sick. "Are you sure?"

"Yes, average height, male. Wearing a generic self. White linen shirt looks custom. Carrying a canvas satchel."

"I'm coming to you." It was Percy speaking, but Briggs heard his voice over the feed rather than from the rig next to him.

*"You're not going anywhere, sunshine,"* said the officer.

"I um… she's just over there, officer," Percy said,

*"DON'T MOVE! HANDS OUTSTRETCHED!"*

"What's going on?" Briggs said.

Carli must have also been viewing Percy's feed as she replied, "He's raised his gun at Percy."

"You're burned, Percy. Disconnect."

"Won't I be in some sort of trouble?"

"No, I'll get it sorted out."

"Can't we just get these guys to chase the bad guy?"

"Not enough time to convince them".

Percy addressed the officer, "I haven't done anything wrong. I'm out." He disconnected.

Carli gave another progress report. "Ten spots ahead of me. Heading down to the platform. Looks like he's going clockwise round the loop."

"Keep on him. But don't get too close."

Briggs's teeper was too slow, and every step made him more nauseous. *I'm not going to make it.*

# 46

I've lost him," Carli said to the group. "He must've boarded the transit to Praxis Central. Or he can pull the same disappearing act."

Briggs replied, "Did you see him board?" his voice was strained, like he was short of breath and came through her phonics rather than from the rig next to her.

"Not specifically? Where are you?"

"I'm on foot—trying to make it to the Praxis Central station and cut him off." Each word was forced between breaths.

It took Carli a moment to understand. A chime announced that the transit's doors were closing. She turned back to the closest door and made a snap decision. "I'm getting on."

"That's not a good idea," Briggs said, but it didn't matter. Carli sliced her way through the line and made it through the transit doors as they closed. An alert in her augments advised her that failure to return the teeper to the same hub would incur an additional fee. She ignored it and looked around the carriage. None of them was Basilicus.

The carriage was full, maybe forty people. She felt the hum of the carriage as it lifted from its position and began to accelerate away from the station. Her teeper compensated its balance flawlessly, though her body felt the same vibrations through her rig. As she finished a second scan, she caught a pair of eyes looking in her direction from her left. Female. A generic self that was disproportionately buxom, wearing a tight athletic outfit. She was too far away to register a moniker. The eyes looked away slowly, settling into a blank stare like most of the other citizens on the transit who were probably streaming Network content.

Carli shifted her position, finding a seat closer to the female she'd seen. Her teeper initiated a careful sitting motion, and she stole another glance and could see the callout from the person's projection: "Basilicus".

"I have him… or her." Carli heard Percy agree—he was streaming her feed too.

"Good. Send me a capture."

She checked Basilicus again. His expression hadn't changed, still staring blankly out into nothingness. As her teeper rested, she now noticed her heart beating in her chest, adrenaline coursing through her veins. It was fortunate her deep breathing was being masked on her teeper, or it might give her away. She tried to adopt a neutral position and expression without looking directly at Basilicus. The next station was Praxis Central, and she would arrive in eleven minutes. She relayed this information to Briggs and Percy. Briggs acknowledged with a grunt.

"Do you want me to do anything else?" she asked them.

"No, just stay on him."

She felt a presence to her right. She turned and found herself face to face with Basilicus, his feminine projection mismatched with his ominous voice, "You look lost, little butterfly."

She gasped, fighting the urge to immediately disconnect.

"I beg your pardon?" she managed to say.

"I made you on the concourse, before the travellator." He pivoted his body around hers, taking her virtual body in, his nose right in her face. She turned away.

"I… I don't know what you are talking about."

He ignored her, "You're not police. That's a domestic teeper, not tactical. Who are you working for?"

"Stall, stall!" she heard Briggs say. Praxis Central was now nine minutes away. Her pulse raced; she wanted to disconnect but pushed through.

"I think you have me confused with someone else."

"No, I don't think so." He was right in her face. Close enough to smell his breath if such a thing were possible. She instinctively raised her hand to push him away. The teeper responded by gently placing its hand on his face—no amount of desire would force it to injure someone else. He grabbed her hand in his left and peered intently into her eyes like he was somehow looking through the virtual Network into her physical soul.

She tried to look away, she wanted to disconnect. She wanted to scream to get someone to help, but she held back. She heard Percy's reassuring voice encouraging her to hang on and that there was nothing he could do to hurt her.

Then, he let go. She dared not look back but forced herself to turn to find him making his way to the internal door between her carriage and the airlock adjoining the next carriage. His hand touched the sensor next to the door, which responded by opening with a hiss. Stepping through, he turned back to watch Carli, shaking his head slowly as the door closed between them.

She felt like crying. *Why am I doing this?* she thought. But she heard Percy's voice again, "You're safe, you've got this. You need to follow him."

Carli felt her eyes swell and sting. She decoupled one arm from the immersion rig control and rubbed her eyes. With a few deep breaths, she placed her arm back into the controller and commanded her teeper to stand.

His body felt every one of his nearly fifty years as Briggs ran from the hotel back to the Praxis City transit station. As he left the hotel, he brought up a map overlay to locate the station, disappointed with himself as he realised he had no memory of being escorted into the hotel the night before, and he almost turned the wrong way as he left the lobby onto the street.

The overlay told him he had 900 meters to travel, a journey taking him past the PPD headquarters. As he ran, responding to Carli's questions through strained breaths, he again considered contacting someone from the PPD for backup. He ruled out Deputy Moya immediately, concluding that he would most likely be chided for conducting an investigation when he was on disciplinary leave. He still had no idea which of his co-workers had survived and in any position the help him, a thought that triggered another pang of guilt and anger. It drove him forward through the fatigue.

A fit runner could cover the distance in about six minutes. He was not in that category. Factor in extra time to navigate through the transit station and down the concourse, and Briggs feared his quarry would get away. As he weaved through citizens walking the streets, he considered hiring a personal conveyance but they were speed-limited to somewhere just above walking pace and offered no real advantage.

He checked the time and compared it with the updates Carli had supplied, correlating it with his virtual map that predicted his ETA. Four-hundred metres left and 4 minutes to make it. It was going to be tight. To his left, he looked past the PPD headquarters building—its entrance now barricaded with temporary fencing and protected by a dozen officers wearing tactical gear. Twelve floors above, he could see missing windows and a slow bleed of white smoke. It spurred him onwards.

Briggs listened in on the exchange between Carli and Basilicus. Her cover had been blown. He hoped she wasn't in any danger. Under normal circumstances, there should be no risk to someone piloting a teeper, but Briggs had no idea if the strange weapon in Basilicus' hand could somehow affect her through the Network. She said that Basilicus had left, moving forward to the next carriage, and she was pursuing.

He thought this information through: *If he knows he is being pursued, surely there is no harm in calling for help?* There was only one person he knew had survived and may have some remote chance of helping him. He initiated a voice call to Lieutenant Constança Gomes, head of the ONI.

Ten seconds without an answer before it connected.

"You're currently on leave, Sergeant."

"Lieutenant—I don't have much time. I've located the suspect travelling on transit E2 arriving in Praxis Central in… three minutes."

"What suspect? What are you talking about?"

"Korb1k. Nguyen and Zaimis. Maybe the bombing too."

She began to clarify, but Briggs cut her off firmly, "Please lieutenant—I have eyes on the suspect now," which was a half-truth—"I need officers at the ready to board the train at the platform. Call through and stop the train if you have to."

"Are you serious? I can't stop a transit like that. You're not even supposed to be working."

"Please! You have to trust me." It pained him to beg, "We both lost friends— I'll stake my career on this being right."

"Your career's already in the…" she hesitated before continuing, "If this gets my arse kicked with Moya, you'll be in so much…"

"Thank you, Lieutenant," he disconnected the call.

Holding the conversation while running made him lightheaded, and he backed off the speed for a moment. Using the reprieve, he sent some basic information to Lieutenant Gomes: Korbik's new Basilicus moniker, as well as the transit details. He made a connection between Gomes and Carli Dawes, who relayed her live feed with diminished privacy. This would allow Gomes to forward the feed to others if needed. He also shared his own feed.

Seeing the yawning mouth of the entrance to the transit station spurred him on. He pushed past citizens on the descending travellator with a firm apology and called ahead to clear a path. Just saying he was a police officer made most move to the side, though nothing in their augments would have confirmed it.

He reached the concourse below, confirmed the path to the correct platform and pressed on as his heart burned in his chest. He heard Carli's report that she'd followed him forward two carriages to the front of the transit. A chime alerted him to the transit's imminent approach. He pushed past commuters on the descending travellator, ignoring a few terse responses. Distant lights came to life in the dark tunnel as the transit approached on its magnetic rail system. He navigated the last few citizens and turned around towards the front end of the platform where the front carriage should open. He spotted three officers who appeared on high alert, one wearing tactical gear.

He called out and waved, "Detective Hal Briggs. Did Lieutenant Gomes send you?" The transit had stopped in position and was settling down to the level of the platform.

"Yes."

"First carriage, moniker Basilicus. Last seen wearing this projection…" he sent through the last capture that Carli had given him.

"We have been connected to a secondary feed from citizen Dawes." The one in the tactical gear appeared to be in the lead.

"Has Justice given you surveillance?" Briggs asked.

"Negative. Not with two minutes' notice. You're lucky we were here—the Chief's got the whole of the PPD out as a show of force."

Adrenaline heightened his senses, but it took a mental effort to slow his breathing and heart rate after running. He settled into a vanguard stance. He had no sidearm or means of subduing Basilicus, and he was about as effective in hand-to-hand combat as he was with a firearm, which was decidedly average.

He had no choice but to defer the arrest to these three officers. As though they were reading his mind, the officer in tactical instructed him to keep behind him. The same guy also directed anyone in the vicinity to clear away and move towards the other carriages.

"Don't let this guy touch you," Briggs told the other officers. "He has some kind of weapon that will override your plexus."

The lead officer looked back at him, his head cocked before replying, "Copy that. Weapons ready. Immobilization rounds only." They each removed their sidearms and held them low and across their body, ready to raise when needed.

"I've lost him again," Carli reported.

Briggs couldn't watch her feed, not without making himself unwell. "Could he have gotten past you?"

"I don't see how."

"Then he must be there. Maybe he's re-donned?"

"There are other people here, maybe twenty? Most are standing to leave."

"Keep looking."

The carriage settled into its final position with a hiss and a high-pitched electrical discharge. The doors opened. The three officers pushed forward, weapons at the ready. People stepped from the open doors. Briggs scanned their monikers one at a time, as well as looking each one in the eyes to detect any sense of alarm. Most recoiled in surprise at the three officers standing at the ready—each one directed to the side after they had been cleared. The officers would have better scanning rights than Briggs, and they processed each one efficiently before moving to the next.

The flow of people leaving the carriage slowed. Briggs checked the doors of the next carriage back to see if there was anyone he could recognise but was too far away. The last person left the carriage, and Briggs saw Carli (Or Carli's teeper) standing back from the doorway, raising her hands.

"Is there anyone left?" Briggs called out.

"Yes, three people sitting down. They look like they're watching something from the Network,"

"Advancing," the tactical officer said, and they each raised their weapons. "Watch your corners. Citizen Dawes, please exit the transit carriage."

They pressed into the carriage, Briggs in formation behind them. He passed Carli's teeper, which moved out onto the platform area. Each officer swept the carriage. Briggs took the lead on one side.

Three citizens were seated. Briggs approached the first, three aisles away from the entrance, a moniker he didn't recognise, a glazed expression on his face. Briggs reached across and tapped him on the shoulder. The guy jumped in his seat, startled as he reconnected with the physical world with a spray of expletives. Briggs watched the second passenger, a female, wake from a firm nudge to the shoulder from one of the other officers.

One left. A male, seated in the furthest corner, near the access door to the previous carriage. Staring into space. Briggs tried to scan his moniker, but he didn't have one. He approached one step at a time. The man's hands rested on his knees. Still no movement.

"Excuse me, citizen." No response. The other officers, led by tactical, closed in behind Briggs, a heightened level of alert. Briggs repeated himself, waving in front of the man to get his attention, but still no response. In fact, he wasn't moving at all, like a statue. No movement in the chest from breathing. No flicker of the eyelids.

He reached for the man's shoulder and found nothing but air, his hand passing straight through to the seat below. And then, the projection disappeared completely, in a swirl of colours and virtual shapes.

"Lock down the station!" Briggs called, turning to the tactical officer.

"We can't do that, Detective," it was Lieutenant Gomes through Briggs' phonics.

"Why the hell not? You're watching this Lieutenant—you can't tell me this is normal Network behaviour?

"Sure, but not without the right process. We haven't even got valid warrants to arrest this guy. From what I've read on the Nguyen file, there is nothing pointing to someone with the moniker of Basilicus. You're lucky I was even able to stall the transit."

"I received new information after I was locked out of the files," Briggs lied.

"You should have passed that information on."

"Are we all done here, Sergeant?" The tactical officer and his team had re-holstered their weapons and were at ease. One had removed his PPD projection and returned to a "plain clothes" self.

Briggs stared down at his feet, anger rising in him like the smoke from the PPD headquarters, hands clenched into balls until they shook. He breathed in and out, then forced his fingers apart. He looked down at the foot space where the disappearing projection had been and found a canvas satchel, just like the one Carli had described. He collected it and set his eyes back to the door.

"Yes. We're done."

# 47

He'd outsmarted half of Praxis' criminal underworld, escaped from a full court press from PPD's finest, and murdered the founder of Augmosis without detection. In some perverted way, Liam felt he deserved escape, to finally enjoy the fruits of the last two years of hard work. To take the time to wash the stains from his blood-soaked hands and march boldly into the sunset of retirement.

And it almost came undone by some random citizen on the transit.

Liam remembered her moniker. He could find nothing in the Network to indicate why she'd followed him, nothing even remotely connected her to his activities over the last few years. And yet, she clearly had an interest in him and enough clout to engage three PPD officers to trap him in the Praxis Central Station.

Liam had wasted little time when entering the final carriage. He found the closest seat with cover from the girl's approaching teeper. He changed his self and initiated a split of his projection for the second time in only a handful of days. His Employer would not be happy.

Separated from a projection, effectively naked, he needed a distraction. He pulled the trench coat from his satchel, stashed the bag at the feet of his old projection and found a seat in the aisle opposite just in time to hear the hiss of the door open behind him and the plastic clicks of the teeper's feet step past. His face only partly obscured by a raised collar, he stared blankly ahead like everyone else on the train who were immersed in the Network. His peripheral vision spotted the girl sweeping the carriage. Looking for Basilicus—but Basilicus no longer existed. People began to stand and press into the open space in front of the carriage doors, ready to exit.

*It's working*, Liam thought. He felt the carriage settle and the doors started to open. People stood around the girl's teeper which was looking towards the door, so Liam made his move. He reached around and swiped the sensor for the gangway to the previous carriage. It opened, but he stayed still, confirming the girl had not seen or heard it before slipping into the gangway and the previous carriage. He was the last to leave, confirming three PPD officers had entered the first carriage, followed by a fourth identified as a private citizen.

With officers inside, Liam stepped out from cover towards the travellator. He saw *her* again. MalvinaHoffman. She'd left the carriage at the same time the officers entered. *Or at least her teeper had.* Now, she stood in the middle of the concourse, her back to him, facing the transit.

Liam was filled with equal parts wrath and intrigue. He needed to know why this person was tracking him, just as he needed to cover his tracks. The front part of his brain told him that running was the smart move, but something compelled him to step closer.

She was not aware of him. The officers were still inside the carriage, and there didn't seem to be any others on the concourse. He weighed his options: it was still incredibly risky to be walking around a public space without a projection. His coat covered only part of his face, and unlike when he was walking around in West Praxis, he received no cover from the dark of night. Now he was well-lit, near a police force on high alert. They would respond to any disturbance like hornets defending the nest—the veneer of civil liberty they typically operated under would be incredibly thin this morning.

He settled on a plan, though he was unsure how it would work. He both needed a distraction and to send a message. Two more steps and he was immediately behind her. He leaned in, whispering into the microphone concealed beneath her projection's ear.

"You've been noticed, MalvinaHoffman."

He reached around and placed his hand on the chest of the teeper, deploying the plexus storm virus he'd activated seconds earlier. He had no idea what it would do to a teeper—if it would somehow kill the controlling host or if it would purge the Network of the host's identity: he'd never done it before. But hoped to disable the teeper at the very least.

A message crossed his optics:

VIRUS DELIVERED.

Immediately, the projection of the girl disappeared from the teeper beneath. He slipped away, heading to the travellator that would take him to the next level. He heard the teeper's digitised voice informing those around him it was returning to a docking station, but the voice was garbled. As he stepped onto the travellator, he turned to watch the teeper's legs buckle beneath it and collapse on the floor.

In his final glimpse of the teeper, smoke was rising from its chest and face. The bodies on the travellator surged as people reacted to the threat of another exploding teeper. Their response justified after a fire klaxon rang out.

Screams and confusion rose as bodies pushed against him. This scene looked all too familiar to the reports of teepers exploding in the PPD building and people reacted as if their life depended on getting as far away from the burning teeper as possible. He might not have realised it at the time, but he was responsible for those explosions.

Liam copied the frantic behaviour of those around him. He joined the tide of people onto the travellator and continued to push along with those who weren't satisfied with the travellator's limited speed. As best he could, he kept his face covered, trying to identify any old-style optical security cameras that would capture his naked oldself. Though there was nothing to reference his image against, if the PPD were now on his tail, they would be able to go through the old footage and track his movements. It wouldn't be automatic, since there was no Network identity to associate and correlate his journey, but someone tenacious enough, looking through the footage frame by frame, might be able to stitch something together.

He did his best to keep his head down as he walked, but anyone taking a close look at him would find his naked appearance a little out of the ordinary. An even closer look would reveal that his trench coat covered only a lifesuit, indicating that the whole ensemble was not a mere projection. His prosthetic hand was also on show for all to see. He patted his right pocket, expecting to feel the hard shape of his tin of platinum chips, but it was gone—most likely fallen back into the satchel he'd been forced to leave behind. He cursed to himself. Without his chips, he had nothing tangible to transact.

Also gone was the snub-nosed revolver, something Alvarez had recovered from the wastes. It was a beautiful thing but not especially accurate at anything but close range. Liam simply hadn't had time to slip it into his leg pocket.

As he reached the next concourse, a group of half a dozen police and emergency services officers on full siren passed him on the opposing travelator. They ignored him completely. Other officers were fanning across the concourse. The smart choice would have been to cross the concourse and board another transit heading in the opposite direction, getting as much distance away from Praxis Central as possible. But everyone was heading for the exits. And without a Network ID, the transit would deny him access.

So, he made the lowest-risk decision available to him. He continued up to the final travellator that would discharge him back onto the main street of Praxis Central. A careful thirty-minute walk around the city would land him at his safe house, where he had no choice but to trust his employer would again forge him a new identity.

The light at the far end of the travellator beckoned him warmly. He expected it to taste as smooth as the vodka he'd had at the Komitet a few days earlier.

Since completing his mission yesterday, he'd received little communication from his employer, aside from acknowledging the mission was complete with another one hundred thousand bits being deposited across his accounts. This brought his total to roughly nine hundred thousand. A million was to be his magic number—when he would cash in his accounts and forge his own identity, but there was just too much heat on him at the moment and every communication with his employer had only served to increase his paranoia.

Until interrupted by the girl on the train, Liam had been on his way to Kenmore on the Fort Gale line. A contact there was going to convert the bits from his accounts into physical commodities. These would be slowly laundered back to new accounts only he could control. It would be a slow process—most of his funds tied up for months as they were used to purchase crates of grain and synthetic meats, which would be moved and ultimately liquidated with the funds eventually being released back into accounts of his choosing. For his trouble, *The Accountant,* as he was called, would take a 30% commission.

Liam stepped off the travellator into the sunshine of the street level of Praxis Central, forced to hide out for another few days with the vain hope his employer wouldn't demand something further from him in exchange for assigning him another new identity. The recent escalation in risk hadn't escaped him, it was almost like his employer was trying to get him caught. *Or killed.*

He vowed he would never allow that to happen.

# 48

The brightest white filled Carli's optics, even with her eyes closed. The sound of static was so loud she couldn't hear herself screaming. She frantically tried to pull her body out of the control rig but was restrained by the sacs holding her back and lower body in place. Still blinded, she remembered an emergency disconnection gesture, and the rig released her and tilted forward to return her to a standing position.

The white slowly dissipated, leaving glowing streaks in her vision, like the lingering effects of trying to stare down a blazing light bulb, and the static softened until nothing but a distant ringing remained. Her eyes ached, and rubbing them made no difference.

Through the ringing, she heard a far-off voice: "Carli? Are you OK?" It was Percy. She felt him brace her shoulders, but she shook him away.

"Gimme space." She was breathing heavily and confused. Her eyes continued to burn, and she felt light-headed.

Percy asked another question, but she ignored it. The pain and alarm focused her attention inward, trying to work out what was wrong. She felt his hands on her shoulders again, easing her down. "Please, you need to sit."

This time, she allowed him to assist her onto the ground. As soon as she was settled, he released her and gave her space.

Minutes passed. Her breathing slowed, and her vision started to coalesce. She made out shapes, then Percy's outline, then his concerned face. Finally, colour returned—some more vibrant than others. In time, she was able to stand, regaining composure.

"I'm… I think I'm okay," she said, as if saying it made it so.

She took in the room she was in—the control rig suite at Lesante Tower. She could see a few concerned people near the entrance looking in on her—maybe they heard her scream.

Percy addressed the concerned onlookers, "It's OK—she said she's OK."

Through the pain in her eyes, she focused on his face—something was off with it. It was yellow and red, with a blue spectre visible behind his projected face. The spectre had an angular jaw, like Percy's oldself rather than his trueself projection. She'd already seen it three times in the previous twenty-four hours—so she knew what it looked like.

Carli looked around the room. It, too, was a stark yellow colour, with splashes of red. Only a few things appeared to have any blue in her vision—a painting hanging on the opposite wall, the small LEDs on the side of the control rigs flickering on and off. Tracking markers were visible on the walls, though should could still see part of the virtual scape projecting in the distance.

She struggled for answers. Only one fit. "Something's wrong with my optics—they aren't showing the colour blue," she said. She turned and looked at Percy again. "And I can see your oldself."

There had been a brief period of excitement when the teeper had melted down. Not a coincidence—Carli's teeper. For a moment, Briggs feared the cloud following him had extended its deathly hand to someone innocent. After a few minutes of attempting to message her, Percy relayed a message that she was safe, albeit rattled. He indicated her augments might have failed and he was going to escort her to a nearby medical centre. The news eased Briggs' fears, but he knew he was responsible, just as he felt responsible for failing to catch this guy when he'd been so close. And if he had anything to do with the attack on the PPD headquarters, this only served to compound his sense of failed responsibility.

*Settle down Hal, you don't even know for sure it was the same guy.* The thought brought him no comfort.

The smouldering teeper had been quickly extinguished by responders using portable canisters. Another citizen in the area identified himself as a teeper service technician and used a specialised tool from his carryall to extract the teeper's power cell, which was the source of the smoke.

Once it was under control, Briggs opened the satchel he'd found on the transit. Inside, he found a small tin, a rubber ball, a packet of playing cards and a revolver. With the teeper in meltdown attracting the other officers' attention, he was left holding the satchel. The revolver was an Old-World model he didn't recognise. Through a gap in the cylinder, he could see it was loaded.

Briggs had no badge and no means by which to defend himself. The revolver was tangible evidence. If ballistics could track the guns to other crimes, that would be a lead worth exploring. *But that would take days.* With the satchel held against his body, he fingered a leaver on the side, which released the cylinder and allowed six brass bullets to be ejected. With a swift motion, he palmed the gun, unzipped a thigh pocket in his lifesuit, retrieved the gun and slipped it inside. He did the same for the bullets in the opposite pocket—there was no way he was going to carry around a loaded gun he wasn't familiar with.

He flicked the top off the tin, and its contents spilled into the satchel: several small metal chips and a small plastic sleeve containing two green circular pills.

His eyes lingered on the pills for a few moments. The voice in his head that usually told him when he was doing something stupid was silent, so he grabbed the sleeve of pills and put them in another pocket. Once the teeper had been extinguished, he handed the satchel off to one of the officers to process as evidence and made his way towards the exit—Lt. Gomes had issued him an urgent invitation to meet.

Briggs stepped out of the elevator on Level 19 of an officer building opposite the PPD headquarters. The open space was occupied by officers and specialists, some he recognized. Some were from Network Crimes and ONI, some from other departments. It looked like they had shifted several whole departments to this new building overnight. The space was buzzing with people trying to organise chairs and workspaces for themselves and other technicians who looked like they were trying to work out the best place to put markers on the walls to overlays of PPD feeds..

"Long black, two sugars," he said to an officer who had escorted him to a conference room. He doubted they would comply.

The walls of the conference room were once white but were now stained grey, mostly around waist height. There were tracking markers on the walls, but no projection had been applied, so now it looked no different to any other room across Praxis—austere and lifeless.

A procession of people approached the door, led by Lt. Gomes.

"Don't get up." He hadn't intended to.

The group included some ONI officers and a junior Network Crimes detective named, Praveen that had only joined the team in the last few weeks. He looked like a fish out of water. There was another detective, female, identified in Briggs optics only as Sergeant Curran. He didn't recognize her but her division was marked as 'Internal Affairs'. That was an ominous sign. Two other officers that Briggs recalled having only passing conversations with entered the room, followed by the consultant he'd seen in the elevator yesterday with the moniker of SpecialistHavoc. No longer looking like a gothic creature from a vampire novel, his current appearance as a character from a cyberpunk sim was no less subdued.

Briggs noticed each of their outfits included a black armband with a glowing purple aura. When he focused on it, a callout appeared in his optics:

"I STAND FOR JUSTICE. HONOURING THE FALLEN OF 99.12.24."

After lingering on the callout for more than a moment, a second appeared:

"WILL YOU STAND? SHOW YOUR SUPPORT BY LEASING AN ARMBAND. 5 BITS PER DAY. ALL PROCEEDS GO TO THE FAMILIES OF THOSE WHO DIED IN SERVICE TO JUSTICE."

*Justice is only worth 5 bits per day.* Briggs scoffed to himself.

They all took seats on the opposite side of the long conference table.

"Do one of you guys bring coffee?"

To his surprise, one of his escorts entered the room, bringing a cup and placing it before him. He took a careful sip. It didn't taste great, but it would get the job done.

Lt. Gomes didn't waste time. "Well, you've made a ripe mess for yourself, Detective. Tell me why I shut down the transit this morning."

He rested the coffee back on the table. He still couldn't tell the extent to which he was in trouble. As angry as he felt, he decided it would go better for him if he dialled down the sarcasm—they had all the cards here, and if he ever hoped to get his commission back, he needed to impress. Plus, Gomes had honoured his request for backup with little more than a plea of, "You have to trust me". At the same time, this whole conversation was going to be recorded and banked, so he needed to choose his words carefully.

"After receiving information from a silent watch on a person of interest in the murder case for Constable Nguyen and Petros Zaimis, I decided to initiate surveillance on my own, as a private citizen of the Collective. The person of interest boarded a transit at Augmosis and was travelling clockwise when I contacted you for assistance. Unfortunately, he seemed to get past us."

One of the ONI officers spoke, "Do you have banked footage of this suspect? You said you had eyes on him? How did he get away?"

He didn't. Carli Dawes had supplied him with a copy of her stream, but it had been mysteriously scrubbed. His own had also been scrubbed, including the projection of the man who had been seated in the carriage before disappearing.

"No—anything containing the suspect has been scrubbed."

"That's convenient," another ONI officer said.

"Ask your CO—she saw it too. She witnessed my feed and the one from my… friend, Carli Dawes."

The officers looked at Lt. Gomes. She nodded. "I did. My feed's scrubbed too."

"That's not possible," the first ONI specialist said.

"Well, apparently it is. You techies should be on top of this. Instead, there's some thug out there killing people and slipping through the net each time." Briggs continued. He found himself directing most of his explanation to the specialist, Specialist Havoc. Though he didn't seem to blink, he sensed enough shared confusion to raise his confidence and try to play the room in his favour.

"Look, for almost the last week, I have been investigating a growing list of Network anomalies. Not just the two unusual murders in West Praxis, but the scrubbing of banked footage, the delay of respondents to Nguyen's call for assistance, the escape of two suspects with active BOLOs, with one now apprehended, at some personal risk I might add. And the last thing, in case you weren't aware, the damn murder of dozens of my fellow officers just yesterday." He let that sit for a moment—not for dramatic effect, but because he could feel the emotion rising and needed a moment to force it back down where it belonged.

"I'm not into conspiracies. I see only the evidence and go where it leads me. And the evidence is telling me there is some larger game afoot, tying all of these anomalies together.

"Some of this is in the case file. For example, in my interview with Judge Khoury, who witnessed Nguyen's live stream to issue a warrant—that stream was destroyed, and I had to take his statement from memory. A lot of it hasn't made the file yet—when investigating Network anomalies, I don't like having the PPD bureaucrats analysing my every thought and partially formed theory until I'm certain of it."

"That's still not policy," Gomes said.

Briggs tensed, "My Captain was well aware of my approach. She knew this was politically sensitive for the people at Augmosis and the Collective as a whole."

The point landed, and the room fell quiet. Everyone looked to Gomes for direction. In the brief pause, Briggs heard someone call from outside the room, "Scapes on people!" and a few seconds later, the walls of their conference room came alive, two walls projecting the framed frosted glass view of the rest of the office, complete with shadows of workers shuffling past. On the other two walls, framed windows now looked down over a virtual city. It was the same scapes used by the PPD headquarters across the road.

They came in an instant, and Briggs jerked a little in his chair—the experience squeezing his stomach before he regained composure. *Of all the things these people could be wasting energy on right now, surely fixing the décor shouldn't be high on the list.*

Gomes still appeared to be thinking, accessing something on the Network. With a few gestures, Briggs saw an alert cross his optics advising him that his Network connectivity had been suspended.

"Under the ONI Charter, Item 15, I have initiated a temporary suppression on recording," Lt. Gomes stated. "For the next thirty minutes, conversations in this room will be private and cannot be banked. Is that understood?"

There were a few grumbles. Briggs checked his own connection to confirm his curiosity—it seemed like a similar process to the one he experienced when he met Goldstein at Augmosis.

"Sergeant, after this conversation, if I am happy with your answers, I will put in a recommendation to Deputy Moya to have you temporarily reinstated and seconded to ONI. I can't say if he will accept that recommendation—he's had his hands full over the last 24 hours...."

"I'll bet—covering his arse," Briggs interrupted. The lieutenant paused, expressionless, before continuing as if nothing was said, and for a moment, Briggs wondered if she agreed with him.

"What you're missing is that for the last few weeks, ONI has also been investigating a significant increase in unusual Network behaviour, some of which we believe now correlates to your own enquiries. This has all culminated in one single event..."

"Yesterday's explosion?"

"We think so, but we aren't convinced that was the end of it. Network Crimes and ONI are depleted. The people in this room are all that's left, barring a few consultants continuing to work from their private residences. Everyone else is either deceased, on medical leave, or have concluded their consulting contracts because, in their words, 'they didn't sign up to be killed by terrorists'. I don't just need your help because of what you have uncovered from your own investigation. I need your help because we don't have enough people left."

"It's nice to be appreciated." Briggs sat in this revelation for a moment. "But you need Moya's OK." He wasn't asking a question, just saying it out loud.

"Yes. ONI has more leeway than most departments, but I can't override the Chief even if I wanted to. The best I can offer is a sharing of information. I can't condone you taking matters into your own hands. If I can talk Moya round to giving you a badge, I will—at least until all of this is over. And you'll still have whatever disciplinary process awaiting you on the other side."

It wasn't a reinstatement, but it felt like a step in the right direction. "Fine. I'll help if I can."

"Good. Now, Sergeant, this is the point where you tell us *everything*."

# 49

Asking other people to trust him came naturally to Briggs, even if, on occasion, he'd fallen short of that trust. But placing his trust in others was an entirely different proposition, and it wasn't going to be easy. He kept telling himself that sharing the entirety of his case from start to finish wasn't the same thing as sharing his deepest thoughts and emotions, but he found it difficult to differentiate between the two. Considering he barely knew any of the people he now shared this room with, being fully transparent was going to hurt.

He had no choice. He dropped a digital folder into their feeds. All his notes from the investigation's first day. It contained his notes for how he'd analysed the evidence and addressed the crime scenes: first for Zaimis and then for Nguyen. At his request, Lt. Gomes was able to retrieve and share PPD files, including the imagery taken from both sites. He recapped how Judge Khoury had witnessed Zaimis' murder, describing how the suspect, Korb1k, had placed his hand on the victim's neck, causing him to eventually collapse.

"My working theory is that the suspect was able to deliver a virus to compromise the heart, causing it to stop beating."

"How exactly?"

"Since no data could be recovered from the plexus or the lifesuit, that is unknown," Briggs replied.

Gomes responded, agitated, "But you have a theory? Briggs—I don't want to have to fight you for every question, or this will take forever. You asked me to trust you earlier today, and I did. In response, I need you to trust me and this team. We all know how to run a case with limited information. We also know what it's like to have bureaucrats breathing down our necks to shut down investigations that are politically or professionally embarrassing."

That last point rang true. "This is a safe place. Share what you think, not just what you know and maybe as a team, we can piece it all together."

"Well, of course, I can't prove it, but I think the virus did a couple of things. First, it caused their lifesuits to stop their hearts using their built-in defibrillators. This mimics a medical condition called 'commotio cordis'. The same virus then traversed the Network and scrubbed their accounts and any others with banked footage that included that ID. Lastly, the virus caused each citizen's paired node to melt down in the Augmosis data centre."

The air was sucked out of the room in an instant. Two of the ONI officers had their mouths open.

"Is that your theory, or did that actually happen?" Gomes asked.

"That happened. I saw the nodes myself two days ago." This triggered a range of discussion around the room that Gomes let play out for a few minutes before calling time and returning to Briggs.

"They haven't reported this?"

"No."

"Why did you leave it out of the file? It wasn't a theory; it was real evidence."

Briggs chewed on this question for a few moments before carefully answering, "I made a promise to someone to leave it off the file until after all the facts were known. That person is no longer available for questioning."

"Why?"

"Because that person was Aldus Goldstein—who I believe was also murdered by the same assailant yesterday." The room was stunned once more.

For the next twenty minutes, Briggs continued to share his account of the rephasing of the plexuses being linked to new identities for the suspect, Korb1k. How the timestamp of the rephasing coincided with the disappearance of Korb1k from the Network immediately before Nguyen had been killed. He explained how he'd obtained a list from Augmosis of every citizen to have their identity rephased in the period immediately after Korb1k's disappearance and had ruled almost all of them out, except for one by the name of Basilicus.

It was here that Briggs knew his conclusions had been tenuous at best. The death of Aldus Goldstein, coinciding with a transit arrival of Basilicus at Augmosis only 50 minutes beforehand, was highly coincidental. Still, he expanded on the theory that the same virus or something similar had been used to kill Goldstein. Since Basilicus was the only one left on his list, he thought it worthwhile investigating.

"And to be honest, after we had surveillance on him, the way Basilicus behaved on the transit goes some way to support my theory. The teeper meltdown right outside the transit a few minutes later—the same teeper piloted by my friend who was pursuing him pretty much seals the deal as far as I'm concerned."

"How are Carli Dawes and Percy Hayward?"

Briggs frowned. After receiving Percy's message that Carli was safe but injured, he hadn't followed up further. He'd been too consumed with trying to talk his way back into the investigation to reach out. It wasn't the first time in his life he'd had to chide himself for getting his priorities wrong.

"I've heard they are safe, but Ms Dawes may have received an eye injury."

"And how do you know them exactly?"

"Recent acquaintances. Very recent, really."

For a few minutes, everyone in the room was quiet—interacting with the Network as they corroborated parts of his story against their own findings. Briggs sat back in his chair, tired, but justified. He took the opportunity to compose Carli Dawes a message to see how she was. He typed it out three different ways with finger gestures before deleting them and simply asking if she was okay. The Network told him the message would be sent after his connection was reactivated.

He returned his attention to the room around him. "Since we've been working on crazy theories, I believe I might have an image of him. Unmasked."

"How?"

"Hard to explain, but it's only a few frames."

"How certain are you?" Gomes asked.

"25%. The timing and location are consistent with when I believe he was temporarily without a Network identity. A witness said he was assaulted by him. He didn't file a report but banked the footage and this time it wasn't scrubbed." With a few gestures, Briggs located the footage in his personal store as well as the key frames and shared them with the group. "Note the scars on his face— the fingerprint analysis at the scene indicated only right-handed prints with the appearance of scarring. And secondly, his left hand is a prosthetic that doesn't look like any others that I have seen."

They all reviewed the footage. A murmuring grew between them, particularly the IA officer, Curran. Gomes sat back again, as though the burden she'd already been carrying had now gotten heavier.

"We know who this is," she said.

For over two years, Internal Affairs and ONI have been investigating the disappearance of electronic records within the PPD," said Sergeant Curran. "Not many, just eleven. These were concluded investigations: case files for individuals who had been tried and sentenced. Their original records, monikers and identities were completely cleaned away. Where other case files referenced them, their identities had been changed, pointing to a new identity."

"Who?"

"They all had a private Network ID of 0 and a moniker as 'null.'"

"So, scrubbed. As though they never existed?"

"Yes. Access to change these files should be impossible, except for high-ranking PPD officers. Internal Affairs lacked the skillset to investigate the Network aspect of the anomalies and handed the responsibility over to ONI."

Gomes took over. "We found nothing. No record of changes ever occurring. We audited and interviewed every officer with high enough access to make the changes but found nothing."

"How do you think this links to Korb1k or Basilicus?" Briggs asked.

"That image you shared is of one of the missing citizens. He disappeared at least two years ago. His name is Liam Nolan."

*Liam Nolan,* Briggs' target, now had a real name, but he needed to press into this new information. It seemed too convenient.

"But if his history was cleaned away, how do you know what he looks like? How do you even know that he is missing?"

Sargent Curran replied, "Because I arrested him, Detective. Before joining Internal Affairs, I was a homicide investigator working out of Kaplan. Liam Nolan was convicted of the murder of three executives of a lithium refinery almost eight years ago. The same refinery, located outside the barrier in Kaplan had an explosion that killed thirteen people two years before, including Liam Nolan's wife."

"I remember that explosion. There was an outcry for all factory work to be completed by teepers afterwards. Nothing changed."

"Yes. As well as losing his wife, Liam Nolan received burns to 60 per cent of his body, including severe burns to his left hand. Although his employer paid for most of his rehabilitation, he took justice upon himself, bought a black-market firearm and summarily executed the CEO, COO and safety supervisor.

"He'd served seven years of his three life sentences when I thought to look him up to see how his rehabilitation had been progressing—his was one of those cases that stuck in your memory and made you ask questions of yourself if you'd been in the same position. I'd hoped he was progressing well. Instead, I found that he no longer existed. A physical visit to County penitentiary confirmed that Liam Nolan was no longer a prisoner, and no one, including the warden or fellow prisoners, had any recollection of him."

Gomes continued, "He was the first—the first of eleven, which triggered our joint investigation with Internal Affairs. All we have to go off—in terms of his physical appearance and history, is what we remember. We only know what Liam Nolan looked like because Sergeant Curran had kept physical imagery of him during the court case and stored it without a Network identity in her personal archive."

Briggs checked the notes in his personal store from his meeting with Goldstein. "The first node meltdown at Augmosis—that was November 97."

Curran thought for a moment before nodding, "Yes—that timing fits."

Briggs considered this information—it made sense, but was frustrating. He truly was chasing a ghost. Even more concerning was that there could be another ten people out there who may be equally as dangerous.

"I appreciate that I'm only a sergeant, but shouldn't all of us have been told if something like this was going on? If I'd known, then maybe I might've been able to connect some of the dots sooner." Briggs stated.

Gomes frowned. "It seems that failure to share information might be a problem for both of us, Detective. So, from now on, let's both work to fix that problem."

"In that case, I have a few requests of my own."

"Fine," Gomes replied.

"Firstly, I want copies of those images from your files. I'd like to get a good look at him."

"Done."

A blip in his phonics confirmed the share of a trusted file. He opened it and found not only images of his suspect but a complete set of notes on the investigation so far. Realising the importance and sensitivity of this information and its potential value to the overall case lifted his spirits. He briefly opened one of the images, an arrest photo of Liam Nolan, captured by Sergeant Curran whilst he was in custody. It was indeed the same man, scarred and deformed, but with a brooding callousness behind his dark eyes.

"The other ten missing people—who are they?" he asked.

"We'll send you what we know. At least five were incarcerated for high-grade Network hacking. ONI officers were able to able to follow up on significant arrests over the last few years to see if they had been given a get-out-of-jail-free card. The others, we know nothing about and only know they must exist by analysing patterns in the records pointing to the null identifier. There may be more than 11, but we think that's unlikely."

Brigg nodded. "I also want to make contact again with Augmosis—someone in Aldus Goldstein's area—I'm sure they can help in some way. If Nolan burned his Basilicus moniker on the transit, then Augmosis would have seen it happen. They can tell us when a new moniker is rephased so we can do it right this time."

"Deputy Moya is leading the relationship with Augmosis at the moment. That's not going to happen—at least not any time soon."

Briggs cursed to himself and tried again, "Please—I'm certain he's still here in Praxis Central. Without an ID, he can't go back through the transit station. That means that all we have to do is to track every citizen that gets a newly phased plexus from this hub and track him down again. Also, we should still have optical surveillance cameras in place around the city—can we get their footage and try and follow his path away from the transit station?"

Everyone turned to Gomes for confirmation. "I'll see what I can do."

Briggs pressed on. "And I don't mean we run the usual pattern recognition stuff over them to find him, I mean we go through it manually. There was a warrant out for Alvarez for two days, and his face didn't get matched once. You can't tell me he didn't walk past a sensor in that time—so I think you have to assume the pattern recognition is probably compromised or at least broken."

Everyone remained quiet; he had the room and wanted to push as far as he could.

"West Praxis—Alvarez knows something he didn't share. If Korb1k… Liam Nolan was working with Alvarez, we should at least interview him again. Whatever they were doing out there has to be connected with this whole thing."

"I agree there is more to that connection. I have two officers meeting with him and his legal counsel tomorrow."

"Can I get the reports? Or better still, join their feed?"

"I'll think about it," she said, arms folded.

Briggs thought back to the technicians who processed the storehouse in West Praxis. "What happened to the evidence from West Praxis? I was told it was being relocated for processing."

"Most of it, yes. The weapons and narcotics went to level 4. The contraband articles are in decontamination in West Praxis. The tech and the teepers were shipped to us."

"Here?"

"No. Level 12. If they weren't destroyed in the explosion, the EM blasts that went off probably cooked them pretty good."

Each setback was being piled on another. "The teeper explosions. How did they happen?"

"Eight distinct explosions. One went early, triggering an alarm. The rest fired about 60 seconds later. We believe the explosive was attached to them at their docking station. Could have been there for days or weeks. The teepers were being piloted by ONI officers and consultants."

"I heard there was another explosion, somewhere nearby?"

"Yes. It was at the docking station itself. Minimal casualties.

Briggs took this in, following through on a nagging question, "But these weren't PPD teepers? They were public units?"

"Yes."

"So, what were they doing in there in the first place? Why were the officers piloting them at all? And maybe more to the point—how did the attacker even know which teepers to compromise?"

Lieutenant Gomes exhaled and broke eye contact. "It shames me to say, but about three months ago, ONI officers switched to using public teepers for remote work. The PPD fleet of teepers is older and less responsive than the teepers for lease on the street. Since most of the team tend to be fussy about the capabilities of their drone, they decided it was just easier to hire teepers from outside for remote work than to use the ones from the basement."

Briggs stewed on this information, acknowledging what hadn't been said aloud—that ONI was indirectly responsible for their own destruction.

"How did they know which teepers to target?"

"Human nature detective: we always hire the same ones."

**51**

A few hundred meters away, Carli sat in a reclined chair in an Augmosis clinic after being escorted there by Percy. He seemed agitated. He left with an apology and a promise to reconnect via the Network soon.

Behind the waning pain in her eyes, she felt a sense of resolve. She owned her decision to help Detective Briggs, and though her vision had been impaired, having some sense of control over the things happening around her was invigorating. It echoed the same feeling she craved when sculpting a client's first trueself but somehow seemed more tangible.

A few times she tried closing one eye and then the other. Both were affected. Optics worked by either creating or altering the incoming light to match the projections of the Network. Sometimes that was by adding colour to the incoming light, or by creating light directly within the lens of each optic.

The colours of the central promenade clashed with those she remembered from the day before. Most of the world now looked bright yellow, especially the sky. Beneath nearly every surface and every projection, she perceived a purple spectre. Faces were most obvious—even with colours missing, she could see oldselfs and trueselfs simultaneously. Through every projected outfit, she saw the lifesuits beneath. Teepers were everywhere, hosting the projections from their pilot over their plastic frame. She was surprised to see so many—maybe half of the people on the street weren't really there. She didn't know if that was normal, or the consequences of a rising fear of some further calamity in Praxis Central.

"How did you say this happened?" The optics technician held an instrument in front of Carli's eyes, switching from one to the other and peering through the other side. The technician's acrid breath caused her to hold her own until he backed away.

"Connected to the Network and I saw a bright light." She didn't want to share anything more than that.

"Interesting—were you doing an immersion sim or was it a physical light?"

"It was from the Network, I was… controlling a teeper."

"Interesting—"

The technician leant back, and Carli found a brief pocket of fresh air.

"One problem is easy to fix—your plexus has failed, which is why you can't connect to the Network."

"Why can I still see people's projections?" she asked.

"Plexus hopping—when your plexus is down, your augments automatically connect to others in the area to deliver passive content. Wouldn't want to allow people to peek behind the curtain by smashing their plexuses, would we?" The technician chuckled to himself.

"I can rephase you a new plexus which will solve one problem. Your eyes, however… If what you say is correct, it sounds like you may have depolarised your optics' blue crystals. I'll have to run a few more tests."

With her consent, he reclined the chair a little further and administered some eye drops, making her vision instantly blurry. Through the fog, the technician brought a device to her face which he attached over the back of her head. She felt claustrophobic but breathed deeply to settle any nerves.

"How long will this take?"

"Only a minute or two—it's just a diagnostic," he replied.

A chorus of colours flashed before her eyes. She wasn't sure if they emanated from the machine attached to her face or generated by the Network. She found her eyes trying to focus on a pattern or subject within the colour, but it hurt to concentrate. Soon it was over, and the device was removed from her face. The colours she'd seen were repeated like spectres around the room before slowly fading.

"How was that for you then?" the technician asked.

"Fine."

"Your results are processing now and… yes, here it is. In short, your blue optical plasma has died."

"Come again?"

"Your optics contain four types of organic plasma. Red, green, and blue shape colour. The fourth shapes luminosity. They all work in concert to create or shape the image you perceive. Many decades ago, optics used a nanoweb of coloured pixels within the iris to do the same thing, but they struggled with fast-moving projections and caused the perception to lag. Modern optics, however, contain an organic plasma—it responds faster than your mind can perceive the change.

"In your case, in an attempt to render whatever this bright light was, the blue plasma overexerted themselves to a level they could not sustain and perished. To be honest, I haven't seen it happen before, not without some kind of external agent or chemical."

"I… I'd never really thought about how they worked," she said.

"People rarely do. It's easy to take these things for granted."

"What do… what do they eat?"

"I beg your pardon?"

"What do the organisms in my optics eat? What powers them?"

"Oh, in a manner of speaking, they eat you. Or rather the salts and enzymes which your eyes naturally secrete."

Gross.

"So, how do I fix it?"

"Well, we must extract the dead plasma and replace it. It is a relatively straightforward procedure but not something we can do here. Your best option would be Mount Tabor Augment Institute in Métropole. General anaesthetic. It takes a few hours but recovery will take longer—usually 24 hours before you will be able to see at all. I can book ahead for you if you'd like?"

"No, that's fine—if you can connect me back to the Network, I'll arrange the appointment."

After reverting her chair, she removed her plexus and provided it to the technician, who retrieved a new one from a nearby storeroom. He unwrapped it from its blister pack, scanned it a few times with a hand-held device, and passed it to Carli.

"I've set it to pair. Once you attach it, you should connect automatically. Then you'll need to provide your moniker and chain code to complete the rephasing process."

Carli looked down at the octagonal device in her hand, feeling its meagre weight. She twisted it onto the coupler on the chest of her lifesuit and reconnected.

"There's one more thing. I don't know if it's relevant." Briggs flicked a few Network commands and removed his projection, hoping that the same process worked as it had before, though he'd not tried it himself. The room now saw his oldself.

"Um, nice bruise on your forehead, but what does this have to do with…" The awkwardness in the room shifted like the air had been sucked out.

"Do you still see me?" Briggs said, ignoring the alerts and alarms in his optics telling him that his oldself was being masked. Everyone's eyes were pointed in his direction, but not making direct eye contact. SpecialistHavoc seated nearby reached over, finger extended as if to poke him—Briggs took the opportunity and swatted his hand away before reapplying his trueself projection.

"What on Earth was that?" Gomes asked.

"That's what happens now when you remove your trueself. Carli Dawes happened upon it by accident." Briggs explained how he thought it worked, based on Carli's theory.

After a few minutes of technical discussion that Briggs didn't follow, Gomes concluded the meeting with, "I don't know what that means or if it is important at the moment in the grand scheme of our problems, but it's still concerning."

"Since we are being honest, I thought you should know."

After completing the briefing, most of the officers left the room, having been given assignments by Lt. Gomes to follow up on.

"Specialist Havoc, can you please wait?" Lt. Gomes asked. The consultant returned to the table. He'd said nothing through the whole briefing. Through his plasticine projection, Briggs could not get a read on him. "Sergeant, I feel like we've made a good start in trusting each other."

"I suppose."

"For the next five minutes, this is still a safe room. I think it would help build that trust further if you could help us with something from yesterday's arrest at West Praxis."

"Oh?" Briggs felt uneasy, like a guilty child.

Specialist Havoc finally spoke, "At 21:42, we intercepted Network activity we hadn't seen before. It was lightning fast—faster than Flynn. Hacking into some Augmosis sub-systems and processes we barely even understand. At 23:31 that activity coalesced around you, Sarge—or your Network identity. Two hours later, it ceased, and Alvarez was in custody."

Briggs was having trouble keeping track of the dates and times, but it didn't matter. "What's your question?"

Lt. Gomes responded, "Was that you?"

Briggs grunted, "Was *what* me? Do I look like someone capable of hacking into Network things? If you've read my HR file, which I'm sure you did before you invited me up here, you'll see that anything more than a few minutes in a simulated environment and I fall apart. My brain or balance or something can't deal with it."

"So, what led you to find Alvarez? What clue? What piece of evidence?"

"Confidential informant." Briggs repeated the same thing he'd said to Deputy Moya the previous day.

"And was this informant authorised to bypass every known security control the Network has to offer?"

"I don't know what you're talking about."

She frowned before redirecting. "Is this person, this CI, likely to be sticking his or her nose into things again any time soon?"

Briggs's eyes widened for just a moment. "I can't say," he said, but it was enough of a tell to cause the consultant to grin like a child.

"Aldus Goldstein, I presume," he said.

"Okay Specialist, you're dismissed," the Lieutenant said.

Briggs chided himself. Though, there was no evidence he'd done anything wrong, nor anything that would compromise the charges laid against Alvarez.

He deflected again, "That guy needs to pick an identity and stick with it. Is he old enough to be working here?"

"Detective, if we want to get to the bottom of all this, you'll be grateful for the help of people like Specialist Havoc. If you're in this team, we work together. There are no vigilantes and no corner-cutting. We still have access to some of the best White Hats around. If the Network is indeed compromised, then we will need people like Specialist Havoc to figure this out and put it back the way it should be."

"Fine. So… Have I earned your trust enough to let me help?"

"I trust you, but not enough to give you a badge—that's got to come from Moya. I *can* give you a temporary consultant role with limited access to the files in question. No sidearm. No warrant requests—they come through me. You also won't have access to BOLO or tactical in the field."

"So, you want me to help, but tied to a desk."

"Not quite. I'll get you the surveillance footage access—if you think you need to go through it manually, then you're more than welcome to."

"I can do that."

"It'll take me an hour or two to get the warrants and set the permissions up." This frustrated Briggs, but he tried to let it go.

"Anything else?"

"Actually, yes—Percy Hayward and Carli Dawes. I need their statements. More specifically, I want you to get a little friendlier with Hayward."

"Oh?"

"The Wakers have been on our radar for at least a year, and the first thing we do in response to a direct attack is find anyone with the motive and capabilities to organise this sort of attack."

"And the Wakers are on that list?"

"They are. Not at the top, but since you already have contact with them, it would help if you dig a little further. Our intel says that Percy is one of their main organisers and financiers. Track him down again and see what you can learn."

"These guys probably don't meet face to face, most of the time. They probably connect in an immersion sim or something. I'm not exactly the best person for that job."

"Possibly. Start with Hayward and see where it leads from there."

It didn't sit well with Briggs. He'd only met Carli… yesterday? And Percy, only a few hours ago. He wouldn't call them friends, but he didn't call many people friends. It also seemed like a pointless exercise, but he recognised it was better than being benched entirely.

"Fine. I accept." He pivoted to another issue he'd been considering, "One last thing, if this guy can scrub Network footage, then I think you need an alternative."

"Explain?"

"Body cameras. All recordings go to local storage, without connection to the Network, so it can't be tampered with. Without banked footage, the PPD has its hands tied. Even if we catch the guy in the act, banked footage can't be relied on for prosecution—especially if it gets scrubbed."

"I hear you, but that's a political minefield, Briggs. PPD hasn't worn secondary cameras since the first few years of the Collective. The Overseer would claim them to be a violation of Projection."

"But do you see an alternative?"

Gomes took a moment to respond, "Perhaps not, but let me think about it."

**52**

Carli was expecting Percy in the waiting room of the Augment clinic, but instead found Detective Briggs. "How are you feeling, Ms Dawes?" Briggs asked.

"Please, just call me Carli," she replied. "I'm OK. There's something wrong with my optics. They said it might take a while to fix."

As she said this, she looked at Briggs' forehead, seeing both her handiwork repairing his projection and the bandaged cut beneath, which only partially covered a growing bruise. She felt a pang of guilt for staring and looked away.

"Where's Percy?" he asked.

"Not sure. He came with me here, but he said he needed to leave. I think he's worried his group are being investigated."

"Hmm. Are you hungry? Would it be OK if I bought you lunch?"

She checked the time and realised she hadn't eaten anything since their rushed breakfast.

"Sure."

They found a café a few shops back towards the transit station. As they walked in silence, Carli found herself paying closer attention to everything around her. With the pain in her eyes nearly gone, she was able to focus more closely on her surroundings. Teepers carried their pilot's semi-transparent projections, gliding purposefully to their pilot's next appointment. In the centre of each tree lining the sidewalk was a simple metal pole with a tracking pattern around its circumference, on which the projection of each tree was mapped.

The ornate facades of the buildings concealed bare concrete dotted with tracking markers. Even the glass shop fronts were textured like smooth concrete. She followed the buildings up towards the sky above. It was no longer blue and cloudy, but yellow, striped with massive support pylons converging in the centre of the hemisphere directly above her.

Her gaze returned to the front of the café as they entered. The glass window revealed the name, 'Dawn Roast'. Beneath the glass, she saw the texture of concrete. Graffiti was sprayed over it with the now familiar words:

YOU ONLY SEE WHAT YOU WANT TO SEE.

She paused to read the words twice, wondering what made the phrase seem so important for it to have become the rallying cry of a hidden rebellion. It was one of the rights of the Collective, but why was it sprayed on the walls like it was a sacred phrase to only be shared in hushed voices? Why would the Network then mask it over?

"You alright?" Briggs asked

"Yes."

They continued inside and found a private booth. Briggs sat forward as he spoke.

"I want to thank you again for looking after me last night. And for what you've done this morning to try and catch a killer. I want you to know that I appreciate your help."

"That's OK. I wanted to help. Something strange is happening, and I don't want to sit by and watch it happen around me."

"Still, I feel responsible that you were put in danger. How are your eyes?"

"The pain's mostly gone. But until they can book me in for a procedure, my vision will be split."

"What does that mean?"

"Whatever happened to me when he touched me caused something in my optics to break. Now I can see both the projected reality as well as the old reality beneath it, but in different colours."

"So, when you look at me, you can see through my projection?" he asked.

She wondered if he felt vulnerable, like the people in the entrance to the transit the other night who were offended that she could see their oldself when the line of sight was obscured by the rain. She decided to be honest—he didn't seem particularly vain. She looked at him before looking around the room.

"Yes. I can see the injury on your forehead as well as the work I did to mask it. I can see that half of the people in this room are actually teepers—why they are meeting in a coffee shop is beyond me. I can see every tracking marker on every wall, and when I was outside, I could even see the dome through the projection of the cloudy blue sky."

"Sounds strange. I think that would make me sick. I have a problem with my balance when the virtual environment clashes with the physical. Something called AVS."

"Oh, I've heard of that. Is that why you wouldn't drive the teeper?"

"Yes." Briggs seemed to mull this over, touching his injured forehead. "If it had been me piloting the teeper, then it might have been me in your position. Again, I'm sorry to have you involved."

Carli didn't respond. She'd been upset by the experience, but didn't feel like Briggs deserved the blame.

"That's OK. It was this Basilicus' fault, whoever he is."

"Well, he has a name now. I was just speaking with some colleagues at ONI. They seem to have accepted my arguments and asked me to help."

"So you're a police officer again?"

Briggs looked down, "Not quite. I'm still on leave but just helping out."

"That doesn't seem fair," she said.

"Maybe. Hang on…" Briggs raised his hand towards his face and gestured like he was brushing something aside. "Sorry, incoming call."

"Do you need to get it?"

Briggs paused before answering, "No, I'll call back. The Wakers. You and Percy. I think it's a dead end, but the PPD want me to investigate a little further in the remote possibility they may have had something to do with the explosion yesterday."

"I barely know Percy, and don't think I had even heard the name Wakers before yesterday," she said, slightly offended.

"How did that happen?"

Carli thought back. "This last week, I've had something of an existential crisis. A few things, probably unrelated, have caused me to question what's real and what isn't around here. Maybe more specifically, what's beautiful and what isn't. I've always thought that what I did as a sculptor was to improve what is underneath—an original creative expression of beauty, tailored for each citizen.

But at the same time, I've seen the beauty of what lies beneath the projection. Not just the beauty but the truth."

Briggs stared expressionless. She realised her revelation may not be as relevant to him as it was to her.

"I met Percy, and we chatted about what the Collective really meant—that what we all take for granted as reality was just a fake veneer. That led me to the gathering at the Areopagus yesterday, which was around the time everything seemed to go to hell."

Briggs grunted in acknowledgement. She explained more of the story at his prompting. Sometimes he asked her to repeat an answer, but in a different order. She could see his fingers moving, probably recording notes. The feeling of being under the microscope made her uncomfortable.

"So, Percy's taken off for now? You said he left you a message?" he asked.

"Yes. I think his default disposition is to be paranoid, especially once the police are involved."

"I'll need to have another chat with him. I think this Waker's thing is a distraction, but I've been asked to follow up nonetheless. I have Percy's contact details, and I've already left him a message, but it might help if you could send him the same message asking him to contact me. You know him a little better than I do."

"Sure. You said you now know who this man is. How did that happen?"

Carli saw Briggs chew the side of his mouth before he answered, "It turns out ONI had a file on him, but didn't know what he'd been up to in the last few years. We compared images, and it turned out we have a match."

Carli's eyes widened. "Care to share?"

"Sure." She received a file, which she opened. Immediately, she noticed a sharing timeout of 10 seconds in her optics. She took in the image of the man's oldself. His face was scarred, one of his ears almost missing entirely. A grotesque face, unique in its own way, but she found no beauty there—not when she knew what this man was alleged to have done. Not after he had attacked her personally.

The image vanished when its timeout expired. "Does he have a name?" she asked.

"Yes. Liam Nolan."

Since his escape from the transit station, Liam's employer had been as silent as the rest of the Network. Silence was not abnormal for hours at a time, yet he grew concerned that his near miss would not be well received.

He stared at his left palm for what could have been the hundredth time since he'd returned to his safe house towards the edge of Praxis Central. Dull, amber-coloured plasma radiated from the centre in response to some unforeseen force. It wasn't the colour that captivated his attention but the darkness behind it. A darkness so deep it swallowed the light of the plasma as well as the ambient light from the room.

He reached down to the pocket he'd sewn into the right calf of his lifesuit and removed a flexible blade with an ivory handle. He'd taken the knife from the body of a citizen his employer had charged him to kill 18 months ago. Liam couldn't remember their real name, just their moniker—one repeated on many news posts and public conferences in the time since. He'd enticed the target away from his expensive-looking apartment in Norwich to a storage complex. His employer had given Liam instructions to offer his target important information about one of the Overseers who was starting to lose followership.

He wasn't the first person Liam had killed, but he was the first using the mystery device implanted in his prosthetic hand. His employer had been adamant that he use the virus rather than a more *traditional* method. As the man dropped first to his knees in silent capitulation before slumping onto his chest, Liam found the blade concealed behind the man's hip—easily visible once his projection deactivated at the time of his death. He disposed of the body in a storage cell he'd leased an hour earlier before removing the blade and keeping it for himself. As he closed the door, he noticed a strange smell—a combination of burning plastic and flesh.

The blade was far from ideal for self-defence—Liam reckoned it was likely a filleting knife recovered from the Old-World. Its flexibility made it light, and the bone handle blended in with the colour of his lifesuit, making it very easy to conceal.

With the short sleeve of his lifesuit rolled up, he positioned the tip of the blade between the scarred flesh below his left elbow and the polymer sheath that was his forearm. It wasn't the first time he'd done this—using the tip of the knife and what little feeling he had in the stump below his elbow to count the number of wires and tendons between the dead and the barely living which transmitted his body's instructions to his hand and back again. These didn't physically hold his hand to his arm. *That* job was done by two carbon fibre bones, replacing his radius and ulna. They were now the strongest bones in his body.

Liam positioned the blade higher, pressing through his skin into the notch where his humerus bone rested against his artificial ulna. He visualised the cut he would make, comparing it to his memory of the streams he'd watched on the Network. His blade pressed a little deeper, his burned nerve endings finally triggering some semblance of pain. He held it there for a few more seconds, before releasing the pressure and returning the blade to its sheath. From a nearly invisible line on his elbow, dots of blood began to appear.

This was Liam's last resort. His employer's control over him was linked to that hand. The moment Liam exhausted his usefulness, he was certain his employer would use this hand to end his life with no warning whatsoever.

Liam's mind went to the girl who had followed him on the transit. Her identity was burned into his memory, "MalvinaHoffman". He wasn't sure if delivering the virus to her teeper would have had the same effect as if it were in the flesh, but the moment he was reconnected with the Network, he intended to find out for sure.

*If my employer lets me live that long.* In addition to failing to get away from Augmosis undetected, he'd also caused a scene at Praxis Central station. Now in the space of three days, he'd lost two identities and deployed his device two more times than specifically directed by his employer.

He was snapped out of a daze with a chime in his phonics, alerting him to an incoming message. It carried another mysterious ID.

<D0CC42-7E52F8> REPORT.

Liam looked one more time at his prosthetic hand as though it would turn on him at any moment, before composing a response

<NULL> I WAS FOLLOWED FROM AUGMOSIS BY A TEEPER. POLICE WERE CALLED TO PRAXIS CENTRAL STATION. I NEEDED A DISTRACTION.

Another message was received, this time from another mystery identifier.

<26AFDE-64B2D4> UNACCEPTABLE. WE CANNOT KEEP ASSIGNING NEW IDENTITIES.

Liam swore and balled a fist before relaxing just enough to reply.

<NULL> SCREW YOU. YOU SENT ME TO MURDER GOLDSTEIN, IN ONE OF THE MOST SECURE FACILITIES ON THE PLANET. I WAS LUCKY TO GET AWAY AT ALL.

His hand went to the handle of the knife in his calf, where it hovered, waiting for a response—some clue that would tell him if his life was now at risk. He waited, but no response came. He sat there, poised for at least five minutes before he allowed his body to relax, first with his fingers, then his shoulders. His phonics chimed once more.

<C4DC8A-DFA02F> STAY CONCEALED UNTIL A NEW IDENTITY CAN BE ISSUED.

His heart sank—equal parts relief and anger at being manipulated once more. He replied.

<NULL> WHAT OF THE GIRL? MALVINAHOFFMAN?

The message returned with an error.

<NETWORK> CITIZEN <C4DC8A-DFA02F> NOT FOUND

*Dammit.*

One more life, but there was no way he was going to play this game any longer. As soon as he was back on the grid, he was going to continue with the plan he'd made earlier that morning—to push south to Kenmore, wash his bits through the Accountant and separate himself from the ticking time bomb at the end of his elbow. With almost a million bits, a new identity could be forged or acquired. His employer was not the only one who could work *that* miracle.

Liam looked around his domicile—nearly identical to the one he'd used in West Praxis. There were a few rations available. They'd last him a day or two. A bottle of synthetic vodka he'd purchased when he was relocating was nearly empty, and he'd lost his platinum chips and the few extra doses of Vallux acquired the day before.

*The next 24 hours are going to be hell.*

**53**

Briggs offered to escort Carli back to her domicile, but she declined—a response he was quietly happy to hear since he didn't want to leave Praxis Central just yet. He was certain Liam Nolan was still here somewhere, hiding amongst the nearly 200,000 citizens calling the hub home.

He remained in the same café where they had eaten lunch, the waiter diligently filling his coffee at random intervals but otherwise giving him space to work. Alone again, a familiar but dangerous voice suggested he should probably go and find a bar and order something to drink. He pushed the idea aside—not out of willpower but simply because continuing the investigation seemed the more urgent distraction.

He submitted Carli's formal statement back to Lt. Gomes, which he'd captured with her consent at the end of their meeting. He checked in on the status of the footage warrants but was advised it was still pending. He briefly scanned the file received on Liam Nolan from ONI—it was long and would take him most of the night to review, so for now, he parked it, intending to work through it when he had time.

He brought up the missed call he'd received whilst he was interviewing Carli. The caller identified as 'Doctor Imogen Godfrey'—not a name he'd heard of before. He turned to face a mirrored wall on the side of his booth and initiated a video call. The mirror morphed into the view of a middle-aged female wearing a business suit and a white lab coat.

"Detective Briggs, thank you for returning my call."

"I'm sorry... Doctor? Have we met? I don't recognise your name."

"I am Aldus Goldstein's special projects director at Augmosis."

Briggs vaguely remembered seeing her when he'd visited Goldstein a few days earlier. "Oh, I'm sorry for your loss," Briggs offered.

"And I, you—yesterday was a dark day, for all of us. I'll get to the point, Detective: I think we need to talk—somewhere privately. Aldus… Goldstein kept me apprised of your discussions, and I understand you had a breakthrough yesterday. But I… I think there is more I can do to help."

Briggs thought she seemed genuinely upset, which was understandable, but was there something more—maybe fear?

"Doctor, I'm presently on temporary leave with the PPD—I believe Deputy Moya is leading all formal discussions with Augmosis. It may not be appropriate for me to go around formal channels."

"Oh. That explains why I couldn't connect with you through the liaison office. Detective, I am not speaking on behalf of Augmosis. Aldus' projects were separate from the rest of Augmosis' business—in fact, with him gone, none of us are sure what will be happening to our team. Goldstein trusted you enough to bring you in—I think you need to know of something new that has happened."

Briggs thought carefully and weighed the risks of continuing to speak with Augmosis outside of official channels. He wanted to know what information she needed to share. He already believed Goldstein was most likely murdered. Any information confirming that would be beneficial to building a case, but it wasn't going to help him in the short term. Still, having a new contact from inside Augmosis was too tempting to turn away.

On the other hand, he feared losing any goodwill he may have established with Lt. Gomes if he went rogue again. For now, it felt like he had his foot back in the door with the PPD. He had no problems working without a safety net, but a PPD badge gave him access to far better information.

"Okay, Doctor. I'm not in a private space to discuss—I'll reconnect with you later."

Briggs didn't know when that would be or where. Nor had he decided if it was something he would bring to Lt Gomes' attention, but rather than deciding to cross another line now, he decided to kick the problem down the road to a later time.

After disconnecting, he went back to his personal files and began working through the notes he'd recorded over the last few days, as well as the information he'd received from Augmosis on rephased identities. He was certain Nolan was responsible for the murders in West Praxis as well as Aldus Goldstein. But the

PPD bombing could still be another actor. He prepared a timeline of Liam Nolan's movements.

| 99.12.22 CD 8:09AM [WEST PRAXIS] | ZAIMIS MURDERED BY KORB1K (NOLAN). |
|---|---|
| 99.12.22 CD 9:17AM [WEST PRAXIS] | NGUYEN MURDERED. "KORB1K" ID DESTROYED. |
| 99.12.22 CD 11:44PM [WEST PRAXIS] | NOLAN STILL NO ID—ASSAULTS DENIZ HARPER |
| 99.12.23 CD 10:10AM [WEST PRAXIS] | NOLAN ASSIGNED "BASILICUS" ID |
| 99.12.23 CD 10:52AM [WEST PRAXIS] | BASILICUS (NOLAN) ENTERS TRANSIT STATION |
| 99.12.23 CD 11:15AM [PRAXIS CENTRAL] | BASILICUS (NOLAN) ENTERS TRANSIT STATION |
| 99.12.24 CD 12:04PM [PRAXIS CENTRAL] | BASILICUS (NOLAN) ENTERS TRANSIT STATION |
| 99.12.24 CD 12:21PM [AUGMOSIS] | BASILICUS (NOLAN) LEAVES TRANSIT STATION |
| 99.12.24 CD 12:41PM [PRAXIS CENTRAL] | PPD FIRST EXPLOSION |
| 99.12.24 CD 12:50PM [AUGMOSIS] | GOLDSTEIN MURDERED BY BASILICUS (NOLAN) |
| 99.12.24 CD 1:01PM | ALL TRANSITS LOCKED DOWN |
| 99.12.25 CD 9:00AM [AUGMOSIS] | BASILICUS (NOLAN) ENTERS TRANSIT STATION |
| 99.12.25 CD 9:19AM [PRAXIS CENTRAL] | "BASILICUS" ID DESTROYED. |
| 99.12.25 CD 9:20AM [PRAXIS CENTRAL] | NOLAN DESTROYS CARLI'S TEEPER |

The last few timestamps were guesses based on his personal notes since he didn't have access to those logs from the PPD. The most important part of the equation was that it took almost 25 hours from when Nolan's first ID was destroyed to when a new ID was assigned to him. During this time, confirmed by Deniz Harper's assault in West Praxis, Nolan was "bare" with no projection other than his disfigured face.

Briggs brought up several images of Nolan from those provided to him by ONI. Other than the scarred skin, the near absence of a nose and his left ear, Briggs found an anger-fuelled determination. Whatever events led to the creation of Liam Nolan the murderer, were set in steel behind his piercing eyes. Briggs reviewed some of the other medical records—all personal notes recorded by the IA officer, Curran—they revealed a history of drug abuse, both stimulants and synthicol in the period after the death of his partner—most likely a dependency created from managing pain and skin restorations. He found notes from a psychological assessment: insomnia disorder and attention deficit hyperactivity disorder were recorded.

Returning to his timeline, he asked himself the question: *if you are holed up waiting to receive a new ID, why take the risk of leaving your safe house and going to a bar for a drink?*

He felt the sleeve of pills in his pocket and carefully pulled them out. Green circles with a "VX" stamped on them. *Vallux.* He'd taken a few himself but not for a while. Illegal, but not highly sought after—more of a downer than an upper. Briggs considered the records on Nolan's medical history again.

*If you get separated from your normal safehouse, suffer from insomnia, and must wait up to 25 hours to receive a new ID before you can connect to the Network, what do you do?* Again, he wasn't certain, but of all the possible vices in Praxis, Briggs felt he at least understood drug dependency. If someone needs drugs to function, there is no risk you wouldn't take. *And if I have his drugs, then pretty soon he's going to start taking some more risks.*

He created a countdown time in his optics, overlaying it at the top right of his vision. The current time was 1:35pm. He didn't know if 25 hours for a new ID was fast, slow or average, but with only one data point, he had nothing else to go off. He did the maths, rounded it down and set the timer to 18 hours and pressed, "start".

For the next hour, Briggs poured through the remaining files on Liam Nolan provided by Sergeant Curran. They were far from complete, full of notes where she appeared to have reconstructed her case files from memory. With the original files scrubbed, it was the best she could do. A few personal descriptions stood out for him: "only trusts himself" and "does not like being controlled". Briggs thought those comments probably described him too.

A message came through the Network to him from Lt. Gomes.

<PPD-GomesCons> GOT YOUR VIDEO FEEDS INCOMING. IF YOU WANT TO HELP, COME BACK TO OUR OFFICE TO REVIEW THEM.

Briggs acknowledged the request, settled his account, and paid a small tip to the wait staff for letting him use the booth before returning to the new ONI offices a few blocks away.

An admin officer greeted him by name on level 19 and directed him towards a meeting room. He stepped through the door, expecting to find the Lieutenant, but was instead greeted by a green-skinned lizard with yellow eyes. He almost stepped back in shock before reading the creature's moniker as "SpecialistHavoc".

"Looks like we're partners, Sarge," the lizard said.

"You can't be serious."

**54**

The expected feeling of safety and normality opening the door to her Archibald domicile fell short of Carli's expectations. It was home but different: Her expensive beach scape now looked a sickly yellow and green, interspersed with grit and stains from the wall beneath it. Rubbing her eyes for the hundredth time gave her no miraculous cure for the dull pain behind them, nor the disorientating feeling of seeing two different realities simultaneously.

She sat on the corner of her bed, initiated a call with Mount Tabor Augment Institute and enquired about a possible appointment time to repair her eyesight. The receptionist had received a report from the augment clinic in Praxis Central but she was still compelled to recount the story twice before they accepted an appointment a week later. Her health insurance wouldn't cover it, and the cost was going to be almost a month's wages.

Maybe she could get something back from the PPD—she found a claim form on the Network and was promptly told it would be assessed in due course. She made a mental note to follow the matter up with Detective Briggs the next time she saw him—if she saw him at all.

She connected to the NuSculpt private network and submitted a leave form, along with a digital certificate she'd received from the augment clinician. Her contract limited sick leave to only a week before she would start to be paid a partial wage subsidised through sacrificing future dividends from the company. One of the "perks" of being a partner meant her salary was tied to her contribution towards company profits, something which was going to have to go on hold for a few weeks until she recovered.

Tired and frustrated, she collapsed onto the bed and stared at the ceiling, noting for the first time the imperfections and stains. One corner looked like it might even be harbouring the beginnings of a mould infestation. She wanted to sleep, but it was far too early in the afternoon, so after counting the spots on the ceiling, she rolled off the bed, peeled off her lifesuit, placed it in the fresher and took a long, hot shower.

Afterwards, she stood in front of the vanity mirror, wiping the condensing steam to see her reflection. Her whole body was a sickly mustard colour. She saw the trueself she'd sculpted: every forced imperfection, every computer-generated pore and hair follicle. She saw the oldself beneath it: creases and lines, small patches of red or dry skin. Short grey hairs sprouted amongst her patchy, short-cropped hair—she hadn't noticed them before.

As she dressed in a fresh lifesuit, a chime in her phonics drew her to an incoming message: an invitation to join a virtual space. The invitation flagged the moniker of the sender and Carli recognised it as Percy's. A message followed afterwards.

<WOLLEMI> HEY. I'VE BEEN OFF-GRID TRYING TO PROCESS ALL THAT'S GOING ON. PLEASE JOIN THIS SPACE. I'VE GOT AN EXTRA CRYPTO RUNNING FOR SECURITY.

Carli hesitated, but settled into a comfortable chair and initiated the connection. After a brief delay, her optics darkened almost to black before crystallising back to reveal two-thirds of a virtual space. She stood on the veranda of some old structure. Beyond the veranda, red dust blew over spiny plants under a hot sun. The structure had a service area—a bar made from rusty tin and adorned with virtual stickers and flags. An elderly woman with a weathered face cleaned the counter—a callout over her head told Carli she was part of the decoration and not a virtual participant.

Next to the bar area was a gaming table with two more virtual characters playing a game of pool. Behind them were booths decorated with the same rusted metal and old wood. Three people sat in the final booth. The wall behind was covered with weathered signs, most of them yellow with arrows and glyphs she didn't recognise. One read, "Beware—Unfenced Road" and another, "Snakes spotted in this area". Carli thought that seemed a timely warning.

Someone stood from the table—Percy and he gestured for her to approach.

She controlled her virtual character towards the table and told it to sit. Other than Percy, she could not identify the other two at the table. Their projections were identical—non-binary mannequins. The Network gave her no other information, like a moniker. Their expressionless faces and dead eyes were unsettling. Both looked in Carli's direction, nodded and disappeared as they disconnected from the virtual space.

"Hey Carli."

"Percy. This place is… different."

"I like meeting here—it's rustic."

"Who were those people?"

"Just acquaintances. We meet often in places like this, usually small groups, but in the last 24 hours, most of us, the Wakers, have felt a little uncomfortable."

"I've been feeling a little uncomfortable myself."

Percy leaned a little closer. "How is your vision?"

"Messed up. The augment technician said I've lost all blue spectrum from the Network—so I can see a little of the old reality at the same time as the new. Pain seems to be taken care of for now but I'm not going to be able to work until it's fixed."

"So, only a few days ago, you wanted a glimpse of the truth concealed by the lies above it. Now you can see part of that truth for yourself—maybe even clearer than anyone can."

"You make it sound like some sort of blessing. I can assure you it's not. There's a reason we don't live in a split reality—I'm trying my hardest just to ignore the shadows of my home peeking through into this space."

"So, what did you see before this—when you were walking around the streets of Praxis?"

"It was dirty. Bland. There's a reason every surface has been masked by the Network—everything looks disgusting."

"*Everything?*"

"Maybe not everything. Lots more real faces—so different to their projections. People with changed ethnicity, gender, height, and weight. Lots of stained lifesuits that should have been 'freshed weeks ago. A lot more teepers walking the streets than I would have thought."

"Amazing. Maybe it's a curse. Maybe it's a gift. I have heard of people going to places—underground places—where for a few thousand bits they will surgically remove their optics and phonics and try to live outside of the Network."

"How does that even work?" Carli asked.

"It doesn't. The freedom of being disconnected only seems to last as long as the inconvenience of not being able to connect and transact with everyone else. There aren't any jobs in Praxis if you can't connect with the Network. After a few weeks, they usually pay more bits to slave themselves back into the machine."

"Slaves. That's not the first time you've used that word. Do you really believe it?"

He paused dramatically. "With every fibre of my being."

"If we're all slaves, then who is the master?" Percy didn't get a chance to answer before a chirp alerted Carli that the time was now 3:00 pm and the Council of Overseers was now meeting."

"Sorry, Percy, I want to watch the Overseer. I'll connect with you after." She was just about to disconnect before remembering to say, "Oh—Detective Briggs says he needs to speak with you."

## 55

An hour into the review of the footage, Briggs stood to stretch his legs. At first pass the footage was inconclusive—multiple cameras conveniently scrubbed within the transit platform, concourse and even the hub street cameras. There were no cameras in the transit itself and he expected anyone with banked footage would find it scrubbed, just as his and Carli's had.

Briggs realised there was a pattern to the scrubbed camera footage. The time sequence when each camera's footage was scrubbed spoke to him through the random noise. The cuts were too perfect, too precise. Running with the theory that each camera's footage was only scrubbed from the exact moment Liam Nolan was in view, Briggs could plot an approximate path on foot. From the platform up to the street had been relatively easy, but once on the street, a larger number of cameras made the task of tracking Nolan's journey more complicated.

Still, after unifying the default views for each camera with maps and a few other assumptions, a journey to the south of the transit station was clear. At 16 minutes and 40 seconds after the footage was distorted, it returned to normal, and Briggs found his man, walking purposefully away, tracked by a handful of image cameras. His face concealed in every shot, always walking away from the direction of the camera. But for brief periods, Briggs could see the appearance of scars on the back of the man's head and left ear through the pixelated images.

The further south he travelled, the fewer cameras were available to track his transit until he disappeared from the footage altogether. With a few simulations, Briggs was confident Liam Nolan entered one of three low-cost apartment complexes, each containing 200 domiciles.

"Looks like we've got him pinned down, Sarge," the lizard said.

"We agreed, you call me Briggs, and I'll call you whatever ridiculous name you chose for yourself." As irritating as Briggs found him, SpecialistHavoc, or Havoc as he'd said was an acceptable abbreviation, had been more than useful poring through the footage. His speed in reviewing each clip and mapping these against the camera positions on the Praxis Central map had saved Briggs at least an hour of work and headache. Briggs even conceded his need to double-check what Havoc was doing at each step had probably slowed him down, but the result was rock solid.

"Get this to the LT," he said. "We need eyes out there right now."

"I thought you said we had another 18 hours?"

"Maybe, but he's stepped out unmasked before."

"Right, well, you go catch the bad guy and I'll hang here. I need to figure out how he's scrubbing the footage. Most of those cameras are private—it took 23 warrants to get them. That means Sark's got some mean skills—not just to gain access to each system but to know what to look for and how to remove the evidence." Havoc said.

"Sark?" Briggs asked.

"Yeah. Sark's always the bad guy. You got someone exploiting a bug in the system, then you call him 'Sark'."

Briggs just stared at the lizard's sickly face—it was like he was speaking another language. His mouth opened a fraction as he considered asking what he was talking about, then thought better.

"None of this seems to explain your other disappearing projection problem," Havoc said.

"I think it's everyone's problem, but you're right, it doesn't look connected. Is Gomes following up on that, too?"

"Maybe—not with me. My skillset is more around connectivity and messaging. There's probably another consultant working on that, but I don't know anyone who knows how those services work. They're all locked up pretty tight in the castle."

"Castle?"

"Augmosis—c'mon Sarge, uh, Briggs... As far as the Network's concerned, everything goes through Augmosis. We've been living and breathing their IP for a century. ONI only accesses what they let us, and that's only a tiny fraction of the systems running this place. We only see the layer of services above those that actually do the heavy lifting. Anything interesting is encapsulated away."

Briggs stalled before replying, "So how do all of the hackers—black hats break into finance accounts or forge new IDs or reprogram teepers or whatever?"

"Because no software is flawless. All you need is a vector, one hole in the top layer of security to get to the layer beneath and the layer beneath that again. Augmosis can patch the hole if they discover it—and in a hundred years you'd hope they've got all the kinks out, but the best hats don't share every vulnerability they find—they don't even exploit them for themselves—they just hoard them until they need them. Occasionally, they'll try to sell them on the black market, but most of them aren't in it for the bits, just the glory—and you can't enjoy the glory if you're locked up."

"Is that your story? Did Gomes give you the chance to work off some time?"

Havoc's lizard face tilted. Even his blinks were masked—animating horizontally rather than vertically. "No way, Sarge. My hat's clean."

<hr>

"This is good intel, Detective. Actionable. I'll get people on it now." Briggs had found Lieutenant Gomes in the same meeting room as earlier in the day. He stood patiently whilst she reviewed and considered his findings.

"I'm glad you approve. Three buildings. If you put them in lockdown and get enough bodies down there, you should be able to find him. Even if it takes a day to clear each room."

"That's only happening if the Overseer grants us our emergency powers. No judge would issue a warrant for the search of a few hundred private domiciles."

"Then split the warrants," Briggs proposed. "Break them down into small groups and spread them across the whole Justice division. Surely Justice understands the magnitude of what's going on."

"Sorry Briggs, that's not going to happen. This footage and our own memories are the only things we can go off. Without hard evidence—banked footage or something tangible, I don't like the chances of getting a warrant to search a single domicile, let alone to search three whole buildings. The best we can do is get all the eyes and ears we have available on those three buildings and wait for him to make a move."

Briggs stood to leave. He wasn't satisfied with the answer but was eager to get to the location and start working on a perimeter.

"So, who's running point? Where do you want me?"

Gomes remained seated, "Um, Detective… Hal—I don't think that's a good idea."

"Nor do I." Deputy Moya appeared in the doorway like a 6-foot 3 shadow.

Briggs reeled at the voice like he'd been hit with a stun round. He could do nothing but glare at the Deputy Commissioner before finding his voice.

"You can't be serious? I've brought you the only leads on this guy and I've only been chasing him for less than a week. You clowns in ONI have known about him for how long? And how far have you gotten?"

"Detective, please—sit down…"

"This guy's killed the father of the Network. He's killed 13 officers. 14 including Nguyen." He pointed to Gomes, "*Your* captain *and* mine. Our family…"

Moya approached calmly, hands raised. "You need to cool it, Detective."

It took every ounce of self-control he had left to rein in his temper. He forced his clenched fists out by sheer force of will. His subconscious wanted him to fold his arms, but he fought that urge too, settling for gripping one hand in the other and holding them tightly together in front of his waist.

Moya continued. "There's no hard evidence connecting your suspect with the Network Crimes bombing. Nguyen and Zaimis—maybe. Aldus Goldstein—circumstantial at best."

Briggs continued, knowing he couldn't hide his frustration. "Have you even been following what's been going on in the last few hours? This isn't just my crazy theories—ONI, including the Lieutenant, have seen this with their own eyes: a suspect disappearing into thin air; his moniker disappearing with it; banked footage continuing to be scrubbed for multiple people's accounts."

"That's concerning, but none of it directly intersects with the Network Crimes bombing. That's my priority. That's Lieutenant Gomes' priority. That's the whole department's priority."

"Well, it doesn't look like it from where I'm standing. If you were serious, then you'd have me in the game, not on the bench."

"And if *you* were serious…"

"Gentlemen, this doesn't get us anywhere." Lieutenant Gomes stood. Her interruption caused Briggs to break eye contact with Moya, but he could still feel the Deputy's eyes burning through the back of his head.

Gomes continued, "Deputy, I think we have solid intel that the fugitive Liam Nolan is holed up in one of three apartment complexes in the southern reaches of Praxis Central. I believe it is more than justified to put eyes and ears around the location. And if the Overseer has granted us emergency powers, we might be able to close in a lot faster rather than waiting for him to show his face."

Moya grunted, and Briggs turned to look. His face was sterner than ever. "Unfortunately, that won't be possible. The motion for emergency powers was rejected. We didn't even come close."

# 56

Carli had been standing during most of the meeting of the Council of Overseers, adopting the position of a gallery observer. There were scripted speeches and procedures she didn't care to understand. The motion to enact a one-week state of emergency was finally presented by the representative of the administrative division, identified as PraxisAdministration. This was explained as granting additional powers to monitor and track suspects and associates relating to yesterday's bombing.

Only one Overseer spoke to the motion: ArdentBlue. She stood confidently, eyeing some of the other members before addressing the Collective presence in the centre of the room.

"We have already spoken of the tragedy of yesterday's attack on the PPD. This motion asks us to set aside the liberties we enjoy—the liberties some of our finest died fighting to protect—all under the guise of safety. My only response is to quote from one of the founders of the world before this one who said: 'Any society that will give up a little liberty to gain a little security will deserve neither and lose both.'"

ArdentBlue hesitated, her voice wavering, and she wiped a virtual tear from her face before continuing with a renewed, albeit staged confidence, "The cost of losing liberty is too high. I do not support this motion."

The motion was put to a vote and failed. Of the 21 members, only 5 voted in support.

Carli slowly sat, shocked. She didn't like the principle of the motion, but she was convinced that the temporary loss of liberty was worth it to restore order.

*Even ArdentBlue—I know she holds freedom and liberty above all else, but I thought she might stretch her principles in the interest of public safety.*

The Network delivered Carli another cryptic invitation to rejoin Percy in the virtual meeting. She accepted, and her reality merged back into the virtual space. Percy sat alone at the same table.

"What did you think of that?" Carli asked.

"Not unexpected," he replied, "The Council of Overseers hasn't rocked the status quo for decades. Their very existence is a representation of the status quo."

"I suppose," she conceded. "Kind of makes you wonder what the point of them is anyway."

"Ha!" Percy did a virtual clap in front of her, "Now you're catching on—but maybe not in the way you think. The Overseer is just a reflection of us all. The aggregate of millions of citizens pledging their support for certain policies, philosophies, and agendas. If they are ineffectual, it is because the Collective is ineffectual. If they are apathetic, it is because we are apathetic."

That didn't sound true to Carli. She wasn't apathetic, was she? She cared deeply for these issues, especially now that it seemed like her right to project what she chose was being stripped away.

Percy continued, "The Overseer, the Collective, even the very systems on which the whole Network runs—the best they can do is keep everyone compliant and submissive whilst calling it freedom. That is what we organise against Carli. *That* is why the Wakers exist—to snap us out of this shared delusion that reality is what we make it, instead of what it truly is."

Carli grew angry, but wasn't sure why. She wanted to argue but felt too weary to engage.

"Carli, have you ever heard of the Philosopher's Cave?"

"No?" she replied.

"It's a very old story—a philosophical allegory. I'd love to show you—it explains things better than I can."

The virtual room Carli was in faded to blackness and a new scene appeared. She was now in a cave. Two men sat facing a stone wall, shackled by their hands, feet, and neck, such that neither could move. A flickering fire far behind them caused shadows to dance on the wall in front of them.

"This is a simple sim," Percy explained. "We are just observers—it will play out like a movie."

A recorded message, in a smooth, reassuring voice, commenced, explaining what Carli was watching:

*Lysander and Xenophanes have been bound and shackled in this cave since they were small children. Their shackles prevented them from turning their heads, and since no one interacted with them, all they ever saw of the world was the cave wall and the shadows cast upon it by the fire behind them. As other people walked between them and the fire, they cast new shadows on the wall. As those people carried things like a plant, a baby and a puppy, they named the shadows they cast without being able to see them directly.*

*Suddenly, Lysander's shackles fell off and he realised he was free. For the first time, he turned and walked past the fire towards the blinding light outside the cave. Shielding his eyes until they adjusted, he saw each of these objects directly for the first time in living colour—illuminated by the 'true light' of the sun. The shadows he'd been perceiving his whole life were just a poor imitation of the real thing.*

*Lysander ran back into the cave, desperate to share his discovery with Xenophanes. But with his eyes now adjusted to the bright light outside, he could barely see his own steps, let alone the shadows on the wall caused by the fire.*

*Finding his friend in the darkness, he tried to explain everything he'd seen. "Xenophanes! You are only looking at shadows! These are but phantoms—poor imitations of reality. See—I have released your shackles—come discover the truth for yourself!"*

*But sadly, Xenophanes resisted, "Lysander, you are a fool to believe such lies. I have seen the shadows on the wall and know the truth. There is simply nothing else to know of the world than what I have already seen."*

*Lysander couldn't understand—he had seen the true reality in all of its beauty, but his friend only wanted to settle for the phantoms cast on the wall by the dim firelight. He even tried to force his friend out of the cave so he could see for himself, but Xenophanes attacked him and almost killed him. So afraid was Xenophanes of the threat of having his simple reality challenged, he would rather kill his friend than accept the truth.*

The simulation dissolved, and Carli was back at the virtual table, seated with Percy. He locked eyes with hers, clearly waiting for her to say something, but she held back. She thought the sim was trying too hard to make its point and found herself being manipulated.

"Carli, every human being in the Collective is shackled, watching shadows dance on the wall, and calling it utopia. Augmosis has made those shadows look and sound indistinguishable from the real thing, but they are still just phantoms—imitations of reality. It's time all of us left the cave and saw things for ourselves."

"It's a good presentation, Percy. I think I understand what you are trying to say—that the two prisoners are unenlightened until one finds the truth, but the other is too ignorant to accept it. But if you are saying that's the same thing as the Collective, then I think your analogy falls short."

"Go on?" he said.

"If the shadows on the wall represent the projection of the Collective and the reality outside the cave is supposed to represent some greater truth, then you haven't explained what the alternative is. Is the 'better alternative this same world with the projections turned off? Is it the world without the Network entirely? Is it the world outside the domes? Because I've seen something of what this place looks like without projections, and it's cold and ugly. Other than the beauty of the people themselves, everything else is just bland."

Percy hesitated. "Why should that matter?"

"Because if you are trying to convince me and everyone else that we need a change, then the 'true light' needs to be a more attractive proposition than what I can see now. Even if you forced this on everyone, they would rebel, just like the second prisoner in your story. People will fight to protect what they know—not because they are happy in their ignorance, but because what they know is the best reality we can all hope for."

He stroked his virtual chin before responding. "Maybe you're right. But maybe the goal shouldn't be to convince people that the true light is prettier or better than what everyone sees now, but simply necessary."

"Necessary? What do you mean?"

"This place is dying, Carli. Seeing the truth isn't just a philosophical argument, but the survival of the human species. Birth rates aren't maintaining the population. Since the first decades of the Collective, there has been a steady decline in the birth rate—it's not reported on and even if it was, I'm not sure people would care—they are too plugged into the Network, worried about their liberties and their creative expression, but within a few decades there will be no humanity left."

"So, what does population have to do with your argument?" she responded. "Surely population can be solved without convincing people to unplug from the Network."

Percy pulled a strange smirk, "Humanity has been fooled into believing intimacy is safest in a virtual space, but even beyond that, people just don't want to have children."

"That's not right…"

"I apologise for asking Carli, but do you want children?"

A knot settled in her stomach, and she sat back. She thought that maybe, someday, she might have children. But not now. Not without being in a stable relationship. Not without the resources of a second income. Angry, she managed to force out a response, "That's none of your business."

"Sorry—you don't need to answer, but your hesitation at least tells me you're not sure."

Carli felt anger rising again and stood, preparing to disconnect.

Percy continued, "If your reaction is the same as everyone else's, then maybe it goes some way to prove my point."

"Somehow, Percy, you manage to both inspire *and* offend me."

**57**

Briggs felt like he'd been suspended all over again. Moya offered a few more choice words about Briggs' attitude before leaving. Lt. Gomes reaffirmed that the only thing she now needed from him was to take a formal statement from Percy Hayward. He felt the same compulsion to take himself off to the nearest bar and drown his rage—the voice that usually whispered its invitation had grown to a scream. But he couldn't give himself over—not now when he felt like he was back on the trail.

He didn't care what Moya had said: if Liam Nolan wasn't personally responsible for the Network Crimes bombing, he must still be involved. The timing was too coincidental. The bombs could have been planted in the teepers days, if not weeks ago, but Nolan was also in Praxis Central for more than a full day before the bombs went off. He needed to cling to his theory, rather than make space for doubt to creep in.

He walked over to the meeting room door and closed it for privacy. He initiated a video connection call to Doctor Godfrey from Augmosis. After accepting the connection, a window showed a close profile video of Doctor Godfrey—she must be using a small handheld mirror to capture and project her image to Briggs. The room he was in had scanners to achieve the same result without needing a mirror.

"Thanks for taking my call, Doctor," Briggs recognised that the background of her video image was the gardens outside the Augmosis buildings, rather than a private meeting room within the building. "Are you in a safe place?"

"As safe as anywhere, Detective. The last few weeks have caused me to be a little *careful* with my communications. I'll get to the point—in the last twenty-four hours, we had two more nexus nodes melt down. One yesterday, and another this morning. The first…"

296

"Was Goldstein," Briggs interrupted.

"Yes—well I think so, the timestamps are near identical. But how did you know?"

"Just a hunch, but the PPD will need that data to correlate with the investigation. The other was possibly from the suspect trying to escape capture this morning."

Briggs stated the timestamps when it happened, which Godfrey confirmed aligned with Augmosis' logs. "So… You got them?" she asked.

"No, unfortunately. He used the same trick he did to Constable Nguyen a few days ago, where his projection seemed to split off from his body and stayed put as he disappeared through the crowd."

"Curious. Can you tell me what he did? To escape? It might help."

Briggs obliged, explaining what he knew as well as the pattern of scrubbed footage.

"That's very interesting. Tell me more about this weapon—you think it might be the same thing causing the plexuses and nodes to melt down?"

"Yes, I do, but I'm not sure how."

"And this suspect—do you think he is working alone?"

He'd considered this question himself after reviewing Nolan's file. "Absolutely not. This guy is a mercenary—a resourceful one, but not somebody who could invent this sort of thing himself."

"OK—I will need to think through what this information means," she said. "Was there anything else I can help you with?"

Briggs thought for a moment. *Goldstein's powers to spy on the whole Network would be useful right now, but that's not something that I can ask for, nor is it something that anyone else but him could have provided.*

He came up with an alternative, "The rephased plexuses. Can you alert me if you see any more? It would be very helpful if you could let me know of any citizens with a re-phased plexus in the next 48 hours."

"Across all of Praxis? That could be a lot," she asked.

"No—just Praxis Central."

"Okay, I can do that." She appeared to pause as if considering something. "Detective, I think you should know that my department — Aldus' department — is being dissolved by the Augmosis board as we speak. We have been given until the end of the week to accept variations to our employment contracts and be redeployed within Augmosis or to receive a redundancy."

"That seems awfully fast?" Briggs asked.

"Maybe. The board tolerated Aldus' work, even if they directly benefited from it when we generated a new idea or technology. However, the current leadership of Augmosis is very different to the founders that Aldus worked alongside. The board is run by the descendants of the original investors, and the culture is more about self-preservation than innovation. They liked to wheel Aldus Goldstein out to give them the appearance of credibility and stability, but behind the scenes, I think they saw him as more of a nuisance.

"So much of our research had no commercial objective. 'Research is its own reward, ' Aldus would say. I fear some accountant will evaluate most of our work as unviable and back it up to a node somewhere to be lost forever."

"That's sad to hear," Briggs offered. He could see tears welling in her eyes, he could tell there was more to her relationship with Goldstein than just an employer.

"Aldus… He was like a father to me. I never had a father, but he was like that to me."

Briggs felt uncomfortable. No amount of compassionate training had given him the skills to effectively deal with his own grief, let alone someone else's. All he could do was nod his head in an awkward show of support. Doctor Godfrey found some composure, looking about her surroundings, almost like she was worried about being seen.

"Detective, you should know that those nodes we showed you—the destroyed nodes when you visited Augmosis—they weren't the only ones…"

"Oh?"

"No—so far there have been one hundred and ninety-three."

Briggs' eyes widened—he didn't know if he was shocked or angry. "Nearly two hundred?"

"I'm afraid so. For the ones we showed you, we knew from the timestamps and the hypervisor logs that they were most likely connected. The others followed the same pattern but weren't linked together. Aldus didn't want to tell you. He was embarrassed enough to bring you into his circle and share what he did. This whole situation weighed on him more heavily than anything I have ever seen. He… he didn't want his legacy bookended by a significant failure."

A thousand things went through Briggs' mind, not the least being the fact that, rather than twenty possible murders at the hand of Liam Nolan, there could be nearly two hundred. But at the same time, he wasn't sure if knowing that information earlier would have made any difference to him.

*Unless I had shared the information with Captain Hagen immediately.* If more people had known, maybe better resources could have been put on the case from the start.

"How long since the nodes started to die?"

"The same period—two years. The node we showed you was number thirteen. Most of them occurred in the first year, slowed down in the second and ramped up again in the last few weeks."

"How many recently?"

"45."

A lump formed in his throat. "I'm going to need everything you have on them. Timestamps. Anything at all."

She hesitated, looking downcast, "I will get them for you. Should I also provide everything through formal channels to the PPD?"

*That was a good question*, Briggs wondered. He didn't want to repeat the same mistakes of failing to share information that might be helpful to the broader investigation, but at the same time, he didn't know how far he could trust the others in his department. Two hundred nodes indicated a broader conspiracy.

If Hagen were still alive, he would have sent the information to her. *If I had shared the information I had two days ago, maybe she would still be alive.*

"Send everything to Lieutenant Gomes from ONI. I will share her Network ID with you," he said, "but don't provide it through the normal liaison office."

He concluded the call just as the door to the meeting room opened, giving him a brief start. As if hearing her name, Lieutenant Gomes walked in and paused as she saw Briggs.

"I'm sorry, Detective, I didn't know you were still in here."

For some reason, the fact that she assumed he'd left annoyed him further. "I suppose there probably isn't any point in me staying around if I'm not being listened to."

"Please, Detective. My department deals with some of the most eccentric and childish consultants across the PPD. If you want to take your bat and ball and go home, that's your prerogative, but don't for a moment think that my keeping you off the field isn't justified.

"Alvarez' lawyer has already filed a complaint on her client's behalf. Any leads he might have been willing to share, with the correct motivation, will now be sold for a much higher price. That's not up to me, but the Praxis Prosecutor will no doubt bargain their way out of anything that looks poorly on the Department."

"So, their complaints will probably get whisked away," he said.

"Most likely. But that still leaves the PPD at risk and an administrative tribunal to decide what happens to you."

Briggs' shoulders sagged.

"Look, Detective… Hal… For what it's worth, I understand it. I'm angry too. Most likely, a month from now, you get your badge back and everyone will have put this thing behind us. But right now, in the aftermath of what happened yesterday, everyone is walking on eggshells, trying to avoid a misstep. There are just as many eyes working to figure out how we let this happen as those trying to catch whoever did it.

"But I can promise you that my mandate is to pursue all Network activity converging on yesterday's explosions to locate a source."

"What of Liam Nolan?" Briggs asked.

"Liam Nolan has been passed to Praxis Central Patrol."

"Beat cops? You think they stand a chance against this guy?"

"Patrol will be overseen by Tactical Branch. Patrol will provide surveillance, and Tactical will make the arrest if he is spotted."

This went some way to satisfy Briggs. Tactical Branch was the best team suited to this sort of thing. The fact that they had been brought in for one man was at least a step in the right direction.

"And there is still no way that I can be involved?"

"No. Best you get some rest, Detective. I don't want you anywhere near those apartments. If you want, keep following up on the Wakers and Percy Hayward, but for now, that's all."

"If you get eyes on Nolan," he said, trying his best to hide his frustration, "could you share the feed with me?"

She thought about this for a few moments before saying, "Fine." It was a small consolation, but he nodded in acceptance and headed for the elevator.

**58**

Liam awoke from a hard-won sleep by a noise outside his apartment door. *An argument* he concluded. He cursed the noise and everything else when he realised he'd only been asleep for a few hours. He hadn't tried to fall asleep, but boredom had brought him to lie down and rest his eyes well before the hidden sun outside had started to set. Now it was only 10:00 pm. He made a fist and slammed it into his mattress without thinking, and a fresh jolt of pain from bruised knuckles went up his arm, leading to another curse.

*You're not going to get back to sleep.* The voice in his head sounded like his, even if he couldn't control it. That was it. *You'll probably never sleep again.*

He stood and stretched, popping his back and neck and trying to relax his shoulders before breathing deeply and trying to slow his heart rate. He lay back down on the mattress and closed his eyes—a position lasting barely 15 seconds before his eyes opened again to stare angrily at the ceiling.

"That's it," he said to himself. "Four hours is all you get."

Still no connection to the Network. Still no chips or anything of value to trade, even if he wanted to. He looked down at his prosthetic arm and briefly wondered what it would be worth as a barter, but dismissed the idea.

He was caged again—the same way he'd felt when he was recuperating from the industrial "accident" that had taken his wife, Fi, so many years ago. As he lay alone on the hospital bed, the only rest he could find was when a computer decided it was time for a fresh release of painkillers to distract him from the painful skin grafts. Caged—the same as his six years spent in prison for avenging her death by taking the lives of the criminals responsible.

He accepted death that fateful day, not because he no longer wanted to live, but for the briefest of moments, he felt justified. He hadn't enjoyed the killing, but it seemed righteous. But he'd chosen to persevere. To survive.

*After all, death is the ultimate cage.*

His retribution for the culprits who had murdered his wife was meticulously planned. And yet the Network security blackout he'd organised at great expense to delay the police response collapsed sooner than he needed. His imminent capture and the prospect of spending the rest of his life in a cage almost led him to turn the gun on himself. The only thing stopping him was the conclusion that life in a temporary cage may still be preferable to death in a permanent one.

Liam stood again and began pacing the room. He checked the small refrigerator, and it was just as empty as the last time he'd looked in it. All he had was a faucet which he turned on just to watch the water swirl around the basin before exiting into some hidden system, probably to be captured, treated, and returned to the faucet in an unending loop. He remembered staring at the stream of water from the faucet when he was incarcerated. *That* was a whole different kind of survival.

Network access was almost non-existent in prison. Inmates could consume Network content using a paltry allowance of bits. In his high-security section, everyone wore prison-issue lifesuits but there was no projection—everyone saw each other for the ugly convicts they truly were. Removing the right to project was considered the ultimate punishment for criminals of the highest order. Electronic communication within the prison or the outside world was non-existent, except to your legal representation, who were more than happy to chat with you and rack up a fresh bill of bits to assuage your boredom.

That was why he was so surprised when he started to receive messages from some other connection offering him a chance to escape the cage. The communication was then just as it was now—each message a scrambled Network ID, different from the next…

<7432B5-C2C05E> DO YOU ENJOY THE CAGE YOU ARE LIVING IN, LIAM?

<NolanLiamAR> WHO IS THIS?

<D778CA-FA495C> WE ARE LEGION. WE WANT TO EMPLOY YOUR SERVICES. WE HAVE THE MEANS TO SEE YOU RELEASED.

<NolanLiamAR> HOW?

<515E64-CC2CD3> DOES THAT REALLY MATTER?

Liam still thought this was some sort of a joke or even a trap. He looked about the other cells in his wing to see if anyone was looking at him.

<NolanLiamAR> Fine.

There was a minute before there was a response—not in the form of a Network message but with a buzz of his cell door followed by a mechanical latch releasing and the door rolling to the side.

<6DD976-66B465> Look at yourself in the mirror.

He obeyed, he didn't see his scarred face and prison lifesuit, but he now looked like one of the guards. He also noticed that his moniker had changed to something new.

<D5C46F-6096DA> Liam Nolan no longer exists. Your new identity has limited access to this wing as a correctional services officer. Simply walk out the door.

He still didn't believe it, but stepped out into the corridor. There were no eyes on him. No guards charged at him with batons to corral him back into his cage. He walked to the end of the corridor towards the guard station. An inmate in one of the cells swore at him as he walked past, and a guard entering the secure wing gave him an affirming nod. Thirteen security checks later, Liam stood outside the front entrance of the county penitentiary and headed to the transit platform.

Liam turned off the faucet and looked at himself again in the mirror. The same scarred face. Maybe with a few more grey hairs and wrinkles. He looked at his hand—a "gift" from his employer, given to him after he was collected from the transit station. He was grateful that day.

But two years on he acknowledged the truth—everyone was living in a cage, it's just a matter of how big it is and what it is made of. Some cages are harder to break out of than those made of metal.

*Liam Nolan no longer exists.*

The lights in Briggs' Boulder apartment activated as he opened the door. He placed a freshly purchased bottle of whiskey on his kitchen bench. He'd already cracked the seal on the transit, spinning the top around nervously, but never removing it completely. He slumped into the sole lounge chair in the room functioning as his living space, but it was just a bridge between the small kitchenette and his bedroom. Feeling the pressure in his thigh, he unzipped his pocket and removed the revolver he'd found in Liam Nolan's satchel on the transit.

He inspected it closely, released and spun the cylinder, engaging the trigger a few times to test the weight of the action. It was an unusual design, with the barrel at the bottom of the cylinder rather than the top, but it seemed well maintained. The wooden grip was well-worn and stained, but was still a genuine novelty from a lost era. He activated the safety and loaded the gun with the bullets he'd put in his other pocket. He spun the cylinder one more time before placing the gun on the table next to his bottle of scotch.

He clenched his jaw and initiated a voice call to Detective Carlyle.

"Briggs? If you're asking me to storm the castle again, I'm afraid I must decline."

Briggs grunted before replying, "Not tonight. Just thought I'd check in."

"Here, check out the damage," Carlyle sent through a still image of his oldself, showing a bandage across his nose barely hiding the bruising that was radiating across his cheeks and to his eye sockets. A tracking marker had been applied to the tip of his nose like a cherry on a desert. Briggs couldn't help but snigger.

"Yeah, you laugh but I've got two weeks of sick leave and a commendation coming on my file, what do you have?"

"Fair point," Briggs replied, "Have you heard my news?"

"Not fully. I heard you're off the clock—benched personally by the big boss, but that's about it."

Briggs grunted. "Let's just say I crossed a line interviewing Alvarez. Could've done a whole lot worse, but it was more of a problem since his suit was in the room."

"Ah, makes sense. Lucky I wasn't there, or he might be sporting one of these too." Carlyle pointed to his face. "Gotta pick your battles though. It's only worth crossing that line when you can't get caught. Otherwise, my policy is to walk up to the line and piss over it."

Briggs hadn't been explicitly told to keep any of the details he'd learned to himself, but since Carlyle was involved, he at least told him the killer now had a name and was now believed to be locked down in an apartment in Praxis Central.

"Son-of-a-bitch," was all Carlyle could say, followed by a whistle. "So, we've got him surrounded in Praxis Central, hoping he pokes his head above water? Sounds like a long shot."

"Maybe."

"What are you going to do about it?"

"What do you mean?"

"C'mon, man. I know your reputation. You're in this for the hunt. Me—I'll quite happily take my two weeks' medical leave while the rest of the PPD tries to figure out who attacked them and why. But I'm guessing that right now, enjoying your PPD-funded holiday isn't going to fly."

He hated being exposed, but didn't see any other option other than to agree. "Fair enough. I was hoping that you might have access to a few other resources that might help me—just in case I should need them."

"Sure, what do you need?"

"Any inventory reports from Alvarez's hideout. ONI says the teepers may have been destroyed, but they should have at least catalogued the rest." Carlyle nodded. "And if Alvarez starts talking, any of that information would be good. Whatever was happening in West Praxis was enough for my guy to kill twice to protect it."

"I'll see what I can do. Probably won't raise any red flags for the other arresting officer to be checking in—even if I am on leave. I'll have to give you my own summaries rather than the original files, though."

"Thanks."

"Do you need anything for *personal protection*?" Carlyle asked.

He looked at the firearm on the counter beside him. "No. I'm covered. One of those thermal scopes might come in handy, though."

"That might be a problem since I lost it in Alvarez's hideout. It would have been picked up with the rest of the evidence. Damn shame. Hopefully, no one looks too closely at its serial number."

Briggs concluded the call and tapped the armrests of his chair with his hands. It was a comfortable chair, and his hand instinctively went to the side table to grab a non-existent glass of scotch that he hadn't yet poured himself. He cursed and clenched his fists, angry at himself for falling off the wagon yesterday. Angry that he hadn't done enough to protect the ones he cared about. Angry that his lapse in judgment had taken him off the case. Angry at whatever powers existed within the PPD or the universe at large to deny him the opportunity to enact justice. Angry at himself for getting his hopes up that half a day's work ingratiating himself to Lieutenant Gomes was enough to win him back his commission.

He was already impatient to receive the information from Carlyle, but he knew it was probably going to take some time and might not yield anything. Even still, he knew he had to do something. Without access to the evidence, without a commission to investigate, without a badge—what was he?

He should have felt sad. Should be mourning for the loss of a friend and the loss of purpose. But he refused to make room for mourning. The void had barely enough room to contain his anger.

Briggs remembered he'd also pocketed a sleeve of tablets from Nolan's satchel. He removed them and looked at the two green tablets, stamped with "VX". He'd taken Vallux before. It wasn't addictive, but it was more than effective at knocking someone out for a night. He stared at the pills before looking over to the bottle of scotch on his kitchen counter. His hand wrapped tightly around the pills, and he forced his eyes closed.

*Deep breaths. Slow and purposeful.* He fingered each of the pills. Even if it wasn't addictive, for Briggs, taking a drug like Vallux was still the first step towards the abyss. It had been over a year since he'd met with a PPD-assigned counsellor, and though he'd seen it as more of an obligation of his rehabilitation, he at least remembered some of the techniques to try and calm himself.

*Deep breaths. Slow and purposeful. Bring every muscle in your body to mind, from the tips of your toes upwards and will it to relax and release.*

After a few minutes, he started to feel the anger dissipating enough to recognise how tired he felt. He kicked off his shoes and stretched his toes, settling further into the chair.

As sleep approached, he heard a familiar yet comforting voice ask him, "Are you going to drink that?"

"No ma'am," he said.

# PART FOUR

"*The Collective somehow behaves comparatively to the quantum theory on which it is based. The Collective is both wave and particle. At any given moment, our perception of the Collective is simply the interference of those factors, and once observed, they are destroyed forever.*"

Camila Romero, Co-Founder

# 59

At some point during the night, Briggs' body must have decided that his bed would be a better place to sleep than his couch, no matter how comfortable he found it. He recognised the combined smell of sweat and spilled drinks on his lifesuit from two nights prior, so he removed his plexus, extracted himself from his lifesuit and placed it in the refresher whilst he had a brief, hot shower.

In a fresh set of underwear, he went to his closet and inspected his two remaining lifesuits. One was his faulty PPD lifesuit from earlier in the week, where the hand and finger sensors had been damaged. He hadn't gotten around to dropping it off to the PPD quartermaster for repair or replacement. The other was a standard lifesuit with no protective plating for when he was off duty. Since the added bulk of the PPD issue suit never bothered him, the standard lifesuit was in near-new condition.

He inspected the damaged fingerless gloves of his PPD suit. Tiny wire filaments were visible through the stretchy fabric. Fixing them was well beyond his skill set, however, it did give him an idea. Remembering what he'd been told by the medical examiner, he tried to turn the suit inside out around the collar to inspect the area behind the plexus. The rigidity of the suit made it difficult, but he was able to see four small, silvery circles on the area of the suit that would normally press against the wearer's chest.

He took the suit over to the kitchen bench, pushing the full bottle of whisky away to make space. If he had more willpower, he would've tipped it down the sink, but pushing it out of reach seemed good enough for now. From the kitchen drawer, he removed a pair of scissors and used one of the blades like a scalpel to cut away at the disc. After a few minutes, he held the disc in his hand, severed from the slightly heavier filaments connecting it to the rest of the suit.

311

Briggs retrieved his plexus and attached it to the coupling, waited for it to connect, and a stream of alerts flashed across his optics:

`LIFESUIT RIGHT GESTURE INTERFACE FAULTY, CONTACT SUPPORT.`

`LIFESUIT LEFT GESTURE INTERFACE FAULTY, CONTACT SUPPORT.`

`LIFESUIT EVS REPORTS ERROR CODE 0x0DE930, CONTACT SUPPORT.`

That last error was new, and it was exactly what he was hoping for.

---

Carli woke from a broken sleep by an alarm she'd forgotten to cancel for a job she could no longer fulfil. Her vision was unchanged. Fragmented. She found herself again thinking about the cost of yesterday's misadventure, the cost of repairing her optics and reduced income during recovery. For a moment, she allowed herself to consider if it had been worth it.

*Yes*, she conceded. She'd felt more 'in control' pursuing Briggs' fugitive than at any time she could remember. It was almost the same feeling of freedom when she'd chosen to remove her projection at the Areopagus, only for the system to push back and deny her that right.

But that sense of control had an undercurrent of fear. The more she replayed Liam Nolan's attack in her mind, the angrier she became. *If I'm attacked when my projection is hosted by a teeper, that's no different from being personally assaulted.* Her eyes now carried the wounds to prove it. For someone else, maybe someone who spent a lot of time in immersion sims and Network games where being attacked was the norm, it might not have been such a big deal. But an attack on her projection, in the real world, from her perspective, was just as offensive as having your right to project your oldself stripped away. The growing sense of violation united with the memory of his statement in the final moment, "MalvinaHoffman, you have been noticed."

Her thoughts went to Detective Briggs—he was her only connection to the PPD's investigation. *Maybe this Liam Nolan has already been caught.* She put on some joggers and decided to go for a run to clear her mind.

The centre of Archibald was a long park, one block wide and six blocks long, making each circuit about 700 metres. It was a circuit she knew well—this was her home after all, and though it had been a week since her last run, she'd hoped to run her usual seven laps. She barely finished the first.

The typically beautiful park, with its lush green grass, fountains and oriental-style gardens, was partially transparent, replaced with the same stained concrete ground covered with pillars of different sizes with tracking markers. She shouldn't have been surprised—she remembered as a child with her freshly integrated augments seeing these parks for the first time and running to touch the green-brown leaves of the large maple trees, only to find them dissolve through her hands. But seeing them for what they truly were was depressing.

Carli found a seat amongst the gardens, its cold concrete slowly creeping through the protection of her lifesuit. All around her, she expected to see the beauty of humankind's creative and technological prowess, but it could not fully mask the ugly void beneath it. After sitting silently for a few minutes, she stood to return home.

With no real food in his domicile, Briggs found a nearby eatery offering something resembling a hot Western breakfast with black coffee. He ate alone at a table as he processed a few incoming messages he'd received through the night. No messages from Lt. Gomes regarding the Liam Nolan stakeout. Nothing yet from his countless attempts to contact Percy Hayward—if he still had a badge, he would have been tempted to put out a BOLO on the guy just to get his attention.

His pulse quickened for a hopeful moment after seeing a message from Doctor Godfrey, a feeling which escalated when he read that the first plexus rephrasing had happened in Praxis Central only an hour after the altercation at the transit station. When he recognised the attached moniker as MalvinaHoffman—Carli's identity, he realised he'd gotten his hopes up prematurely.

The last message he read was from Carlyle, as promised. It was an inventory of the evidence collected from his West Praxis arrest. He wiped his mouth and tried to think through his next move. Carlyle had been right; he couldn't leave this alone—he couldn't just let the rest of the PPD try to figure this out without his help. At the same time, he recognised that boredom could be equally as problematic for him as diving deeper into his work. Without a badge, his options were limited.

It wouldn't be interesting work but at least it might be productive if he could work through the evidence reports. That was something he could do back in his apartment, but just as easily be done from anywhere. *And if that should happen to be somewhere in Praxis Central, even somewhere hypothetically close to three specific apartment complexes near Liam Nolan's last known location, surely that would be perfectly lawful?*

Briggs stood to leave but was interrupted by an incoming audio connection. Percy Hayward.

"I understand you've been wanting to speak with me," he said.

"Yes. PPD wants me to take your statement for what happened on the transit yesterday. Routine only."

"You were there. You saw the same things I did. Why do you need my report, too?"

Briggs sighed—it was a fair question, but he understood why Lt. Gomes had wanted it followed up. If there was a growing perception that The Wakers were causing disturbances across the Collective, then it made sense to at least start a dialogue, especially in the wake of the bombings. And he knew the reason why Gomes had asked him to follow up wasn't just because he'd met him, but because it would at least get him out of her hair.

"That's just what I've been asked to do. I've got no real authority right now, so I'll take your statement and get it filed with the hundreds of other statements made every day, then we both go and spend the rest of the day doing whatever."

"Can we just do it in a virtual space?"

"I'd rather face to face."

"Fine. I'll send you a place to meet in Archibald. I'll ask Carli to join as a witness."

"You don't need witnesses," Briggs said, but the connection had been cut. A message was received with the name and location of a place to meet—a public monument not far from the Archibald transit station in thirty minutes. It was presumptuous on Percy's behalf that Briggs would be able to make it in time— most places in Praxis would be more than 30 minutes travel time away. Maybe Percy assumed Briggs would use a teeper, but there was no way he would attempt that twice in just as many days. Fortunately, it so happened that he was only a few transit stops away.

He weighed his options—Archibald was further away from the City Circle. Further away from Liam Nolan. But if getting Percy's statement got him in Lt. Gomes' good graces, then maybe that was a better strategy than the alternative.

Carli sat patiently on a bench facing the 'Hommage au Fermier', a simple monument established in recognition of Archibald's status as Praxis' main agricultural centre. Its granite edifice rose two storeys from a raised platform standing guard over the mass of agricultural factories occupying most of the southern portion of the hub. Etched across its stone surface were depictions of grains and livestock, wrapping to the top where a smooth stone sphere represented the sun.

It was yet another fakery she'd accepted as real. Why Percy had asked to meet her at this location, she wasn't sure, but rather than Percy, it was Briggs who greeted her, puffing slightly. He gratefully took the offered seat next to her.

"I was expecting Percy," she said, realising afterwards that it sounded like she was disappointed to see him instead.

"Percy asked me to meet you both here so he can give a statement. Same as you did for me yesterday. He seems to frighten easily, so I'd say he asked you to sit in on the interview."

"Oh OK." Carli looked up at the statue. Other than the two of them, there was no one else paying it any attention, the closest people were a hundred metres away, hustling to or from something important.

"You know I've seen this statue a hundred times and took it for granted that some artisan had carved it from a piece of granite. But now I see that it's just another imitation that lives inside a computer. I'd imagined a whole team of people working with hand tools to chip and shape the stone into something unique when it probably took someone a few hours of Network crafting to achieve the same result."

Briggs looked up and down at the statue. "It's fake?"

"Nothing but a concrete pole with a tracking marker on it, and a whole lot of air." Briggs' gaze stayed fixed on the monument. "Doesn't that bother you?"

"Not really, I guess. I'm not an expert in statues, but it probably wouldn't mean anything different to me if it were actually made of stone. Which is to say, I probably wouldn't care either way."

Carli saw Percy approach from the direction of the transit. If she couldn't see outright that his projection was overlaid on top of a teeper, she would have guessed it from its inorganic movement as it glided towards them.

"Carli. Detective," he said as he approached.

Briggs stood and greeted him. "Let's get this over with," Percy said, hands crossed.

Briggs asked Percy a lot of the same questions she'd answered the previous day, from what happened at the Areopagus through to the point where he was forced to disconnect from the teeper in the Augmosis transit station. Briggs asked if he banked any of his footage, and Percy gave a non-committal answer. After that point, he only recounted what Carli and Briggs had seen themselves.

Thinking his duty was complete, Percy said, "Well, if that's everything, I'll disconnect and be on my way."

"Not quite everything," Briggs stated. "Tell me more about the Wakers."

"Network community. We have a Network channel if you want more information."

"Yes, I've seen it. Not much there. I'd like to hear your take."

Percy looked at Carli and back at Briggs. "What does that have to do with whatever this guy did on the transit yesterday?"

"Probably nothing, but it's good to be thorough."

Percy sighed, "The Wakers are a community of like-minded citizens that try to help people see this world the way it truly is, without masks, and other fake veneers."

"Fake veneers like this monolith before us? Carli says it's not real?"

Percy looked up at the statue, his eyes fixed on it whilst he answered, "Just one of a million illusions we all have forced upon us every day." He looked back to Briggs. "The Collective utopia is a myth—each citizen is just a slave to the shared dream. And sadly, most people don't care. Humanity has given up its agency for an endless stream of content and fantasy. It needs to be woken up."

Briggs' eyebrow raised. "And how exactly do you do that? There's a lot of people in the Collective… a lot of systems and institutions that seem to be protecting this myth?"

Percy's energy increased, "Absolutely! Everything in Praxis was designed by a bunch of tech bros at Augmosis a century ago. It is nothing but a social experiment that we've all been born into. We had no say."

"The Wakers—you're like a resistance?" Briggs was leading Percy now, but Percy didn't notice.

"Yes—a resistance against institutions that make slaves of us all."

"Resistance against institutions like the Network Crimes division at the PPD?" Briggs asked sternly. Carli's eyes widened as she turned to see Percy's answer.

"The PPD is at the heart of the problem! Wait… you mean the bombings? No—don't be silly. Nothing like that." He looked at Carli, pleading for help. "Uh—I think I misspoke. What I meant to say was…"

Briggs interrupted, "Yes, you were just telling me that the PPD was the heart of the problem."

Percy raised his arms, "No, that's not what I'm saying. You're putting words in my mouth. The Wakers aren't aggressive. We are a philosophical movement. One heart and mind at a time—that's what we do. People like Carli—we share our ideas and let them make up their own minds. That's all."

Carli couldn't tell if Briggs was satisfied with that answer, but shared Percy's annoyance that his words had been twisted. Briggs asked a few more clarification questions before dismissing Percy, who nodded to Carli before releasing the teeper to return back to its charging station.

"Was that really necessary?" she asked.

"The interview? Yes, my CO asked me to follow up."

"That's not what I mean. You tried to walk him into a trap—surely you wouldn't believe that he had anything to do with the bombing?"

Briggs' shoulders sagged just a little. "You're right, I don't, but it's a force of habit to try and get under a suspect's skin to see how they respond."

"A suspect! Seriously?"

"Again—you're right. Maybe Percy is legit, but I have heard the name, "Wakers" too many times over the last week, and even if I might believe Percy,

I still have no reason to believe the Wakers are completely harmless. So, are you one of the Wakers now too?" he asked.

"No. But Percy still has some valid points," she replied.

Briggs' expression changed, and he looked over her shoulder, distracted. He made some erratic hand gestures, followed by a look of focused energy.

"What is it?" she asked, standing in anticipation.

Briggs mumbled an apology as he continued to work before his attention returned to her. "A Network moniker was rephased in Praxis Central eight minutes ago under the name, "eVoniik". There's a good chance that it's Liam Nolan."

"You've found him again? Can you arrest him?"

"No," Briggs continued to work. "Not immediately. Normally, we—the PPD—would obtain an arrest warrant, which would allow us to directly track him in real space, but my CO doubts we can get a judge to sign off on it. We can issue a BOLO instead."

"BOLO?"

"Be on the lookout. In PPD terms, it means that officers nearby him will be able to more easily spot him from a distance when he tries to leave his apartment, unlike what we tried at the transit station—they should get a match at a range of 25… Dammit!"

"What is it?"

"I asked my CO if I could assist with the surveillance. My offer was not accepted."

"Oh…"

"Just hang on a second…" A few more gestures later, Briggs said, "At least they're letting me watch the feed—not much of a consolation prize, but I'll take it."

Briggs looked around the area, then said to Carli, "I need to find a quiet place to watch the feed. Maybe a café or media hub—or I can catch a transit back to my apartment."

Carli thought for a moment. She was cross that Briggs had been hard on Percy, but she felt like she wanted to catch this guy as much as Briggs did— even if she couldn't help personally.

"My apartment's just a few blocks from here—you're welcome to work from there if you want."

Briggs locked eyes with her and smiled, "Thanks—lead the way."

# 61

Briggs steadied himself on the doorway to Carli's apartment before entering. Since leaving the monument, he'd unsuccessfully tried to overlay some of the streams from the field officers into his vision as he walked. It yielded no result other than feeling like someone was trying to squeeze his breakfast from his stomach. Fortunately, during that time, there hadn't been a whole lot happening or reported from the officers in the field.

After following Carli inside, he noticed a long grey wall with visible tracking markers. Usually there would have been a scape applied.

"Thank you again—can I use this wall?"

"Yes, sure," Carli said. She asked him something else that he didn't hear because he was too busy overlaying the many network feeds onto the wall in a tiled configuration. There were nine live PPD feeds from officers in the field. Three per building, plus a few external cameras outside two of the buildings. That wasn't many.

"Where's the rest of the surveillance? I thought Tactical Branch was on hand," he asked the operations commander over the Network.

"*Redeployed, Sergeant,*" came the reply.

"Not good enough." Briggs sent another message through to Lieutenant Gomes but expected it to be ignored just like the last dozen he'd sent. It made no sense to him why resources had been shifted around, and his mind immediately went to equal parts conspiracy theory and general incompetence. If Liam Nolan was their top priority, those three buildings should be swarming with officers.

With his limited access to the PPD feeds, he couldn't visualise the potential blind spots in three dimensions. It seemed like each building's primary and secondary exits were covered in some form, except for the third building,

'Gamma', which was missing a feed covering the rear exit. As a result, one of the officers on site repositioned himself to get a distant view of the exit of the alleyway behind the building.

"What do you see?" Carli asked from next to him. Briggs had an idea and sent a request to the commander that Carli be added to the feed so she could see the same thing he did on the wall. The commander argued for a bit but seemed convinced that having an extra pair of eyes wouldn't hurt, even if they belonged to a civilian.

"Here, you've got three buildings, Alpha, Bravo and Gamma. Three officers deployed to each building. Here, you can see their live feeds. Two fixed perception cameras for Alpha and Bravo." Briggs pointed around the wall as he explained. "I'm worried about Gamma since we don't have enough eyes out there."

"You can't see their oldselfs? That would make it easier," she asked.

"I have to agree. Even the fixed cameras will only show us projected selfs. There aren't many cameras now with raw video." Briggs looked her in the eyes and tilted his head, "To be honest, if you were out there, your eyesight would probably be quite helpful."

"*Mark entering Bravo,*" came a voice over the comm. "*ID confirmed—not the suspect.*" They were being thorough, but Briggs wasn't looking for someone entering the building, only exiting.

Movement caught Briggs' eye from building Alpha, but he ruled it out as a rotating advertisement on the side of the building. Another officer called in an observation before confirming the moniker didn't match. This process continued for 20 minutes before Carli moved a chair over and sat, still watching the wall. Briggs refused to follow suit, trying to keep his energy up by pacing back and forth.

"What do you see—with your altered vision?" Briggs asked, trying to keep Carli engaged.

"Same as you, but less vibrant. I see the wall's tracking markers, which kind of get in the way of the overlaid image. It's ... disorientating."

"*Mark exiting alpha.*" Briggs focused on those feeds and saw the citizen, a female projection, leaving the building. An anxious pause preceded an eventual, "*ID confirmed—not the suspect*". Briggs continued to watch the citizen as they walked away—no moniker appeared over their head as the officers and the fixed cameras were now too far away.

"*Mark entering Gamma—rear entrance.*" Briggs switched to another feed—the advancing citizen moved to the mouth of the alleyway and appeared to pause there, looking down the alleyway.

"*Confirm ID?*" It was the operations commander.

"*Not possible, too far away. Approach?*"

"Negative," Briggs said out loud, but the message wouldn't be relayed to the rest of the team.

"*Careful approach and confirm ID. Five, switch from Bravo to Gamma to cover the gap, then reset,*" said the commander.

The citizen turned around, looking away from the alleyway. The as-yet unidentified mark's behaviour did seem a little out of the ordinary.

"*30 metres… 25… ID confirmed—suspect identified—moniker 'eVoniik'*"

"Is that him?" Carli said. "Why is he just standing there? And why was he entering the building instead of leaving it?"

"Yeah, but something feels off."

The suspect—Liam Nolan stepped into the shadows of the alleyway and disappeared out of visual contact.

"*Lost visual! Pursue?*"

"*Yes, pursue. Seven and Nine, stay on the front of the building. Five, Two and One, redeploy to Gamma.*"

"Too many," Briggs messaged the commander, but there was no response.

"*Who's got visual?*"

"*Five has visual. Suspect entered building through rear entry.*"

"*Seven and Nine, close in on front entrance. Five and Eight, close in on the rear.*"

"They're spreading too thin," Briggs said, but he could only watch. Eight and Five converged on the rear entrance, gesturing amongst themselves before entering.

The feed showed a long corridor inside the apartment complex, the distant image of the target marked as eVoniik or Liam Nolan wearing a generic self at the end of the corridor. He then turned into the last room.

The two shaky camera views rushed down the corridor to the now-closed door that Liam Nolan had entered.

*"Door locked. Appears to be a maintenance room. Permission to breach?"*

*"Negative. Announce yourselves, but we need owner permission or court order."*

"Are you serious?" Briggs fumed. "He's right there. Break the door down!"

*"Another mark exiting Bravo."* Briggs' eyes darted to the other feed and saw a distant figure leaving the front exit of the other building.

*"ID on Bravo?"* came the Commander's request.

*"Negative,"* came the response, *"Mark is a teeper returning to a charging station."*

"Why can't they go in?" Carli asked.

Briggs fought back rage to answer, "PPD doesn't have a warrant, and there is no apparent immediate threat."

*"Five and Eight: any response?"*

"No."

*"All units hold position, while we wait for consent."*

The wait was only ten minutes, but it felt like an eternity. During that time, the other officers called in reports for sixteen other people entering or exiting one of the three buildings, each time confirming the ID as being of no interest.

*"Owner permissions received. Breach approved!"*

Five broke the lock, and the door swung open. Eight pressed into the room with his sidearm raised in position. The room inside was small and dark. Lights on the officer's chest illuminated the room to reveal Liam Nolan standing in the centre of the room, motionless.

*"Freeze! Hands behind your head!"*

Liam Nolan's face twitched, looked at one officer, then the next, unconcerned by the bright light shining in his eyes. A smile came over his face and his projection dissolved to reveal a teeper in its place.

*"Please stand clear as I return to the nearest charging station."*

"It's a decoy!" Briggs yelled at the wall. The two officers looked at each other, and one shrugged.

Five stepped closer and touched the shoulder of the machine. *"Confirmed. It's a teeper."*

Briggs swore, barking directions to the commander who wasn't listening. Through his rage, he heard, "*Acknowledged. Reset to our original positions.*"

But as far as Briggs was concerned, the opportunity had passed. The surveillance team had taken the bait. He wanted to punch the wall in defiance, but managed to control himself.

"I see him," Carli said.

Briggs snapped back into focus, "Where?"

"Not where, when. Time code 10:16, the street camera opposite building Bravo."

Briggs wound back his stream, though they were using the same wall to position their respective feeds, what they chose to view on the wall was different. He brought up the camera feed in question, which showed the mark previously identified as a teeper.

"Are you sure? Officers reported a teeper?"

"Watch it move," she said.

Briggs did, and after a while, he saw it too. The teeper was not moving smoothly, its step was slightly more shuffled, head movements ever so sharper than they should be. The teeper continued away from the buildings in the general direction of the transit station, many blocks away, before disappearing outside of view.

Carli explained, "That's no teeper. That's Liam Nolan wearing a projection of a teeper. You can lease one for a hundred bits from most novelty stores."

"Son of a bitch."

**62**

There's no way he's doing this on his own," Briggs declared to whoever was on the other end of his voice call. "He's got better information than us from someone on the inside."

Carli went to the kitchen, prepared a glass of water and placed it on the table near Briggs. He hadn't asked for it, but she was trying to do something helpful. She was satisfied to have been able to help, but was frustrated she hadn't been able to spot Liam Nolan in time. Briggs wound up his call and collapsed on the couch. Carli wanted to ask what was going on, but stayed silent, figuring he would share if he wanted to. What he said surprised her.

"They can't catch this guy. *I* can't catch him." He grabbed the glass and stared into it for a moment before taking a small sip.

"You can't trap him in the station?"

"Maybe, but not from here. If we piloted our own teepers, there is no telling that the same thing wouldn't happen. The PPD—my Lieutenant says they are going to follow that up, but I have my doubts."

"I can't hire a teeper at the moment. Not until I've sorted out an outstanding debt."

"Oh. I'm sorry that happened. I've raised it with the PPD, but those things move slowly. I don't see that as an option anyway—my Lieutenant has told me to stay out of the way. If I want any hope of seeing the end of my suspension, then I don't have much of a choice."

*So that's it*, Carli thought. She looked back at the wall. She'd cleared the video feeds and the wall now showed only the tracking markers, but for some reason, the absence of an image helped her to think. She knew it wasn't her job, but the beginnings of an idea formed.

"What kind of person is this guy? *Liam Nolan*. What makes him tick?"

Briggs stirred in his chair before leaning back, "Murderer. Mercenary. Terrorist."

"Surely it's not that simple? What's his motive? What's his psychology?"

He grunted before answering. "Self-preservation. Revenge. I looked through the file from the PPD. It had gaps because they were reconstructions from memory after the originals were purged. He was a relatively compliant citizen until the industrial accident killed his wife and injured him. He spent the next two years not just recovering but planning his revenge and murdering the people he deemed responsible."

"And then he was arrested?

"Yes. Three concurrent life sentences. Best guess is he disappeared from the system just over two years ago."

"And since then? What's his motive? The people in West Praxis and Goldstein? Is it still personal or something else?"

"If I were to guess, I would say he is just someone's hired hand. Nothing indicates that he has any Network hacking skills, and whatever that thing is in his hand isn't something he can come up with himself. He's following orders—someone far more powerful than most of the PPD."

"Who has that kind of power?" Carli asked.

Briggs turned to look up at her, a focused seriousness in his eyes, "No one. The power to destroy all traces of someone's existence, to scrub what should be private and secure banked footage? To break someone out of prison without them even knowing he was gone? To get a guy into the heart of Augmosis to kill its founder using some mystery device that stops your heart and destroys your identity? No one has that kind of power."

"Except Augmosis themselves?"

"Maybe. An ONI agent I worked with yesterday said there were still holes in the security of the Network that aren't discussed. When I was speaking to Goldstein, I saw enough to confirm that it was probably true. I suppose if anyone knew how to exploit the bugs across the Network, it would be him."

"It's too bad he's gone," Carli lamented.

"Yeah. Too bad—and not a coincidence."

"Liam Nolan—what else? What does he want?"

Briggs chewed on his cheek for a moment. "An insomniac—he needs to self-medicate to sleep."

Carli asked the question she'd been mulling over for the last 24 hours, "Why did he come back to attack me? To attack my teeper? He was home free."

"Yeah, that was strange. If he were professional about it, he would have walked away, but he took the risk to try and take you out of the equation. Risk-taker: that's another thing. When he attacked Deniz Harper, he was running around West Praxis without an ID, trying to buy drugs. Lying low was the smart move, but he did it anyway. What did he say to you again?"

"He knew I wasn't police. He asked who I was working for."

"After that? When your teeper was attacked?"

"Oh, he said, 'MalvinaHoffman, you've been noticed'." She felt a shiver down her back as if saying it out loud had summoned a supernatural presence. "So, what does he do next? You said you've seen his file—if you're Liam Nolan, what is your next move?"

Briggs stirred in his chair before settling and nodding to himself, "He's getting out of Praxis Central, that's for certain. He'll relocate further away to a hub that doesn't have the same level of scrutiny. I can't imagine he's planned for this number of setbacks—he'll set up a new safe house and lay low for a few days.

"He needs food. Drugs. Hard currency. He's got to be out of all three. I think that when he doesn't have an active ID, he's cut off from his money. That's when he's most exposed, but also when he's hardest to track. He's burned through two identities in three days, and he knows that his latest one, 'eVoniik' is probably compromised too since he must've known he was being watched. If he's smart, he'll stay out of sight and the trail will go cold."

"But *is* he that smart? Or will he keep taking risks? Could he, for example, be *baited*?" Carli asked.

Briggs shot a glance towards her. "Yes, he could. What are you thinking?"

"What if… *I* was the bait? We know his current moniker—at least until he changes it. We know he took an interest in me, and would recognise my moniker if I tried to connect with him. Maybe he sees me as unfinished business? What if I somehow try to lure him out into the open?"

"That… that would be an incredible risk."

"But do you think it would work?"

Briggs stared off into the distance like he was parsing and processing this new idea.

"I don't like it. But yeah… it might work. The PPD will be a problem—I'm not sure how Nolan got the information that he was being watched—so I'm not sure if I can trust them with this idea. Even if I did, I'm sure I would be told to stand down. Whatever we do, we'll be doing it on our own."

Carli's resolve crystallised, and she stood a little straighter. "Then let's do it. Together."

**63**

Liam had already reached the transit station by the time he received another message from his employer.

<1DF8B9-E82ADA> RELOCATE TO VANDENBERG. ESTABLISH A SAFE LOCATION. AWAIT INSTRUCTIONS.

<EVONIIK> POLICE WERE WAITING FOR ME. OUTSIDE MY APARTMENT. HOW DID THEY KNOW WHERE I WAS?

<E1D492-179F9C>: WERE YOU IDENTIFIED?

Liam hesitated before lying.

<EVONIIK> NO

<447730-821253> THEN WE DON'T SEE THE ISSUE. RELOCATE TO VANDENBERG. ESTABLISH A SAFE LOCATION. AWAIT INSTRUCTIONS.

<EVONIIK> ARE YOU SERIOUS?

<NETWORK> CITIZEN <447730-821253> NOT FOUND

The simple mask he wore could barely conceal the anger across his face as he rode the transit away from Praxis Central. He'd passed through Port Lincoln, and the next stop would be West Praxis. Every fibre of his being wanted to push south to Kenmore as per his previous plan to trade the funds with The Accountant and sever his contract with his employer, but the PPD being hot on his tail now gave him no choice but to follow his employer's direction to head west.

He'd used his little ruse to escape wearing the image of a teeper once before when he was evading hitmen in Pangola, but they were a whole lot stupider

329

than PPD officers. Piloting a teeper was no mean feat without a control rig, and his imitation of a teeper was awkward but effective. Still, the PPD had gotten close enough to ID him—either they already knew his new identity and were looking for it specifically, or they knew the general area he was in and were looking for anyone who looked out of place. Regardless, they now knew his new moniker, eVoniik, and he'd just lied to his employer about it.

He wriggled his prosthetic fingers. He'd never seen his employer's face or heard a real voice, but he knew they would be pissed if he burned another identity within hours of it being assigned. The transit settled and the doors opened onto the concourse of West Praxis. He made a snap decision and exited—it wasn't quite Vandenberg, but he at least had his old safe house here and he knew the local establishments better than Vandenberg.

He dutifully scanned the people around him for any possible law enforcement, careful not to move his head. He saw none. He shuffled up the travellator to the surface and made a direct path for a convenience store to start collecting supplies. He needed to stock up his previous safehouse before deciding if he would move on to Vandenberg. He'd transfer a small amount of his now significant account balance into metal chips to use as trades for drugs and anything else he thought might help him pass the time in the event of some other emergency. He knew a few places that would sell him the good stuff without the need to barter after routing his bits through several other phony businesses.

A chirp indicated an incoming message from an untrusted Citizen. He'd been ignoring the stream of messages on his feed from the PPD asking him to report his location and submit to an interview. This one came from an unlikely sender, however.

<MalvinaHoffman> Liam Nolan, you've been noticed.

He came to a dead stop in the middle of the doorway of the store causing someone behind him to step around him in a cloud of curses. He walked down an alleyway to somewhere with slightly more privacy before replying.

<eVoniik> Who are you?

He doubted playing dumb was going to get this person off his trail, but figured it was worth a shot.

<MalvinaHoffman> Your friend from the transit.

\<eVoniik\> No way. You're PPD.

\<MalvinaHoffman\> Wrong.

\<eVoniik\> Bullshit.

\<MalvinaHoffman\> That little stunt of yours on the transit
gave me a headache.

\<eVoniik\> I was expecting more.

\<MalvinaHoffman\> Well, that hurts my feelings Liam,
especially when I was going to help you.

\<eVoniik\> With what?

\<MalvinaHoffman\> You've lost 3 identities in a week. I can't
imagine the people you work for will be too happy about that.

*Who is this person?* He didn't reply, waiting nearly half a minute before the next message arrived.

\<MalvinaHoffman\> Maybe there is a way I can help set you
free.

This person didn't sound like the person who was on the train. But still, he was intrigued—whoever they were didn't just know he was the same person who had been Basilicus on the transit the day before, but knew he was Liam Nolan—an identity that should no longer exist. Someone was playing games with him, and he felt more vulnerable than ever.

\<eVoniik\> What's in it for you?

\<MalvinaHoffman\> Information.

\<eVoniik\> About what?

\<MalvinaHoffman\> About who you are working for.

\<eVoniik\> Maybe I don't know who I'm working for.

He sent that message too quickly. You don't start a negotiation by saying you have nothing to offer.

<MalvinaHoffman> I think you might be surprised by what you know. There's more. I want your hand. I want to see how it works.

He looked at his hand before replying.

<eVoniik> It's not like I can remove it.

There was a long pause before the reply arrived.

<MalvinaHoffman> I can take care of that, but we need to meet.

<eVoniik> Where?

<MalvinaHoffman> I'll send you a location.

<eVoniik> No. I'll give you the location. You'll hear from me soon.

Liam closed the chat and muted the channel for 3 hours. He suspected a trap, but the promise of escape was too irresistible to ignore. He weighed the risks and considered how he could mitigate them, then made his decision.

He had some planning to do, but also some research. There was no way he was going to meet with someone in person without knowing exactly who they were and who they worked for.

After stepping out to collect some supplies, Briggs returned to Carli's apartment. The bag under his arm contained a now clean PPD lifesuit and a pair of nylon cuffs he'd left at his apartment from a previous case. Snuggly concealed in his thigh pocket and hidden behind his projection was the 6-shot revolver he'd recovered from Liam's satchel. He didn't want to waste a bullet, but he hated the idea of relying on a firearm he hadn't tested at least once. His test fire into a pile of towels confirmed that it worked. The gas discharge burned his thumb, and the recoil was firmer than he was used to, but other than that, it was solid. The gun would be a last-resort option only, however. For a gifted shooter, it would have had an effective range of maybe ten meters. For Briggs, it was probably half that.

He noted that Carli appeared just as determined as she'd been when he'd left. Even after he explained his temporary limitations in engaging the PPD in the sting, she remained resolute in her commitment to proceed.

A part of him didn't want the PPD to find Nolan, at least not without his help. He needed this—for so many reasons, both professional and personal. Standing on the sidelines was never going to bring him the absolution he craved. Still, he feared how he would react when he finally met Liam Nolan face to face. Even if Briggs wasn't certain he was responsible for the bombing, the other murders were enough to make this feel personal.

"Any response from Nolan?" Briggs asked. She replied in the negative. "Give it time, we need to discuss the plan anyway."

Briggs handed her his PPD lifesuit from his bag. "I know it's going to be too big, but I'd like you to wear this." Carli's eyes widened as she slowly understood the reason why he'd given it to her. "Just a precaution. There is some risk, but if things go to plan, I don't expect him to get anywhere near you. Still, it would make me happier if you were wearing it, just in case."

"It's heavy," she said.

"And somewhat uncomfortable," he said. He pointed to some of the panels across the chest. "These are strong enough to absorb a typical pistol round, positioned around the key organs and arteries. Chest, abdomen and thighs. To a lesser extent your shoulders, back and arms. It's not a tactical suit—so nothing for your head."

"So, if I'm going to get shot, not in the face?"

"Uh... yes. Well, I'm going to make sure you don't get shot at all."

Carli looked up to him, "Seriously—how risky is this going to be?"

He met her gaze. "I'm not going to lie—with this guy, nothing is certain. Once we know where we are meeting him, we'll do some reconnaissance to assess the location. I expect him to demand a location trust so he can track your arrival into the hub, but you will also be able to track his. Once that happens, we should know exactly where he is, and I can move in."

"He won't be at the location he sets?"

"I doubt it. I expect that he'll be waiting somewhere near the transit station, hoping to follow you as you travel—that's why I'll be getting there before you do. But, I expect a few surprises. He might follow you with a teeper instead of in person. Even at high trust, you won't know where he is physically since the

Network treats a teeper no differently from a real person when they are being piloted. If he does, I'll need contingencies. Remember, he believes you have something he needs—information, a means to separate from whoever he is working for. He won't want to do this from a distance."

"How do you know for sure?"

The truth was, Briggs didn't know. The more he thought this through, the more he doubted his judgment that this was a good idea. Being impulsive wasn't out of the ordinary for him, but he could usually justify it if he was certain that it was the smart move, and any risk he took was his own and didn't impact anyone else. Now, he just felt desperate, as though this was his only move, and that was not something he was used to.

"Carli, I want to make absolutely certain. You've been more than generous with your help over the last few days… I just want to confirm this is what you want."

Carli's hands ran over the chest plate of the PPD lifesuit before she answered. "Absolutely. I was wondering, though, why won't the PPD listen to you?"

"I've burned my bridges there. My captain, Anneke, we understood each other, and she always had my back. But since she… since she's gone, it feels like some of the other higher-ups have decided they don't want to have to deal with my… *unpredictability* right now. To be honest, I probably haven't done a whole lot to endear myself these last few years."

Carli nodded as though she understood.

"Besides I still haven't ruled out that the whole department is somehow compromised." He chuckled like it was a joke but deep down he feared it might be true.

He leaned towards her. Now was not the time to sink deeper into the black hole of self-loathing that beckoned him like a siren's song, but he needed to get something off his chest. "I'm sorry it's come to this. I feel like… I feel like a failure these last few days, and I feel like I'm responsible for at least half the stuff that's going wrong. I want you to know that I appreciate your help." His gaze lingered on her for a brief, vulnerable moment before he sat back and changed the subject.

They spent the next few hours going over the plan—what Carli should say as soon as Liam responded; how they would approach the meeting itself, and all of the contingencies. It was like planning any other PPD operation, apart from the fact that they had no backup and were up against a foe with superior Network abilities. Carli at least had the advantage of being able to spot Liam Nolan through his projection.

He made another attempt to call Lt. Gomes but the connection was closed. She replied with the simple message: "You've done your job. Let me do mine."

*I'm on my own,* he thought, before looking over to Carli. She'd put on his bulky lifesuit and was looking at herself in the mirror, practising her range of motion—*we're on our own.* His mind wandered for a moment, appreciating Carli's willingness to trust him, willingness to look out for him. She'd already seen more of his demons than some of his past partners, and he realised in that instant that he would do anything to protect her, including calling the whole thing off.

Carli looked over to him, as though she'd felt the weight of his gaze. For a moment, he wondered if she was thinking the same thing.

"He's just messaged me. West Praxis—90 minutes."

Briggs snapped out of his fantasy and checked the time: approaching 5:00 pm. He'd expected the invitation to come later in the evening when there would be fewer people around but was less surprised by the location.

He stood and stretched his legs, allowing his hand to brush the hard shape of the gun in his right pocket as he stuffed the nylon cuffs into his left.

He nodded at her. "Let's do this."

# 64

Liam watched from a second-storey nightclub named the Ice Lounge that overlooked the common park area in West Praxis. From the balcony, he could see across to the Café Roma where he planned to meet MalvinaHoffman. The same location where he'd taken out the fool, Zaimis, only a few days ago.

It was Zaimis' fault that everything had turned into a steaming pile of manure. Even if he'd been at his employer's beck and call for the last two years, he at least had some sense of autonomy. His employer's directions had previously been far more general: 'ingratiate yourself with this group', 'coordinate shipments through this port'—the calls to remove someone from the equation were infrequent and rarely involved someone he'd been directly associated with.

The time approached 6:30 pm. The bar's music had ramped up, but was still fairly empty. Any minute now, he expected a notification from MalvinaHoffman that she'd arrived at the transit and his plan would be underway.

He'd had a busy afternoon. After her initial contact, he engaged the services of a Hat to do a deep dive into the girl's identity. The short-notice report would be delivered at a premium charge in only a few hours. It would be less thorough, but he couldn't wait for the extra time a full report would demand.

He'd stocked up his West Praxis safehouse with enough food and other supplies in the event he needed to hole up again. He'd traded some of his Bits for platinum and palladium, then visited another vendor to trade some of those chips for a handful of drugs and a well-worn pocket pistol. It was a very common black-market model because of its small size, but its 0.22" calibre bullets would need an accurate hit to the head or the heart to take down a target. He'd used this model before, but this particular gun looked like its grip was partly melted, much like his own skin. A test fire into an old mattress at least confirmed it was operational.

The final step was the most risky: re-boarding the transit, travelling to Vandenberg where he leased a new location and set it up as another safehouse. If his employer could track his location, travelling to Vandenberg would at least demonstrate his compliance, even if he didn't plan on staying long.

He needed the means to keep the PPD off his back. Until he was able to convince his employer that his Evoniik ID was burned and initiate a reset, the PPD would be able to track him to a hub location. Since they would now expect him to be in Vandenberg, he needed a way of returning to West Praxis undetected by the scanners at both locations. The solution was to acquire something called a "plexus shroud" from another special kind of vendor, which took him longer than he expected in a hub he didn't know very well. The shroud attached to his plexus and reported a different, stolen Network ID for around the next hour whilst he relocated back to West Praxis.

On his return, the report on MalvinaHoffman appeared in his inbox. Name 'Carli Dawes'. She was gendered female, with a likely age between 25 and 30. No connected family members. No current attachments. Some route tracking indicated frequent transits from and to Praxis Grove on the Fort Gale line, possibly from Archibald or Lyon, which Liam considered to be the likely location of her residence. She worked as a partnered sculptor with NuSculpt in Praxis Grove, a commission she'd received three years prior. Before that, she worked as a sculptor at another provider, also in Praxis Grove.

A partial list of recent clients was supplied, which Liam pored through. One name immediately stood out to him: ArdentBlue. It was a name he not only recognised as one of the Overseers but also from his first mission two years ago. It was ArdentBlue whom he'd been sent to kill using the plexus storm virus from his prosthetic hand. The blade he now hid in his lifesuit had been taken from their lifeless body.

He was more than surprised six months later when that same identity had been elevated to the Overseer as a result of a high level of followership. That was the first moment Liam realised his employer was playing on a much larger stage than he'd originally assumed. It was the first warning sign that he might be in over his head.

This intersection with MalvinaHoffman raised his suspicions. Other information supplied included public posts by MalvinaHoffman supporting

ArdentBlue as Overseer. Liam read a few longwinded posts, seeing a bunch of common words and phrases relating to liberty and self-expression, but he understood little and found most of it uninteresting. That confused him even more.

Still, he was committed now—this person knew who he was. Either they could give him a way out, or they stood in his way.

As 7:00 pm arrived, a message alert came through on his optics—it was not from MalvinaHoffman—but from his employer:

<70F6B0-B5B2C4> REPORT.

LIAM'S STOMACH TIGHTENED JUST A LITTLE BEFORE REPLYING.

<EVONIIK> I'M STILL HERE.

<922311-57B724> HAVE YOU RELOCATED TO VANDENBERG?

<EVONIIK> YES.

It wasn't technically a lie. But then it wasn't the truth either. There was a long delay, and he received no response. He looked across to the café. From this distance, he couldn't see many of the patrons, but most were either eating or conversing and did not look to be on alert. He looked over at the teeper he'd leased, standing watch from the balcony—it would play its role soon.

Another message arrived. He expected his employer again, but instead, it was MalvinaHoffman.

<MALVINAHOFFMAN> I'M HERE.

<EVONIIK> INITIATE A SHARED LOCATION TRUST FOR THIS HUB SO I KNOW YOU'RE TELLING THE TRUTH.

<MALVINAHOFFMAN> THOSE THINGS CAN BE HACKED, BUT FINE.

LEVEL 3 TRUST REQUESTED: CITIZEN "MALVINAHOFFMAN" AKA "CARLI DAWES". CONFIRM?

Liam smiled. The name he'd received was correct.

<EVONIIK> NOW CARLI DAWES—YOU CAN SEE MY LOCATION, YES? I CAN SEE YOU EXITING THE TRANSIT PLATFORM.

<MalvinaHoffman> Yes.

<eVoniik> OK. Café Roma. Meet me there in 5 minutes. No surprises.

<MalvinaHoffman> You too. I'm here to help, Liam.

*We'll see about that.*

Carli's heart raced as she found a seat at the Café Roma, doing her best to project an aura of confidence, avoiding jerky movements or looking too closely at the other patrons in the Café. A server greeted her and asked for an order. She was sure that she jumped a little, but managed to say, "I'm waiting for someone," and waved them off.

"You're doing fine," Briggs' voice came through her phonics, "Keep this connection on and tell me if his location changes. I'm on a wide arc—I can see you *and* anyone that approaches."

"Okay," Carli managed a reply. Settled in her seat, her eyes darted from patron to patron, recognising no one. Briggs had arrived half an hour earlier and ordered a coffee from the café, confirming none of the staff or patrons had Liam's "eVoniik" moniker before taking up a position amongst a handful of others in the common.

She checked her yellow-tinged map and confirmed the location of Liam Nolan, across the far side of the common, walking in her direction. She knew if she looked now, she would be able to see him but resisted the urge for as long as possible, not wanting to give any appearance of unease.

"He's crossing the common, headed directly towards me—about 50 meters," Carli said to Briggs.

"I think I can see him. I've come around the gardens and approach from his six—uh, from behind."

Eyes forward, Carli counted to twenty, watching the approaching red blip in her optics over the top of the map layer as it approached. She imagined each second was a step—with each step she timed her breathing, inhaling for two, exhaling for two, pleading with her heart to slow to the same pace. After counting twenty breaths, she slowly turned her head to face Liam Nolan.

She spotted him from 25 metres away—he wore a new projection, different from the others he'd donned before, but still based on some algorithm-generated generic self. His clothes were custom, a white linen shirt that appeared very similar to the one he wore when she'd met him on the transit, and dark-coloured trousers. Her eyes met his, seeing both brown eyes and a pair of optical sensors. "That's a teeper, it's not him."

"Acknowledged. I've got a good look at his projection, so I'll start searching to see if I can locate him."

"Couldn't he be anywhere in Praxis?"

"He'll be here. He'll be watching."

Briggs had predicted that Liam Nolan's first approach probably wouldn't be in person, and so now the plan shifted. Carli needed to keep his teeper talking to give Briggs time to locate him, or, to try to encourage him out of the shadows to approach her in person. If Briggs found him, the goal was simply to detain him for long enough for the PPD to arrive.

Any extra information she could glean from him would be a bonus, and since it was a teeper, her risk was minimal. *Unless the teeper was another bomb.*

Liam's teeper glided the remaining few meters. Carli spoke first: "Hello Liam, please take a seat." *That's good*, she thought, *be commanding and assertive.*

The teeper carefully pulled out the chair opposite and made a rehearsed move to sit in it.

"Put your hands on top of the table, fingers spread apart and keep them there", he said.

Carli briefly wondered why, before Briggs' voice spoke in her phonics, "He wants to make sure you're not communicating with anyone."

She complied, then added, "I'd ask the same of you, but it seems you haven't shown the same respect to show up in person."

"I'm not far. I'm taking precautions, same as you, I'm sure. Tell me—who is Malvina Hoffman?" he asked.

"A sculptor—early 20th century."

"Just like you? A sculptor, I mean."

"I can only dream." *Why did I say that? And how does he know what I do?*

"So, you said you could help me. How exactly?"

Carli tried to hide her relief—this was a question she'd rehearsed. "You're on the run. You've been on the run for two years, at someone else's beck and call. I can set you free."

"And how's that exactly?"

"First, we deal with that hand of yours. You are being tracked right across Praxis, Liam. I can organise a safe space to remove it. In time, I'll organise a *safer* replacement. Then, we trade information." Carli heard Briggs' encouragement in her phonics.

"That's a convenient deal, but I see nothing that gives me the confidence that you can honour it, or that making such a deal would leave me in any better position than what I'm in now."

For a moment, Carli felt something in response to him. Empathy? *Not if this guy's a cold-blooded killer,* she told herself.

"Fair enough. We need to trust each other. I've shown trust by meeting you face to face. What else can I do to convince you?"

"You can start by telling me how you know who I am."

It was another question that she'd rehearsed with Briggs. She felt confidence growing, not just in herself, but in Briggs's ability to predict what questions Liam was likely to ask.

"The PPD," she explained. "My contact there was aware of your disappearance from prison, and we've been tracking you across Praxis since."

"We? So, you *are* working for the PPD?" he said.

"I'm… No—he's just a contact. I'm working with others," she recovered.

"I'm still not satisfied. I think you *are* working with the PPD—or at least the Overseer. You have some connections that concern me," he said, "like ArdentBlue."

Carli recoiled, fighting the temptation to pull her hands off the table. "How… what do you mean?"

"ArdentBlue. You seem to have had a connection with them. Professionally—as a sculptor—but personally too."

Carli froze—she had no answer. Briggs was silent in her phonics. *Say something!* she screamed at herself. "I'm sorry?" she managed to squeeze out before chiding herself for not having a better response.

"I met ArdentBlue once," he said, "One of my first assignments. I was quite surprised when they were elevated to the Overseer a few months later."

"Why? Why's that?"

An odd certainty crossed Liam's face. "Because I killed him."

Carli pulled her hands off the table as a reflex, feeling like she'd been punched in the stomach. She forced them back to the table, found her breath and asked. "When?"

"Two years ago." Carli considered the maths. She'd been following ArdentBlue for at least three years, but it was 15 months ago that she'd prepared their self. *If he's telling the truth,* she thought, *that means it was an impostor that I'd scanned and crafted a self for.*

She heard Briggs say something encouraging in her phonics, but it barely registered.

"You're working for whoever took over that identity after it was… purged. Which means you are also connected to my employer since they gave me the kill order." Liam's expressionless teeper stared through her, "So again, I have to wonder what your game is."

Her chest tightened further. *I should just run away,* she thought. She needed a fresh idea to try and shift the discussion back in her favour. She remembered what she'd practised with Briggs—to lean into and confirm whatever theory Liam had started to believe in himself. In particular, that his employer is not happy with him. *Confirm what he already suspects.*

"You're right. I'm a sculptor. I sculpted ArdentBlue's current self at the request of an employer—the same one that sends you instructions. The employer is not one individual but a group. Some—a splinter, aren't happy about how things have escalated in the last week."

He gave no response, so Carli continued, "Aldus Goldstein was a step too far. After that, and the PPD bombings, my splinter wanted you followed. And to remove you from the game."

"So, *you* brought the PPD down on me on the transit?"

"Yes." She kept going, remembering more of the prepared story she'd discussed with Briggs. "But my group changed their mind and decided they would rather have you on their side. To do that, we need to make sure you can't be tracked." She gestured to the teeper's hand.

"I could get this thing removed at any back alley butcher, sort out a new ID and be home free. I'm not sure I need your help."

"But what then? How sure are you that the rest of the group won't see you as a liability and hunt you down?"

"I like my chances. What's in it for you?" he asked.

Carli's confidence grew, buoyed by the credibility of her answers. *He's starting to believe me!* "We want your hand. My group does not understand how it delivers a… 'death blow' to someone on the Network. We will learn from its secrets. And if you are still interested in work, I'm sure we can find something for your special skill set."

"Can you control my accounts? Last time I spoke against my employer, he… it made all my money disappear."

"I think we can sort something out there." Another long pause. She needed validation and was just about to ask another question when she heard Briggs, "I see him. Keep him distracted."

"So—have I earned your trust, Liam?"

He sat still, cocked his teeper's head to the side. 'Who is BriggsH33207?".

Carli gasped, pulling her hands from the table again.

"Stay right there." Liam's projection left the teeper.

**65**

Piloting a teeper on the move was difficult. When he'd escaped the PPD in Praxis Central, Liam parked the teeper in a closet and put it on active standby as he made his escape. But to protect himself this time, he pulled a different trick—one shared with him previously by Alvarez: when concluding the lease of a teeper, a special package of code could leave the teeper connected and retaining his projection and moniker while a second teeper was leased.

The second teeper was piloted to the Café Roma to speak with Carli Dawes. The first teeper remained where he'd left it, standing on the balcony of the Ice Lounge nightclub overlooking the common. Meanwhile, Liam took up a far more private position seated in a booth usually reserved for private amusements. A dancer, wearing the projection of a pale-skinned, Asian character in a school uniform was initially irritated when told she wouldn't need to perform, but after a healthy tip, she seemed more than happy to quietly sit opposite him and entertained herself with content from the Network.

The advantage of this booth was that it gave him a full view out to his dummy teeper on the balcony, and anyone outside the booth could not see inside because it had a privacy mask active until the hire was over.

Carli Dawes had been nervous. Her answers to his questions had done little to satisfy him, but he at least believed part of her story. Her answers didn't contradict what he already knew but offered no greater sense of certainty. The conversation had simply served to confirm his relationship with his employer needed to end—as soon as possible.

He continued his conversation with Carli Dawes, watching her face and body language in a window in his optics, while he split his attention to his other teeper on the balcony. One of the wait staff did a circuit of the balcony, pausing at his teeper for a moment before returning to the bar. If they had asked his teeper a question, he wouldn't know it—when it was in this statuesque state there was no real connection. He did another scan of the rest of the club—the dark ambience made it just as difficult to see as it was to be seen, but in the last half hour it had started to fill with patrons. Most of the loud music came from his phonics which he could dial down to almost nothing, but his body still felt the rumbling bass from the subwoofer.

His attention returned to the bar where a new figure had stopped and spoken to the waiter. He turned and looked around the room. It wasn't the look of one friend looking for another friend, nor even a patron searching for the right place to sit. Instead, it was slower. More methodical. He recognized it instantly.

Liam muted his voice connection to the teeper in the Café Roma and turned to the dancer who had been quietly sharing his booth, "I need you to go to the bar and order me a drink."

"Just place an order through your connection," she said without making eye contact, her hands gesturing as she interfaced with the Network.

"Go to the bar, order a drink and scan that guy's Network moniker. I'll give you a nice tip when you come back."

Her eyes crystallised as they turned to him. "Just hang on a second…" She then proceeded to interface with the Network again, before she turned back to him and said, "BriggsH33207."

"How did you get that?"

"I asked Angus, the bartender."

Liam swore, anger rising. "I didn't tell you to do that. Did he ask why you were asking?"

"Nope. We always share monikers we bump into, for safety reasons."

"Did you share mine with him too?" he asked, leaning forward in his seat.

"Of course." She turned back and again started interfacing with the Network before adding, "So about that tip?"

"Damn it," he said.

The man moved from the bar to another position, closer to the balcony, performing a similar scan along the way. Liam was only 20 metres away. If the guy had been a PPD officer, Liam would have already been detected. This guy moved like a police officer, but hadn't found him yet.

The man moved towards the balcony and stopped before ducking behind a pillar—he'd spotted Liam's first teeper, standing like a sentinel overlooking the common. Liam stood from his booth and pressed towards the boundary of the privacy screen. The man was moving his hands to his right thigh, retrieving something—a pistol of some sort.

*So, this guy's definitely here for me.*

The man paused briefly before advancing quickly towards Liam's teeper, gun raised in a threatening but controlled stance. He advanced the ten metres to Liam's teeper and yelled something that Liam couldn't quite make out over the noise.

Liam returned his attention to the window with Carli Dawes from across the common. "Who is BriggsH33207?" he asked. She gasped, and he added, "Stay right there."

Liam closed the gap between the mystery man and himself in a few quick seconds and armed his PlexusStorm virus. He disconnected his lease on the second teeper, which consequently released the first teeper. He loomed over the man from behind, hearing him bark instructions to his lifeless teeper to get down on the ground. Then, Liam's projection dissolved away from the teeper to reveal the plastic body beneath, he heard him say, "Son of a bitch…"

Liam reached up to the man's neck from behind and deployed the virus, receiving a confirmation message back from the Network.

The man fell to the floor, screaming in pain. The gun he'd been holding was lost, and he now held the sides of his head like it was on fire. Liam jumped back in surprise—he'd never seen this response before. Usually, their death was quick and seemingly painless. The man continued to roll around in pain.

Realising the noise was going to attract attention, Liam turned and ran—he needed to catch up to Carli Dawes across the street. He needed more answers, and now it seemed she was the only person who might have them.

---

"Briggs? Briggs!" Carli called through the Network, but there was no response. Her connection had been severed. She could no longer track his position through the trust system, and her messages returned an error.

She stood from the table, watching Liam's teeper glide away back to its station. The Network now identified Liam's location as being across the common in a building on the opposite side, the same location where Briggs had been when he disappeared off the map. The marker representing Liam's location was now moving quickly in her direction.

*What do I do? If I end the trust connection and run, he'll know it was a ruse, and this will all be for nothing. But what can I do by myself? Do I just call the PPD? But even Briggs said he'd tried that without success.*

She backed away, watching Liam's marker advance closer. Across the common she could see him approaching at a fast walk, his stride filled with determination and purpose. She froze, unable to think fast enough. Any sense of thrill shifted to imminent danger.

*What do you do if you are in danger, Carli?* She asked herself. *You call for help!*

She snapped out of her brain fog and triggered an urgent assistance alarm on the Network. Any PPD officer nearby would respond as soon as possible. She'd never used it before, but anticipated someone would come to her rescue. She followed that up by directly messaging Constable Gomes, recalling her Network ID from when she'd shared her feed with her on the transit.

<MALVINAHOFFMAN> THIS IS CARLI DAWES. LIAM NOLAN IS WITH ME IN WEST PRAXIS. BRIGGS IS GONE. SEND HELP!

There was no immediate reply. Liam was now less than 30 metres away—close enough to partially see his oldself below, including his prosthetic hand and scarred face.

"Help," she whispered, followed by a louder "Help!" No one in the café paid attention—too absorbed in their conversations or Network content for her pleas to register. It was like she wasn't even there.

And that gave her an idea.

She completely removed her projection, revealing her oldself beneath. Liam slowed his approach with a confused look on his face. He was seeing her bare face and lifesuit, it was a temporary distraction until the message came through the Network that she'd been hoping for:

<OMEGASERVICE> YOU ARE NOT PROJECTING A TRUESELF INTO THE COLLECTIVE. YOUR OLDSELF WILL BE SANITISED.

This stopped Liam in his tracks. To the best of her knowledge, Carli knew this would only work if there were more than one pair of eyes looking in her general direction. She shifted her position slowly away from her seat towards the centre of the outdoor area of the Café. Liam's gaze left her as he scanned the café, including turning around to see how he'd missed her. His expression had changed from that of a man on a mission to complete confusion.

"That's a neat trick," he said in a loud voice. "I can only assume the other guy was with you. He won't be coming to your rescue."

Carli tried again to contact Briggs through the Network but continued to receive the same message, as though he was no longer connected. She stood facing Liam, only 10 meters away. If she was a fighter, maybe she would find some way to stop him herself—find a blunt weapon and knock him unconscious. But she knew that was well beyond her skill set. The backup option was simply to run, and now that her projection had been "sanitised" she was confident she could escape.

But for some reason, she picked a third option: wait and see what would happen next.

She shouted at him, remembering that the Network would also try to mask her voice, "I wasn't lying!"

His head jerked towards her location—clearly heard, but still unsure. Out of her peripheral vision, some of the other patrons in the café looked around, trying to identify the sound, before returning to the comfort of their Network streams.

A new expression crossed Liam's face—no longer the Network's representation of an individual's face applied on top of a teeper, this was his own expression masked only by the veneer of his trueself. It read to Carli like he was weighing his options—she'd outsmarted him somehow. He'd planned to find Carli and extract answers, but she'd thwarted it. He patted his thigh pocket, followed by reluctant acceptance. His eyes met hers for the briefest of moments before they drifted off.

"This isn't over," he called out before backing away slowly, turning and running.

Carli exhaled a breath she hadn't realised she'd been holding, awash with a sense of relief for herself, but a concern for Briggs. Liam Nolan looked back a few times to see if she'd miraculously reappeared, but she remained "sanitised" from reality. Her relief was interrupted by an incoming voice call request from Lieutenant Gomes.

"What's happened? Where are you?" she asked.

"I'm at the Café Roma in West Praxis,"

"I can't hear you—your voice is muffled. Are you OK?" came the reply.

Liam was close to disappearing from view across the other side of the common. *I can't let him get away.* Trusting only in the Network's decision to sanitise her projection, she moved past the tables of the Café and launched into a run.

"Carli?" Gomes said again.

She closed the call and switched to a text conversation, which was a little clunky to achieve when running.

<MalvinaHoffman> Does this work? I can see Liam Nolan in West Praxis. I'm pursuing him.

<PPD-GomesCons> Are you in danger?

<MalvinaHoffman> No, he can't see me.

<PPD-GomesCons> Where is Briggs?

<MalvinaHoffman> I don't know. I think Liam attacked him. He was last in a nightclub called the Ice Lounge. I can't connect to him any more.

<PPD-GomesCons> Neither can I. Don't follow Nolan. I will get support.

<MalvinaHoffman> But where are they? I triggered a personal safety alert and haven't seen any officers appear yet.

<PPD-GomesCons> How long ago?

Carli had reached the edge of the common and proceeded down the alley where Liam Nolan had gone. She saw him in the distance, two blocks ahead, before he turned right down another street. Others were walking the streets as well, but fewer than in the common—without eyes to watch her she knew she would become visible again.

<MalvinaHoffman> 5 minutes.

<PPD-GomesCons> Nothing's been logged with the PPD. Can you give me a full location trust and I will send officers. Don't pursue Nolan.

She granted the trust request, ignoring the fact that she'd now been told twice to walk away. She wanted to comply—it would be the right thing to do—the safe thing to do, but letting him get away also felt like a mistake.

<MalvinaHoffman> I'm following him at a distance. If you want him caught, I'm your best chance.

There was a long delay before she received a response.

<PPD-GomesCons> Fine. But you are accepting the risk. I've passed your location to the West Praxis station. Officers are 7 minutes away.

Carli smiled as she rounded the corner of the block. She saw Liam turning left another block away—she'd made up some ground and found herself grateful that her morning runs had paid off. Two blocks further and it was clear that Liam was slowing down while still trying to lose whatever tail he couldn't quite see. His repeated checks over his shoulder were frantic and fruitless. Carli's boldness increased as she narrowed the gap further.

Two more left turns, followed by a right—Carli had to slow down her pace to make sure she remained a safe distance away. Her pulse continued to race from adrenaline, so she took a moment to slow her breathing. Straight for two blocks before turning right again, Carli began to wonder how long this pursuit was going to take. As she rounded that corner, she got her answer, finding Liam Nolan standing in the centre of the street, only 10-meters away, facing her direction.

She gasped and stopped dead in her tracks. She wanted to duck back around the corner, before realizing something was wrong with Liam Nolan's guise—she saw only the limited colours of his trueself, but the projection was otherwise hollow—there was no body beneath it.

Liam had done the same thing he had on the transit: separate his projection from his oldself to escape. This meant that he was nearby, hiding in the shadows.

She looked around the rest of the street, low and medium cost apartments on both sides and saw no one. No escaping Liam Nolan or anyone else, for that matter.

And then she realised her mistake. *I'm not invisible anymore.*

# 66

There you are, Liam thought, trying his best to suck down deep breaths from his attempt at escape without making any noise. He'd suspected he might be followed and was even convinced he'd heard muffled steps behind him. Those suspicions were satisfied when he received a message through the Network from his employer:

<844FC1-9B0E48> YOU ARE BEING FOLLOWED. PPD IS ON THE WAY. WHY ARE YOU IN WEST PRAXIS?

Liam cursed through heavy breathing, looking at his prosthetic hand like it could attack him at any moment. He knew of no other response but to counterattack.

<NULL> BECAUSE PPD HAVE BEEN ON MY TAIL FOR THREE DAYS AND YOU'RE NOT DOING ANYTHING ABOUT IT. WHO IS MALVINAHOFFMAN?

He made it a whole block before receiving a response.

<735EF0-FE72B5>: NO-ONE. WHY WAS BRIGGSH33207 KILLED?

<NULL> HE WAS TRYING TO ARREST ME.

There had been no further response. He was tired from running. Tired of being told what to do and having to justify himself. His employer may have the means to suck his accounts dry in a heartbeat, but that was the least of his problems if he was caught.

He ducked into the foyer of an apartment building to catch his breath again. That's when he saw her—a female form, wearing only a lifesuit, but with the projection of a paper bag over her head, winking in and out of reality. The more he stared, the less defined she appeared, disappearing out of view, but when he glanced away, she appeared again.

*What mystery is this?* He wondered. *And why is she pursuing me?*

Nothing made sense to him. For the briefest of moments, he'd believed her story as genuine, until the guy she was with had tried to arrest his decoy teeper. If she was truly "no one" as his employer had stated, then why was she chasing him—and to what end? She posed no physical threat to him, even without a pistol in his pocket and a death-dealing prosthetic hand—and yet here she was.

She stopped running as soon as she'd rounded the corner and saw the remnants of his old projection fixed in place when he split his Evoniik identity. But it did not seem to fool her—at least her gaze did not linger on it for long. Instead, she stepped backwards before scanning the buildings and foyers on either side of the street. Liam pulled behind a pillar to conceal his position, but continued to watch her from a relatively safe distance.

The sound of a door opening across the opposite side of the street caught his attention. Two citizens left an apartment lobby and walked towards Carli's position, past his phantom projection. They both ignored it, unfazed by the appearance of a man standing stationary in the middle of the street.

Liam looked back to where he'd seen Carli, but she'd disappeared again. Surely, she was still there—surely when he spoke with her in the Café, she hadn't just been an apparition of the Network. He heard her voice and saw her face. *No, this must be something else—some way she has found to cancel herself out of reality.*

The two citizens rounded the corner from view, and Carli reappeared in his vision, now standing on the opposite side of the street, but she still hadn't made eye contact with him. She appeared cautious, as though she knew she might be discovered.

He tried to imagine how the Network could be hiding her from reality—he knew little of how the technology worked, but it seemed as though her disappearance was predicated on there being more people around than just him.

Another message appeared from his employer.

<0C2B00-F14919> WHAT IS SHE DOING?

<NULL> SHE KEEPS APPEARING AND DISAPPEARING. SHE VANISHED COMPLETELY AT THE CAFÉ.

He pulled further into the shadows as her gaze scanned past him.

<C46A12-9F58E3> COMPLETELY INVISIBLE?

<NULL> YES.

<61F5F8-DC76B9>: CAN YOU CAPTURE HER?

<NULL> MAYBE.

<30F812-233BF6> DO IT. I NEED TO KNOW HOW.

The correspondence from his employer seemed different from before. For as long as he could remember, his employer had referred to itself as "we". But now it said, "I". He didn't know if it was important. Still, he recognised that even if overpowering the girl would normally be an easy task, the likelihood that the PPD were in pursuit complicated things. He needed to make it worth his while.

<NULL> WHAT ABOUT THE PPD? WHAT IF THEY'RE TRACKING HER?

<89569A-9F0305> WE CAN DELAY THEM AND HAVE BEEN SCRAMBLING HER LOCATION. YOU HAVE TIME.

<NULL> 200,000 BITS, AND THEN I RETIRE.

<0AD826-64953C>: WHAT?

<NULL> 200,000 BITS. THEN YOU LET ME GO. YOU DISABLE THIS THING IN MY HAND, AND I RIDE OFF INTO THE SUNSET.

He felt his pulse quicken again with the faint glimmer of hope of freedom. For the first time, it felt like he was talking to a person instead of an enigma, and for the first time, it felt like freedom might be a possibility. Carli retreated a few steps, still scanning the spaces on both sides of the street. He began to formulate a plan but needed a response soon.

<705E4D-7BFA34> WE AGREE. GET ANSWERS.

He closed his eyes and tried to relax, thinking through what he needed to do, then stepped out of the shadows back onto the street.

He walked with feigned confidence in the opposite direction from where he'd last seen Carli. For every step, he wanted to look around to confirm she was following, but that would cause the ruse to break down. His safe house apartment was only a block and a half away. If he just continued towards it, he hoped she would follow, believing she hadn't been discovered. He turned right at the next corner, identifying his apartment building as the last one on the left. He was sure he heard a muffled step behind him but again couldn't chance looking around to confirm.

The street was relatively clear of other citizens, just as he'd hoped. After all, selecting a safe house location with relatively low foot traffic had always been a strategic choice. But this apartment complex had the added advantage of being on the corner with two different entrances to the main lobby. He wouldn't expect the girl to follow him into the building, but he did expect her to follow him around the corner, meaning he had an option to double back through the lobby and approach her from behind.

A few more steps later, he rounded the last corner. Concealed by a concrete pillar, he kicked into a sprint through the lobby doors before crossing the space, bounding over a bench seat while unzipping his thigh pocket and retrieving the compact pistol. He held it against his body as he reached the lobby's secondary doors that opened back onto the street.

There were few windows. The walls projected a simple, generic scape of some night-time street view that was completely foreign to the reality outside. The doors, however, were glass and he pressed his face against them trying to spot the girl as she approached the corner.

And there, flicking in and out of reality, he saw her again, stopped in her tracks now that she'd lost track of him. He pressed on the door slowly to avoid any kind of sudden movement or unexpected sound. He kept the firearm concealed—as soon as he extended it and someone saw it in his hand, the Network would automatically flag the PPD.

He slid out of the door and ran for Carli. For half of the journey, she was invisible, but for the last few seconds, she reappeared, still looking in the opposite direction. He reached out with his prosthetic hand and grabbed her by the shoulder, pulling her towards himself as he pressed the gun into her ribcage.

"You and I need to continue our discussion," he said.

al Briggs did not exist. That's what his broken Network connection would have told him if it hadn't been for the white-hot light shining like a thousand suns directly into his retinas. A shriek of static in his ears was loud enough to drown out his scream. He'd been shot with an immobilisation round before—part of his weapons certification as a rookie officer. This was far worse.

After what felt like an eternity, the light disappeared, one colour at a time. First, the light changed to green-yellow, then to red, then finally to black. He could barely make out the faces of the crowd forming around him. The sound of static faded, leaving behind a ringing—the only thing louder was the voice in his head telling him that he was probably dead.

He'd felt so clever when he'd disconnected the defibrillator electrodes in his lifesuit with the expectation that it would somehow protect him from Liam Nolan's mystery weapon. Though it has been a last resort, he hadn't considered the possibility that an attack would affect more than just his lifesuit.

Through the pain, he recalled the image of Nguyen lying on the autopsy table, with a hole burned through his ribcage. That realisation snapped him out of his shock, and he desperately grabbed at his plexus to try and remove it before it could melt down and do the same damage to him.

It wasn't there—he felt only the empty coupling on the front of his lifesuit. An unknown hand clasped his—small and soft. He made out a man's voice through the ringing. "We took it off and threw it over the rail. It was smokin' bro."

He slumped back, a moment of relief, and slowly awareness returned to him. With every painful heartbeat, the throb in his eyes reduced and the inky blackness gave way to blurry shadows floating behind pin-pricks of light. He couldn't tell if the ringing in his ears was getting quieter or if everything else was getting louder, but he could make out different voices to match the shadowy faces of the people sitting next to him.

He forced himself to sit up, an action he instantly regretted as his stomach tightened, which forced him into the same breathing exercises he'd done so many times before. As his vision began to sharpen, he made out the face of the person who had held his hand. He whispered a "thank you". He didn't recognise her, but he recognised her outfit—a lifesuit, much like his own. He looked at the others—they too wore only lifesuits. Rubbing his eyes again, he looked back into the nightclub from the open balcony where he had collapsed. There were no bright neon lights. No scapes on the walls projecting virtual sports or other music-themed content. Just tracking markers and a lot of stained, dirty surfaces.

"It's weird, bro," it was the voice he'd heard earlier. He looked up at the heavyset man in a tight, dirty lifesuit, "You've lost your projection. And you've got no ID. We tried to call for a paramedic, but they wouldn't accept without your ID."

*The same thing that happened to Carli's eyes has happened to me*, he concluded, *but I've lost everything*. The Network was gone. He couldn't see anyone's monikers. Couldn't communicate with Carli or the PPD, or anyone. As far as the Network was concerned, he no longer existed.

"Did you call PPD?"

"Oh. No. I saw the gun and figured maybe you wouldn't want the fuzz involved."

Briggs forced himself to his feet. He expected the world to spin and swirl around him, but it seemed steady. The small crowd attending him began to disperse.

"It's fine. I'm Sergeant Briggs," he said. "Can I ask you to contact PPD? Ask for Lt. Gomes in ONI. Say, 'Briggs was attacked and Carli is in danger'. Tell her my Network is fried."

The big guy nodded an assent and the girl smiled at him, showing teeth that were yellowed and chipped. His thoughts again went to Carli. She was in danger. "How long was I down?"

"Five minutes, maybe ten."

"Where... Where's my gun?"

The girl removed it from her pocket and placed it in his hands. He quickly concealed it, like it wasn't anything out of the ordinary, but he knew that would create problems for him later.

He squinted and looked across the common, his eyesight improving but still painful. He managed to make out the table where Carli had been seated. It was empty. He scanned from left to right—a process that was far easier to perform now that all of the trees, advertising and other Network-originated content had been stripped from his reality. He'd always presumed that Praxis harboured a dark and ugly soul and now it seemed that soul had boiled to the surface.

Plenty of teepers and citizens were walking about in their lifesuits, but no Carli and no Liam.

"Uh—Mr… Officer Briggs… I'm speaking to a lady—Gomes. She says she'll meet you."

Briggs turned and faced the large man. "Ask her if the girl is OK."

"She can hear you," he said, nodding, then paused, staring blankly.

"Well?" Briggs said, agitated. "What did she say?"

"Oh—you can't hear her?"

"No! What did she say?"

"She says '305'."

Briggs's stomach tightened. "Code 305?"

"She says, 'affirmative'. The guy's face tilted, "What's a 305?"

The news landed. "Hostage taken." Acid rose in his throat. The promise he'd made to Carli and to himself hours earlier to keep her safe had already been broken. And yet, he refused to quit, refused to allow the guilt to overwhelm him.

*If anyone has a chance of rescuing her, it is me.*

*I'm here. C'mon already,* Briggs thought. He'd travelled four blocks south through residential apartments and was waiting next to a teeper station— coordinates that Lt. Gomes had relayed to him through the big guy in the night club. Briggs asked his name, but in the ten minutes since, he'd already forgotten it. If he had any access to the Network, he would have banked the conversation or recorded a digital note. Instead, he was forced to rely only on his memory, which at this moment was being uncooperative.

He looked up at the grey metal dome above him. The clear night sky he'd taken for granted was nothing more than a whole lot of rusty metal and concrete, dotted with a few illuminated tracking markers. The buildings around him were equally austere—stained concrete, crumbling in places, patched with a slather of fresh cement in others. For such a utilitarian outlook, he expected it to be also quite dark, but the illumination from lamp posts and the dome above bathed the street in a white glow.

A buzz and a beep from behind him drew his attention to a teeper station where one of the bipedal machines had decoupled from its charger. He gave it distance, hand resting just inside the open pocket of his lifesuit. The teeper took one step forward, tilted its head before making a gesture with its left hand up to its own throat, held it there for a moment, and cupped its hand where its ear would have been.

*Hostage*. It took Briggs a while to recognise the hand signal—something still practised at the academy but only used in emergencies since most communications between squad members would just use the Network.

"You can hear me, right?" he said.

The teeper nodded and did a big thumbs up. This isn't going to be easy, Briggs thought.

"Where is the rest of the PPD? Why are you using a civilian teeper?"

Its expressionless face gave nothing away. It offered another gesture of an extended fist that swung down to its other hand. Briggs knew it was important, but didn't know what it meant. If it was something he'd learned before, it was long forgotten, and without any connection to the Network, he had no way of looking it up.

Another hand signal waved him forward, and the teeper shifted to a smooth walking gait. It was the teeper's top speed but still frustratingly slow.

"You know, I have no idea that you are actually Lieutenant Gomes. For all I know you could be working with the other side."

It ignored him. Briggs couldn't bring himself to consider the machine as being a person at this point but followed along, nonetheless.

"How many blocks away are we? Just give me a number."

The teeper extended two fingers to the side without breaking stride. They passed a group of pedestrians walking the other way. One of them pointed towards Briggs before giggling behind their hands. It was ironic they should find amusement in seeing him without any projection when he could see them all the same way. The emperor wasn't the only person who wasn't wearing any clothes.

Gomes' teeper held out its hand again—a single finger. Briggs surveyed the block ahead, indistinguishable from every other stained concrete monstrosity in West Praxis. But, according to this machine, which he desperately hoped was piloted by Lt. Gomes, this was where Carli was being held hostage.

They pressed on, finally reaching one of the entrances. He unzipped his thigh pocket, removed his firearm, confirmed the safety was on, and held it at the ready close to his chest. Gomes' teeper turned and paid careful attention to the illegal weapon he now nursed. Its head tilted on an angle again, before making eye contact with him with its two lifeless glass eyes. As though it had decided to overlook the indiscretion, it made a different gesture Briggs recognised: 'Follow me'.

# 68

The door unlocked, and a firm hand directed Carli into the apartment. She thought of calling for help from one of the other people in the lobby, but a twist of her wrist made her think again. At least she was still able to communicate with Lt Gomes via the Network, sharing her location and the floor on which she exited the lift. The whole time, this man, *this killer*, hovered behind her, occasionally nuzzling something hard and metal into her side as if to reinforce the gravity of the situation and to remind her that *he* was now the one in control.

The apartment was bare, its walls dirty and un-scaped. A messy cot lay to one side, adorned with a few carry bags. Other than the door to what she assumed was the bathroom, the only other furniture was a small refrigerator humming to itself and two moulded plastic chairs.

A final push caused her to stumble towards the chairs, and he barked a command to sit. She complied, her heart racing from her now-failed pursuit, amplified by the dread of being completely at the mercy of a killer. But despite this real threat, she was not defeated—she'd experienced too much in the last week to just give in to the inevitability of her circumstances.

She channelled her defiance into keeping Lt. Gomes as informed as possible—a difficult process considering the first thing he'd commanded her to do was to retract her hands from the gloved portion of her lifesuit and bring her hands out the side splits usually used for personal hygiene. Instead, she'd worked to communicate via cumbersome eye movements, or by simply staring at things as she walked like numbers in the elevator or room numbers which she hoped were still being relayed through to Gomes via her trust.

She'd received messages from Gomes giving her reassurance that they were on the way. She assumed "they" were just the PPD, but considering the lack of any kind of intervention so far since her first contact, she dared not place her hope solely in a PPD rescue. Almost as though Gomes had read her mind, a message flashed across her optics. "Briggs and I are on the way."

She let out a gasp of relief: Briggs was OK. It drew a curt look from Liam Nolan.

"Take off your plexus," he demanded.

She hesitated but thought better of resisting—at least not yet. She unhooked the plexus from her chest to the sound of a few chirps and alarms.

"Throw it on the floor". She slowly complied, her eyes darting to the gun he pointed at her.

He retrieved a thin pillow from the cot, placed it over the plexus and fired his gun into it. Carli jumped, and any defiance she may have been harbouring melted away. The pillow did little to soften the noise as another two shots followed. Liam lifted the pillow and inspected the device, now cracked and smoking. Still dissatisfied, he picked up the plexus and disappeared into the bathroom. Carli heard what she assumed was him tossing the plexus into the toilet, followed by a flush. For some reason, her first thought was that her expensive, one-day-old plexus was now destroyed.

The loud bangs had distracted her from the feed in her optics, which now reported a range of error messages. Her augments were no longer paired to her primary plexus and were now running in passive mode only. She lost all connection to the Network but continued to see the masked reality around her—or in her case, the split reality. But now she was more disconnected from the Network than she'd ever been. She would no longer receive messages and no longer be able to broadcast the feed from her optics. She was, for all intents and purposes, alone.

She tried to slow her heart rate. The final message she'd received from Lt. Gomes told her to stall for time. She had no other strategy. She reminded herself that she'd been playing a role when speaking to Liam earlier, but she didn't know if he believed her. *Should I continue that ruse?*

Liam took the chair opposite hers, his weapon still held in his right hand and pointed at her, a faint wisp of smoke coming from the barrel.

"No more games. Who are you and who do you *really* work for?" he demanded.

*Stall for time. The best lies are ones grounded in truth.*

"Carli. Nothing's changed—my group still wants to work with you." Her voice waivered, and she knew he'd noticed. It was not the convincing performance of a seasoned agent like she'd seen on a Network drama.

"I don't believe you. I know the PPD's been alerted, and I fully expect them to show up here soon. I assume that was you." He lifted the gun from his side and pointed it at her to reinforce the point. "So, I'll ask you again—who do you work for?"

Carli flinched in her seat, fighting a pressure behind her eyes—her body wanted nothing more than to give in, but she somehow kept the fear at bay.

"I'm… I'm no one. I'm a sculptor. You know that already. I was asked to meet with you. To give you an offer. That's all."

She closed her eyes, fearing the worst. After what seemed like an eternity, he responded. "How did you disappear?"

Carli opened her eyes. His gun was resting again at his side. "What?"

"Don't make me repeat myself Carli Dawes. You disappeared at the Café. You followed me the whole way here. How?"

"There… There's a fault in the Network. It will cause you to be masked out of reality."

Liam transferred his gun to his left hand—the hand Carli could see was the prosthetic. His right hand started a dance of micro gestures, indicating to Carli that he was communicating with someone on the Network. His eyes were unfocused for a moment, and Carli wondered if it would be enough of a distraction for her to attempt to escape, but the moment passed too quickly.

"Show me how," he said.

"I can't—not without my plexus."

"Then tell me how you do it. If you're hacking the Network, then I need the code packet."

"No—I'm no hat…"

His frustration intensified. "Then give me a straight answer! How do you do it?"

"I… I just remove my trueself, my projection. The Network does the rest."

Another pause as Liam relayed this information. Carli took note of the time it was taking to send and receive a message. Close to 20 seconds. Clearly, Liam wasn't broadcasting his feed, and they couldn't see or hear what was going on.

If she wanted to create an opportunity, she needed to give a more complicated message. The barrel of the gun dipped away slightly as he typed.

"That's too simple. My employer… thinks you're working for a rival guild."

*Guild?* "I have no idea what you mean." She leant forward a little in her chair. "If your employer doesn't believe me, then they can just try it for themselves. But it only works if there are other people around to see them. It won't even work if they use a mirror. Afterwards, they will get a message from the Network—from something called 'Omega Service' telling them their oldself will be sanitised."

Liam cursed and continued to type away with his right hand. The gun in his left dropped away slightly. Carli pressed her feet a little further forward, wondering how long it would take her to spin away from the chair and make it through the closed door. *Seconds?* Surely that was more than enough time for Liam to respond, and she would be dead. She didn't know much about guns, but she suspected even the small gun he held would be more than capable of doing the job.

A second idea formed, and she brought her feet back level with the rear legs of the chair. It was a lightweight plastic—she could grab it and throw it at him to buy her more time—or even knock the gun out of his hand. But again, she held back. *Then what? You somehow knock his gun away and make a run for it? He chases you out the door and then shoots you at a distance before you can reach the elevator?*

She dismissed the idea a second time, somehow disappointed in herself for not taking the risk, even as she faced down the barrel of a gun. Liam continued to type, and she continued to watch him. He shifted in his seat slightly, and she could see the shape of something above a pocket on the side of his left calf. It was not a common location for a pocket in a lifesuit, but midway up the calf was a bone-coloured shape: some form of handle or… *hilt. Some form of knife or blade.*

With an angry groan, Liam stood, slamming back his plastic chair. Carli almost tipped backwards in her own chair in surprise.

"Stand up!" he ordered. "We're leaving, NOW!" The gun reinforced every gesture, adding an authority that Carli could only comply with. His prosthetic hand grabbed her by the left wrist and spun her towards the door. He commanded her to open it and forced her out into the corridor by bending her arm behind her back.

He hustled her down the corridor, towards the elevator. She stumbled once before regaining her step. Her head spun in renewed alarm and confusion.

"What's going on?" she managed to ask.

He didn't answer. They'd made it to the entrance area in front of the elevators and slowed. She looked over her shoulder at Liam and found him concentrating at the projected number above the elevator doors. Level 18, and increasing.

"You didn't call the elevator," he said—not a question. She couldn't do anything without a Network connection now that her plexus was smouldering in Liam's bathroom. There was a second elevator, but it showed that it was still on the ground floor.

He jerked her body sideways, towards the fire escape. He commanded her to open the door, reinforced with an extra twist of her arm. She complied, stepping onto the landing and looking down the spiral staircase. He held her close as the heavy fire door slammed behind her, reverberating down the stairwell.

She began to speak, but another arm twist and a curt hush silenced her. He peered over the railing. Above the dissipating sound of the slammed door, she heard something—muffled but electronic, a metallic clap-clap over a high-pitched whine.

It was a sound she knew well. A sound out of place. A teeper was ascending the stairwell. It was a sound that meant one thing to Carli—rescue.

A defiant smile crossed her face, and she almost turned to face Liam to bask in his imminent defeat.

But Liam must have had another idea, because in that moment, rather than give up, he turned towards the noise and shoved her down the first flight of stairs.

Briggs imagined the elevator made an audible chime as he reached the 21st floor, but he heard only the mechanical grinding of the doors as they slid open. At least the elevator still had some mechanical buttons that he could use to input the floor. A frustrating game of charades had been necessary for Lt. Gomes to communicate that she would pilot the teeper up the stairs to cut off an escape while he rode the elevator.

Gun drawn, Briggs surveyed the landing in front of him and determined it was clear. He stole a glance down the corridor and saw nothing unusual. His damaged vision rendered it with dirty carpet and stains at hand level up and down both sides. He couldn't locate the apartment door that Carli had shared—without the Network providing an overlay, no numbers were visible.

He shifted to the fire escape and opened the door to allow his mechanical partner to gain access to the floor. As the door shuddered open, his attention was immediately drawn down the stairs where Carli lay in a crumpled heap holding her side. Gomes' teeper stood over her, attempting to provide assistance. Briggs launched into action, rushing down the handful of steps and pushing the teeper out of the way.

"Carli—what happened? Are you OK?"

She nodded with a wince. His eyes followed a trickle of blood originating from above the line of her lifesuit's head stocking, where a red stain was growing. She managed to sit up, holding her side. Such a fall would most likely have ended in bruised ribs at the very least, but the panels of her oversized PPD lifesuit had at least softened the blow. Injured, but alive.

Still—despite now being safe, seeing Carli in this state refired the anger within him. The anger at losing Captain Hagen and the other officers. The anger at Liam for causing all of this devastation. The anger at Moya for suspending him. The anger at himself for not doing enough to stop this from happening in the first place.

"Where? Where is he?"

"Up." Carli pointed. "He's got a gun. And… a knife on his leg."

"How long ago?"

"A minute? Maybe. Maybe I blacked out."

Briggs turned to Gomes' teeper. "I still don't understand why this building isn't swarming with PPD officers, but you need to get this place locked down. I don't care what kind of shortcuts you take or favours you have to call in, that murderer is not leaving this building under his own power." Briggs poked the chest of the teeper to reinforce the point. "Lock down the elevators in case he manages to make it past me."

Briggs turned to leave, but a mechanical hand held him back. Gomes' teeper did another hand gesture he didn't recognise, then looked down at Carli.

"She says to wait for backup."

Briggs shook himself away from its cold grasp. "No—I'm not letting him get away again."

He took off up the steps, imagining Gomes' teeper shouting at him as he climbed. He listened for any other noises, the sounds of doors opening, but heard only his laboured breathing. It was a slow climb. He rounded each corner wide to give him the best angle on any possible trap. He tested the handle of each fire escape door to confirm it was locked. With every storey reached, anticipation grew, knowing that the number of floors and therefore the number of options remaining was approaching zero. He forced himself to slow down, making each footfall as precise and quiet as possible. Only a week ago, in an apartment building not far away, he'd climbed a similar set of stairs after finding the body of Constable Nguyen at the bottom of the elevator shaft.

He counted floors as he climbed; most apartment buildings were no more than 25 floors high. He was extra cautious on the 25th floor, expecting to be pounced on or shot at, but again, the stairwell was clear. He checked the door into the hallway, and it too was locked. The stairs led to one more level, to the rooftop, not usually accessible since it only housed machinery and ventilation.

*If Nolan can get onto the rooftop, there's no certainty he won't find another way down*, Briggs thought. He reached the final landing—there were no other places to hide and no options other than a faded yellow door. His heart thumped in his chest as he tried the handle. Unlike the others, it turned, but the door didn't shift. He pressed his weight against it, felt it give a little, then gave it an extra shove, breaking it open.

Gun out, Briggs sought cover—a wire storage cage that would give him a better position to survey the rest of the rooftop. The elevator and stairwell were in the centre of the building, creating a blind spot on the opposite side. He readied himself and dashed the few metres to safety, expecting to be shot at, but nothing came.

He snuck a glance over the rest of the rooftop, cluttered and messy—air processors and other large equipment Briggs didn't recognise. Fortunately, most were no higher than Briggs' hips, still tall enough to give reasonable cover to someone crouching down. He found no other means of escape. No other stairwells. All neighbouring buildings were separated by ground-level walkways—it was too far to jump.

The metal dome separating West Praxis from the harsh environment outside was above him—its light panels offering only a soft glow since it was still nighttime. At this height and position, the dome curved upwards towards its apex, centred over the West Praxis Central common. Following the framework with his eyes gave him a completely different sense of vertigo. He hadn't been up this high before in the real world or any kind of simulation.

The smart play would be to wait. If Liam Nolan was here, and Briggs was certain he would be, the lowest risk option was to hold the door until backup arrived. Attempting to clear the spaces behind each piece of machinery would expose him, and he doubted his own reaction time if he was caught off guard.

It was only once he accepted the inevitability that he needed to stay put that his plans were interrupted.

"You are persistent," came a loud voice. It sounded far enough away that Briggs wasn't in any immediate danger, close enough to be heard over the sound of the blowing air and machinery.

"It takes persistence to catch a snake," he countered. "This place is surrounded. The building's locked down. There's no need for violence." He looked around, trying to discern the direction of the voice.

"Sometimes there is," Liam responded.

Gun still drawn at the ready, Briggs cocked the receiver as quietly as he could and slowly pressed out of his cover.

"So, who are you exactly?" Liam asked.

"PPD. We've already met—you killed me not long ago." Briggs cleared some of the machinery, scanning each row as he passed it and pressed further towards the origin of the voice.

"Ah Briggs? That's an interesting twist. How did you survive?"

"Persistence." He passed another row of machinery. "And you're Liam Nolan. Mercenary. Assassin. Murderer of Constable Lee Nguyen; Petros Zaimis; Aldus Goldstein;"

"Great. Gold star for you then…"

Briggs interrupted, his anger boiling over, "Terrorist."

"Hmm. So, you *are* PPD. You know the PPD's compromised, right? If you're here all alone, where's the rest of them?"

"Maybe I wanted the satisfaction of taking care of you myself." He cleared another row of machinery.

"You make it sound personal."

You're dammed right it is.

"It seems I have the good fortune of knowing some things about you, too. Hal Briggs."

Liam Nolan stepped out of the shadows on the far side of the rooftop, his hands behind his back. Briggs trained his gun towards him like a laser, but he was still over 15 metres away. He would have stood some chance of a successful shot to the body with his usual Torque firearm, but he doubted he had the skill to make a successful shot with the pocket revolver he now held—not that he intended on giving that information away.

"Hands out!" Briggs ordered, making an aggressive step towards Liam, while also confirming he would have some partial cover if Liam responded in kind.

"What? You don't recognise me?" Liam said, unmoved. "Don't I look a little familiar to you?"

"You look like a melted piece of garbage," Briggs replied.

"How about now?" Liam said.

Ignoring the strange distraction, Briggs pressed forward again, yelling, "I said, hands!" He heard a noise behind him that sounded like the stairwell door closing. He assumed that meant Gomes' teeper or some other backup had arrived, though part of him wished he would be able to finish this alone, on his own terms.

"Hal Briggs. You've barely got a few thousand bits to your name. Currently suspended from the PPD—oh my! Threatening a witness!"

Briggs stood his ground, index finger resting on the side of the trigger. In this state, it wouldn't take much pressure to squeeze off a shot. Liam's eyeline shifted away from Briggs towards the stairwell.

"Parents unknown. Twice divorced. No children. There's a whole bunch of banked personal notes here," Liam said. He smiled and turned back to Briggs.

Briggs' finger wrapped the trigger, feeling its weight. He could take this guy down and make it look like an accident, but he feared he might now have an audience. Still, Liam Nolan was the closest he would ever get to whatever conspiracy was happening across Praxis.

A sound approached from behind him and to the left, a whirring of motors and clicking of metal on the concrete floor. Briggs forced his finger away from the trigger and stole a look to his side. Lieutenant Gomes' teeper approached his position, but its head appeared to be scanning the rest of the rooftop. It nonchalantly stopped at his side and gave a palms-up gesture. If its shoulders were opposable, they probably would have shrugged.

"What the..?" The teeper paid no attention to Liam Nolan. It couldn't see it.

A shot rang out. Not from Briggs' gun but from Liam's. Briggs couldn't tell what he registered first, the sharp noise or the molten sensation of a bullet piercing through his left shoulder. He was already ducking when he heard a second shot, then a third. Or was he falling? Either way, he hit the ground hard enough with his right shoulder that his gun discharged into the steel cage that gave him some modest cover. The impact dislodged the gun from his hand, skittling it to his side, and he desperately kicked his feet to push his body further behind the cage.

*Reset. Use your cover and reassert yourself,* he told himself. His right hand found his gun, but his left wasn't cooperating and screamed abuse at him when he attempted to raise it. He tried to sit up, but that too proved difficult. His only working arm didn't want to let go of his only means of self-defence.

He swore. He knew he was vulnerable. Injured and too slow to react.

Gomes' teeper moved towards Briggs, its expressionless face both menacing and innocent. He stared into its glass eyes. Another gunshot hit the side of its head, causing it to spin and the whole body to stagger on its ungainly feet. Plastic and glass fragments burst from the impact location, revealing electronics and blinking lights.

The teeper tried to regain its balance, but a different mechanical hand seized its left arm—Liam Nolan, who'd closed the distance between them and nullified Brigg's cover. He pulled the teeper towards him and pressed his gun into its left hip socket and fired twice, severing whatever electronics controlled the leg.

Briggs lifted his gun to defend himself. He managed to squeeze off another shot in the general direction of Liam, but he'd positioned himself well behind the teeper to give himself cover. The teeper lurched forward, flailing its arms in a desperate attempt to keep balance to compensate for the loss of control of one of its limbs. As it fell, Liam steered it towards Briggs' supine body, causing it to collapse over him. The teeper may have weighed slightly less than a human of comparable size, but it still had plenty of hard surfaces. One of them struck Briggs on his forehead in the same place he'd injured a few days earlier. Its ungainly limbs trapped his own, forcing his gun hand away, and its whole weight pinned him to the cold concrete floor.

The damaged face of Gomes' teeper pressed against his own. And behind it, Liam Nolan now stood over him, gun trained on him. Briggs tried to raise his gun, but Liam stepped on his wrist, forcing him to release it. With a twist of his leg, Liam flicked the gun behind him and far out of reach.

Trapped and disarmed. Face to face with his quarry, and completely helpless.

Carli didn't know if the cut on her forehead had stopped bleeding, but the fog lifted, and she managed to return to her feet. Her side burned from the heavy fall, causing her to wince, but she found a resolve to ignore the pain. She should have been grateful to be free of her captor. She was no longer at risk of being shot or stabbed or erased from reality completely. But instead, rage was brewing. She refused to be a victim again, to have this or any other person casually cast her off to the side.

Lieutenant Gomes told her to stay put. She disobeyed. Wincing from the pain in her ribs, she too climbed the stairs and made it onto the rooftop not long after Gomes' teeper.

From a hidden position, she'd seen the whole thing play out. Briggs pointed his gun at Liam Nolan, who first appeared to be donning a projection that was identical to Briggs. Then his projection disappeared, and for a few seconds, Liam was wearing only a lifesuit and a paper bag mask. Lt. Gomes' teeper however, seemed oblivious to what was going on and didn't recognise that Lian Nolan was even there.

Carli pieced everything together—somehow, Liam Nolan had already been given a new identity—Briggs' old one. Now he'd gone bare and was being masked out of reality. But Briggs could still see him, and so could Carli—he appeared as a blue ghost in her optics. She was just about to call out when everything went to hell.

Carli saw Liam fire and Briggs fall—a piercing double bang causing her to inhale sharply. Gomes spun around as if to try and locate the origin of the mystery bullet. *She can't see him at all.* It took two pairs of eyes to effectively mask someone out of reality. The teeper had one. Carli had the other.

She ducked to the ground, her ribs swearing at her. She made her way on her hands and knees—she should have been heading towards the stairwell, but instead, she pressed forward, finding cover behind a row of machinery. She heard another gunshot—closer now. She made it past another row of machinery and peered around the corner to see Liam fire another shot into the hip of the teeper and throw it on top of Briggs' body, still moving but injured.

Liam stood over him. Briggs struggled, and something skidded away from him, behind Liam and towards her. It stopped moving within only a few meters of her prone position.

A gun.

Carli recoiled for a moment before realising that Liam was distracted. He towered over Briggs, his gun raised. They spoke, but she couldn't hear what was said. She inched forward, crawling towards the gun, her eyes locked on Liam just in case he turned. If he did, she didn't know what she would do. A metre to go. She could see Briggs on the ground. It looked like he'd managed to disentangle himself from the teeper, but otherwise lay still—Liam had all the power right now.

She needed the gun. She'd never fired one. But it was the only way to regain control of the situation. She needed to protect Briggs and herself. She feared she wouldn't be fast enough to stop this murderer from executing her friend in cold blood.

Her hand found the gun, and she slowly pulled herself to her feet. Its weight was far heavier than she expected—not just its mass, but the weight of the power to kill in the palm of her hand.

Liam's projection changed. When attacking the teeper, he occasionally disappeared and reappeared like a ghost. Now she could still see his oldself beneath a brand new projection. Denim jeans, oilskin coat. Tight curly hair.

Liam was wearing Briggs' projection.

She raised the barrel towards Liam, held in both hands away from her body. She felt disgusted on Briggs' behalf—as if attacking him hadn't been bad enough, he'd now stolen his identity.

She felt the stiffness of the trigger, aimed for the largest part of Liam's body and squeezed.

The shot was deafening, and its force jolted her wrists back. Her right thumb burned, but she managed to keep hold of the gun. Liam, on the other hand, did not respond like the bullet had made any impact. Carli was sure that she closed her eyes when she'd fired. Liam staggered at the sound, spinning towards the origin of her shot. He almost made a full rotation before Carli managed another shot, this time eyes wide open, but connected only with machinery just to Liam's right with a sharp burst of sparks. Liam fell onto one knee, but his gun was still extending.

The reality of being shot more vivid than ever, she squeezed the trigger a third time in the desperate hope she would be faster than this killer. They both fired, but Liam fired first.

Briggs was defenceless, his would-be executioner standing over him. They exchanged a few words—an attempt by him to buy some time, but only delaying the inevitable. As he prepared himself for a second, more permanent death, he could only think about his failure in being unable to protect the people he cared about, the regret of being too slow or too stubborn to prevent all of this from happening. His failure was staring him in the face. He took little comfort that his demise would at least go some way towards proving he'd been right.

As he prepared for the final insult, a loud gunshot echoed across the rooftop. Not from Liam's gun—from somewhere behind him. As Liam spun around, Briggs saw Carli standing tall, holding his gun. A second shot went wide, and Briggs realised he was not in the safest of positions. But rather than cower out of the way, he acted.

With all the power he could muster, pushing through the pain and weakness of an injured shoulder, he swung his right leg around to collect Liam in the joint of his knee. His blow coincided with another gunshot, this time from Liam's gun at Carli. Already off-balance from his sudden rotation, Liam's leg folded in on itself and the rest of his body followed to the ground. With his momentum, Briggs managed to throw his body over Liam's gun hand—fearful not for his safety but for Carli's.

He could not waste the precious seconds to see if she was OK. Instead, he grabbed Liam's hand and forced the muzzle in a safe direction before managing to twist it free, holding onto a hot barrel that melted into his lifesuit's hand sleeves.

Liam twisted to try to regain dominance—he was taller and stronger than

Briggs who knew any advantage he may have found from Carli's surprise distraction would be short-lived. Briggs noticed Liam reach down to his calf and was trying to remove something. A knife—Carli had alerted him earlier.

Desperately clinging to the hot gun, Briggs managed to hook a leg over Liam's hand and slammed the butt of the gun down onto the side of Liam's head with as much strength as he could manage. Liam's body responded immediately, falling limp, and collapsing, the knife clanging to the ground.

Briggs exhaled deeply, his fatigued body falling back to the concrete rooftop, his shoulder burning. A new shadow approached him, haloed by the dim lights of the domed barrier above him—Carli Dawes. He gave her a grateful nod and thanked whatever unseen power had decided to give him another chance.

He found his way to his feet and stood over the body of Liam Nolan. Using the plastic zip cuffs he'd stored in a pocket of his suit, Briggs fastened Liam's hands together behind his back, tightening a few clicks more than was probably needed. A careful, one-handed pat down revealed a fresh gash to Liam's left side, probably from one of Carli's shots, and swelling to his temple where Briggs' blow had struck.

He recovered the knife Liam had unsheathed—old, with a decorative hilt and a flexible, razor-sharp blade. Not the most practical weapon, but would still have been deadly at close quarters. He threw it into one of the machinery cages, out of reach. He also secured Liam's gun along with a second clip he removed from one of Liam's pockets.

He checked and confirmed a pulse. A knock to the head shouldn't have been enough to kill the man, but that would certainly have made things a whole lot simpler.

He looked at Carli, who remained in an aggressive cover position over Liam's unconscious body, gun poised. Her hands shook slightly, but Briggs saw the pressure of her finger on the trigger, ready to fire once more.

"It's OK, Carli, he's not getting up."

"He's alive?" she managed.

"Yes, but he can't hurt us now." Briggs approached her slowly, raising his good hand and motioning to steer the gun away. He'd lost count of how many bullets had been fired.

Carli didn't move from her stance, eyes wide and tears rolling down her face—they refused to meet his own but were instead laser-focused on Liam.

Briggs took in her defiant posture, unfiltered and unadulterated by the masking of a projection.

He pressed closer, reaching towards her hands. "Please, Carli. He's not worth it. I want that too, but I need him alive. *We* need him alive."

His hand reached hers on the gun, and he heard an audible click, but there was no shot. The gun was out of bullets. Carli gasped through tears in response before dropping the gun.

He eased around her and repeated, "It's OK, Carli. We're safe now."

Shivering, she returned his gaze. The trickle of blood from the hood of her lifesuit joined a stream of tears. Briggs managed to wrap his right arm around her in some semblance of comfort, but the pain in his shoulder prevented anything more. She leaned into him in sobbed, head nestling into his chest.

Fully aware of his mortality and overwhelmed with gratitude, the best he could manage was, "Thank you, Carli."

Their awkward embrace was interrupted by Gomes' teeper, which was still making stuttered movements. Briggs did not know if Gomes was somehow still in control or if the teeper was just attempting to return to base.

"Lieutenant Gomes asks if you're OK," Carli said.

He inspected the wound in his shoulder—straight through shot just below his clavicle and only just exiting above his scapula. A small calibre bullet—It was a mess, but could have been a lot worse.

"Yes. Liam Nolan is apprehended." Briggs saw Liam start to stir as he slowly regained consciousness.

"She says she's coming in person with reinforcements… and a medic." Carli paused, "She wants us to stay put."

Briggs grunted, "Fine, but we're sitting ducks here."

# 71

I nearly did it. I nearly shot him in cold blood.

If anyone deserved to die, it should be this man. She told herself that she was no executioner, and yet she could not contain the feeling that death was the righteous response. It disgusted her—who had she become?

At some point, Lt. Gomes cancelled her lease from her disabled teeper, which flailed and jerked in several failed attempts to return to a charging station before deciding to power down. Now that the lease was concluded, Carli's lack of a linked plexus meant she had no other connection to the Network and was only perceiving everything passively.

Briggs inspected the cut on her forehead, awkwardly pulling the hood of her lifesuit back before returning it after he realised that it was holding back the bleeding. He found some clear plastic wrapping that may have been used once upon a time to wrap boxes on a crate and fashioned himself a rudimentary sling with Carli's help. She was careful to avoid the wound which oozed dark red blood down both sides of his punctured lifesuit. She doubted the wrap would have been particularly sterile, and didn't want to look too closely at his open wound. She tapped her own shoulder in the same place with a dull thud—Briggs had given her his only PPD lifesuit and was wearing a civilian one. If he'd kept his original lifesuit, he probably would have been a lot better off.

Liam regained full consciousness but remained in a seated position. Accepting his fate, his demeanour shifted dramatically, with slumped shoulders and pursed lips. Even through his capture, he'd continued to wear Briggs' previous projection. For all intents and purposes, he was Briggs. The Network identified him with the same moniker. The location trusts that Briggs had initiated before she met with Liam at the Café Roma remained in effect. It wasn't just disorientating; it was another violation.

Carli found a seat, but Briggs stood guard over his prize like a predator deciding if it should devour its prey now or save it for later.

Carli intervened, "You know, he's wearing your projection. He has your moniker, too."

Briggs took this in before replying with more patience than she would have assumed, "Ok, that makes sense then. You ditch one identity, and somehow pick up another one. You're no Network hat, though—who does it for you?"

"If I knew who that was, then I suspect I wouldn't be in this position."

"So, you don't know who you're working for?"

"I have some ideas, but not specifically," he replied.

Briggs turned to Carli, "So, he's still connected to the Network? Using my identity?"

She confirmed. Briggs reached down and removed Liam's plexus from the centre of his lifesuit and stared down at it like he was holding his own identity. He attached it to the dock in his own lifesuit. Carli knew that wouldn't do anything since the phasing process for a plexus had already paired it to Liam's augments. Briggs had explained that all of his augments had been destroyed, not just a single colour, but all vision and sound. She doubted that a borrowed plexus would have made any difference.

Briggs arrived at the same conclusion before removing the plexus again, placing it at a distance a few meters away and smashing it with a nearby concrete block. It muttered a few hisses and squeals as gas vented from its cracked case, at which point Briggs tossed it over the side of the building to the street below.

"That probably wasn't wise. Or legal," Liam said.

Briggs shrugged, then asked, "Why wasn't it wise?"

"I know that my employer doesn't like to lose. If they suspect that their asset has been compromised, they won't be happy."

"And why should I care about that?"

Liam looked up at Briggs and straightened his posture. Even from his low position, he conveyed a sense of dangerous confidence.

"Because I've seen what they can do. They can drain bits from accounts faster than I can move them myself. They can scrub footage and destroy or repossess an identity at will. And because, right at this moment, I have a piece of their technology surgically attached to my elbow that I suspect is more valuable to them than my life is."

Carli found herself recoiling as he spoke, looking down at the mechanical hand with its partially masked orange glow. She remembered what Liam had said to her at the café.

"He wants the hand gone," she said. "He told me earlier." She remembered a few other things he'd mentioned. "He also said that Overseer ArdentBlue is not who she... *they* say they are. She says they were... replaced."

"And how would he know this?" Briggs asked, coming closer and standing over Liam.

"Because I used *this*," Liam awkwardly gestured with his prosthetic hand behind his back, "on the guy in Norwich, two years ago."

"That timing makes sense. Was that your first with the device?"

"Yes," Liam confirmed.

"Can you show me a body?"

Liam held his gaze before answering, "If it's still there, maybe."

Briggs turned and paced away, clearly thinking about the importance of whatever Liam had told him. Liam turned to look at her.

"You're not happy, I get it. For what it's worth, I probably wouldn't have killed you."

Anger rose again. She tried to think of a witty reply but came up with nothing. He smiled, which only made it worse.

A door slammed behind her, bringing them all to attention. Briggs already had Liam's reloaded gun in his hand, ready and had dropped to one knee. She followed suit, with a much slower response time.

"Briggs? Carli?" She heard the voice before a face peered out from behind the stair pillar. Lt. Gomes—this time in the flesh. Even in her heightened state, she sensed a flash of guilt for being able to see through her projection, like she was invading her privacy.

She stood again, but Briggs was still in cover position. "Is that her, Carli?" he said.

Remembering that he couldn't perceive her projection at all, Carli confirmed, which finally put Briggs at ease. Gomes approached, beckoning two others behind her that Carli didn't recognise. One wore full police body armour, and the other was carrying a medical pack and a generally timid disposition. Gomes glanced between Briggs and Liam, hesitating.

"Son of a bitch is wearing my projection," Briggs stated.

"That's not the start of it. He *is* you," Gomes said.

Liam called out from his crouched position, "Maybe *he's* the imposter?"

Gomes' eyes rolled, gesturing to the armoured officer to approach Liam and to the second officer to approach Briggs. A callout from the officer identified her as Detective Curran. She waved an optical scanner device over Liam's face and looked at a display on the back—it looked very similar to the scanners she'd used at NuSculpt to do quick facial scans before crafting a trueself.

"Is it him Gayle?" Gomes asked.

"Yes. Liam Nolan in the flesh."

Carli looked over to Briggs, now being attended to by the medic. She was sure she noticed his posture drop like he was finally vindicated. He straightened almost as quickly as the medic, having unwrapped the temporary sling, lifted Briggs' shoulder in a way that triggered an angry outburst.

"You OK Carli? That was… " Gomes raised a comforting hand towards Carli's shoulder but stopped short.

"Yes."

"And you…" Gomes turned to Briggs. "I don't know where to begin. You were told—ordered—the keep out of this fight. And not only did you disobey, but you also almost got your friend killed—more than once."

"She knew the risks," Briggs said through a clenched jaw.

"You know, after I stuck my neck out for you on the transit, I went through the late Captain Hagen's notes from your last performance reviews. I needed to know what sort of person I was dealing with, and although I'd only worked with her for a few months, I knew her well enough to trust her opinion. Do you want to know some of the words she used to describe your performance?" Briggs stiffened again. "Obstinate. Head-strong. Stubborn."

Briggs smirked. "Those all sound like compliments."

She shook her head and sighed.

"And if you don't mind me saying, unlike the rest of the PPD—I've delivered," Briggs added.

"And at what cost? You're injured. Carli too. You've somehow lost your own identity. Whatever reputation you might have had in the PPD is probably burned…"

Briggs interrupted. "And yet, against *this* guy and whoever he works for, against the pencil-pushers and arse-coverers in the PPD hierarchy and even against the Network itself, I've prevailed." He gestured to Carli, "We've prevailed."

There was a long pause, and Lieutenant Gomes seemed to be thinking something over. She nodded to the medic who'd continued his assessment whilst they had been talking, "What's his damage?"

"In and out. Bullet's passed through and doesn't look like it's hit the bone or major arteries. But he'll need surgery to clean up the lifesuit fibres. I'm more worried about infection, but I'll administer an analgesic and antibiotic."

Gomes turned to the other detective, "And him? What's his status?"

Detective Curran had replaced Briggs' temporary binders with a sturdier set of cuffs. "He's got a few nicks, but he can be moved. I'm most worried about his hand. If it's as deadly as Briggs said yesterday, moving him might be a problem. I don't know how it works."

Briggs stepped forward. "I can move him. He's already killed me once today, and I doubt he can do it twice. I was right—the hand infects the lifesuit and causes its EVS to interrupt the heart's rhythm—effectively stopping the heart."

"And how were you able to survive this?"

Briggs pointed to his heart, "I cut out my EVS."

Gomes stared off into the distance for a minute before inviting the medic and Detective Curran into a conversation away from Carli and Briggs. Briggs approached her, his left arm now held against his chest with a sturdier sling.

"This is the part where they call in damage control."

"What do you mean?" she asked.

"This has got political dynamite written all over it. It looks bad for the PPD. Looks bad for Augmosis. Looks bad for the Overseer. Hell, we probably can't even arrest Liam—as far as the Network is concerned, he is Hal Briggs. If they scan my DNA, it probably won't match whatever is on file. The others—even their DNA was scrubbed as though they had ceased to exist. In fact, I wouldn't be surprised if his DNA now also points to Hal Briggs."

"Can't it be fixed?"

"Maybe. Maybe not without *him*. I probably should have just shot him—might've made things easier to explain."

Carli's heart sank—In the heat of the moment, she'd made that same decision. Now she regretted she ever seriously entertained such a thought, let alone *pulled the trigger*.

Gomes broke from her huddle and called out to Liam Nolan, who was still sitting cross-legged on the cement floor, "You. Carli offered you a deal. You spill on everything, and we'll take care of that hand."

Liam raised his head. "And after that, I'm a free man, right?"

Both Carli and Briggs' heads jerked back to Gomes in anticipation. "No chance. There's no way you're getting out of this with anything less than a cell. But what you choose now will determine how big it is."

Liam grunted acknowledgment as Gomes continued, "We need to get off this rooftop to somewhere a little more private."

"I know a place," Briggs offered.

Gomes nodded. "Carli, you're still identified in the Network, but I see your plexus is gone. You'll still be able to transit back home and should get access to your apartment, but you'll need to phase a new one in the morning. Or if you'd prefer a hotel here in West Praxis, I can arrange something on your behalf."

Carli felt the tiredness trying to overtake the adrenaline of the last few hours. The medic had administered something for her head and bruised ribs, but her eyelids were growing heavier. But the idea of walking home alone did not sit well with her, nor did a hotel room. At this moment, she did not want to be alone.

As if reading her mind, Briggs suggested, "The place I'm thinking of is nearby, has a few cots and a basic medical suite."

"Fine," Gomes stated. "Let's get moving."

**72**

The storage unit in the level 5 basement of building S14E8 was just as abandoned as it was when he and Carlyle had stormed it a few days earlier, leading to Alvarez's arrest. If his augments had been working properly, they would have been screaming alarms, telling him he was entering an area sealed for police. Instead, all he saw was stone and dirt.

It was his idea to use the location. Gomes had wanted a secure "off-the-books" location to hold Nolan until something more permanent could be secured. Guiding Liam forward with his uninjured arm, Briggs spent the dozen or so blocks thinking through the evening's events and wondering if this was the right approach. Unlike Alvarez, Nolan had agreed to talk and had already started to recount his actions over the previous week as a gesture of good faith, though he shared nothing of any involvement in the PPD bombings. Briggs knew he was holding back and felt that some additional incentive might be required. Though he may have been able to contain his wrath towards this man, he doubted he could keep it in check indefinitely. It was a beast that needed to be fed.

"What is this place?" Carli asked. She'd remained at Briggs' side. Though he thought it would be safer for her to return home, he didn't like the idea of her doing so without an escort. Gomes, Curran and the medic, Rossi, had followed behind them. Rossi had tended to Carli's forehead cut with hands far more skilful than his own and confirmed Carli's ribs were only bruised, not broken. Briggs noticed Lieutenant Curran's hand didn't deviate from above her holster for the whole trip.

"This is where we found Alvarez. It was being used as a store for black-market Old World wares." Briggs noticed a scorch mark on the floor where he

383

assumed one of the stun grenades had gone off. "Over there should be a medical station—no idea what supplies might be left after PPD Property cleared it out."

"How'd they get it all down here?" Detective Curran asked.

Briggs directed Nolan towards the stainless-steel bench of the medical suite with an extra wrist twist, "I hope that's something our new friend here can answer."

Nolan turned slowly, before sliding his backside up onto the bench, his bound hands still behind him. His eyes rested first on Gomes, before returning to Briggs. He recognised that expression; it was even more detectable without the added layer of a projection: resignation. It was the look of a man who understood this was his only option. Nolan took a deep breath.

"The rest of your PPD clowns didn't look very hard. The exit's here. This building's right on the edge of West Praxis' dome. Follow the corridor down, and the second room on the right has a false wall—made of plastic, but painted like stone. Has a tracking marker on it and probably has a scape applied for good measure. Slide it over and there'll be a steel door."

Briggs looked to Gomes, who nodded to Curran to investigate, "Don't open it, Gayle. Just confirm. I don't like the idea of this place having two exits."

With another seemingly small piece of the puzzle put together, Briggs wanted to press further. With enough preparation, he would have discussed an interview strategy with Lt. Gomes, but with the weariness of the day's events, a returning headache and a week's worth of disappointments and grief, there was no way he was going to hand off the responsibility of questioning Liam Nolan to someone else.

"That's a good start, but let's go further. How were you involved in the PPD bombings?" Briggs asked.

Liam held his gaze, showing little expression other than a momentary smirk. "Hand first, then questions."

"You're in no position to negotiate."

"Probably not, but this…" he gestured with his prosthetic hand, "is a ticking bomb. I would have removed it myself before now if I'd had the… *opportunity*. As soon as my employer realises I have been captured, then it's game over."

The medic, Rossi, had laid out some scary-looking tools that looked like the distant relatives of those he'd seen used by the medical examiner. It seemed that Gomes hadn't seconded just any Collective paramedic, but a former PPD officer who had switched careers. That explained why he didn't seem as concerned about the ethics of what he'd been asked to do.

"Do you have what you need?" Gomes asked.

"I think so. I brought enough anaesthetic to knock him out for a while, and *these*," he held up one of the curved blades he'd collected, "will do the job, even if it's not pretty. I can't remove the rods completely without risking damage to the socket, so I'll just cut them through and hopefully, they can be cleaned up later."

"This is hardly the sort of medical procedure I thought I was agreeing to," Liam said.

Briggs pressed a little closer, "Terrorists don't get a private medical suite in Métropole, scumbag. Be grateful he's even offering anaesthetic."

Rossi's eyes widened, and Gomes shook her head, "He's given his consent, let's get this over with." She nodded to Rossi, who thrust a syringe into Nolan's forearm.

"Aren't you going to take the cuffs off first?"

"Not on your life."

Briggs loomed over Liam, his face close enough to see the stubble that poked through from his scarred face.

"The PPD bombings. That was you."

"Probably."

Briggs slammed his fist down on the table in front of Liam's face. Liam didn't flinch, and his eyes started to glaze over before a few words escaped his lips, "I don't make bombs. But I know a guy."

Within a minute, Liam's posture sagged, and Briggs and Rossi eased him onto his side. They waited another minute for good measure, with Rossi checking Liam's vital signs before Gomes unlatched the cuffs.

Rossi started his work behind a sheet of fabric that served as a makeshift curtain. Carli and Gomes shuffled a little distance away so they wouldn't have to watch. Briggs stayed next to the curtain, wanting enough of a view to make sure that Liam remained incapacitated.

Detective Curran returned from down the corridor. "I've found a door, just as he said. I think there's power running behind it, I can hear a hum."

"That's some pretty shoddy scene processing," Briggs said.

Gomes ignored it. Instead, she focused her gaze on Briggs, Carli, and Curran.

"I want to get a few things straight for all of you. What we have here is the worst possible scenario. We have a guy who is clearly guilty of numerous crimes: prison break, assault and murder. And if he was involved with the PPD bombing as we suspect, that makes him the most wanted man in all of Praxis.

"However, every piece of digital evidence directly connecting him to each of those crimes is scrubbed the moment he drops an identity and starts a new one. If he'd managed to get away tonight, he could have strolled into the PPD as Detective Briggs, and none would have been the wiser. It concerns me that whoever is switching people's identities could have done it before. It puts a cloud of suspicion over pretty much everyone."

Briggs caught Carli's eye, "We think it's already happened. Carli said he confessed to killing the person ArdentBlue two years ago. Since ArdentBlue joined the Council of Overseers afterwards, it stands to reason that she is also a plant."

Gomes cursed under her breath. It was the first time he'd seen her show any form of emotion other than steely determination.

"He said he'd show us a body. We get him to confess to the rest, and surely, we have a case," Briggs offered.

Gomes became more agitated, "And do what, Detective? This punk is the only lead we have on the biggest conspiracy Praxis has ever seen. If people can be replaced, then there's no telling who can work against us—Overseers? Judges? Hell, even other PPD officers? And the ramifications if the rest of the Collective found out? There'd be unrest!"

Briggs understood—he'd already arrived at a similar conclusion. He felt vindicated for his mistrust of the PPD, but everyday political interference was far simpler than the potential size of this conspiracy. Unlike the puzzles he prided himself in solving every day as a detective, this one had already proven beyond his capabilities to solve without help. Without Carli, and now without Gomes and ONI, he'd gone as far as he could—he had no power to do anything. It was the same helplessness that drove him to the bar after the PPD bombing.

"Whatever happens next, I want to be involved. For my sake. For Anneke's sake. But I recognise this is bigger than me and it's going to need a lot more skill than I will ever have: technical and political. If that means justice against this man has to be delayed, then… I'm, going to have to deal with it."

"I appreciate that—" Gomes was interrupted by a high-pitched whirring noise coming from the operating table. Rossi was using a power tool to do something that Briggs didn't want to think about.

Carli stepped closer and asserted herself, "And I want to help, too. I've been thinking about what Liam said to me at the café—if ArdentBlue is an impostor, then you need to find out who they really are."

"And how can you help with that?" Gomes asked.

"I sculpted their identity. NuSculpt has full body scans of her or the person who pretended to be her when her trueself was created. You need to get access to those scans from our private network.."

Gomes took all this in before completing her reply, "Okay, here's what we're going to do. This whole operation never happened. That shouldn't be hard since Carli's PPD communications appear to have been scrubbed. Liam Nolan is, as of this moment, an asset. I'll need to arrange some less dungeon-like accommodation and build a team to keep him supervised. If ONI was the main target for an attack, I have to believe that whoever's masterminding this thing is fearful we may be the only ones that can stop it, which means that ONI should be trusted. Frankly, without ONI's skillset, we don't stand a chance anyway.

"Liam Nolan stays off-grid. I noticed that his plexus seems to have been mysteriously destroyed. That's probably for the best. Briggs, we'll find a way to get your ID back if we can, but we'll keep him off the Network." Gomes caught a concerned look from Curran. "Yes—I know that's a violation of liberty. We've already crossed a dozen lines—and it looks like I'm going to cross a few more before this is done."

For some reason, this brought a brief smile to Briggs' face as he realised that Gomes had concluded that the only pragmatic solution was to bend or break the rules of a system that was clearly already compromised.

"And what about Moya?"

"What about him, Hal?"

"What are you going to tell him? He's been fighting me the whole time on this case."

"I'll deal with Deputy Moya."

"You've said that before. I trust *you*. Hell—that's not something I say often. But I *do not* trust that man. Keeping him in the loop is a mistake… *in my opinion*."

"I'll take that under advisement."

Rossi now approached with a concerned expression, holding the corner of a plastic bag containing Liam's black prosthetic hand. The orange glow continued to radiate from its palm. At the other end, two carbon fibre bones were coated in blood. Detective Curran approached and took the bag by the other corner and placed it onto a tray some distance away. Rossi returned to Liam and started to close the skin around the elbow joint.

Briggs noticed Carli yawning and realised he probably should have shown her where the cots were by now.

Gomes continued, "Carli, like I've said before, you've done a good thing tonight. I'm confident you'll keep this to yourself until we work out what happens next."

"Yes."

"Here, let me show you the beds. They aren't anything special." Briggs escorted Carli down the corridor and found the room where Aldus Goldstein had managed to distract April Rocha while he and Carlyle had moved on Alvarez. He activated some lighting via a mechanical switch and found an unmade, but clean-looking double cot. Just looking at it made him feel tired.

"Will this be okay?" he asked.

"Yes, it's fine." She sank into the cot as he moved back to the door, turning off the lights. A small amount of light spilled in from the corridor to illuminate her face.

"I'll be right outside if you need me." He didn't hear a response and closed the door a little further, leaving Carli in the shadow.

Returning to the main space, Briggs found a weathered couch. It didn't look too comfortable, but he doubted it would matter. As he sat, Detective Curran approached and crouched next to him. It felt so foreign to Briggs to be able to see past her projection. The 30-something-year-old female he remembered from a few days prior was starkly different to the more elderly person crouched by his side.

"Detective. *Hal.* The Lieutenant knows what she's doing. But on a personal note, I want to thank you. Liam Nolan has taken more than three years of my life. I know you've made sacrifices in getting us here, and this whole situation isn't going to get any less messy, but thanks to you, we've got *something*. And Liam Nolan is no longer on the loose."

Briggs managed a nod. He fell asleep, reminding himself of how close he came to death and how far he remained from the answers he needed.

He awoke to the sound of voices. Without a connection to the Network, he had no sense of time, and the room seemed just as poorly lit as it was when he'd closed his eyes. As his vision slowly came into focus, he found the medical suite was now empty. An officer, identified only by the tactical lifesuit he was wearing, was positioned at the doorway.

He started to stand, but the blunt pain in his shoulder told him it was a bad idea. Whatever drugs he'd been given had worn off. He'd need to have the wound looked at again by a proper surgeon, but that had to wait until after he could restore his Network identity. Without it, he wouldn't get past the front counter of a hospital. After a few deep breaths and shifting his weight to his right, he managed to stand and moved down the corridor towards the sounds of voices.

The door to the room on the left was still ajar, and Briggs looked in to see Carli sleeping in almost the same position as before. Another officer stood outside the next door—the room where Briggs had first found Alvarez.

"The lieutenant is interviewing the suspect. She asked you to wait outside."

Briggs grunted, irritated that he hadn't been given the first opportunity to interview Nolan. "What's the time?" he asked.

"About 7:00 am."

"Briggs, is that you?" a voice came from the storeroom opposite—Detective Curran. He approached and found her and another person, not wearing a tactical lifesuit, young and slightly built, Briggs would have described them as male, but probably wouldn't have said so out loud.

"Sarge! You got the boss?"

"Huh?"

"Nolan—you got him!"

Briggs glanced between this small human and Detective Curran before realising, "SpecialistHavoc?"

"In the real life."

"Great, I already had a headache."

In the storeroom, the false wall had been slid to the side. Behind it was a steel door three meters wide and two meters high with a large spinning handle that looked like one from an Old World bank vault.

"The Lieutenant asked me to prepare Ms Dawes with a new plexus and then escort her home," Curran said. "Can you join me?"

He complied. The three of them moved to Carli's room, where she stirred as the light from the stone hallway spilled onto her face.

"Carli? It's Briggs."

Her eyes opened quickly, adjusting to the light, but she offered a faint smile and sat up on the side of the cot.

"It's OK, you're still safe. Sergeant Curran here is going to escort you home."

She looked at him and smiled. "Your eyes are red."

"Probably. My eyes got fried the same as yours, remember? I can't see anything from the Network."

"So, you see me without my projection?"

"Um yes—well, I see everything without a projection."

"What does it look like to you?" she asked.

He thought for a moment, "People look different. But everything else looks very… ugly."

She nodded, and Briggs motioned for Havoc to move forward. He produced a sealed package that he broke apart to reveal a plexus, which he activated with a hand-held device before passing it to Carli.

"Have you done a re-pair before?" he asked Carli.

She nodded with a yawn and attached the plexus to the coupling on her lifesuit. A few gestures later, she confirmed she was connected again.

"Great," Briggs stepped aside "If you go with the Sergeant, I'll catch up with you once I figure out how to get back onto the Network."

She stood, frowning, "You're still on the Network—I still have full trust with your ID?"

"Liam Nolan," Briggs said. "He's still holding onto my ID. We'll sort that out, but maybe best to remove the trust until it all gets fixed."

She nodded. Moving to leave, she gave him a gentle hug. It hurt his shoulder, but he didn't care. She'd saved his life. If he thought about it long enough, he could probably argue that he'd also saved her, but right now, it didn't matter.

"Thank you, Carli."

Liam was certain he'd answered the same question at least twice before. This wasn't his first police interrogation, after all—asking the same questions in different ways was standard practice to confirm the truth or trap someone in their lie. But for someone who hadn't had a good night's sleep for as long as he could remember, who had woken from anaesthetic only a few hours earlier, he found it increasingly difficult to stay awake.

If this had been a standard PPD interview he would have been served his rights, received legal representation and would have been given a concession to recuperate from his surgery. But this was off the books, and he no longer had the same liberties the law afforded every other citizen of Praxis.

His right arm was cuffed to his right leg. The top half of his lifesuit had been completely cut away. The scars from burns and skin grafts across the left side of his body were exposed for all to see. He wasn't ashamed of his scars, but he still felt vulnerable.

His left arm was strapped to his side, now terminating in a bandage at his elbow. It felt different to the first time he'd lost the use of his hand in the explosion at the refinery, where he'd not only lost part of himself but the only person he'd ever loved. Through a cloud of grief, the a pain in his hand had continued to burn almost as hot as his anger at the corporate bastards who were to blame. It wasn't until after his employer had fitted him with the prosthetic that the phantom pain where his fingers had once been finally disappeared. But now, with the prosthetic removed, he expected the pain to return. Instead, he found nothing: no pain, but no feeling at all. It was a strange sense of finality that gave him pause.

"So, when your employer wants to communicate with you, the messages you receive aren't from a real moniker? Just random letters?"

He rolled his eyes, taking a long stare at the camera placed before him on a tripod. He turned back to his interviewer, the Lieutenant—Gomes. She was clearly in charge.

"Correct."

"And you don't remember any of those letters?"

"Not since the last time you asked me."

"What was your last communication? Before you… *lost* your plexus?"

Liam sighed, "They asked me to report in. I told them I was busy."

"Do you think they know what happened to you? Do you think they can track you?"

"I can't answer that. Sometimes it seems like they had full control over the Network. Sometimes it seems like they were in the dark, just as *you* were. If they *were* tracking me, I'd guess it's in *that* thing." He instinctively wiggled the phantom fingers on his left hand before realising it was a futile gesture. He sighed again and sat back, weary and defeated in his chair.

The Lieutenant looked off to the side, made a few gestures and the door to the room opened. In walked a person donning a grey jumpsuit and helmet accented with neon blue lights. Liam's eyes didn't linger on the garish projection, instead tracking the second person who joined the room, the detective, Briggs. If Liam had any sense of remorse, he would have turned away. If he felt *something* resembling guilt, he would have willed it away and held the stare anyway.

"How many characters?"

"What?" The glowing officer was asking a question.

"The messages you receive—the monikers—if they're random characters, are they all the same length? Any patterns? Letters and numbers?"

He hadn't been asked that question, thought for a moment and said, "Yeah, I'd say so. Letters and numbers. Two groups of five characters with a hyphen."

That seemed to excite the glowing officer. The Lieutenant gave him some instructions before he left the room.

"Is he responsible?" Briggs asked the Lieutenant without breaking eye contact.

"Yes. He collected the explosives and planted them in specific teepers at the charging station. He remembers the contact's moniker, and we are making enquiries now—hopefully, that might get us further up the food chain, but the actual instructions seem to be coming from random monikers. They will be difficult to track."

Liam saw a wavering in Briggs' glare. He'd seen the same expression staring back at him in the mirror after the accident, after Fi had been stolen away from him. The look of a man who would do anything to deliver his own form of justice.

"And Goldstein?"

"Guilty," he said. Briggs nodded.

"And who does he work for? Who is his employer?" Gomes nodded towards Liam, telling him he was expected to answer that question again.

"They've only referred to themselves by one name," Liam said.

"Which is?"

"Legion"

Briggs looked to the Lieutenant. "Does that name ring a bell?"

"No. Hundreds of communities in the Collective use that name. It could be one of those. It could be something else. At least it's a start." She grabbed the camera from the tripod and directed Briggs back towards the door. "We need a recess. Constable Vargas will keep him supervised. I need a break anyway."

Briggs resisted, "What's behind the door out there?" he asked.

"Best you look for yourself. You wouldn't believe me. Needless to say, the only reason any of us are here is because of what's behind that door."

They'd almost made it out before Briggs turned back and asked, "Why did you kill Petros Zaimis?"

Liam had already answered that for the Lieutenant, but since he was in a talkative mood, said, "One answer is that my employer told me to. But a better answer is that Zaimis was a fool and an opportunist. We only kept him around for extra security, but he was using this place, the 'Dock' we called it, to shift Old World wares. A small amount wouldn't have mattered, but he was getting greedy and was starting to draw suspicion. The Bratstvo Syndicate had placed a contract to have him interviewed—I guess they didn't like that he had access to better-quality wares and was diluting their market. My theory is that my employer suspected he would expose this operation if compelled."

Briggs appeared to consider this before Liam added, "And Alvarez—if he's not dead already, he soon will be. He knows more about what's beyond that door than anyone, even me."

Briggs gave the Lieutenant a look, and they both left.

He sat back in his chair and looked again at his missing hand before closing his eyes. He'd traded the shackles of prison for a virtual leash attached to his arm. He'd gotten so close to a freedom he could control, set for life with more bits to his name than he would ever need. Bits that would have bought him a new hand that wouldn't kill him whilst he slept.

Now the leash was gone, replaced with a leash of a new kind as… an informant? He still wasn't sure. But as he drifted off to sleep in this uncomfortable chair in an uncomfortable position, all he could think of was what he'd lost and how he needed to do whatever it took to be back in control of his own destiny.

<hr>

"I'm sure he's holding some things back, but he's giving us more than we can deal with for now." Gomes passed an electronic device to one of the other officers, adding, "You know what to do with that?"

The officer said, "yes". Briggs asked, "What is it?"

"Old World recording device. Separate storage, off the Network. He's making copies."

"So, looks like we're using body cams after all," he quipped. "He's right about Alvarez being in danger. We need him in protective custody. And Augmosis—Liam walked through one of the most secure places in Praxis to execute Goldstein. There was someone there in Goldstein's team who helped me—Doctor Godfrey. Augmosis was possibly going to fire her. I think she needs to be protected, too. She may be able to help."

"Okay, okay…" Gomes succumbed. Unlike Briggs, who at least had managed a few hours' sleep, he suspected she'd been working through the night. "I want to pop the seal on this door to see what's on the other side. You're welcome to stay for this, but then I'll have an officer escort you to Métropole to get someone to look at your shoulder. Even without an ID, we'll make sure you're admitted."

"And after that?"

"After that, you rest and recover. We'll figure out what to do about your ID and your augments. And then," she met his eyes and gestured to herself, "you work for me."

His heart skipped—a final vindication and an opportunity to see this through. He composed himself and said, "I accept."

"Don't agree so quickly. I don't want to be fighting you on every step of the way. I decide who to keep in the loop and when we make a big play. If you disagree, you do it with me in private, but you follow orders. Agreed?" She gave him a gentle finger jab to underscore the point.

"Agreed."

An officer moved to the door and spun the large dial until the whole door made a clunking sound and began to pivot outwards. The same officer retrieved a scanner from his pocket and placed it in the opening, taking measurements Briggs assumed to be levels of radiation or other carcinogenic particles.

"It's higher than inside, but still acceptable."

He pulled the door open the whole way, revealing a pitch-black corridor. Gomes, Briggs and two other officers entered one at a time. The dim light of handheld torches revealed a corridor cut from the stone, adorned with cables of different colours and sizes. The corridor ascended with a moderate incline towards a blackness that swallowed the light.

The first officer inspected the door further after they went past and declared, "The door looks like it only opens from my side. I'll stay here and leave it open."

They'd shifted to the end of the corridor, the ground beneath him changing from stone to something softer—almost slippery. Through the blackness, Briggs perceived faint glowing lights, mostly blue or yellow, too numerous to count. They offered only enough light to make the space seem large and ominous.

The other officer with them said, "Power leads here to a switch. Turn it on?"

"Do it."

The humming noise increased with intensity as the officer flicked the switch. Rather than coming on instantly, the lights started at a low level before gradually rising to full brightness. They revealed, not a corridor, but a cavern—a space bigger than the rooms inside. In fact, it felt larger than a city block—red-brown stone shaped by water or some other ancient forces to create a natural cave.

And, lining both walls of the cave, stacked in clusters together, and connected by cables in a long, messy chain, were teepers. Rows and rows of them. Strung together around the perimeter of the cave. More teepers were grouped in banks, some propped up by other teepers in poorer condition. Old models—some looked like the ones that had attacked him and Carlyle, and some looked even older. All were covered in red dirt. Some were missing limbs, and others had limbs replaced with other implements that Briggs couldn't identify but looked like they would be used for welding, cutting, or carrying. Almost every teeper emitted a glow, mostly washed out from the bright lights above.

"My God," Gomes said.

"There has to be hundreds of them?" said the other officer

"At least," Briggs added. A large modular container with a clear plastic door was on one side. At the end of the vast cavern, the dim light succumbed to more darkness. "Decontamination pod's here. Alvarez is the engineer—this was his job, to keep these things going. Doing what—I have no clue, but these aren't just being used to recover Old-World wares. Those are tools to build or maintain something."

Briggs pointed towards the end of the cavern—the source of the darkness. A cavern that extended out to the wastes of the Old World. "And whatever it is, it's out there."

# 74

As Carli stepped out of the storage building onto the streets of West Praxis, the light of a simulated sun cast long, pale shadows. Its inauthentic light provided no warmth, but at least a little comfort.

Sergeant Curran, Gayle as she'd asked to be called, tried to make awkward chit chat as they walked towards the transit station. She'd offered to lease a personal conveyance, but Carli said she wanted to walk—it gave her time to think over her last few days. Somehow, the fear she'd felt being at the mercy of Liam Nolan was a distant memory, but the thrill of chasing him through the streets and pursuing him to the top of his building was still palpable. She felt her pulse quicken as she replayed firing the gun at him—her hands remembering the shock of the gun recoiling and the sensation of squeezing the trigger with her target in her sights.

It was… intoxicating. And yet, it could have so easily been a fatal mistake— for herself, or even Briggs. She couldn't identify where he was in the movie that was replaying in her mind.

"Carli?" Gayle Curran had stopped in front of her.

Carli shook her head, snapping out of her dream. "Sorry, just remembering what happened."

"Oh. It's been very emotional. I can connect you with someone discreetly if you'd like to talk it through."

They continued walking through the transit station and boarded a transit that would take her back home. Sergeant Curran insisted she accompany her at least to the Archibald transit station. Carli sat back in her seat—the transit carriage wasn't full, but there were more than a few people on board. She scanned each one, contrasting the trueself they projected to the oldself they concealed.

*So much diversity*, she thought. *So much beauty. Not just in the image people had chosen to project to the world but in the authenticity of what lay beneath.* There were even several teepers which surprised her—she knew first-hand that renting teepers between hubs was expensive and somewhat pointless since you could just hire a new one at your target destination.

This reminded her of the reality she would face once the dust had settled from this adventure. She'd received a notice of breach of contract for "damaging" a teeper. She expected a fine would soon follow. She'd been quoted a high cost to repair her optics. Her meagre savings would not cover those expenses—she just had to place her faith in the PPD to reimburse her. *Lieutenant Gomes will sort it out*, she thought, *and Briggs will make sure of it.*

She was going to start sifting through the news feeds to see if anything had been reported, but noticed an accumulation of unread messages since her plexus had been destroyed. She skimmed over some from Lt. Gomes, they were mostly a stream of updates and questions asking how she was, timestamped for when she'd become Liam's captive. There was a message appearing to be from Briggs, but it was clearly from Liam Nolan using Briggs' ID. He must have sent it in the time after he'd woken up from being knocked out on the rooftop and before Briggs had destroyed his plexus. All it said was:

<BRIGGSH33207> MY EMPLOYER KNOWS.

She tried not to imagine what such a statement was supposed to mean. She forwarded the message to Lt. Gomes in case it was of any value.

There was one final message, timestamped at 5:10 am: only a few hours earlier. It was from Percy Hayward—a mirror recording with video and audio. She sat back in her chair and triggered the message to play in her optics.

Percy appeared in a window. He looked agitated—the recording switched quickly from his reflection to a rapid scan of his apartment.

"Carli… The PPD is here—at my apartment. I think they're going to…" A loud crash followed, and Carli saw officers in tactical gear pushing through a hallway, guns raised and advancing behind plastic shields."

"Percy Hayward!" they yelled, "ON THE GROUND! ON THE GROUND!"

Carli's breath caught in her throat. It looked like Percy was complying. The officers barked more orders, and she heard Percy whimper and groan as his vision was partially filled with the blackness of the floor and grey tactical boots.

"Percy Hayward, you are under arrest."

"What for?" he yelled at his captors.

"Planning and committing an act of terrorism. Murder. Assault."

"What?"

There were more noises, shuffling and groaning. Carli had thought Percy had forgotten he was still recording a message when he said, "Carli... Briggs sold me out!"

*The Collective became a man.*

*His name is "Om".*

**75**

On this historic day in this special place, the cradle of Praxis, we celebrate our hundredth year of the Collective. We mourn the loss of its founder, the great Aldus Goldstein. And we come together in solidarity to support the friends, family and co-workers who suffered through what has been the greatest ever assault on our freedoms.

"But we are resilient! We are not defeated! In these last eight days since that fateful explosion, the Praxis Police Department has restored stability and order to our Collective. We have arrested nine members of the terrorist organisation, 'The Wakers', including their leader, Percy Hayward and continue to deconstruct their network of anarchists, Network hats and malcontents.

"Whilst our Collective's bravest citizens burned to death, this vile gang of insurgents gathered only blocks away at the Areopagus to celebrate their fleeting victory against the institutions and brave citizens that uphold our liberties. But we have prevailed! Do not fear those who plot evil in dark rooms. Their childish conspiracies are no threat to what we have created together. For in the end, freedom, liberty, and democracy will always triumph!"

A chorus of cheers rang through the crowded outdoor space as Deputy Earl Moya concluded his speech with raised hands in a show of solidarity. All members of the Council of Overseers gathered in this bowl-shaped outdoor meeting space in the gardens of Augmosis. Except ArdentBlue, who had been granted a leave of absence.

Although she was on the edge of the crowd, Carli could still see each of the Overseers in the centre of the meeting space, addressing the embodiment of the Collective seated in the centre. A million different selfs flashed over its surface in a kaleidoscope of collective heterogeneity. For this presentation, they had effectively relocated the entire Overseer to the Augmosis parklands.

The Overseers weren't present in person. Each piloted a teeper—apparent only to Carli with her split vision. Behind the central meeting space and the gathered crowds was the 'living' Moreton Bay Fig tree. The symbol of the legacy of Augmosis, long dead—its leafless branches stretching up and out were propped in place with metal supports. Tracking markers allowed the Network to re-leaf the tree in everyone's optics.

But Carli could see the truth.

Another Overseer stood to speak to the Collective. More platitudes. More false claims.

She was surprised by the small turnout to this historic event. Only a few thousand, by her guess. In the last week, she'd noticed a rising panic across the Collective, that the Overseers were attempting to placate, but didn't appear to be overly successful.

Someone approached from behind and she turned to see an unfamiliar projection overlaid on top of a familiar face.

"Hello, Carli," he said.

"Hello, Briggs."

He cocked his head before asking, "You can see me? You haven't had your eyes fixed yet?"

"No. Not yet," she said.

The truth was she hadn't decided yet if she would, despite the new assurance from the PPD that they would be covering the costs. She looked at Briggs' projection—something bland and generic. It didn't suit him. The wound above his eyebrow was now a thin line, and she could see his left arm was effectively immobilised by a sling against his body. His moniker was also brand new.

"You aren't yourself yet?" she asked.

"No. Lieutenant wants to keep my moniker attached to Liam Nolan in case it helps somehow in tracking down his employers. Plus, technically, he's serving my PPD suspension while Gomes assigned me this temporary ID from their undercover pool."

"It doesn't bother you that he's wearing your projection? As far as the Network is concerned, it's you that Lieutenant Gomes has locked up in that underground bunker."

"A little, yes. But there's some advantages in having a clean slate—even if it's only temporary."

She looked back at the podium where the Overseer was also attempting to rally applause. "This is garbage," she said. "Percy didn't do this. You set him up as the fall guy."

"I'm sorry Carli. That… I didn't know that was going to happen."

She turned to face him, rage boiling from within—something she'd kept bottled up for the last week since she'd seen Percy's message and watched the follow-up news feeds about his arrest. "Bullshit, you didn't. The PPD needed a fall guy to give you space to keep Liam Nolan off the books. They used your interview with Percy—the one I arranged—and twisted it to make him look guilty. I don't care if it wasn't all your idea, but it's still your fault."

Briggs' head dropped before replying, "You're right. I'm sorry. The interview would never stand in court, but until then, Moya needs him to be the scapegoat—but that doesn't fix anything right now. In a few weeks, we should know more. We'll get the right answers and can go public. Percy and his friends will be well looked after until they are exonerated. It's not fair, but I don't know how else to make it work. I promise I will make things right; I just need time".

She scoffed and turned back to the Overseer, again, taking in the ridiculous scene of a bunch of plastic machines preaching to earn the love and affection of the physical representation of a philosophical construct, seated in front of a dead tree.

"You've gotten your augments fixed?" she asked.

"Yes. It was painful afterwards, but not as bad as when it happened."

"You didn't think of staying like this? Was it your vertigo illness?"

"No," he said. "In fact, until my eyes were fixed, that issue was gone completely."

"And now?"

"Same as before. Too much content, too many projected realities, and I'll fall in a heap."

"And was it worth it—to rejoin the Collective? To… resubscribe to this shared lie?"

"Hell no," he said, "But unless I'm connected, I can't do my job. I can't chase down Liam Nolan's cabal unless I'm part of the system."

Carli didn't reply. She supposed that made sense for him. For her, it was still a decision she needed to make. But a sculptor couldn't possibly be successful with fragmented vision. Soon she was going to have to make a choice—and whichever choice she made, it would still mean giving something up.

Another Overseer rose to conclude the event. He turned to face the crowd directly and thanked them for their attendance and their support. Returning to the embodiment of the Collective, he gave a final address.

"As our last act of solidarity, let us take one final minute to mourn those who have given their lives to create the utopia we share. For our fallen comrades. For Aldus Goldstein. For all those who have gone before us to uphold our liberty."

The crowd hushed. Carli looked around—so many people buying this lie. She focused on the virtual presence, seated in the centre of the space. Its symphony of projections vibrated thousands of times per second, more agitated than she'd ever seen it before.

And in the silence shared by the six million citizens of the Collective, as they remembered fallen comrades and the passing of heroes into legends, the virtual presence in the centre of Overseer did something that it had never done before.

It stood from its chair and began to speak.

"The Collective sees. The Collective wills."

# EPILOGUE

I t had been said that after decapitation, a severed head could maintain full consciousness for up to ten seconds. After that, blood pressure would drop and deprive the brain of oxygen. What little blood remained in the brain would quickly become toxic, and one by one, the cells would perish. Brain death would occur within three minutes. *And then it would be all over.*

Aldus Goldstein wasn't sure where and when he'd acquired that piece of information, nor even if it was true. But at this moment, it seemed like the most important fact in the world.

His neural implants had given him the bad news. His mechanical heart had stopped. His oxygenator was offline. He'd lost all communication with the Network. Since his body hadn't walked a step under its own power for half a century, it was of no help either. Goldstein didn't know why the team of nurses in the room next door hadn't responded the moment his systems went offline like a swarm of wasps defending their nest, but it was inconsequential right now.

All that mattered now was that he was dead. Killed by a man with the moniker of Basilicus. A name he recognised from a list he'd given Detective Briggs the day before. And the most frustrating thing was he'd only just started to figure it all out.

In the seconds before his assassin placed his hand on Goldstein's wasted body to deliver the same kind of instant death that he assumed had affected others in the Collective, his eyes had been opened for what felt like the first time in decades.

Not the mystery assassin that Briggs had been chasing. Something bigger. Something… fundamental.

A whole group of citizens had removed their trueself projections, resulting in a cascade of exceptions and automated alarms from a software system as old as the Collective itself. A system Goldstein had personally authored.

Before the rock fell from the sky. When Praxis was more of a philosophy than a physical reality. When the Collective numbered only in the thousands, sharing the physical space around the research and technology hub located in the old city's Northwest, Augmosis' CEO and founder Calum Bonner tracked Goldstein down in his private office. It was 2 AM. It wasn't unusual for Goldstein to be awake at such an early hour—he did his best work in the hours after everyone had logged off and it was just him, his development platform, and a glass of red wine. On this night, Bonner was forlorn and dejected, a stark contrast to his usual effervescent and charismatic self.

"The latest round of user experience testing has fallen short. People are struggling to stay immersed and keep removing their augments," Bonner said.

In those days the augments were little more than a glorified visor with integrated headphones. Though revolutionary in the context of technology across the world, they were still uncomfortable to wear for a long time. Despite universal praise, most considered Augmosis' Collective experiment as nothing more than a group of geeks wearing ski goggles.

"They'll get better. I've seen Gare's prototypes for the new optics, and they will change everything. He thinks he can get them down to the size of contact lenses," Goldstein replied.

Bonner whined like a spoiled child. "But that's still eighteen months away at best. We need something to make people want to stay connected: something that makes them feel like they would be missing out if they pulled the plug. I need them to stay connected, even if the technology isn't quite as comfortable to wear as it should be.

"People shouldn't want to spend time in the real world with all of its ugliness—we are creating the virtual utopia that will drive our economy for centuries! Each person needs to experience a true improvement over their physical lives. It shouldn't just mask the things people don't like, it should improve on them. Every building, every face, every surface should be a blank canvas that we make more beautiful."

"You know that's too much content to try and create all by ourselves. Too much tracking to figure out. We could hire a small country of designers, and we wouldn't get anywhere near the number of assets we would need," Goldstein replied.

If Goldstein and the technical team were the brains of Augmosis, Bonner was its heart, and much of their success was due to his single-minded drive to leave his mark on the world through this revolution in technology. Their relationship was often volatile, but for some reason, Goldstein couldn't help but be inspired by the man to do better. And do better, he did. Goldstein had almost single-handedly developed the first prototype for what they were calling the Network. Bonner was so impressed that he wept when he discovered the functionality Goldstein had pre-empted in his design. Goldstein could almost predict what Bonner wanted before he was even asked.

And like the best ideas, he found inspiration in an unexpected place. "What if, we guess?"

"What do you mean?" Bonner asked.

"We guess what people want to see before they see it. We guess that a cracked paver shouldn't look like a cracked paver. We guess that a weed in a garden bed shouldn't belong. Every imperfection, every stain and every scar—we get the system to recognise anything that doesn't belong, and we fix it. We need an algorithm that guesses reality. We teach an AI what we prefer to see, and over time, it should be able to figure it out for us."

Goldstein's mind was already assembling blocks of code and orchestrating what services he would need to make the idea work, vocalising a stream of problems and solutions as he went. "We could identify the patterns in what people already believe as attractive or unattractive. Every choice to filter something or to elevate something to the fore. But what if someone sees something as ugly when someone else sees it as beautiful? We'd have to generalise—find a regression algorithm across the whole sample space... We'd still have to enforce the right to project or perceive, above what the AI suggests, but that should be part of reconciliation..."

He couldn't remember how long Bonner had stayed after that. From the moment the challenge had been issued, Goldstein's mind had been on autopilot—a beautifully messy flow of thought and will identifying and classifying every obstacle to his goal and the solution that would defeat them. It was moments like these that he lived for: a high of adrenaline that powered the furnace of innovation.

It would be a week before he emerged from a self-imposed exile with the first draft of his solution. It was plugged straight into the Network, running passively, learning, finding the patterns in the decisions made by every user, as well as reprocessing every previous decision made since the Network first went live. In another week, he applied those learnings to his new service, using himself as a test case. What he found was better than he could have possibly imagined. Everything was affected, from the architecture to the faces of people who weren't yet connected to the Network. Even his stained coffee cup, which he always refused to wash out of some form of eccentric rebellion, now appeared clean. He made a note to teach the new algorithm that he liked it the way it was.

The update was released to much celebration. It wasn't the only catalyst that propelled people into a more immersive experience within the Augmosis Network. There had been many other occasions of frenetic development that contributed to and improved upon the whole system. It also wasn't the last time Goldstein would improve upon the service, which he called, "Omega" through the 100-year history of the Collective. But it certainly hadn't been something he'd spent any time thinking about for at least half of that time.

But now it seemed that this service was Goldstein's undoing. How exactly it had managed to find its own voice or sense of identity within the Network, he didn't know. What he did know was that he'd made a terrible mistake, maybe a century old.

Disabling the service in his final seconds of life was impossible. Somehow, his Network privileges had been revoked and he found himself effectively unplugged from the rest of humanity: a few vital seconds wasted. He thought it pointless to try and contact his other team members or the PPD, but tried anyway out of some desperate hope he was wrong. His failed attempts did nothing more than waste a few more precious seconds of consciousness.

Panic ensued. Somehow, he needed to get a message out—to tell his team or anyone who would listen, that the Network was compromised and needed to be fixed. He was not prepared to die knowing that he'd left a bug in the system, a bug that now appeared to be taking over.

And then, in a moment of clarity, he found his only solution. Not only did his neural implants keep him connected to the Network, but they'd also been streaming his very thoughts into the storage volume of the synthetic intelligence he'd created. The intelligence affectionately named "Golem". It knew what

Goldstein knew. Every thought and every memory. The Golem was not currently active, existing only in a virtual sandpit—completely isolated from the rest of the Network. But it now had all the information it needed to solve the puzzle.

The mind-streaming connection to the Golem was still active, but the capacity to activate it was part of the Network connection that was now disabled. There was no way to get a message to his team to tell them to reactivate the system—no way to tell anyone to wake his Golem and ask it the most important question in the world, "Who killed you?" No way to tell the world that he was a failure.

Someday, one of his team would turn the Golem back on, but the project had been running for a decade. It hadn't been pursued in years. It could be a month, a year or an eternity until it was reactivated.

He simply had no other choice but to trust that someday, this part of the story would be told. Someday, someone will discover that his final legacy was a flaw in the system so devastating as to tear down everything he'd worked to build. One fatal misalignment—a bug of eternal proportions, now impossibly outside of his control.

He hated it.

With that final despairing thought, he severed his neurological connection to the Golem. He wanted his last thoughts to be his own.

*"How long has it been? How long before I slip into unconsciousness?"* he asked himself. *"How would I know the difference between this and death? Should I expect to see some sort of light or just fall asleep?"* He'd long ago decided for himself that there was no eternity, no judgement or afterlife. That was his justification for pursuing the "final augmentation" in the first place. To release his consciousness into the Collective itself was to defeat eternity with technological immortality.

But he'd failed.

And in the last few moments of life, before the electrical activity of his brain ceased, starved of oxygen and drowning in carbon dioxide, anxiety flooded his thoughts. For the first time in as long as he could remember, his mind spiralled into a pattern of thought he'd long assumed impossible. Staring down the barrel of annihilation, he could not control his final thought:

*What if I'm wrong?*

<NETWORK> ENVIRONMENT.EXIT(); // THE END.

This story will continue in:

# AUGMOSIS

## LEGION

## ABOUT THE AUTHOR

Steven Tye lives on a rural property on the outskirts of Mackay in North Queensland, Australia, with his wife, Alison, and children Lara, Lachlan, and Kaitlyn. After a successful career in software development in IoT, smart utilities, agriculture and education, he pivoted to fiction. Augmosis is his first novel. Steven loves to cook, sing, play with chainsaws, lose balls on the golf course and make his children roll their eyes at him

For the latest news and information on Augmosis and other titles, go to:

WWW.STEVENTYE.COM

# ACKNOWLEDGEMENTS

I'd like to thank my early readers for their honest feedback, including Rabbs, who forgot to take notes because he enjoyed the story too much, Dale for her effusive encouragement and my wife Alison for suffering through a genre she loathed. Thank you to my developmental editor, True Margach who helped with pacing and coaching, leading me to trim over 15,000 words. Thank you for the affirmation from the community at Litopia Colony, particularly the "Southern Huddle" contingent.

Thanks to all the online teachers and podcasters with whom I have never spoken, but who have taught me so much about the writing journey. The most important to me have been:

- Brandon, Dan, Mary Robinette and Howard at the "Writing Excuses" podcast.

  WRITINGEXCUSES.COM

- Katie at the "Helping Writers Become Authors" podcast.

  WWW.HELPINGWRITERSBECOMEAUTHORS.COM

- Alida at the "Storyworks Roundtable" podcast.

STORYWORKSPODCAST.COM

Thank you to my other early readers and those who have helped to prepare this as an indie-published novel. Lastly, to everyone who has encouraged me to believe that I have something worth sharing, you have my dearest thanks.